FIFTEEN SECONDS

Before turning to full-time writing, Andrew Gross was an executive in the sportswear business. Andrew has written six novels, four of which were Top Ten bestsellers in the UK. He has also co-authored five *New York Times* Number One bestsellers with James Patterson. He currently lives in New York with his wife Lynn and their three children.

ANDREW GROSS

Fifteen Seconds

HARPER

This novel is entirely a work of fiction.
The names, characters and incidents portrayed in it are
the work of the author's imagination. Any resemblance to
actual persons, living or dead, events or localities is
entirely coincidental.

Harper
An imprint of HarperCollins*Publishers*
77–85 Fulham Palace Road,
Hammersmith, London W6 8JB

www.harpercollins.co.uk

This paperback edition 2012

1

First published in Great Britain by
HarperCollins*Publishers* 2012

Copyright © Andrew Gross 2012

Andrew Gross asserts the moral right to
be identified as the author of this work

A catalogue record for this book is
available from the British Library

ISBN: 978 0 00 738427 3

Set in Meridien by Palimpsest Book Production Limited,
Falkirk, Stirlingshire

Printed and bound in Great Britain by
Clays Ltd, St Ives plc

All rights reserved. No part of this publication may be
reproduced, stored in a retrieval system, or transmitted,
in any form or by any means, electronic, mechanical,
photocopying, recording or otherwise, without the prior
permission of the publishers.

This book is sold subject to the condition that it shall not,
by way of trade or otherwise, be lent, re-sold, hired out or
otherwise circulated without the publisher's prior consent
in any form of binding or cover other than that in which it
is published and without a similar condition including this
condition being imposed on the subsequent purchaser.

MIX
Paper from
responsible sources
FSC
www.fsc.org
FSC® C007454

FSC™ is a non-profit international organisation established to promote
the responsible management of the world's forests. Products carrying the
FSC label are independently certified to assure consumers that they come
from forests that are managed to meet the social, economic and
ecological needs of present and future generations.

Find out more about HarperCollins and the environment at
www.harpercollins.co.uk/green

Everyone is guilty of something, or has something to conceal. All one has to do is look hard enough to find what it is.

—Aleksandr Solzhenitsyn

Prologue

It had all gotten a little blurry for Amanda, behind the wheel of her beat-up, eight-year-old Mazda:

Her recollection of what she'd been doing only twenty minutes before. Katy Perry's voice on the car radio: "*I just kissed a girl . . .*"

The road.

She zipped in front of a yellow school bus crawling along ahead of her, the realization beginning to settle in that this wasn't the right way.

Truth was, things had been going downhill quickly from the time she'd woken up this morning. First was her pathetic, out-of-work dad, waking her out of a deep sleep—"*Why're you always yelling at me, Daddy?*"—threatening to throw her ass out of the house for good if she didn't change her ways.

Then her boss, who always seemed to be on her case. Sure, she'd missed some time. I mean, washing hair at that stupid salon, like it was some fancy-ass boutique in Milan or France or somewhere. And her tight-ass instructor at the local cosmetology school, Miss Bad Hair Tease of 2001. *At least know how to do it if you're gonna teach the shit, right?* I mean, there had to be some reason the bitch was stuck in a shit bucket like Acropolis, Georgia, right . . . ?

Not to mention ol' Wayne, her so-called boyfriend. They'd had another one of their famous blowups last night. Amanda was sure he was nailing the checkout girl at Ruby's Market, Brandee or something, with her big rack and all, and that cheesy, fake-gold necklace with her name in large script.

And here she was—one more missed class away from an F, and late again. That class was the only thing keeping a roof over her head these days. Amanda switched lanes, barely squeezing ahead of a slow-moving SUV with a mom and kid in it. *"C'mon, c'mon,"* she yelled. "I see you— *okay*?" She turned up the music. She just couldn't handle this kind of shit today.

The only way she could even think straight anymore these days was popping a couple of thirty-milligram Oxys like she'd done when she brushed her teeth. Always did the trick.

Especially with a Xanax chaser.

Katy Perry sang, *"It felt so wrong, it felt so right . . ."*

and Amanda sang with her, dancing with her hands off the wheel.

She heard a loud honk. Like a foghorn in her head. She realized she'd been weaving just a bit. *"All right, all right . . . Jesus, keep your ass on, bitch."* Last thing she needed was for the police to be on her butt today. Nineteen years old. With no money. Flunk out and get your ass tossed in jail.

Just like me, right . . . ?

Blinking, Amanda scanned for the turnoff to the school. She knew it was around here somewhere. It was just that everything seemed a little fuzzy about now.

Next to that Burger King, right . . . ?

She pulled into the turn lane. Suddenly horns blared at her from all directions. *Okay, okay . . .* A red pickup swerved, narrowly avoiding her, the driver twisting his head in anger as it zoomed by.

"Asshole . . ." Amanda turned to cuss him out. She stared back at the oncoming traffic. *"Holy shit."*

That's when it finally dawned on her that she'd been driving on the wrong side of the road.

"Deborah Jean? Deborah Jean? Honey, look what you forgot . . . !"

Deborah Jean Jenkins's mom ran out of the house, holding her grandson's "didee." The soft, blue terry cloth that always seemed to make eight-week-old Brett smile as he clung to it with those adorable, tiny little fingers of his.

Not that he was smiling much at all these days. In fact, the poor boy was really colicky or something, and was barely taking his formula. His dad was still two months from coming home from Afghanistan. He hadn't even seen his own son yet. Only on Skype. He had a position waiting for him at the Walmart. Then they could get their own place. Start their lives over again.

"Okay, Mom, thanks . . ." Deborah Jean said with a loud sigh, going back to pick the didee up from her by the front stairs.

"You want me to come along, honey?" her mother asked.

"No, Mom, I think the two of us can handle this perfectly well ourselves. It's like, *what*—a fifteen-second drive right down the road . . . What can happen in fifteen seconds?"

"Well, okay . . . Just make sure you buckle my grandson in there nice and tight."

"I promise, Mom," Deborah Jean said, rolling her eyes with a tolerant smile.

She took Brett back down the walkway to where her minivan was parked. "You're going to be a very important person in this world one day . . ." she told him. "A doctor or a lawyer, maybe. You'll make us all very proud. And when you *are*"—she gazed into his bright blue eyes—"I want you to promise me something. I want you

4

to promise, dude, that if *I* ever go on like that when you're all grown up, you're just gonna tell me to shush up! Can I count on you for that, Brett? Huh, can I?"

Deborah Jean tickled her son's chin with her knuckles as she suddenly heard a rumble from behind her. She turned.

To her horror, a rust-colored car had busted right through the white fence off the street and was heading up the lawn right toward the house—*toward her*—seemingly out of control.

"Stop! Stop!" Deborah Jean shouted as the car careened off the large elm in the yard, barreling down on her. *"Oh, Lord Jesus, no . . ."*

She tried to shield Brett, turning directly into the disoriented eyes of the young woman at the wheel. The last thing she ever heard was the terrified cry of her mom, who never ever stopped worrying over the oncoming engine's roar:

"Deborah Jean! Deborah Jean!"

When Amanda came to, her car was resting among the hedge work of a large, white house.

A house? She blinked foggily. *How the hell did she get here . . . ?*

A shrill voice beyond the car was shrieking, *"Deborah Jean! Deborah!"*

Would you stop? You're busting my head, lady.

Through her haze, Amanda wasn't sure what had

5

happened. The car just seemed to go out of control, like it had a mind of its own. Her door was hanging open. Fuzzily, she pushed herself out of the car. She knew she'd done something really bad. The woman kept screaming, *"Brett! Brett!* Oh my God, someone please help!"

Who the fuck is Brett? Amanda wondered. Her head was really killing her now.

Suddenly people were everywhere. "Someone cut me off," Amanda muttered to someone rushing by. No one seemed to be helping her, only the woman who was screaming.

"Hey, I'm hurt too," Amanda said. Blood rolled down her cheek. *"Can't you see? Whatever . . ."*

This was like some really bad dream. *It's time to wake up now!* she told herself. But blinking, she knew that whatever was going on, it was really real. Really bad too.

"Deborah! Deborah Jean, my daughter! Help her, please!" the bitch with the piercing shrill wouldn't stop screaming. Then she looked squarely at Amanda: "What have you done?" Her face twisted in anguish. *"What have you done?"*

"I couldn't help it," Amanda said, coming around the car to see.

A woman was pinned under her car. She was kind of pretty. Her eyes were glazed and very wide and her lips moved ever so slightly, though her voice was faint.

"*Brett . . .*" she murmured.

That's when Amanda saw that she was clutching something under there. Something bundled in blue. A blanket.

A baby's blanket. And people were standing around with their eyes filling up with tears. And there was blood everywhere.

You've done it now, Amanda said to herself.

Just like me.

PART ONE

PART ONE

CHAPTER ONE

You get *ten days*, someone once told me. Ten days in all of your life that qualify as truly "great." That when you look back through the lens of time stand apart from everything else.

All the rest is just clutter.

And driving my rented Cadillac STS somewhere outside Jacksonville, just off the plane from Ft. Lauderdale, looking around for Bay Shore Drive and the Marriott Sun Coast Resort, I thought that today had a pretty fair shot of ending high on that list.

First, there would be eighteen holes with my old college buddy from Amherst, Mike Dinofrio, at Atlantic Pines, the new Jack Nicklaus–designed course you pretty much had to sell your soul—or in my case, remove fifteen years of wrinkles from the face of a board member's wife—to even get a tee time on.

Then it was the Doctors Without Borders regional conference I was actually in town for, where I was delivering the opening address. On my experiences in the village of Boaco, in Nicaragua, where, for the past five years, instead of heading off each August on some cruise ship or to Napa like most of my colleagues, I went back to the same, dirt-poor, flood-ravaged town, doing surgeries on cleft palates and reconstructive work on local women who'd had mastectomies as a result of breast cancer. I'd even put together a fund-raising effort at my hospital to build a sorely needed school. What had begun, I'd be the first to admit, as simply a way to clear my head after a painful divorce had now become the most meaningful commitment in my life. A year ago, I'd even brought along my then-seventeen-year-old, Hallie, who freely admitted that at first it was merely a cool way to show community service for her college applications. But this year she was back again, before starting at UVA, snapping photos for a blog she was doing and teaching English. I'd even included some of her photos as a part of my presentation tonight: "Making Medicine Matter: How a Third-World Village Taught Me the Meaning of Medicine Again." I wished she could be there tonight, but she was going through exams. Trust me, as a dad, I couldn't have been prouder.

Then later, after everything wound down, I had drinks lined up at the Marriott's rooftop bar with one

Jennifer H. Keegan—former Miss Jacksonville, now regional field manager for Danner Klein—whose visits to my office were always charged with as many goose bumps and as much electricity as there was product presentation. The past few months, we'd bumped into each other at cocktail parties and industry events, but *tonight* . . . hopefully basking in the afterglow of my moving and irresistible speech, with a couple of glasses of champagne in us . . . Well, let's just say I was hoping that tonight could turn a day that was "really, really *good*" into one that would reach an all-time high on that list!

If I could only locate the damn hotel . . . I fixed on the green, overhanging street sign. METCALFE . . . That wasn't exactly what I was expecting to see. Where the hell was Bay Shore Springs Drive? I started thinking that maybe I should've waited for the Caddie with the GPS, but the girl said that could be another twenty minutes and I didn't want to be late.

Bay Shore had to be the next street down.

I pulled up at the light, and started thinking about how life had bounced back pretty well for me after some definite rocky patches. I had a thriving cosmetic practice in Boca, annually making *South Florida Magazine*'s list of Top Doctors, once even on the cover. I'd built my own operating clinic and overnight recovery center, more like a five-star inn than a medical facility. I'd put together a successful group of three storefront medical clinics in

Ft. Lauderdale and up in Palm Beach, and even appeared periodically on *Good Morning South Florida,* "Dr. Henry Steadman Reports" . . . Dubbed by my daughter as "the go-to Boob Dude of Broward County," my reputation cemented as creator of the Steadman Wave, the signature dip I'd perfected just above the areolae that created the seamless, pear-shaped curvature everyone was trying to copy these days.

It wasn't exactly what I thought I'd be known for when I got out of med school at Vanderbilt twenty years ago, but hey, I guess we all could look back and say those things, right?

I'd played the field a bit the past few years. Just never found the one to wow me. And I'd managed to stay on decent terms with Liz, a high-powered immigration lawyer, who five years back announced, as I came home from a medical conference in Houston, that *she'd* had one of those "days that made the list" herself— with Mort Golub, the managing partner of her practice. It hurt, though. I suppose I hadn't been entirely innocent myself. The only good thing that came of it was that I'd managed to stay active in my daughter's life: Hallie was a ranked equestrian who had narrowly missed going to the junior Olympics a couple of years back and was now finishing her freshman year at UVA. I still went with her to meets around the South, just the two of us.

But I hadn't had a steady woman in my life for a

couple of years. My idea of a date was to cruise down to the Keys on weekends in my Cessna for lunch at Pierre's in Islamorada. Or whack the golf ball around from time to time to a ten handicap. All pretty much "a joke," my daughter would say, rolling her eyes, for one of "South Florida's Most Eligible Bachelors"—if he was trying to keep up the reputation.

Traffic was building on Lakeview, nearing I-10, as I continued on past Metcalfe. I saw a Sports Authority and a Dillard's on my left, a development of Mediterranean-style condos called Tuscan Grove on the right. I flipped on a news channel . . . *Another day of U.S. missiles pummeling Gadhafi air defenses in Libya* . . . The dude had to go. *Tornadoes carve a path of death and destruction through Alabama.*

Where the hell was Bay Shore Springs Drive?

Yes! I spotted the name on the hanging street sign and switched on my blinker. The plan was to first check in at the hotel, then head over to Mike's, and we'd go on to the club. My mind roamed to the famous island green on the signature sixteenth hole . . .

Suddenly I realized the cross street wasn't Bay Shore Springs at all, but something called Bay Ridge West.

And it was one-way, in the opposite direction!

Shit! I looked around and found myself trapped in the middle of the intersection—in the totally wrong lane, staring at someone in an SUV across from me scowling like I was a total moron. Behind me, a line of cars had pulled up, and was waiting to turn. The light turned yellow . . .

I had to move.

The hell with it, I said to myself, and pressed the accelerator, speeding up through the busy intersection.

My heart skipped a beat and I glanced around, hoping no one had spotted me. Bay Shore Springs had to be the next street down.

That was when a flashing light sprang up behind me, followed a second later by the jolting *whoop, whoop, whoop* of a police siren.

Damn.

A white police car came up on my tail, as if it had been waiting there, a voice over a speaker directing me to the side of the road.

I made my way through traffic to the curb, reminding myself that I was in *North* Florida, not Boca, and the police here were a totally different breed.

I watched through the side mirror as a cop in a dark blue uniform stepped out and started coming toward me. Aviator sunglasses, a hard jaw, and a thick mustache, not to mention the expression that seemed to convey: *Not in my pond, buddy.*

I rolled down my window, and as the cop stepped up, I met his eyes affably. "I'm really sorry, Officer. I know I cut that one a little close. It was just that I was looking for Bay Shore Springs Drive and got a little confused when I saw Bay Ridge West back there. I didn't see the light turn."

"License and proof of insurance," was all he said back to me.

I sighed. "Look, here's my license . . ." I dug into my wallet. "But the car's a rental, Officer. I just picked it up at the airport. I don't think I have proof of insurance. It's part of the rental agreement, no . . . ?"

I was kind of hoping he would simply see the initials *MD* after my name and tell me to pay closer attention next time.

He didn't.

Instead he said grudgingly, "Driving without proof of insurance is a state violation punishable by a five-hundred-dollar fine."

"I know that, Officer, and of course I have proof of insurance on my own car . . ." I handed him my license. "But like I said, this one's a rental. I just picked it up at the airport. I'm afraid you're gonna have to take that one up with Hertz, Officer . . . *Martinez*." I focused on his nameplate. "I just got a little confused back there looking for the Marriott. I'm up here for a medical conference . . ."

"The Marriott, huh?" the policeman said, lifting his shades and staring into my car.

"That's right. I'm giving a speech there tonight. Look, I'm really sorry if I ran the light—I thought it was yellow. I just found myself trapped in no-man's-land

17

and thought it was best to speed up than to block traffic. Any chance you can just cut me a little slack on this . . . ?"

Traffic had backed up, rubbernecking, slowly passing by.

"You realize you were turning down a one-way street back there?" Martinez completely ignored my plea.

"I did realize it, Officer," I said, exhaling, "and that's why I didn't turn, not to men—"

"There's a turnoff two lights ahead," the patrolman said, cutting me off. "I want you to make a right at the curve and pull over there."

"*Officer* . . ." I pleaded one more time with fading hope, "can't we just—"

"*Two lights,*" the cop said, holding on to my license. "Just pull over there."

18

CHAPTER TWO

I admit, I was a little peeved as I turned, as the cop had instructed me, onto a much-less-traveled street, the police car following close behind.

Through the rearview mirror I saw him pull up directly behind me and remain inside. Then he got on the radio, probably punching my car and license into the computer, verifying me. Whatever he would find would only show him I wasn't exactly one of *America's Most Wanted*. I couldn't even recall the last time I'd gotten a parking ticket. I glanced back again and saw him writing on a pad.

The son of a bitch was actually writing me up.

It took maybe five, six minutes. A few cars went by, then disappeared around a curve a quarter mile or so in front of us. Finally, the cop's door opened and he came back holding a summons pad.

A couple of them were filled out!

I sighed, frustrated. "What are you writing me up for, Officer?"

"Driving through a red light. Operating your vehicle without valid proof of insurance . . ." He flipped the page. "And driving down a one-way street."

"Driving down a one-way street?" My blood surged and I looked up at him in astonishment. "What are you talking about, Officer?"

He just kept filling out the summons, occasionally eyeing my license, which still rested on his pad, and didn't respond.

"Wait a minute, Officer, please . . . !" I tried to get his attention. I wasn't exactly the type who lost his cool in front of authority. I mean, I was a surgeon, for God's sake, trained to control my emotions. Not having proof of insurance was one thing—a completely minor offense. And driving through a red light? *Okay . . .* Maybe I had sped up through a yellow.

But driving down a one-way street? Who needed that on their record? Not to mention I *hadn't* driven down a one-way street.

I'd never even started the turn.

"Officer, c'mon, please, that's just not right," I pleaded. "I didn't drive down a one-way street. I know I stopped . . . I may have even contemplated it for a second before realizing it, the street sign had me all confused. But I never got into the turn. Not to mention, I'm also pretty sure I *don't* need proof of insurance if the car's a rental. Which it is! It's all in the boilerplate somewhere . . ."

"I don't need an argument on this, sir," Martinez replied. I could have said anything and he was just going to continue writing on his pad, ignoring me. "If you want to challenge the charges, there are instructions on how to do that on the back of the summons. It's your right to—"

"I don't want to *challenge* the charges!" I said, maybe a little angrily. "I don't think you're being fair. *Look* . . ." I tried to dial it back. "I'm a doctor. I'm on my way to play a little golf. I don't need 'driving down a one-way street' on my record. It makes it sound like I was impaired or something . . ."

"I thought you said you were on your way to a medical conference," the cop replied, barely lifting his eyes.

"Yes, I did, *after* . . . Look, Officer, I acknowledge I may have sped up through the light. And I'm really sorry. But please, can't you cut me a little slack on the 'one-way street' thing? You've already checked out my record, so you know I don't have a history of this sort of thing. And, look, regarding the insurance . . ."

"This is now the second time I've had to give you a warning," Martinez said, finding my eyes, his voice taking on that I'm-the-one-wearing-the-uniform here tone. "Don't make me ask you again. If you do, I promise it will not go well . . ."

21

I sat back and blew out a long exhale, knowing I had taken it about as far as I could. It was true, if there was one thing that did irk me, it was the arbitrary use of authority, just because someone had a uniform on. I'd seen that kind of thing enough in Central America, *governmentales* and useless bureaucrats, and usually for no one's good but their own.

"Go ahead," I said, sinking back into the seat, "write me up if you have to. But I didn't drive down a one-way street. And I do have a right to state my innocence. It's not fair to just keep telling me—"

"That's it! I warned you!" Martinez took a step back. *"Get out of the car!"*

"What?" I looked at him in disbelief.

"I said get out of the car, sir! *Now!*" There was no negotiation in his hard, gray eyes. It all just escalated in seconds. Later, I couldn't even recall who had actually opened the door, him or me. But the next thing I knew I was out on the street, spun face-first against my car and roughly, with my hands twisted behind me.

"Hey . . ."

"Sir, you are under arrest, and your vehicle is being impounded," Martinez barked from behind me.

"Under arrest?" I twisted around, jerking my arm back. "Under arrest for what?"

"For obstructing an officer in the act of performing his job," he said, yanking back my arm and squeezing the cuffs tightly over my wrists. "*And* now for resisting arrest!"

"*Resisting arrest?*" I spun again. I couldn't believe what I'd just heard. "Officer, please, this is crazy!" I pleaded. "Can't we take a step back here? I'm not some thug. I'm a respected surgeon. I'm speaking at a medical conference in a couple of hours . . ."

He turned me back around, shooting me an indifferent smirk. "I'm afraid you're going to have to work out that little detail from jail."

The next thing I knew, I was thrown into the back of Martinez's police car, my knees squeezed at a sharp angle against the front, unable to comprehend how this had happened. Maybe the cop *had* told me to shut up, but I was only protesting my innocence. I was never threatening. I wasn't sure what I should do, or whom I should call. They were expecting me to give a speech at the conference. I'd have to let them know. My stomach sank. *And Mike*—I looked at my watch. I was supposed to meet him at Atlantic Pines in an hour! I needed a lawyer. I didn't even have a fucking lawyer! Not *that* kind of lawyer. There was Sy, who looked over my business stuff. Or Mitch Sperling, who had handled my divorce. Oh God, I could only imagine Liz's reaction when she found out. "You always think you know all the answers, don't you, Henry . . . ?" she would say, smirking with that gloating eye roll of hers.

Not to mention how she would play this out with Hallie.

As if in seconds, several other police cars showed up

on the scene, their lights flashing. Six or so cops jumped out, diverting traffic at the intersection behind me, conferring with Martinez, radioing in. I couldn't believe this was happening

Who the hell did they think they actually had here—*Timothy McVeigh*?

As I watched, Martinez and several cops talked outside their vehicles. I twisted against my restraints for a little legroom, which, like I'd always heard, only tightened them further. I sucked in a few deep breaths, trying to calm myself and figure out what I was going to say: that this was all just some crazy misunderstanding. That I was a doctor, on my way to a medical conference. To be honored tonight. That I didn't have as much as a parking ticket on my record. Things had simply escalated out of control. For my contribution to which, I was truly sorry.

But nothing I had done merited being cuffed and carted off to jail!

A second cop—this one muscular and bald, with a thick mustache and his short sleeves rolled up—came over and opened the rear door.

"Sir, we have a couple of questions to ask you. And as you're already in enough trouble as it is, my advice is to be very careful how you answer."

Already in enough trouble? This was growing crazier by the second. But I wasn't about to exacerbate it further now.

"Okay." I nodded back to him.

He knelt so that his eyes were level with me. "Where is your wife?"

"My wife?" It took me a second to respond, blinking back in total surprise. "You mean my *ex*-wife? I'm divorced. And I don't know *where* she is. And what the hell does she have to do with this anyway?"

"I'm talking about the woman you were seen driving around with earlier this morning." His iron-like gaze never wavered from me.

"What woman? I don't know what you're talking about," I said, almost stammering. "There was no other woman with me. I just flew in to the airport. I drove straight here until the officer over there stopped me."

"Sir . . ." The officer's look had the kind of intensity he might use on a felon or something. "I'm going to repeat my instructions, about answering carefully . . . You say you didn't have a woman in your car? Approximately one hour ago? *Downtown?"* The question was starting to make me just a little afraid. And it seemed he already knew the answer he was looking for.

"I don't have the slightest idea what you're talking about!" I shook my head. "And I appreciate it, but I don't need to be cautioned on how to reply. I haven't done anything wrong, other than to go through a yellow light."

The cop blew out a snort, with a thin smirk that was quickly followed by a cynical glare. Then he slowly stood up, shut the door, and went back over to his crew. A group of seven or eight of them conferred again for some time. Traffic was stopped in both directions; six or seven officers standing around, looking my way. I felt my heart race and I realized I may need someone to get me out of this situation. *Who the hell could I call?*

A few minutes passed, and Martinez and the bald cop came back over. They slid into the front seat and looked at me through the glass.

The next question got a lot more serious.

"Sir, when was the last time you were stopped by the Jacksonville police?" Martinez asked, staring into my eyes.

Huh? I laughed a nervous, back-of-the-throat chortle. *"Stopped by the police?"* I uttered, my mouth completely dry. "I've *never* been stopped by the police. Listen, I don't know what the hell's going on, but—"

"You're saying you weren't pulled over in downtown Jacksonville earlier this morning?" Martinez asked me again. "Around nine a.m. With a woman in this car?"

I was shaken by the total seriousness in his eyes.

"No. *No!* I have no idea what you're talking about. Nine a.m. I had just gotten off a plane! You can check my itinerary. I think it's in my briefcase in the car. Or in the rental agreement. Look, I don't know who the hell you guys think I am, but you've obviously mixed me up with . . ."

Martinez removed his sunglasses. "Sir, what were you

26

doing in a federal office building in downtown Jacksonville an hour ago?"

My heart stopped. As did just about everything inside me. I just sat, with my hands bound, realizing just how serious this was. Being stopped for a traffic violation was one thing . . . But having 9/11-like kinds of questions thrown at you—in cuffs; in the back of a police car . . .

"*Look.*" I stared back, sure that my voice was shaking. "I don't know who you think I am, or what you think I've done, but look in my eyes: *I'm a doctor.* I'm on my way to the Marriott for a medical conference at which I am delivering a speech later. I sped up through a traffic light because I was confused about the area trying to find the damn hotel. Actually, I'm not even sure I *did* go through the light . . . And I surely didn't drive down a one-way street, which in any event, all seems kind of trivial now in light of what you've been asking me.

"*But that's it!* I wasn't stopped earlier by the police. I didn't have a woman in the car. And I damn well wasn't in a federal office building in downtown Jacksonville! I don't know whether you have the wrong car, or the wrong information, the wrong whatever—but you definitely, *definitely* have the wrong guy!"

I steadied my gaze as best I could, my heart pounding in my chest.

"You just better hope you're right," the bald cop finally said with an icy smirk, "'cause if it turns out you're screwing with us in any way, you have my promise I'll put a fat one up your ass so deep you'll be shitting lead for the rest of your life. Which, I assure you, no one will be betting will be very long. You getting me, sir?"

"Yeah, I'm getting you," I said back to him, my gaze heated too.

The cops got out again, Martinez asking for my Social Security number. Then he and another older trooper who seemed to be in charge stood talking for a bit, and out of the blue, I thought I saw Martinez smile.

Smile?

Martinez patted him on the arm, and a short while later the senior cop got back in his car and headed off. As did the others. Even Baldy, who tossed me a final glare that to me said, *Don't let me meet up with you again.*

I started to think this seemed like a positive sign. If they were transporting a dangerous suspect to jail, they wouldn't all be driving off. I even let out a hopeful breath. Maybe I would get out of this with only a ticket. A ticket I didn't deserve maybe, but it damn well beat jail!

Finally, Martinez came around and opened the rear door again. This time his tone was different. Softer. "I'm not going to apologize," he said. "I told you several times to keep your mouth shut, didn't I?"

This time I wasn't looking for any moral victories. "Yes, you did, Officer, and I guess I—"

"And I haven't violated any of your civil rights . . ." He stared at me. "Isn't that *correct* . . . ?"

Sitting there, unfairly, in the backseat of a police car, my wrists aching from the cuffs, I took a chance and smiled back at him. "That part, I'm not sure the jury isn't still out on . . ."

He gave me a bit of a chuckle in return. "Turn around. I'll get you out of there. Truth is, I suppose the streets are kind of confusing back there. Bay Shore West is only a couple of lights down the road. We do try to be friendly here . . ." He took off the cuffs and a wave of relief ran through me.

"Your sidekick back there . . . I assume he's just the friendly type too?"

"Rowley?" Martinez snorted. "Me, I'm a teddy bear." He slapped me amicably on the shoulder. "Him? Guess he's just a little embarrassed by the misunderstanding. Let's just say, better you don't run into him again, if you know what I mean?"

"No worries," I said, wringing my hands free.

He said, "I'm going to write you up a warning. For speeding up through a yellow light. No proof of insurance required. That sound okay?" Martinez winked, like the whole episode was just some kind of a shared joke between us. "Just take a seat back in your car."

A warning? If the guy had said up front that all he was doing was writing me up a warning, we could have avoided the whole mess . . .

I got back in the front seat of the Caddie, glancing back once or twice through the rearview mirror, as Martinez, back in his car, wrote on his pad.

And suddenly it all began to make sense to me—how they were all just standing around grinning, like it was some kind of joke . . . How, *what if there never was any other person in a federal office building?* Or someone who had been stopped earlier. With a woman in the car. How what if they were all just covering Martinez's ass for totally overreacting. He'd probably told them that he had this rich, out-of-town doctor in cuffs, and they all stared back at him, like: *Are you out of your mind? You're arresting him for that, protesting a traffic violation . . . ?*

My blood was simmering, and I could feel myself growing more and more angry at how the whole thing had gone down.

That's when I saw an old-model blue sedan, a Ford or a Mercury or something—I wasn't the best at those kinds of things, and nor was I really paying attention— pull up next to Martinez's patrol car.

Yeah, that's what I'm sure it was, I said to myself—*a cover. To give him some justification for what he did, yanking me out of my car. There probably never was any other person or woman in any car. In fact—*

Suddenly I heard a loud *pop* coming from behind me. Like a whip snapping.

Then another.

I spun around and saw the blue sedan pull into a frenetic U-turn, screeching away from Martinez's car.

Everything was scarily still. Just this total absence of movement or sound. Including my own heartbeat.

What just happened?

I looked in my mirror as horror began to grip me. Martinez was slumped forward against the wheel.

Oh shit, Henry . . . I leaped out of my car, this time no one barking at me to remain inside, and hurried back to Martinez.

His police light was still flashing and the driver's-side window was down. Martinez was pitched forward, his forehead against the wheel. The warning pad was still in his lap. There was a dark, dime-size hole on the side of his head, a trickle of blood oozing.

I found a second wound, a blotch of matting blood, near the back of his skull.

He wasn't moving.

"No, no, no," I shouted. *How could this be . . . ?*

My heart surged into fifth gear. I ripped open the door and did a frantic check for a pulse or any sign of life. There was none. Martinez must have been dead when his head hit the wheel. I let him fall back. There was nothing I could do. Except take a step back from his car in disbelief.

He'd been killed directly in front of me.

My head whipped around and I realized that the blue sedan, which had made a sharp right onto Lakeview, was speeding away. In front of us there was this blind curve, other cars finally driving by, stopping at the light across from me. Some drivers appeared to glance over, watching me coming out of Martinez's car. Maybe seeing the body slumped there. Probably not sure at all what had just happened.

But they damn well would be soon.

I had to do something. I'd just seen a cop being killed. And I'd seen who had done it! At least, I'd seen the car he was driving. I bolted back to my car and grabbed my cell, frantically punching in 911.

Then I stopped.

A tremor of hesitation wound through me. *What was I going to say?* That an unidentified blue car carrying the person who had done this was speeding away? Half the police force in Jacksonville had just seen me in the back of Martinez's car. *In cuffs.* Almost carted off to jail. All those incriminating questions hurled at me . . .

Not to mention, all these people driving by now. Seeing me come out of Martinez's car.

Away from his body.

The body of the policeman who had tried to arrest me!

My hesitation escalated into outright panic as I realized just what they were all going to realize.

The whole fucking world was going to think it was me.

CHAPTER THREE

Okay, think, Henry . . . Think! I knew I hadn't done anything. But I'd just seen a cop executed. And now the killer was speeding away. I was the only one who could identify him. And at the same time, exonerate me!

What was I supposed to do, just sit here until the cops came back again and automatically assumed it was me?

I didn't think on it a second more. I thrust the ignition on and swung the Caddie into a U-ey, then pulled up to the light on Lakeview. All I remembered was that the killer's car was blue. I hadn't been able to determine the make. Or a plate number. I had noticed that the plate wasn't from Florida, but more like an off-white ground with blue numbers . . . And as I hit Lakeview, pushing my way to the light, a couple of letters on the plate came back to me—*AMD*, or *ADV* . . . I tried to recall. Or was it *ADJ*? And I thought I'd seen a four somewhere . . .

But something did come back to me with certainty as I took off after it. A kind of insignia. A dragon maybe—red, with a long tail. Or a winged bird of some kind. That might make it easier to find.

I swung a right onto Lakeview at the first break in traffic. I hit the gas, weaving in and out of cars, pulling ahead of as many as I could. The guy had a minute or so on me. But there were tons of lights. And traffic. So he couldn't just take off crazily and risk being stopped. For all I knew he could have turned off onto a side street by now. Or pulled into a strip mall and switched cars. I fixed on that plate and that image I had seen. And looked out for the police. They'd tossed me in cuffs for a meaningless traffic violation. *What would they do to me now if they thought I'd killed a cop?*

I knew I had to call it in. Only a couple of minutes had gone by, and the police probably didn't even know what happened yet. I reached for my phone and punched in 911, still no sight of the car. After a few seconds, a female operator came on. *"Emergency . . ."*

"I've just witnessed a murder!" I shouted. I placed my phone on speaker. "A policeman! In his vehicle. On . . ." Suddenly I realized I didn't even know the name of the street Martinez had had me pull onto. *"Christ,"*

I said, stammering, "I don't know the street. It was off Lakeview. Near Bay Shore Drive . . ."

"Sir, you say the victim was a policeman?" the operator replied, her voice responding to what she'd heard. "In his patrol car? I'm going to need your name. And the location you're calling from. Are you still at the scene? Are you able to give us the patrol car's number?"

"No, no." I wasn't sure what I should say. "I'm driving on Lakeview. The person who did it took off in a blue sedan. I'm chasing him now!"

"Sir, I am going to ask you to please pull over and go back to the scene," the operator instructed me with urgency.

Damn. I had to stop at a light. I pushed myself up and tried to see over the tops of the stopped cars.

Nothing. The son of a bitch was getting away! I tried to concentrate on what I'd seen on the plate. A dragon or a snake, or a winged bird. *Red,* I was thinking. Yes, it was red. All I knew for sure was that the plate definitely wasn't from Florida. But I couldn't completely visualize it. Everything had happened so quickly.

"Sir, I'm going to need you to return to the scene of the crime," the 911 operator said to me again. "And I'm going to need your name."

The light changed. I drove on. *My name . . . ?* I was about to give it, the accelerator pressed to the floor, doing sixty on a crowded, suburban street. Seventy. *"It's . . ."*

35

Then I stopped.

A few lengths in front of me was a blue sedan that looked like the one I saw, and it was weaving in and out of traffic. *"Hold it!"* I said, as if I'd been jolted by EKG paddles. "This may be him!"

"Sir, I don't need you to be a hero . . ." the dispatcher shouted at me. "Just give us some identifying characteristics. We'll take care of it from there."

Hero . . . ? I wasn't trying to be a hero. I was trying to do what was right and at the same time save my own skin! Go back to the scene? Without a plate number or some identifying characteristics. I knew I'd have one helluva time explaining myself back there.

I was forced to stop at another light. But so was the blue car, which was approximately ten cars ahead of me. I saw a road sign for I-10, one of the main highways, *straight ahead*! That's likely where he was heading. That's where I'd be heading! The light changed, and the blue car drove on ahead. I leaned and caught a quick enough glimpse of the plate before it was blocked, and again I noticed the light ground, just like I'd seen.

"Sir . . ."

I knew I'd lose the guy for good with the dispatcher continuing to bark at me. I waited a few agonizing seconds for the cars in front of me to move, every nerve in my body bristling with electricity and urgency.

Then I just said, *The hell with it, Henry. Let's go!*

I swung into the turn lane and sped up to the

intersection, and went right through the light. I was already in up to my eyeballs anyway!

"The guy is in a blue sedan heading down Lakeview toward the entrance to I-10!" I shouted into the phone. Which caused the dispatcher to warn me to stop for a third time.

I ignored her. I spotted the car again—maybe ten or twelve vehicles in front. I kept speeding up, dodging ahead of other vehicles in front of me, making up ground.

Eight cars now.

Then, to my astonishment, I spotted another blue car! This one was one or two in front of the one I was chasing.

Which was the right one?

Neither had in-state plates, but the second one—the one in front—did have something else on the back plate, and as I squinted in the sun, I saw it began with an *A*! I pressed on the gas. The speedometer climbed to seventy. Now I was only a handful of cars behind them. Five or six. We were rapidly approaching the highway. I yelled to the 911 dispatcher, *"There's a second car!"*

If one of them got on the highway and the other remained on Lakeview, I'd have to make a choice.

The first car I had spotted put on its blinker and began to veer toward the highway, picking up speed. I couldn't make out the plates, other than an *AD* or maybe a *J* or something . . . I couldn't see part of the plate. The second car stayed on Lakeview. And it had that thing on the plate.

I had to make a choice.

I yelled to the operator, "One of them is veering onto I-10. West. The other is staying on Lakeview . . . *I'm staying,*" I told her.

The first car veered onto to the ramp, heading onto the highway. I went past it, underneath the overpass, praying that wasn't Martinez's killer getting away.

I hit the accelerator, pulling myself closer to the second blue car. It had light-ground plates, just like the one at the scene. I started to make out the number. AB4 . . . I didn't know. That could have been it.

And some kind of image too . . .

I sped up, inching closer, until I could finally make out the plate number in full. AB4- 699.

It was from Tennessee. And the image I saw . . . It was a U.S. Army medallion.

And there was a sticker on the back window. *Honk if you support our troops.*

Could that be it?

As I pulled up even, I saw a woman behind the wheel. And a kid in the back. In a kiddie seat. The one thing I *was* sure of was that the person driving the murder car was a man! I drove alongside of her, staring in futility and frustration. The woman leered back at me like I was some kind of nutcase and changed lanes.

"*Fuck!*" I slammed my palm against the steering

38

wheel. The killer was heading away on I-10. *Fuck, fuck, fuck, fuck fuck!*

All of a sudden reality sank back into me. I had to go back to the scene and tell the police what I knew. I had to face a bunch of pissed-off, angry cops who might well slam me onto the ground and slap the cuffs on me again.

"I need your name, sir!" the 911 operator kept insisting.

Would they buy for one second what I'd been saying? That I was chasing after a blue car. The killer's car. With nothing concrete to identify it. These same cops who had just seen me in cuffs, in the back of Martinez's car. Having argued with the very policeman who was now dead! And taken off from the scene!

"You have to find the car," I said to the operator. "It's heading west on I-10. It's a blue sedan. Out-of-state plates. I think the first letters were *AMD* . . . Some kind of image on it, a dragon or winged bird. I'm heading back to the scene. Someone has to have spotted it."

I hung up and began retracing my route along Lakeview, nervously going over what I was about to face. Up ahead, it appeared as if traffic was being diverted off the main road. By now they'd probably found Martinez's car. They all knew who I was anyway and what car I was driving. I'd have some explaining to do. How I didn't kill Martinez. Why I'd run from the scene.

39

I decided to give myself up to the first policeman I saw.

About a mile from the scene, police cars had blocked Lakeview and were pushing traffic onto a side street. I knew I'd need a lawyer. A good one. A criminal attorney. As I inched closer to the cops, to my impending capture, I started going over in my head who I could call. I inched to about eight car lengths away, and spotted two navy-clad patrolmen waving cars away.

My eyes stretched wide.

One of them was that asshole. Rowley. *Baldy.* The one who just winked at me maliciously and said, "Just never let me catch you again!"

He'd wanted to rip me a new one over nothing more than a traffic violation. Now one of his own had been murdered.

He was the last person on earth I wanted to hand myself over to!

I thought about pulling out of my lane and finding someone else. But there wasn't anyone. Not here. The line of cars kept creeping forward. I had no choice but to inch closer, or draw attention to myself. The kind of attention I didn't need right now.

Suddenly Rowley looked up and scanned down the line of cars, and to my dismay, his eyes seemed to lock like a magnet on the sight of my white Caddie.

Then they fixed directly on me.

Every cell in my body froze. I put up my hands where he could see them. I didn't know what else to do.

Then I watched as the sonovabitch shouted something to his partner and reached for his gun.

To my horror, he started running up the line of cars toward me.

I started yelling, *"No, it wasn't me*! *It wasn't me!"* And he was shouting something back, *"Out of the car! Out of the car!"*

Oh, shit!

And then he aimed!

My heart almost clawed its way up my throat as I vividly recalled what he had warned me of if our paths ever crossed again. A warning bell inside me rang: *Henry, you have to get the hell away from this guy! Now!*

I jerked on the wheel and forced the Caddie out of my lane.

I turned around and saw Rowley's weapon aimed directly at me! *He's going to shoot, Henry!* My heart clawed its way up my throat. No way I could simply make myself a sitting duck for him.

I hit the gas.

Suddenly the front windshield exploded, glass raining all over me. He *was* shooting!

Oh my God!

"No, no," I yelled back in horror. *"It wasn't me!"*

I whipped my head back and saw Rowley again, this time in a shooter's position, two hands on his weapon, steadying, eyes trained directly at me.

He's going to kill me! I screamed to myself.

I floored the accelerator, the Caddie screeching into the oncoming lane, as another shot crashed through the side window, shattering it, narrowly missing my head.

"How the hell is this happening?" I screamed in the car. *"It's not me!"*

I spun a U-ey, jolting up onto the pavement and hitting a street sign, ducking my head as low as I could, and sped off in the opposite direction on Lakeview as two more shots slammed into my chassis, clanging off the rear.

I didn't know if I was making the biggest mistake of my life, but I was sure that if I didn't get out of there, I'd be dead.

I cut a sharp right onto the first cross street I encountered, and then an even quicker left onto a residential lane. I floored it again and for the first time checked behind me.

No one was there.

CHAPTER FOUR

At the Jacksonville Sheriff's Office, on Adams Street downtown, it was Carrie Holmes's first day back on the job.

She knew it wasn't going to be an easy one. It had been four months, the four toughest months of her life, since that day. The day her world had fallen apart. But she knew she had to get back into the world. Back to the person she was before . . . Before "the day my heart died too," as she always referred to it.

Take a deep breath, she told herself, stepping off the elevator onto the detectives' floor.

Life starts over—now.

Carrie worked for the JSO. *Community Outreach Director*, her business card read. A glorified way of saying she took care of matters in which the department's duty interacted with the public, building goodwill in the parts of town where the department didn't have much. Softening the outrage after an incident in which excessive force was used, or worse, an officer-involved shooting. Overseeing police-sponsored community events. A new chief had been appointed since she'd been gone. Erman Hall. More of a numbers guy who was given a mandate on issues like the tough immigration law and budget control. She'd heard that everyone was trying to curry favor with him.

Truth was, Carrie was kind of surprised she hadn't already received her "pink slip" in the mail. Let's just say "Community Outreach" wasn't exactly a priority in a time when cops were being pulled off the street and station houses closed. She'd always expected she'd become a detective herself—her dad had been a chief in New Hampshire for twenty-four years and her older brother, Jack, was a supervisor with the FBI in Atlanta. With a master's in criminology from the University of Florida, she'd always thought that becoming a detective was the path she would take, but with Rick on duty overseas, and then starting up his law practice, and then Raef, she took the job that opened—in Administration—and it just kind of stuck. The brains of the family, her dad always said, *and* the looks!

Not that any of that really mattered now. Brains, looks, but nothing had prepared her for what had hit her. Nothing could.

To lose your husband and your son . . . Well, almost your son . . .

And on the very same day.

Now it was time to start over.

Carrie hugged a few people hello as she made her way back to her office. This was harder than she'd thought. Everyone was tiptoeing around on eggshells, not wanting to say the wrong thing: "How are you doing?" "So great to have you back!" And, of course, "How's Raef?"

"He's doing really well," she replied, as upbeat as she could. "He's at my folks'." It seemed the best thing for a while that he remain with her parents in Atlantic Beach, which was closer to the hospital. "We hope to have him back in school soon."

Of course, no one mentioned Rick—except just to shake their heads, eyes glossing over a little, and to say how sorry they were.

"Well, you give that boy a big hug from me!"

She ran the gauntlet of well-wishers back to her desk. She found a card there—signed by most of the office, detectives and administration. *Great to have you back!* That brought a little tear to her eye. And made her smile.

So did the handful of photos that were still on her shelf. Rick finishing the Marine Corps Marathon in D.C. last year. In 3:51:29. His personal best, by far! Raef looking very ferocious in his pee wee football gear. That nice one of the three of them at her folks' last Thanksgiving. All decked out.

Carrie felt herself starting to get sad.

She looked at the mountain of files and memoranda that had been arranged on her desk by Andrea Carson, her deputy, and then the phone started to ring: people she dealt with on the force and even a local press contact, all glad to hear she was back. She started to read through a few of the files, trying to catch up on what was happening. She knew she'd have to ease herself back into the routine.

Andrea knocked on her door, folders in hand. "You ready?"

"Ready." Carrie nodded with a smile. "Come on in."

That's when she noticed that a crowd had gathered underneath the TV in the detectives' bullpen. Things seemed to have gotten a little hectic. Lots of people running around.

She stood up—the captain's office door had been closed a long time now. Then she saw the chief, the new chief, with whom she'd hoped to grab a couple of minutes, heading out of the office with Cam Winfield, the department's press liaison—not looking at all as if "community outreach" was high on his list of priorities right now.

Something had happened!

Carrie stepped out and found Robyn, Chief Hall's secretary. "What's going on?"

"Didn't you hear?" Robyn's eyes were wet with tears. "One of our guys was just shot on the street. *Killed*."

"Oh no . . ." Carrie's blood came to a halt. *"Who?"*

"A patrol officer out of Southeast. Named Martinez." The chief's secretary sadly shook her head.

"Robert Martinez?" Carrie sucked in a painful breath. She knew Martinez. She'd worked with him once or twice, in Brentwood on a community center there. He was a part-time basketball coach. He had a wife and a couple of kids. *"On the street?"* she asked Robyn.

"Shot. Point-blank. After a routine traffic stop." The chief's assistant shook her head. "Right in his car."

"Oh God . . ." Carrie felt her stomach fall. She tried to recall, Jacksonville hadn't had an officer killed in the line of duty for at least a couple of years. "Let me know if there's anything I can do . . ." she said, and shook her head kind of uselessly. *"Please . . ."*

She went back to her desk, an empty feeling in her gut. She went on the KJNT news website and brought up a live feed from the scene. "Police Officer Reportedly Killed on Lakeview Drive," the headline read. The shot was from an airborne copter cam. Carrie minimized it and brought up Martinez's "green screen." There were several commendations. One censure years ago for excessive force that was never prosecuted. She thought of his wife, Marilyn. She would call her. She knew firsthand how tough this was going to be.

"Carrie?"

Bill Akers stuck his head inside her workstation. Akers was her boss, a captain, in charge of operations, and her department reported in to him.

Carrie stood up. "I just heard . . ."

"Listen, Carrie . . ." Akers blew out a breath. "I know it's your first day back and all . . ."

"Don't worry about that," she answered. "What can I do?"

"We're setting up a hotline. A lot of personnel are in the field or following up on leads. We've got a manhunt going. You mind manning a phone? Anyone calls in who seems legit, take down their info. A detective will get back to them as soon as they can."

"Of course I'll take a phone," Carrie said. "Whatever you need. Is there a . . ."

"*Suspect . . .*" Akers filled in. "Yeah, we have a suspect. We've got a picture of him on the screen now."

He led her over to a terminal in the detectives' bullpen and showed her a head shot from Florida Motor Vehicles. "Apparently the guy caused a ruckus after Martinez pulled him over for running a light. He's driving a white, rented Caddie. Name of Steadman. Henry. The guy's a doctor, if you can imagine. Some big-shot plastic surgeon from down in Palm Beach."

"*We're sure?*" Carrie stared back at the screen. The suspect had a nice face. Bright, intelligent eyes. Wavy, long brown hair. Stylish glasses. A warm smile.

48

Successful, nice-looking plastic surgeons generally didn't fit the profile a cop murderer.

"Damn sure." The captain nodded firmly. "Bastard just fled the fucking scene."

CHAPTER FIVE

I drove, accelerator pressed to the floor, in a state between bewilderment and outright panic.

The front windshield had a spiderweb crack and my right rear passenger window was completely shattered, glass splayed all over my lap. My pulse felt like it was in an atomic accelerator and my heart had crawled so high up my throat I could have reached in and pulled it out. I had no idea where I was heading. Just *away*. Away from Rowley and those trigger-happy cops.

I looked at my hands on the steering wheel and they were shaking like branches in a storm.

Okay, Henry, okay . . . What do I do now?

It was clear I had to turn myself in, but I had to find a way that wouldn't end up getting me killed. I ran through all the possibilities of where to go, whom

I could trust. And only one person came to mind.

Mike. Whom I was supposed to be meeting for golf in a little over an hour!

He was a lawyer . . . A real estate lawyer, perhaps, but he'd have partners, contacts. I knew he was very well connected in town. He'd know what to do. No one could possibly logically believe that I was a cop killer.

I thought, if I could simply get to him, he'd be able to negotiate a safe handover. I couldn't have killed Martinez. I had no motive, no gun . . . ? I didn't even own a gun! I hadn't even shot one since . . . I racked my brain. *Since camp, for God's sake!* When I was a kid!

I'd been to Mike's home once. I remembered that it was in an upscale section of town. *Avondale*, he'd told me. I was already supposed to meet him there. He'd mentioned that it wasn't too far from Atlantic Pines. Which meant I couldn't be too far from him now.

Meanwhile, I had cops on my tail and I was driving a shot-up car.

The residential road I was on was coming to an end, leading into a more commercial thoroughfare. I made a right, and anxiously drove a block or two, then pulled into the first business I saw—a Sherwin-Williams paint store—and wove around to a lot behind the store.

I figured I was safe here for a short while. But I knew I couldn't go on in this car. It was a mess, and every cop in the city would be looking for it.

I grabbed my cell and brought up Mike's number. It

went to two, three rings . . . *"C'mon, Mike, please, answer!"* I was begging. Then, agonizingly, I heard his voice-mail recording. *"You've reached Mike Dinofrio . . ."* the familiar voice came on. *"I'm sorry I'm unable to take your call now, but if you—"*

I clicked off. Why the hell wasn't he answering? I was supposed to check in with him when I reached the hotel. *C'mon, Mike, please. . .*

Frantically I tried again. Again, his voice mail. This time I stammered through a harried message:

"Mike— it's Henry! I don't know if you've heard, but something crazy has happened. I really need your help. And now! Just call me back, *please*. It's vital, Mike . . . *and quickly*! Please . . ."

I hung up and let out a long breath. I rested my head back and closed my eyes. I was safe here—for a while. But sooner or later a customer would drive in. I didn't know what information had been released on the airwaves, if my car was hot—they surely knew who *I* was—so I turned on the radio. All anyone had to do was see my front windshield and it would be clear . . . I waited, seconds seeming like minutes.

I just about jumped with relief when my phone suddenly rang.

"Henry, it's Mike . . . !" he said. "I was out polishing my clubs. What's happened?"

I filled him in on what had happened, trying to keep it from sounding as if I'd lost my mind.

"They think you did *what*, Henry?"

"They think I killed the cop, Mike! *Me!*"

"That's crazy, Henry!"

"I know, but, Mike . . ." I told him I needed a place to go. That I had to turn myself in.

He didn't waste a second answering. "Tell me where you are. I'll come and get you . . ."

"*No*. No. These people are crazy. I don't want to put you in any danger. It's best I come to you."

"You're sure?" he asked unhesitatingly. "I could—"

"Yes. I'm sure."

He gave me his address and told me it was only about fifteen minutes away. I said I'd figure out a way to get there. "I'll be waiting for you," he said. "Don't worry. We'll make this come out."

"Okay. Okay . . . Mike, thanks a lot. I don't know what to say. I didn't know where else to turn."

"Don't even say it, Henry. We'll figure this out. I'll do whatever I can to help."

I blew out of a long, relieved breath. *"Thanks."* Then I couldn't believe what popped into my mind. "Sorry about the golf, dude. Looks like we may have to put it off for today."

He chuckled grimly. "You just be careful, Henry . . ."

I hung up and jumped out of the Caddie, getting ready to leave. I grabbed my satchel case out of the backseat. I figured my iPad might come in handy. And a golf cap. Anything that might conceal me a bit. The rest . . . clothes, papers, my speech, what did it matter now?

They already knew who the hell I was anyway!

I locked it up and headed out onto the street. Southside Boulevard. It was a pretty commercial thoroughfare—an auto supply store, a Popeye's Chicken. On the other side of the street, a couple of blocks away, I saw some kind of motel. A Clarion Inn. I put on my sunglasses, pulled my cap down over my eyes, and hustled across the street. I stopped in the middle as a police car sped by, lights flashing, almost giving me a heart attack! But mercifully, it continued by. And just as mercifully—there was a taxi in the driveway when I reached the motel.

"You free?" I knocked on the driver's window.

"Sorry, waiting for a fare," he said. He picked up his radio. "If you need a car, I could . . ."

"How about a hundred bucks?" I reached inside my pocket and pulled out a crisp, new bill. "I need to get somewhere fast."

The driver shot up. "I could always call them another car, is what I meant to say." He turned on the ignition. "Hop on in."

I did and pushed the hundred-dollar bill through the partition. I read off Mike's address. "I need to go to . . ." Then I caught myself and gave him a street number that I figured would be close by. No reason he had to know exactly where I was going. " . . . 33443 Turnberry Terrace."

"That's in Avondale, huh? I think we can get you there."

I leaned back as the taxi pulled out onto the street and closed my eyes. The driver called in to his dispatcher. "Base—this is seventeen. My fare's fifteen minutes late and some guy's got an airport emergency, so I took him on. You may want to check with the Clarion and see if these people still want a car . . ."

I sat back, away from the driver's line of sight. My heart rate calmed for the first time since I left Martinez at the scene. The driver tried to catch my eyes in his rearview mirror, asking me questions I didn't need to hear: "From around here?" "Shame about the weather, huh?" It was cloudless. Eighty degrees. I grunted a few halfhearted replies so that, given how the guy had just basically saved my life, he wouldn't think I was rude. He drove a little farther, and as he pulled onto I-10, I saw two police cars staked out at the entrance ramp. I pressed deep into the seat as we went by.

"You hear what happened?" the driver asked.

"No," I replied. "Sorry. *What?*"

"Some guy just plugged a cop right back there on Lakeview. Traffic's all to hell. They won't let anyone by."

He turned on a local news station. First it was the weather, then a couple of car ads. Then the announcer came back on. "Now back to our lead story of the

55

morning . . . The brazen execution-style killing of a Jacksonville policeman near Lakeview Drive . . . Police say they have a possible suspect who has fled the scene and remains at large . . ."

I immediately felt the sweats come over me, the announcer saying how the suspect had been detained over a traffic violation. And how he had fled the scene in a white Cadillac with Florida plates.

My stomach forced its way up.

The possible suspect I was hearing about was me!

"The slain officer, whose name is being withheld, pending family notification, is a decorated, fifteen-year veteran of the force . . ."

If I wasn't sick already, that got me there. The guy had been a prick to me—I still didn't know why he had pulled me out. But there was no reason in the world that he had to die.

We crossed a bridge and drove past another exit or two, then we pulled off at Riverside Avenue and entered a neighborhood of large, upscale homes. I knew we were close.

"Can you believe that shit?" the cabbie said, trying to catch my eyes in the mirror. "What kind of bastard does that, you know what I mean . . . ?"

"Yeah, I know." I shifted my face away. *Please, just get me there.*

We wound around some residential streets. I recognized the area from my time here before. Then I spotted a street sign for Turnberry Terrace. No need the cabbie had to know precisely which house I was headed to.

"This is fine," I said, grabbing my satchel. "You can let me off here."

CHAPTER SIX

I waited until the cabbie drove off before crossing the street. The homes here were sprawling and upscale— Tudors and colonials with well-manicured lawns and pretty landscaping.

I knew Mike had done well. He had worked on some big land deals in the past few years. Just being here made me feel a bit more hopeful. Mike would hear my story. He'd be able to negotiate something with the local authorities. In spite of how everything looked, it would be clear: the lack of any motive; the impossibility of how I could have gotten my hands on a weapon; how I'd only ducked into Martinez's car to check how badly he'd been hurt. Even why I'd fled the scene . . .

It would be clear I wasn't the killer.

A mail truck drove around the circle, stopping at each house, and I waited, one resident stepping out in her bathrobe to take in her mail, until it headed back down the block. Then I found Mike's house, a stylish, mustard-colored Mediterranean.

I began to wonder if my identity had been released. *Dr. Henry Steadman. Prominent cosmetic surgeon from Palm Beach. Wanted for murder. He fled the scene in a white Cadillac STS. . .*

By now Mike must've heard.

Cautiously, I went up the driveway, praying that I wouldn't run into Gail, his wife, first and have to explain this all to her. She would probably freak. I knew Gail had her own real estate agency in town. She and Mike had two kids—one away at college. The younger one, I figured, would already be at school.

One of the three wood-paneled garage bays was open, and I recognized Mike's silver Jag there.

I let out a sigh of relief.

I hurried up to the house and rang the front doorbell, expecting Mike to open the door instantly, but no one did. I rang again, one of those formal-sounding, church-bell chimes.

Again, no one answered.

I was about to try one more time when I pushed on the latch and the front door opened.

I stepped tentatively into the large, high-ceilinged house, facing a kind of spacious living room with a lot of art on the walls, a huge mirror, and an arched Palladian window.

"Mike . . . !"

Through the window, I saw a large, fenced-in backyard with a good-size pool and a pool house in the same architectural style as the main house. I waited for him to come out and called again, *"Mike . . . where are you?"*

Suddenly a tremor shot through me. Surely he'd heard by now. Maybe he hadn't believed me as much as I thought. I mean, we were old friends, but not exactly *close* friends. I started thinking, what if he'd left, or even worse, notified the police. *What if—*

No. I stopped myself. *Jesus, Henry, you're acting crazy. You've known the guy since college. You're just being paranoid,* which was kind of easy right now.

I couldn't say I liked the idea of sneaking around someone's house with half the police in Jacksonville searching for me. Someone could just blow me away with a gun—and it would be entirely legal! I stepped into the foyer, trying to recall the layout, feeling a little edgy.

"Mike?"

I turned right and found myself in the kitchen. Some plates on the counter, recently used. A half-picked-over muffin. A jar of almond butter—which made me smile, remembering Mike was always kind of a health nut.

Suddenly things began to feel a little odd to me. *"Mike, where the hell are you . . . ?"*

I went back through the living room. The family room was just as I'd remembered, with pictures of the kids all over and a large Tarkay watercolor of a Parisian sidewalk café.

Mike's office was just down a hallway. He had taken me in there on my one visit and showed off his collection of sports memorabilia, his pride and joy.

The door was half open. Reflexively I knocked and called out again. *"Mike?* You in there, guy . . . ?"

To my relief, I saw him sitting in a high-backed, leather chair at his desk, glasses raised on his forehead as if he was looking over a report, wearing a red golf shirt—which accounted for why I didn't see it at first.

My first reaction was to blow out my cheeks and go, "Jesus, buddy, am I glad to see you . . ."

Then I stopped.

He *was* sitting there, except that he hadn't moved or made even the slightest sign of recognition. His eyes were wide and glassy and staring through me.

Two dark blotches were on his chest.

"Oh my God, Mike . . . !" My legs grew rubbery and I suddenly felt my stomach lurch up my throat. *"Oh, no, no, no, no . . ."*

I ran over. You didn't need a medical degree to know that he was dead. His pulse was nonexistent; his body temperature was already getting cold.

61

"*Oh, Mike, Mike . . .*" I said, tears forcing their way into my eyes, and I basically sank, numb and not understanding, into a leather chair.

I'd known Mike for more than twenty years. Since we were freshmen at Amherst. He was on the golf team. He was one of those glass-half-full kind of guys, who'd give you the shirt off his back. Which was basically what he was doing for me now.

Or had been about to do.

I sat there with my head in my hands, looking at him, trying to figure out how this could possibly have happened. My friend was dead! How could anyone have possibly known that I would come here? Or even put the two of us together. How—

Suddenly it was clear.

I realized with mounting alarm that two people were now dead. *Two people.* And that I was the only connection between them!

I felt the sweats come over me and my insides slowly clawed their way up my throat. *Oh my God, Henry. . .*

Someone was targeting me.

It seemed crazy, impossible. Who? And why? What could I have done? Just an hour ago I'd been driving into town, thinking that this was going to be one of the best days of my life. *Now* . . . Now two people were dead. Brutally murdered.

And I was the only link between them!

No, no, this was crazy . . . It couldn't be.

My thoughts raced wildly. I stared at my friend's life-less body while tears of grief and utter disbelief made their way down my cheeks. I realized now that I couldn't explain myself. Not any longer. I'd be looked at as a suspect here as well. In *two* murders now. The first maybe I could explain . . . But *this* one, completely unrelated, my friend, at the place I had chosen to flee to . . . All they'd have to do was check my phone records to see that I'd just called him. My prints and DNA were probably everywhere.

Even on his body.

"Who's doing this to me?"

I heard a car drive by, and suddenly I knew I had to get out of there. *Now!* A housekeeper might show up at any second. Or Gail could come home. My name was already all over the airwaves as a person wanted in connection to a murder.

How could I possibly explain this one now?

I ran back to the kitchen and grabbed a cloth and started wiping down anything I could remember I had touched.

The doors. The coffee mug. Around Mike's office.

Him.

Then I didn't know if I should have done that. It only made me look as if I was covering up. Made me look guiltier.

I saw Mike's cell phone on his desk. I knew it was crazy, but by now mine was probably being monitored

63

by the police and I had to make a few calls. The first one to Liz. She had to know. *Oh God, how would I possibly explain this?* I felt completely nauseous.

"*Mike . . .*" I said, swallowing, placing my hand on his shoulder. "I'm so sorry, dude. I know you were only trying to help. I know you—"

I clasped his lifeless hand. What else was there to say?

I went out through the garage. Mike's silver Jag was just sitting there. His Callaways leaning against the trunk. Crazy as it was, I had no other way to get out of there.

And I couldn't possibly make myself look any guiltier than I already had.

I found the key on the front divider, and the engine started up.

I drove out, closing the garage door behind me. Tears stung in my eyes. I wanted to call Gail and let her know what horror awaited her back at home. But how could I? Until I figured it out.

I knew, once she heard the news, she'd automatically assume it was me.

I drove out the driveway and backtracked along the same route I had taken earlier, toward the highway. I had no idea where I was going, or whom I could turn to now.

In a few minutes I hit I-10 again. I knew I was safe in Mike's car, at least for a while. But that was going to cave in fast.

I looked in the rearview mirror, just to make sure there weren't any cops behind me, and, for the first time, actually focused on the Jag's rear window.

Suddenly my eyes tripled in size.

The window had a decal on it—an image I was sure I had seen before. *What the hell is happening, Henry . . . ?*

I pulled over to the side of the highway and spun around, frozen in shock.

It was the identical image I'd seen on the back plate of the blue car as it pulled away.

Not a dragon, as I had originally thought. But a kind of bird. With a sharp beak and bright red wings. A long tail.

A gamecock.

A mascot. From the University of South Carolina.

I remembered, Mike's oldest son was a sophomore there.

CHAPTER SEVEN

The squat, stub-necked man stepped up to the officer behind the glass, his pink face framed by a felt of orange hair around the sides of his balding head.

"Amanda Hofer," he said, and pushed his ID through the opening while the officer took a good look at him. "I'm her father."

The duty guard at the Lowndes County Jail inspected it and pushed it back to him. "You can head down to Booth Two."

Vance Hofer put his license back in the thick, tattered wallet and stepped through a security checkpoint, taking out his keys and loose change. Then he continued down to the visiting room. It had been a long time, he thought to himself, a very long time since he'd felt at home in a place like this. A lot of things had happened and not many of them good. He eased himself into a chair in the small booth, stared at his reflection in the glass.

He'd lost Joycie to cancer about a year and a half ago. Lost his job at the mill a year before that. Medical insurance too. Then he'd fallen behind on the house. Not to mention how he'd been forced to come up here in the first place, thrown to the wolves down south on trumped-up charges he couldn't defend.

Life was bleeding him, Vance reflected, one cut at a time.

But this last one—what had happened to Amanda. Well, that was one more cut than he could bear.

They brought her out in an orange jumpsuit, hands cuffed in front of her. She looked a little overwhelmed and scared. Who wouldn't be? Maybe a little afraid of seeing him too. Her hair was all straggly and unkempt. Cheeks sunken and pale. And when she saw him, who it was who had come to visit, she had this cautious look that he took as both worried and even a little shamed. Like a proud animal not used to being caged. She sat down across from him with a wary smile and shrugged her shoulders slightly.

"How ya doin', Daddy?"

He nodded back, not knowing what to say. "Amanda."

Truth be told, Vance hadn't known what to say to his daughter in years. He saw her as little more than a whining, pathetic child who never owned up to anything she'd done. Who'd always blamed every bit of what went wrong in her life on someone or something else. Which made Vance sick to his soul, since, if he stood on one thing, it was that each of us had to be accountable for what we had done in life.

No matter how bad.

Still, she was his daughter. He'd tried to raise her as best he could, knowing he had always had a paucity in the way of softness or understanding, until things started to go downhill in the past year. And he hated that—that he'd let things get away from him. That someone with as clear a ledger when it came to right from wrong had to look through the glass and see his own seed, his wife's baby, and say, in a corner of his bruised, unforgiving heart, *That's my daughter there.*

"How's Benji, Daddy?" Amanda asked. Her stupid cat. Not even her cat, just a mangy, scrawny stray who lived in the woods outside and only came around 'cause Amanda was stupid enough to feed it. "Are you leaving a little something out for him? He likes a little raw chop meat maybe. Or maybe some tuna fish."

"He's doing just fine, Amanda, just fine," Vance said, though he was plainly lying. He'd heard a couple of hopeful purrs a few days back, but now the critter must have wised up and was no longer coming around. "He stops by every couple of nights or so. Been asking for you, 'Manda."

That made her smile.

"I talked to my lawyer," she said, the momentary

68

lightness in her soft eyes darkening. "They want me to plead, Daddy, to what they're calling 'aggravated vehicular manslaughter.' Otherwise he says they're going to go for second-degree murder."

Vance nodded.

The whole thing had been played out all over the news, so much that he couldn't even watch TV anymore. Such a nice, young thing that gal had been, and married to someone serving our country, a Marine in Afghanistan. Not to mention that baby . . . Only eight weeks old. The poor guy hadn't even seen his son yet. The D.A. wouldn't let up. Not with Amanda so juiced up and not even knowing what she had done and all. It was clear he was pushing for the max. Vance couldn't even blame him.

It was an election year.

"Sounds like something you ought to weigh carefully, honey."

"Aggravated manslaughter's punishable by twenty years, Daddy!" Her eyes grew scared and wide. "I didn't mean to hurt no one. I didn't mean for this to happen. I wasn't myself. *Those things* . . ." She wiped her eyes and pushed back her hair. "We're talking my whole life, Daddy! I don't deserve this. I'm scared. You have to help me. You do . . ."

"I know you're scared, Amanda," Vance said, looking at her. "But you're gonna have to take responsibility for what you've done. You killed a woman, honey. And her baby . . ."

And after, how she'd just walked around in a big daze crying how she was hurt too. Those animals . . . Her so-called friends. Look what they'd done to her. Vance had fought for right from wrong his whole life, and this was what it had left him. "No one can make that go away, darlin'. There just ain't much I can do."

"*Twenty years, Daddy!* That's my whole life! You know people. I know you can help me." She was crying, his little girl. Thick, childlike tears. But crying for whom? Herself. *"You have to!"*

"I can't help you, honey." Vance lowered his head. "At least, not in that way."

"Then how?" Amanda stared back at him. "How can you help me, Daddy? You were a cop, all those years . . ." Her tone was helpless and desperate, fragile as thin glass, but also with that edge that dug into him with recollections he didn't want to hear. "You were a cop! That has to mean something."

A fire began to light up in Vance's belly. First, like a match to kindling. Then catching, fueled by the anger he always carried, and his shame. The people demanded justice. She'd killed two perfectly innocent people. He understood that better than anyone. His daughter had to pay the price. They'd been bleeding him, one cut at a time, over the years, *one at a time* . . . And deeper . . .

"How you gonna help me, Daddy?"

It got to the point you couldn't take no more . . .

Someone had to pay.

Vance leaned forward and said in barely more than a whisper, "Who gave you the pills, 'Manda?"

"No one gave me the pills, Daddy. You don't understand. You just get them, that's all. I needed them."

"Someone gave 'em to you, honey. *So you tell me who? I'm pretty sure I know who.*" His eyes fixed on hers. "You think, if the situation was reversed, that boy'd be protecting you?"

She snorted back, angry, "You're wrong, Daddy. You've always been wrong."

"Who gave 'em to you, honey?" Vance put his beefy palm on the glass partition, hoping she'd do the same, but she just sat there. "For once, do the right thing, hon. Please. Who took my little girl from me?"

"No . . ." For a moment she looked back at him and shook her head, and then there was anger in her eyes. "That's your answer, Daddy? That's how you're gonna help me? I'm sitting here, looking at my whole life taken away, and all you want to know is who took your little girl?" She screwed up her eyes and gave him a cajoling laugh, daggers in them. *"You* done it, Daddy. You took her. You took that little girl. You know what I'm talking about. You want to know so bad? Well, take a long, hard look at the truth, Daddy. It wasn't the drugs. It wasn't Wayne. It was *you.* Take a good look at what you see"—she pushed herself back and lifted her jangling hands—" 'cause you're the one who's responsible! *You."*

71

She stared at him, her once-soft, brown, little-girl eyes ablaze. "You think you're gonna help me . . . ?" She nodded to the guard and stood up, brushing the stringy hair out of her eyes. "What're you gonna do, Daddy, hurt them all? Everyone who took your little dream away?" She took a step away from him, crushing his heart, though he didn't know quite how to say it.

Then she turned and faced him one more time. A smile crept onto her lips, a cruel one. "You may not be in this prison," Amanda said, like she was stepping on a dying insect to put it out of its pain, "but that don't mean you're any freer than me now, does it, Daddy?"

CHAPTER EIGHT

My eyes locked on the gamecock, the question throbbing through me if some kind of connection could've existed between Mike and the person who had just shot Martinez, or if this was just some crazy coincidence.

Either way, I drove back on the highway, knowing I was safe in Mike's Jaguar, at least until someone discovered the body. Which could be any moment, of course. I tried to think how I could explain this. It would hardly be a secret that I had headed to Mike's after I left Martinez. There was the cabbie; not to mention my prints and DNA probably all over everything. Gail would tell them how we were supposed to play golf that morning. I'd taken his phone and car. As soon as he was found, everything would be linked to me. I veered off the highway at a random exit, pulled the Jag into the lot of a Winn-Dixie food market, and just sat there.

I needed someone to help me now. Someone I could trust.

Amazingly, the person who came to mind was Liz.

My ex-wife and I had stayed on decent terms since we split up. Decent because she had moved on, even if I hadn't completely. Whatever had once come between us—our diverging careers; that she could be a total bitch at times; and oh yeah, that she had started up with the lead partner in her firm while we were still married—we still trusted each other, at least when it came to Hallie's best interests.

Liz was a terrific immigration lawyer; she dealt mostly with people trying to get a green card for their house-keepers or a visa for their relatives from Cuba. But if there was a better person to call who would know how to get me out of this hole, I didn't know who.

I dialed her number at work and her secretary, Joss, came on. "Liz Feldman's office."

"Joss, is she there?" My voice shook with urgency. *"It's important!"*

"I'm afraid she's in a meeting, Dr. Steadman. Can I have her call you back? It shouldn't be too long."

"No, it can't wait, Joss. I need to speak with her now. I need you to pull her out of that meeting."

"Give me a moment," Joss said, obviously picking up the anxiety in my tone. "I hope that everything's okay . . ."

"Thanks. I really appreciate that, Joss."

It took another thirty seconds but finally Liz came on, in her usual bulldog style. "Henry, you just can't pull me out of a meeting like that. Is—"

"*Liz!*" I cut her off. "Listen—this is important. I'm in trouble. *Big trouble.* I need your help."

"What's happened?" she shot back. Then she gasped. "It's not—"

"No, Hallie's okay," I said, anticipating her concern. "It's nothing to do with her. It's me. I'm in Jacksonville . . ."

I tried to explain it all as rationally as I could. How a cop had pulled me over for running a light and began to hassle me. "It was weird—it was like he thought I was someone they were looking for. He pulled me out of the car and told me I was being arrested and slapped a set of cuffs on me . . ."

"Arrested? Well, you know how you can run your mouth off, Henry," she replied in form.

"Liz, this isn't a joke. Just listen! And I didn't do anything—at least not enough to get pulled out of my car. But that's not what's important now. *The cop was killed!*"

"Killed?"

"Yes, Liz. Right in front of my eyes, Liz. After he let me go, someone pulled their car around next to his and shot him, point-blank, right through his head. I saw the entire thing."

75

"Oh my God, Henry, that's horrible. Are you all right?"

"No, I'm not all right! I mean, I'm not injured. But the police believe *I* did it!" I told her how the other police cars had been called to the scene and all those crazy kinds of questions they were barking at me.

"But that's not the issue now! The guy who did it took off and I took off after him. I saw something on the car, but I couldn't catch up. So, basically, the cops saw that I was in cuffs in the back of this dead patrolman's car and then I fled the scene."

"Well, you have to go back, Henry. That much is clear. Now!"

"I did go back, Liz. And they opened fire at me!"

"Opened fire! My God, Henry, are you all right?"

"Yes, I'm fine. I mean, I wasn't hit. But my car was totally shot up. The windows shattered. I managed to escape and ditched it. But now I'm on the run. They think *I* did it! Not to mention my fucking prints are all over his car!"

"*Your prints?*" I heard her struggling to put it all together. "How did your prints get in his car, Henry?"

"Because I watched him being shot, Liz! While he was writing me out a summons. Because I'm a doctor and I ran back to check on him, but he was already gone. But anyone driving by at that particular moment saw me leaning into his car. Find a news station. I'm pretty sure my name is out there as a suspect."

"A suspect? Henry, they obviously somehow believe

you were someone else. Whoever it was they were asking all those questions about. All we have to do is clear this up and . . . So what did you do, after you saw what happened? You called 911, right?"

"Yes, I called 911, of course. But I also went after the car. There was something about it that caught my eye as I watched it speed away . . . I don't know, maybe it was instinct, but suddenly I thought, this son of a bitch just shot someone right in front of me and he's getting away. And I was the only one who saw it. So I went after him, but I couldn't catch up. On my way back, I ran into one of the officers who had been hassling me earlier—trust me, Liz, this guy was a total asshole—and he spotted me behind the wheel and pulled out a gun."

"You didn't give him any reason to shoot?"

"Liz, please don't be a lawyer here! Maybe I panicked. When's the last time *you* had someone aiming a gun at you? The guy had threatened me earlier. So, *yes*, I pulled the car out of my lane and he opened fire and the window caved in. I mean, what was I going to do? I thought he was trying to kill me, Liz!"

"Look, I don't know if I made the right decision or not, but I was scared for my life . . . So the net, net is, I basically ran from a murder scene—the murder of a cop! A cop who had me in handcuffs not ten minutes before. *With my goddamn prints everywhere!*"

"Okay. Okay, Henry, let me think . . . Did you manage to catch the plates? On this blue vehicle you spoke of?"

"Some of it. *AMD* or *ADJ* . . . It all happened so fast. But they were definitely out-of-state. South Carolina. I know that because I—"

"Henry, listen . . . Here's what we're going to do. We're going to find a way for you to turn yourself in. You had zero motive to kill this officer, right? You said he was letting you go. And you surely had no gun . . ."

"For God's sake, I don't even own a gun, Liz! You know that. Not to mention I'd just gotten off a plane."

" . . . And it's perfectly understandable," she kept rationalizing, "why you panicked and felt you had to run. They were shooting at you. From what you told me I think we can easily—"

"Liz, listen!" I interrupted her. "There's more . . ."

"*More*, Henry . . . ?" she uttered haltingly. "What could possibly be *more*?"

I sucked in a breath. "A lot more, I'm afraid. I can't just turn myself in. That's what I was trying to tell you. It gets a whole lot deeper than that."

CHAPTER NINE

"You remember Mike Dinofrio—from Amherst?" I reminded her that we had all met once for drinks at the Meisner Center in Boca a couple of years back when he was in town.

"Yeah. I think so," she answered vaguely, not convincing me that she did. "So . . . ?"

"He's a lawyer as well. From Jacksonville. We were supposed to play golf today before my conference. I had no idea where to go when I drove away from the scene, so I ditched my rental car and found a cab . . ."

"A cab?"

"Yes, Liz, a cab! I couldn't exactly drive around in my car. Every cop in the city was looking for it. The fucking windows were blown out. And so I went there. To *his* house . . . Mike's. To find a way to turn myself in."

"Okay . . ." I could feel her losing patience.

"Well, I just left it, Liz—*and he's dead*!"

"*Dead?*" Her voice dropped off a cliff. "Your friend . . . ?"

In the ensuing pause, I could sense her struggling to make sense of it all—my somehow being stopped by the cop, pulled out of my car and cuffed; the officer shot dead; me, racing madly from the scene on some wild-goose chase. *Then Mike. . .*

And to my rising worry, I felt her starting to fail.

"*Yes*. He was a lawyer, Liz. I thought he could help me turn myself in. The cops were shooting at me and I had no frigging idea where to go. And now he's got a couple of holes in his chest and, so help me, Liz, I have no idea why or what's happening! All I know is that now *two* people are dead. Two people who I'm pretty sure that the only connection between was *me*! What the hell is going on?"

She didn't reply, and the longer the pause became the more it began to worry me. "I don't know, Henry," she finally answered me. "Why don't *you* tell me just what's going on?"

"No, please, Liz, don't you dare go there on me. I need you to understand. You know damn well, whatever it is, I'm not capable of that! I'm up here at a Doctors Without Borders conference. I'm supposed to be delivering a speech tonight, on my work in Nicaragua, and to play a little golf, for God's sake! *The rest . . .*"

"Okay, okay . . ." Liz paused, hearing the agitation

80

in my voice. "Look, Henry, I'm sorry about your friend, but right now all I'm thinking about is you. Is there *any* chance your friend Mike might be connected in all this? To the cop, or to this guy they were supposedly looking for?"

"I don't know." I ran the idea around in my mind. "No, that would be impossible. No one even knew we were getting together. But then again . . ."

"Then again *what*, Henry?"

"The thing I was trying to tell you before . . . What I saw on the shooter's car, on his license plate, when I went after him. There's one on Mike's car too. It's a gamecock. A mascot. From the University of South Carolina. I'm staring at it now!"

"*A gamecock?* What possible connection does that have with anything?"

"I don't know the connection, Liz!" My voice rose at least an octave. "Mike's son goes there. I don't know if it's a connection at all, or just a coincidence. But you just asked if he could somehow be involved."

"All right, all right . . . You let me handle that," Liz said. "We have to find out who that other person is. The one the cops mistook you for. But right now what you have to do is to just stay out of sight for a while. And for God's sake, if the police find you, Henry—please don't resist! Just throw your hands up and let them take you, okay? They think you killed one of their own!"

I blew out a breath. "Okay . . ." Then I followed it

81

up with, "Oh God . . ." as an unsettling thought formed in my mind. "You've got to tell Hallie, Liz. Before she hears it from her friends, or on Facebook or something. My name's going to be all over the news, if it's not already. By tonight, the whole damn world is going to know. *They may already know!*"

"All right. I understand. You're right. I'll do it when we get off the phone. Speaking of which . . ." She paused, emphatically. "I see this isn't your phone. Just whose are you calling me on?"

I swallowed, knowing how this was about to go over. "Mike's."

"Mike's!" She let a couple of seconds pass. "That's a joke, right?"

"No, it's not a joke, Liz. I realize how it looks, but how could I possibly use mine? I found it on his desk. And it's not like I can deny ever going there. My DNA is all over his place. I thought it would buy me some time."

"*Some time*? Jesus, Henry . . . And now, why do I think I already know the answer to my next question . . . ? Just whose car are you driving around in?"

I felt an empty space in my stomach. This one would go over even worse. "It was better than my car, Liz. Every cop in Jacksonville was looking for mine!"

"Oh God, Henry . . . Just get your ass off the street. I don't want to see you end up like Bonnie and Clyde. Go to a motel. Or a public space somewhere. Someplace you won't have to show your ID. Let me talk to some people. I'll be back with you soon as I can."

"Liz . . ." I said, stammering, a tide of emotion finally welling up inside me. It had been a long time since we had talked to each other like this—in what you might call friendship, even trust. "I can't tell you how much . . . Just thank you, Liz. You must know how much this means to me . . ."

"Twenty years, Henry . . ." Her voice seemed softer than I'd heard in years. "It's not like we were enemies."

"No, I guess you're right. We weren't."

"But listen, Henry . . ."

I hunched over as a police car sped by, hoping to hear something soft and compassionate from her, maybe *I'm sorry about the way things turned out.* "Yes . . ."

"That car you're driving makes you look like a killer. I would ditch it as soon as you can."

CHAPTER TEN

She was right. Mike's Jag did make me look guilty.

Guiltier.

And it was only a matter of time before an APB was out on it as well. I had nowhere to go, but I had to get off the street until Liz could work a miracle. At least for a couple of hours. I had my iPad; that was one way to communicate. I just needed a safe place to hold out.

I flicked on the radio and found a news channel. It took no more than a minute to hear the news I dreaded come on:

"Our continuing story this morning is the execution-style slaying of a Jacksonville police officer off Lakeview Drive. Dr. Henry Steadman, a prominent South Florida surgeon . . ."

A sickening feeling filled up my belly, my hands on my head. I couldn't believe I was actually hearing my name in connection with a homicide investigation! A double homicide. It was only a matter of time until Mike was discovered—and his missing car. *Okay, Henry, think—is there anyone else you know here you can trust?* Was there anyone here who I could count on? Just to stay off the streets. For a short while. Who would believe me?

I thought of Richard Taylor, the head of the Doctors Without Borders conference who had invited me to speak tonight. But I didn't want to involve them. I couldn't ask that.

Then Jennifer came to mind. *Miss Jacksonville.* I could explain it all to her. I knew she'd see me for who I was. Not some crazy cop killer. I recalled that she was staying at a different hotel from mine. The Hyatt.

Hopefully she'd already made it to town and checked in.

I took Mike's phone and punched in the number I had for her. I knew it was kind of a long shot, but that's what we were playing now. It took a few seconds for her to answer, probably not recognizing the caller ID—Mike's—but sure enough, after I heard her voice, a little tentatively perhaps, I felt better.

"This is Jennifer Keegan."

"Jennifer—it's Henry Steadman. Please don't hang up. I don't know if you've heard, but something crazy has happened."

"I *did* hear!" Jennifer replied. She sounded surprised,

but not upset that I was calling. "We've all heard, Dr. Steadman! *What's happened?* They're saying such incredible things . . ."

"Jennifer, I'll explain . . . Just trust me—it's not at all what you might think. I just need to be somewhere safe, for an hour or two, until I can negotiate something and get this whole crazy thing resolved. That's all. Can I trust you, Jennifer? I know I have no business asking this, it's just that . . . It's just that, to be honest, I don't have anywhere else to turn."

"You want to come *here*?" she asked, clearly surprised.

"Just for an hour or two, that's all! I have someone working on turning me over. I won't put you in any harm. I promise. *What do you say?*"

CHAPTER ELEVEN

"*Yes,*" she replied, without hesitation. "I knew this all had to be something crazy. I'm at the—"

"I know where you are—" I cut her off. "And you have no idea what this means to me, Jennifer. You can't. You're a godsend. I'll be there in half an hour."

It took about twenty minutes to get there, and just to be safe, I entered the hotel grounds at the adjacent golf course, and left Mike's Jag on the second level of the two-story garage.

I walked the short distance over to the main lobby, telling myself I had no reason to be concerned, that no one was looking for me here. That I looked like any golfer, in my khakis, my golf cap, and shades. That Mike's stolen car wasn't on any news reports yet.

I stepped into the glass-roofed, atrium lobby. It was

packed with people from maybe a dozen trade-show groups and conventions. There was some kind of arena football game in town and a throng of boosters wearing black-and-aqua Shark caps and logo sweatshirts were gathered near the entrance, probably heading to some kind of rally.

Everything seemed benign, nothing to worry about. Not that I was exactly trained to spot undercover police if they were there. I scanned the lobby . . . lots of noise, people moving everywhere . . . and spotted the elevators. Jennifer told me to go to room 2107.

I put down my cap and was about to head across the floor when I saw him.

My chest tightened.

Not someone in uniform, but in a plain, navy-blue windbreaker, leaning against the wall near the restrooms while scanning the crowd.

He might well have just been hotel security, if it wasn't for the terrifying realization that I had seen him once before.

From the back of Martinez's police car.

He was one of the policemen who was milling around when Martinez stopped me.

Every nerve in my body slammed to a stop.

I turned my back to him. I didn't know what to do, except that I had to get out of there now. In truth, I was petrified to even take a step. The guy clearly hadn't seen me yet. He just stood there as if he was waiting to meet a friend. I eased my way toward the football boosters.

Why was he here now?

Then the answer came clear: Jennifer had turned me in. It was a trap! They were waiting for me. Who could even blame her? The only reason I wasn't spread-eagled on the floor with a gun to my head was that I hadn't come in through the front entrance, pulling up in my white Caddie, as they were clearly expecting me to do. They must not know about Mike yet. I figured there were several of them, stationed all around. My whole body went rigid with fear. I searched around for the best way out.

And then my cell phone rang.

I would never have even glanced at it in that moment—I was petrified it would draw attention to me—had I not thought that it could well be Liz, and I didn't want to miss her. Slowly I melded into the crowd of boosters. I pulled out my phone and glanced at the screen. It wasn't Liz.

It was Hallie.

I didn't want to answer, but it rang two, then three times, and I felt as if the trill was echoing around the lobby, calling everyone's attention to me. I just saw my daughter's name on the screen—*Hallie, Hallie* . . . And I didn't know if Liz had spoken with her and if she knew. Knew all that had happened.

So I just pressed the green button before my voice

recording came on and muttered softly, set to call her back. "Hallie . . ."

But the voice I heard wasn't hers. It was a man's voice, both muffled and unrecognizable.

And what he said on my daughter's phone jarred me more than anything that had happened today.

He kind of chuckled as he asked, "So how you liking it all so far, Doc?"

CHAPTER TWELVE

I froze.

I realized right away who was on the other end. That I was speaking to the person who was responsible for all this. Who had killed Mike. Martinez.

And he was calling on my daughter's phone.

"Who are you? Where's Hallie? *Where's my daughter?*" I demanded, my body heaving with mounting dread.

"Oh, we'll get to all that pretty soon. I promise," the man said. "But if you ever want to see her again—*alive*, that is—I think there's just one little thing you oughta know . . ."

"Go on," I said. I ducked behind two boosters introducing their wives.

"If I happen to hear that you get caught by the police, or even turn yourself in . . . Or if it comes out in the

91

press that your little girl is missing, meaning if you tell 'em, Hallie here's gonna end up with a bullet in that smart, pretty brain of hers. And that's if I'm feeling generous. *You hear?*"

The crowd was loud and buzzing all around. I tried to think if I had ever heard the voice before, but it was Southern, slangy, and wasn't clear.

"You hearing me, Doc?" he said again, like ice this time. Waiting.

"Yes." I swallowed, razors in my throat. "I hear."

"So here's a little present for you—just so there's no doubts, about our arrangement."

My heart started to race. Suddenly Hallie got on, her voice shaking with fear. *"Daddy . . . Daddy, is that you?"*

"Yes, hon, it is! It's me."

"Oh, Daddy, I'm so sorry . . . Please just listen to what he says. He'll do it. I know he will. He's crazy! Just do what he says. Please. He—I love you, Daddy," she blurted as the phone was yanked away from her in midsentence.

"Just wanted you to have a sense of what's really at stake here, Doc. Pretty little thing, if I say so myself. And she surely can ride."

"You touch a hair on her head and I'll kill you myself, you son of a bitch! So help me God . . ." I shouted above the noise, my blood on fire.

"Now don't you be giving me orders," the man said.

"That wouldn't go over well. Long as you heard exactly what I said, about if I hear the cops find you."

"What is it you want? Why are you doing this to me? I have money. I can pay you. Please . . ."

"We'll get to what I want. In a while. First, go get yourself a new phone. One of those disposable ones. Text the number to Hallie here. Okay? That is, if you ever want to hear from her alive again."

I shuddered.

"So get on now, y'hear?" I could hear the laughter in his voice. "You keep yourself safe. Remember, longer you stay out there, Doc, longer your little girl lives."

"Listen! Don't hang up! *Listen* . . ."

I heard the phone click off, and all trace of my little girl with it. I pushed the button to call her back, but no one answered. I was left staring at her name on the cell-phone screen.

My knees felt weak.

I turned in the crowd, every corner of me filling up with a mounting sense of dread. He was right! I had to get out of here! I still had the cop to worry about. Liz had told me just to give up if anything went wrong. But now I couldn't do that. Now I had to do everything I could to get away!

I scanned the lobby and realized there was no way I could go back the way I'd come in. If the police were waiting for me here, there were probably dozens of them all around. I glanced back at the one I had seen, still protected by the crowd.

A heavyset man in a green Sharks headdress shifted from my line of sight just as I did so.

Suddenly the cop and I were eye to eye.

My heart felt like it exploded. He looked straight at me, seemingly trying to pierce through the golf cap and the shades . . .

Then, suddenly, he did just that!

I watched his eyes grow wide and his face light up with recognition. He took a step toward me. I moved away, pushing my way through the throng of boosters. I thought I heard him shout something, echoing, above the din of the lobby. I began to run.

Then I heard him call out: *"Steadman!"*

I spun and saw him pull out his radio, signaling the others. I slithered through the dense booster gathering, thirty or forty strong, and came out directly in front of the elevators. A door opened in front of me. I didn't know where it would take me, other than *away*. Which was all I wanted right then. I jumped in.

The cop was already running after me. *"Steadman. Stop!"*

Bystanders turned. The cop still had to cross the lobby and make his way through the crowd. I jammed my finger against the heat-sensored panels. Pushing on every upper-floor—30 . . . 32 . . . 34.

The doors didn't close. *C'mon, goddammit, shut!*

I watched, in mounting horror, as the cop elbowed his way through the shocked crowd. Midway through, he stopped, his eyes locked on me in the elevator, still thirty feet away.

He pulled out his gun.

C'mon, c'mon, close! I realized he saw me as nothing more than a cop killer. He'd be justified to shoot. He wouldn't hesitate for a second. *They already hadn't hesitated!* I kept pressing on the arrow. And on the upper floors.

Close.

The cop finally made it through. Suddenly we were face-to-face again. He leveled his gun at me. I realized he could squeeze off a shot at any second and I'd be dead. *Close, you sonovabitch. Close!*

That's when the doors finally started to shut. The cop sprinted toward me, aimed, and squeezed off a shot, which slammed into the doors as I ducked behind them.

Another made it into the car, ripping into the wood walls. *The guy was crazy! What if there were other people in here?*

A third clanged off the handrail.

The doors finally squeezed shut an instant before he made it over to me. I could hear the cop holler, *"Shit! Shit!"* and bang on the doors as the elevator started to rise. All the higher floors were lit up now, and I knew in that instant that all that would happen if I went up there was that I'd be trapped and captured . . . and then Hallie . . .

As if by instinct, I hit the button for the third floor. The elevator came to a sudden stop. I bolted out, knowing it would keep on going up, floor by floor, all the way to the top.

I ran down the hall, searching frantically for the fire exit. I didn't know how many cops were spread about—or would be, in a matter of minutes. But the elevator was heading up to the roof. They'd have to check around up there. They'd have to search all the upper floors. Room by room.

By that time the entire building might be on lock-down.

I had to get out of here fast.

At last, I found the emergency stairwell and bounded down the stairs, two at a time, my heart almost in spasm. I was completely winded and gasping by the time I reached the ground floor. I fully expected to run right into some trigger-happy policeman who would force me to the ground with a gun at my head.

Mercifully, no one was there. I pushed open the pneumatic door and, with a *whoosh*, found myself outside.

Thank God. I didn't wait to get my bearings—I just sprinted, fast as I could, away—spotting the golf course to my right and realizing I was heading toward the clubhouse. Where my car was parked!

I spun around and didn't see anyone behind me. No one shouted my name. I just prayed that I wouldn't feel a bullet ripping into my back. Ahead, I saw the garage, which I figured was reserved for golfers. I knew I couldn't use Mike's car anymore. The police might have found him by now, and if they hadn't, they surely would soon. Any second it might be over the airwaves . . . and then I was cooked.

I ran inside the garage and spotted one of the green-vested valets hustling to get a car and I waited behind a stanchion until he climbed inside a Lincoln—and I saw him feel under the seat for the key. Then it started up. I had a flashback to my old parking-attendant days, one of the jobs I did to get myself through med school. I counted the seconds until the Lincoln drove off, then I ran over to a red GMC parked nearby. The door was unlocked and I felt frantically under the seat for the key.

Shit. *Nothing*. I had to try another car.

I hopped out and tried a blue Lexus SUV in the next bay. I figured there was a security camera here and that someone might well be watching me right now. Heisting a car.

This time I found the keys under the floor mat.

I started it up and drove out of the garage, leaving Mike's Jag behind. It didn't matter that my DNA was all over it. I wasn't about to deny taking it. I knew I had only a short time before all exits from the hotel were shut down. I drove out to the front gate. There was a guard there. I'd had to talk my way past him the first time, but now he gave me just a lackadaisical wave, as if to say, *Hope you hit 'em well. See you next time.*

I made a right, knowing I was only minutes from the highway. I was so excited, I wanted to whoop out loud.

But then a sober realization ran through me, and my whole body began to tremble.

I suddenly realized that if there was even a chance I was only a person of interest an hour ago after fleeing the scene of Martinez's killing, that possibility was now long gone.

My daughter was in peril. And I was a full-fledged suspect in two murders now.

CHAPTER THIRTEEN

The evening was sticky and warm and Vance Hofer waited in his car, hidden off the dirt road that led to the trailer. He kept his car lights off.

There were two vehicles parked in front. One was a beat-up, red pickup he had seen around his house a dozen times, which he knew belonged to Wayne, the waste of good spit Amanda thought of as her boyfriend. The other was a silver Kia with an "I Heart Daughtry" decal on the back and a pair of pink felt dice dangling from the inside mirror.

For a while Vance had heard sounds of laughter coming from inside. Music. A party going on. Something crashing onto the floor. More laughter. It made his blood curdle.

Then, for the longest time, he heard nothing at all.

He sat there, feeling his life's futility coursing through his body, to the tips of his rough, workman's hands. How things hadn't quite worked out the way he planned, yet he smiled, thinking the story wasn't quite over yet. He needed only one thing—something clear and fixed in this world of uncertainties—and that one thing was that someone take responsibility for what had gone down. That at the end of the line, someone had to pay for what had happened to that poor girl and her baby, not to mention Amanda, and what was happening tonight might only be the first step. When it was all over, the person he would likely find would be the one who had profited the most.

From what had befallen his little girl.

That was what was wrong with life, Vance thought, how no one ever did . . . pay. The ones who bore the guilt. Those people always squirmed their way out, with reams and reams of legal arguments, hiding behind oily lawyers. The banks, who had taken his home; the functionaries who had pushed him out of his job; the fools in Washington and on Wall Street, even those people out in Hollywood—they did just fine, while the rest of us had no career, no home, no insurance. You were just a cipher, left with nothing. Just silt running through your hands. Only the little people had to pay. While the rest went on . . .

And for a man who was brought up knowing what happens when right and wrong collide, this was a heavy cost.

There is wheat and there is chaff, the Bible says. Wheat and chaff.

And it was simply a matter of separating the one from the other: those who had been harmed from those who were responsible. You didn't need no fancy degrees or badges or fitness hearings.

Someone just had to own up. That's all he was saying.

His little Amanda was just at the end of the line.

Vance just kept his eyes on that trailer, knowing pretty soon the door would open.

Wheat from chaff. He flexed his fingers. Someone had to own up and it would start right here.

That's all.

CHAPTER FOURTEEN

I pulled into a McDonald's off the highway certain that after fleeing the Hyatt half of the Jacksonville Sheriff's Department that hadn't been actively looking for me before was probably looking for me now.

I felt Mike's phone vibrate.

I dug it out and looked at the screen. It was Liz. Thank God. She sounded off the planet. I figured I knew why.

"Henry, I just heard on the news. *What the hell did you do up there?*"

"Someone set a trap for me, Liz. I don't know if you heard the whole story, but—"

"Henry, I told you to give yourself up if they found you again! Not to resist."

"I couldn't give myself up! Liz, I have something bad

102

to tell you. Don't freak out. Have you heard from Hallie? In the past few hours?"

"*Hallie*? No. Not since lunch yesterday. She was going riding." I could hear her grow nervous. "Why are you asking about Hallie?"

"Because I received a call. In the lobby of the Hyatt, just before the cops there spotted me. Liz, don't freak out. Hallie's been taken."

"*Taken?*" I could feel tears rushing into her eyes. "What do you mean *taken*, Henry? By whom? How do you even know?"

"Because I heard from her, Liz. It's the person who did these things today. Who killed Mike and that cop on the road. He called me at the Hyatt before the police found me. He has her."

"*Has her?* Oh Jesus, Henry, no . . ." I could almost feel the blood rushing out of her face. Knowing that someone who was fully capable of cold-blooded murder had taken our daughter. I heard her sniff back sobs. This was awful. One minute she was just trying to help me out of a mess. Now she was in it herself. Up to her eyeballs. Same as me. Then she said the only rational thing she could say. "We have to go to the police. You got a partial ID on that car. They might be able to trace it!"

"No, Liz. There are things I have to tell you. That's exactly what we can't do. *We can't go to the police*."

"Henry, I'm sorry about what's happening to you, but some madman has our daughter . . . !"

"Liz—listen! Hear me out! I went to the Hyatt because I knew someone there who I hoped could get me off the streets until you negotiated some kind of deal. But I got a call in the lobby, just before the police saw me there. He put Hallie on and she sounded okay. Scared out of her mind, but I got the sense she hadn't been harmed. But the guy who took her, who's doing this, he said if I went the police on this—if I turn myself in or even if I get caught, or if he hears on the news that Hallie's missing, he's gonna kill her, Liz. Just like he did Mike. And Martinez. I won't even tell you what he said he'd do. Just that the longer I stay out, the longer she lives . . . That's why I had to run. It was one in a million that I even got away. That's why we can't go to the police!"

Liz was silent. I needed her to be rational, yet I knew that what I'd just told her violated every rational instinct she had. Her daughter had been abducted and we couldn't even report it to the police!

It was killing me too.

Liz lashed out. "What have you done, Henry? What have you done to put our daughter's life in danger this way?"

"I haven't done anything, Liz. I don't know what's going on."

"So what do you want me to do? You tell me this insane story about cops pulling you over and putting you in cuffs. Then everywhere you go people are being killed. And now our daughter's been taken by this . . . this person who's got some vendetta against you. Who's killed people! Goddammit, Henry, why don't you just tell me what's going on?"

"Please, Liz, don't go there on me. I need you to understand. I need you now too. You know damn well I'm not capable of anything they said I've done. I don't know why this is happening! I'm up here for a conference. I'm supposed to deliver a speech tonight. I got pulled over for a traffic violation I didn't commit. The rest . . ." My voice started to crack. "I don't know what's happening, Liz!"

"And you're saying we can't even do the one sensible thing that could save our daughter's life! You can't be serious, Henry! What do you expect me to believe? What else should I believe?"

"I am serious, Liz. Deadly serious. I heard him. He'll do it, Liz. He's already done it. We can't."

I just let her sob it out for a while.

Finally Liz said, "He's doing this for a reason. What does he want from you, Henry? *Money?* There's got to be something he wants?"

"I don't know what he wants yet—other than to watch me suffer. Other than to enjoy seeing me completely trapped."

"So what are you saying? We just let him keep her and do nothing. I don't know if I can do that, Henry . . ."

"You have to, Liz. For Hallie's sake. I don't know who

105

this person is and or what he thinks I've done, but he's targeted me. I think Hallie will be okay, for a while, crazy as that sounds. He needs her to get to me.

"You're willing to put our baby's life on the line . . . I can't."

"We have to, Liz. I don't see any other way. I can try to find that car . . ."

"You don't even have a clear memory of it, Henry. A blue car. From South Carolina. You don't even remember the plate number! It could be chopped up to parts, repainted, hidden in some garage for months for all you know."

She was right. "But there's that gamecock thing . . ."

"Gamecock?"

"The image I saw on the shooter's car. The mascot. From the University of South Carolina. I saw one on the back window of Mike's car too."

"Mike's car?" Liz paused. "Do you think your friend is connected in this?"

"I don't know." I had run the idea around in my head. But no one knew Mike and I were even getting together. Only my assistant, Maryanne. And she'd been with me for fifteen years. I'd trusted her with much bigger things than this. "I don't see how. We have to come up with a cover, Liz. For Hallie. In case people worry at school. We have to say she came home . . ."

She sucked in a harried breath. "All right. All right."

106

"At least for a day or two . . ."

"Okay, I'll think of something. Henry, I'm scared. We don't even know what we're doing at this. Hallie's life is on the line. What do we do if he just kills her and we're . . . I don't know if I can live with that."

"Liz, if you break down, they're just going to use it as a way to get to me. The guy's not going to do anything now. He won't. I'm telling you, he wants *me*. He told me to get a disposable cell phone so he can contact me again. Maybe we'll know more then. In the meantime, don't contact me. The minute they find out about Mike . . . this phone will only lead them to me."

"I know." I felt her about to start weeping.

"You just stay strong, Liz. I'm gonna find our girl, Liz, and bring her home. He's not gonna hurt her until he can get to me."

"This is bad, Henry. Isn't it?"

"Yeah, Liz," I said. I was trying not to think of it. "Let's not pretend any other way. It's bad."

Hanging up, I suddenly felt about as alone as I'd ever felt in my life. In spite of trying to pump up Liz, I really didn't know what my next step was going to be, other than finding that car.

That car was the only thing that could save my daughter's life.

And Liz was right. We were way, way out of our league. What resources did I possibly have? On the run. In a stolen car . . .

I flipped on the car radio, and it didn't take long to hear the account of my escape from the Hyatt.

They had my name, but I didn't hear any description of the car I'd escaped in. Which was good. With any luck, the owner might be on the golf course for a couple more hours, so for the near term I could get around.

But what I did hear, which suddenly seemed like a path for me, was a public hotline number to call with any tips related to the crimes.

CHAPTER FIFTEEN

At the sheriff's office downtown, Carrie was manning the tip line.

She'd taken six or seven calls. A couple of them were clearly bogus. One had Steadman held up in a high school with a cache of ammo. Another had seen his Cadillac speeding away and caught his plates, info they already had. A cabbie had called in, saying he'd dropped off someone resembling Steadman at an unspecified street corner in Avondale. That one they sent a team to check out. Several others called in from the Hyatt, having witnessed the shooting in the lobby. One caller had Steadman going from room to room on the thirty-third floor, terrorizing guests. Another had him sneaking away, dressed in a waiter's uniform.

When the lines went quiet, Carrie logged online and checked out Steadman's website. She watched a clip of him from *Good Morning, South Florida* describing the pros and cons of Botox. Steadman was handsome. Sharp cheekbones. Intelligent blue eyes. Stylishly long brown hair. He had a successful business. And a fancy Palm Beach address.

Not exactly the profile of your usual fleeing cop killer. The guy even spent his vacations fixing cleft palates and helping to build schools in Nicaragua. Lots of group shots with happy villagers. Some of the photos were taken by his daughter. It was hard to connect that image with that of some crazed killer who had put two shots at point-blank range into a policeman.

A light flashed on the message board and Carrie picked up. "Sheriff's office. Officer Martinez tip line. This is Carrie Holmes . . ." she said into the headphones.

"I have some information on the killer," the caller said.

"All right, go ahead . . ." Carrie grabbed her pen.

"I didn't do it. Any of it. I swear, it wasn't me."

Carrie's heart came to a stop, as if an electrical wire sent a jolt through it. Silently, she snapped her fingers, trying to catch the attention of one of the other detectives to get on her line.

She put a hand over her speaker. *"It's him!"*

"What do you mean by *any* of it?" Carrie said back, hoping to engage the guy. She pushed the record button. She also routed a message to Akers's secretary: *Get him over here!*

"There's more . . ." the caller said, his voice trailing off. "You'll see."

The whispers of *"It's him! Steadman!"* crackled around the floor and a crowd of detectives gathered around Carrie's desk. The chief of detectives, Captain Moon. Carrie's boss, Bill Akers. Even Chief Hall, who had just come back from the shooting scene. Carrie's heart began to beat loudly and she could feel everyone in the room silently urging her with looks and signals to keep Steadman on the line. *Three minutes,* Carrie knew from training. Three minutes and they should be able to triangulate a fix on where he was.

"Who am I speaking with?" she asked him. "I'll need your name and some proof of who you say you are. You can imagine, there's a lot of people calling in on this . . ."

"I think you know exactly who you're speaking with," the caller said. "Martinez had a bullet wound in his left temple and another higher up on the skull. His driver's window was down. He probably still had my driver's license in his hand . . . You want my Social Security number? I think that's sufficient."

Carrie's adrenaline shot through the roof. She knew she had the killer on the line.

She tried to get him to keep talking. "You said *any* of it, Dr. Steadman. And you said, 'there's been *more.*' Has there been another incident?"

Steadman didn't answer. Instead, he waited a few

111

seconds and changed the subject. "Are you a detective, Carrie?"

The question took her by surprise. She glanced around, at the elapsed time on the screen. Going on a minute. Why not tell him the truth? Sometimes people in these situations just needed someone to talk it out with. "No. I work in community outreach," she said. "I just agreed to man a phone. It's actually my first day back from being away for a while."

By now several of the staff were listening in on the call.

"Well, I bet the community outreach department has a lot more company at the moment than it's normally used to, right, Carrie?" Steadman said with a chuckle.

"Yeah," Carrie said, holding in a smile herself. "This is true."

A minute fifteen.

"You mind if I ask you something?" he asked. His next question threw her for a loop. "You have kids, Carrie?"

More than threw her for a loop. *Where was he going with this?* It was almost like he somehow knew what was going on with her. Today of all days, bringing up kids. She hesitated for a second, not sure if she should give away anything personal like that, but Bill Akers nodded for her to keep engaging him. *Ninety seconds.*

"Yes," Carrie answered. "A son. He's nine."

"I have a daughter myself," Henry Steadman said.

"Hallie. Super kid. She's an equestrian. She almost qualified for the junior Olympic team last year. She's finishing her first year of college. At UVA. She's the world to me. Just like yours, I bet?'

"Of course," Carrie said, feeling a flutter go through her.

"Then you'll understand what I'm about to say . . . though you probably won't believe me. *None of you*," he said, firmer, "since I assume there's a bunch of you crowded around by now."

Carrie didn't answer, but she smiled.

"But *I swear*—on my little girl—'cause I still think of her that way—and right now she needs me more than anything in the world—that whatever it looks like, whatever anyone may think, I had *nothing* to do with what happened to that policeman today . . . I was back in my car, waiting for him to finish up my ticket, when a blue sedan pulled next to him and someone shot him through the window. It sped away and I went after it—to try and ID it—that's all—which was the reason I left the scene. You understand what I'm saying, Carrie? This is exactly the way it happened. *On my little girl!*"

"That's bullshit," Captain Moon said dubiously. "Five different people saw him coming out of Martinez's car."

"And not to mention that *I* was the one who called 911 . . . It was a blue sedan. I don't know the make or the model, but I do know something about it. It had South Carolina plates. You've got to find that car."

"What make was it, Dr. Steadman?" Carrie asked, glancing again at the clock. They had been on two minutes now. "The car. Were you able to make out the plates?"

"No, not the numbers. But they were definitely South Carolina. I'm sure . . ." He stopped himself. "And I have no idea what make," he said with a sigh of frustration. "I would only put you in the wrong direction . . ."

"Just keep him going, Carrie," one of the detectives whispered, pointing to his watch.

"I hear you, Dr. Steadman. But all I can say is—and I think I'm giving you pretty sound advice here—whatever you've done or haven't done, you have to turn yourself in. Everything can be sorted out then. I promise you, you'll be treated—"

"I think you know exactly how I'll be treated." He cut her off. "You all know what happened today, as I was trying to head back peacefully to the scene. And at the Hyatt. You want to help me, Carrie, look for that blue sedan. The plate number began with *AMD* or *ADJ* . . . There must be security cameras around somewhere that would've spotted them. There has to be some way."

Two and a half minutes.

"And remember what I told you. On my daughter, Carrie. I know you'll know what I mean. I wish I could turn myself in. I wish . . ." There was a long pause and Carrie almost thought he was about to share something. He finally said, "Just look for that car. I think it's already

114

clear, whether I turn myself in or they eventually catch me, no one there will look."

"Dr. Steadman . . ." Carrie pressed. "What did you mean by—"

The line went dead.

Carrie sat back and blew out a breath for the first time. Almost two and a half minutes. A phone number had come up on the screen, but it wasn't for Steadman's; it was for a completely different phone. A White Fence Capital. Steadman had likely stolen the phone from somewhere.

"Excellent work, Carrie," Chief Hall said. "Certainly a lot of excitement, no, for what I understand is your first day back?"

"Yes, sir," Carrie acknowledged. Though she found herself wanting to ask if they should follow up on the blue car.

"Well"—he squeezed her on the shoulder—"you did just fine . . ."

Then suddenly someone shouted from the detectives' pool. "There's been another shooting!"

Tony Velez, one of the homicide crew, ran up. "In Avondale! This must be what Steadman was just talking about. Victim's name is Michael Dinofrio. His wife came home from exercise and found him dead at his desk. Two in the chest. His car's gone. A silver Jaguar. And the kicker is . . . guess who Dinofrio was supposed to be playing golf with right about now . . . ? At Atlantic

Pines. *Steadman,*" Velez finished, looking around the table.

"I took a call from a cabbie," Carrie said, suddenly remembering the location, "who claimed he drove someone resembling Steadman from the Clarion Inn near Lakeview to an address in Avondale . . ."

"That's about a half mile from where Martinez was killed," Bill Akers said.

Frantically, Carrie checked back on the call screen, locating the time of the call and drop-off point. 11:02 A.M. "33443 Turnberry Terrace." She looked up. "That's only a block away."

Suddenly she knew what Steadman had meant when he said, "You'll see, there's more . . ."

Then Sally Crawford, who'd been tracing Steadman's call, said loudly, "The phone Steadman just called in on . . . White Fence Capital. It's a real estate partnership here in town." She turned to face the chief. "Michael Dinofrio is the CEO."

Carrie felt a flush of embarrassment come over her. If there was any doubt before about Steadman's connection to these murders, there wasn't one now.

The son of a bitch just called in on the second victim's phone.

CHAPTER SIXTEEN

It took close to two hours, but the trailer's front door finally opened. Vance saw a woman step out into night, wearing a tight red halter and a denim jacket hanging from her shoulder, her blond hair all mussed up.

He watched from his perch in the woods. Good ol' Wayne, the guy Amanda was supposedly in love with, came out, shirtless and in jeans, with a beer in hand. The girl spun around and pressed up against him and gave him a lingering kiss, Wayne's hand snaking down her back and onto her shorts until it came to rest on her behind.

Vance couldn't hear what they were saying, but it wasn't too hard to figure out.

She turned and continued down the steps, a little wobbly, to her car. "You know one thing . . ." she said, turning back, and pointing at Wayne. "Whatever it is you got, it sure does make my register ring."

"Ring-a-ding-ding," Wayne sang, and took a swig of his beer, the two giggling like fools.

The girl stumbled to her car and waved as she drove away, passing right by Vance. After a short while, when Vance was sure she wasn't coming back, he picked up the black satchel from the seat next to him. He got out of his car, lifted the trunk, and took out a heavy lead pipe, the words *the responsibility starts now* drumming through his mind. *Wheat from chaff.*

Just no knowing where it ends.

He stepped up to the front door, hearing the TV on inside. He knocked.

It took a few seconds for the door to open. Wayne appeared, with that same shit-eating grin on his face, still holding his beer, surely expecting someone else. "Forget something . . . ?"

"Yeah," Vance said, staring into Wayne's shocked eyes. "I did."

Vance swung the pipe and struck Wayne in the kneecap, probably shattering it right there, and when Wayne buckled on one foot with a yelp, Vance jabbed the butt end into the boy's jaw, sending him across the floor in a groaning heap.

Vance shut the front door.

CHAPTER SEVENTEEN

"Where the hell am I?" the boy moaned, groggily, finally opening his eyes.

The room was dark. Vance had turned off all the lights. Wayne was hog-tied, his arms behind him, dangling from a crossbeam on the ceiling. He couldn't move. He could barely even breathe. He just hung there, his feet bare, blood pooled in his mouth and all over his shirt.

"Who's there?" Wayne called out into the darkness. "What's going on? Why are you doing this to me?"

Poor kid had no idea who had even strung him up there.

Vance rose up and shined a flashlight into Wayne's eyes. The boy squinted, blinded, turning his face away. "*Who is that?* Mr. Hofer? Why the hell are you doing this to me, Mr. Hofer?" The kid was shaking. "What's going on?"

"What am I doing here, son . . . ?" Vance said, pulling out a chair and sitting down on it in front of Wayne. "I'm simply here to ask you a few things. And how you answer them will go a long ways toward determining whether you ever walk away from here . . . So you think about what I'm about to say, and then we'll see. Okay, son?"

Wayne nodded, scared out of his mind.

"Good." Vance continued to shine the light on him. "First is, what did you do to my girl?"

"I'm s-sorry, Mr. Hofer," Wayne said, tears and mucus streaming down his face and falling onto the floor. He'd always been scared of Amanda's old man. The guy was crazy. Even Amanda said so. The stories she would tell of him, when she and Wayne were high. How he had this violent streak. How he would just hurt things—stray cats, squirrels, Amanda's mom. And what he used to do on the force. How he once busted a man's wrists with his nightstick while the guy was writhing on the ground. Used it in other ways too, he'd heard. Got him thrown off the force.

"You mean her? *Brandee?* She ain't nothing to me. She's just a friend. Amanda's still my girl."

Vance shook his head. "I don't mean about the girl, son. The girl could fuck you to kingdom come for all I care. You really think this is about her? You want to go on living out that putrid, dog-shit life of yours?"

" 'Course I do!" The kid was openly crying now, almost shitting in his pants. "Please, let me down, sir. You know I do. You—"

"So then I'll say it again, how you answer's gonna go a long way toward determining how we get that done, Wayne. So you tell me . . ." Vance stood up and faced him now. "You tell me where you got the drugs from, son. I'm talking the Oxy. That's why I'm here."

"*Oxy?* We only just smoked a little weed," Wayne said. "That's all. We weren't hurting no one . . . We jus—"

"I don't mean tonight, you stupid fool," Vance said, feeling his temper rear. "The Oxy that my little girl was taking. Who just got her life stolen away by whatever it was you pushed on her. That's where she got them from, right?" Revulsion pooled in his eyes. "The stuff she was on. From you, right, son?"

"No, no . . . It wasn't from me, Mr. Hofer. I swear. " Wayne was hanging like a side of beef, the blood rushing into his head. "I don't even know what you're even talking about, sir . . . I—"

"You don't know what I'm talking about?" Vance humphed cynically, almost smiling. "What Amanda was high on when she killed that poor, young gal and her baby . . . While her husband was serving his country over there. Now, I know it was you, son, so there's no sense playing this out. The Oxy, where'd you get 'em, boy?

That's all I want to know. Then I'll hoist you down."

"I don't know . . . I don't know," Wayne groaned. "She didn't get 'em from me . . ." He shook his head back and forth like it was on a pulley. "I promise. I swear that, Mr. Hofer . . ."

"You swear . . ." Vance tightened his grip around the lead pipe, the muscles in his wide forearms twitching. "Son, we both know that's a damn lie. And lying won't be the thing to help you now. But here's a bit of the truth. I lied as well. You're gonna have to pay for what you've done. Everyone is. Everyone up and down the line. Till I find where it came from. No way around that. That's just where it stands, son."

Wayne was trembling now, barely able to garble words back. "What I've done? *What have I done?*"

"All those lives you stole, son. The girl and her baby." Vance stared at him. "My Amanda too."

"No . . ." Now the boy was squirming and sobbing, tiring himself out twisting all over the beam. Every time he jerked his legs, the rope tightened around his neck. "I didn't do anything to them. I didn't give her any drugs! I swear . . ."

Vance went over to the black bag he had placed on the chair. "Son, we can do this two ways, and I'm afraid you're not gonna like either of 'em, but one surely more than the other. But I think we both know by the time I walk out that door"—Vance opened the bag—"it's gonna be with those names."

122

"*There are no names!* You hear me, Mr. Hofer, there are no names!"

It was still dark and Wayne could barely see. He just heard things from wherever Vance was moving around. Things that made him scared. Like a sharp hiss— followed by the sweet smell of gas, *propane,* and then a *whoosh,* which sent an electrical current of fear jerking through his upended body.

He shat down his pants.

Then Wayne looked up and saw the blue flame from a welding torch in Vance's hand, coming closer to him.

"Listen, please, Mr. Hofer, please . . . *Listen!*" he screamed. Suddenly his answers changed, and he began stammering. "These aren't like regular folk. They're not from around here. They're truly bad people. I can't give you their names. I can't! They'll kill me."

To which Vance replied, chuckling, "What do you think I'm doing, son, just playing around?" He adjusted the flame to high and brought it close to Wayne.

"Now, you can stay up there, whimpering like a child, long as you like. Trust me, I've got all night. But whimpering ain't gonna help you in this situation. I want to hear you talking names, son. Otherwise . . ."

Wayne's eyes bulged as the flame came close, darting back and forth. "*I didn't do anything to them!* I swear. I didn't." The heat was close to his face. He began to sob. "I didn't!"

123

"Well, that's just where you're wrong, son. Where you and I disagree."

Vance grabbed one of Wayne's bare feet and put the blue flame against his sole, the boy's skin sizzling and his leg kicking around like a half-killed bass and a shriek coming out of him that might have been heard in Lowdnes County.

"Please, Mr. Hofer, please . . ."

"Where you got the Oxy from that you fed my daughter? You hear me? I can make this last forever, son, or I can make it quick. Either way, by the time I leave, I'm going to have what I want."

He placed the blue flame on Wayne's foot again, the kid jerking and crying and howling bloody hell. And a stink going up. *"Names, son . . .* It's only going to get worse. I think you must be hearing me now. No one's leaving here without those names."

CHAPTER EIGHTEEN

He got them. Names.

Though it took longer than he'd liked—Wayne thrashing and screaming how these were bad people and they'd come and kill him, which seemed to suggest he didn't fully appreciate what was happening to him right now.

The lad was passed out now. Still. The whimpering had stopped, though his feet smelled like meat on a spit and were puffed up bloody ugly, swollen and blistered and blue.

Hell, they wouldn't be much good to him now anyway.

Vance lowered him from the beam, the ropes still horse-collared around Wayne's neck. He surely could have saved the kid a lot of pain and aggravation. But he had to pay—that was clear. Just like that girl and her baby had paid.

Just like Amanda had paid. Forfeited half her life just for being young and foolish.

Now Wayne had to pay too.

Vance hoisted up the body by the armpits. He figured as long as he had the apparatus all rigged up, he might as well put it to some use, and cinched the rope tightly around the kid's neck, placing it the noose under his chin. Then he began to squeeze.

Squeeze. With all the strength he had from those years of running that lathe.

All those years on the force and the way they'd pushed him aside without much of a thought to him.

Squeeze.

Wayne jerked awake, his eyes bulging. He made a gurgling noise and twisted to see what was happening. Strangled whimpers emanating from his throat as Vance tightened the noose, the boy suddenly understanding what was going on, his arms thrashing around behind him. Vance telling him in a soft voice, "No point in struggling, son. I told you plainly, you had to pay for what you've done."

Wayne, grasping at Vance's sides, jerking his head back and forth in some desperate, futile effort to say, *"No, please, no . . ."* But that just made Vance squeeze even tighter, spittle seeping out of the young man's mouth and onto his chin. His fists striking with diminishing force against Vance's thighs. His words barely even intelligible . . . His eyes stretched to the back of his head.

Please.

Vance didn't let up. Not until there was no more fight in the boy. Or gasping for air. Not until he fell back on the floor in a curled-up heap.

He'd told him it had to be done.

Then he loosened the noose from Wayne's blotched neck and undid the makeshift winch and pulley and let them aside. He wrapped the long rope over his arm into neat circles, unscrewed the propane tank from the welding torch, and put them carefully back into his bag.

Not much blood, he thought, pleased with his work. Just a few drops of spittle on the floor, which he wiped with a cloth and disinfectant. Then he put his arms under the dead boy's armpits and lifted him up over his shoulders. Young Wayne was a sizable lad, though Vance had expected more of a fight out of him. Vance carried him outside and into the woods to the spot he had prepared. He'd already dug the hole, about forty yards in, amid a thicket of brush and brambles no one would ever find. Sweat picked up on Vance's back as he carted the heavy weight in the humid night.

When he got to the hole, he was wheezing a bit. He dropped Wayne, faceup, and puffed his cheeks so as to catch his breath.

He thought, *Maybe I ought to say something*, staring

down at the young face. *You probably weren't a totally useless fool, though my daughter liked you, so who knows . . . Still, events don't happen of themselves. They have a cause, and you were part of that cause, son. So here you lie. . .*

He rolled Wayne's torso inside the ditch and then kicked in his legs, which didn't seem to want to go in. Then he started to fill up the hole with the shovel he had hidden here in the bushes.

When he was finished, he smoothed things out as best he could, but no one would ever find him here. No one but that tramp Brandee would even miss him likely.

Wheat from chaff, he said to himself, leaning on the shovel. *The lowest rung on a tall ladder.*

But he would do what he had to do and find his way to the top.

Vance took the shovel and headed back.

He had names.

PART TWO

CHAPTER NINETEEN

Carrie drove to her parents' house in Atlantic Beach after work that day. Raef had just come back from the physical therapist.

It was a small, three-bedroom ranch backing onto a public golf course near the beach, but it was near the Wolfson Children's Hospital, where Raef went every day to the rehabilitation center. He'd gotten most of his major muscle movement back, along with the majority of his speech. The therapists were still working on the fine-motor movements, such as writing and catching a ball; running was yet to fully come. But it was all improving. The doctors thought that in a couple of weeks' time Raef would be able to move back in with her and, after the summer, be back in school.

They were hopeful that one day he wouldn't even

show the slightest sign that his brain had been deprived of oxygen for almost two and a half minutes.

"Hi, Mommy!" He ran up to her like any happy nine-year-old, maybe showing just a little weakness on his right side.

"Hey, Tiger!" Carrie exclaimed, lifting him in the air. "Ooof, you are getting to be a real handful. You know that, guy!"

"Roberta said I was very good today." Roberta was one of his therapists at Wolfson. "We played catch. *Look* . . ." He picked up a blue-and-red, soft-cushion baseball, tossed it in the air, and caught it in his right hand, his lagging one. Papa and I have been practicing!"

"Pretty soon we'll see him pitching for the Marlins." Nate, Carrie's dad, the ex–New Hampshire police chief, walked in. Then his face became more serious. "So how'd it go, baby? Some first day back. We saw the news."

"I'll tell you about it," Carrie said, with a roll of her eyes. "I've got quite the story. *But first* . . . I want to see my Number One Dude here in action. See if he can handle my best heater." She took the cushiony ball and pretended to rub it up like a real pitcher. "What do you say, A-Rod . . . ?"

"If you throw it slow, Mommy."

"Slow it is. Just the right hand, Raef." She went into a windup and tossed it to him underhanded from around four feet away. Raef plucked it out of the air.

"Whoa!" Carrie said, eyes wide. "Awesome job!" She turned to her dad, who was nodding with a glow of grandfatherly pride. "You're not joking. I think he might well be filling out that pitching rotation pretty soon."

Raef grinned proudly. Every time Carrie looked at his freckled face, she saw Rick's smile. He surely did have her husband's will and determination. He never once felt sorry for himself. Most of the tears he shed were when he was trying to comfort her. Even now, her thoughts roamed to the incident that had taken Rick, and as always, the memory seemed to come to her against her will.

She was down in St. John's County. At the opening of a JSO-sponsored youth center there. She got the call from Rick. Trying his best to appear calm—that was his way, after two tours in Iraq—but it was impossible not to hear the worry in his voice. "Carrie, I don't want you to panic, but something's happened . . ." The ensuing pause became the dividing line in her life. *"To Raef!"*

She remembered how every nerve in her body seemed to go dead.

He'd fallen on the soccer field at school and never got up. No one was really sure what precisely had happened yet, but "his right arm started shaking and then he said his leg felt numb and then he just fell . . ."

Carrie knew from her husband's tone that he was trying to hold it together as well. *This was bad.*

"He's not conscious, honey," Rick said, sucking in a

bolstering breath. "But the EMTs are there. They're taking him to Memorial Hospital."

Oh my God! That was close to a two-hour drive from where she was. With traffic. Only about ten minutes for Rick. "I'll meet you there," he said. *"Okay?"*

"Okay," Carrie answered shakily.

"And, Carrie, *baby* . . ."

"Yes," she said, her eyes already overrun with tears and her heartbeat racing.

"He's gonna make it, Carrie. I promise he will. He's gonna come through this—you know that, don't you?"

"I know that, Rick," she answered weakly.

She knew it because *he* was saying it. Because nothing could happen to Rick. He was part of the first Marine platoon to arrive in Iraq, and he did two rotations as a field commander, ending up with the rank of captain. He had come through the war fine. Everything always came easy for him. He played third base at U of F and probably could have been drafted as a pro. He had a 3.8 GPA as a history major. He was on the short list for a Rhodes Scholarship to Oxford, but instead decided to enlist. He was the most capable man she knew.

Raef had to be okay if Rick was saying it.

"I'm on my way," she said, already heading toward her Prius. "I'll see you there."

"You drive safely," he told her. "I love you, baby."

"I love you too."

The drive should have taken close to two hours, but

she made it in an hour and a half. A patrol car escorted her, flashing lights and all. When she got to the hospital, she ran through the sliding-glass doors of the emergency entrance, her heart out of control. "My son! He's being operated on," she blurted to the attendant at the desk. "Raef Holmes. He's in the OR . . ."

"Second floor to the right," the attendant said. "I'll call up. You can take the elevator . . ."

Carrie bolted up the stairs. She pushed through the OR doors, searching frantically for Rick. She didn't see him anywhere. He must have stepped out for a second to make a call. Instead a nurse introduced her to the surgeon. "My son's in there. *Raef Holmes* . . ."

"Your boy's had what we call an AVM," said the surgeon, a young-looking Asian in green scrubs. "An arteriovenus malformation. It's a tangle of abnormal arteries and veins in the temporal lobe of the brain. We operated on him to relieve some of the pressure. He's a strong kid, but I'd be lying if I told you anything other than that it's touch and go right now. We've got him sedated in the ICU. We placed him in a coma—"

"*A coma!*" Carrie put a hand to her mouth. *My poor baby. . .*

"To control the swelling. The next forty-eight hours will be key. But, Ms. Holmes . . ." The surgeon took her by the arm and walked her over to a bench. "I'm afraid there's more . . ."

135

More. Carrie remembered saying to herself, *What could possibly be more?*

Then she focused back on Rick. Why he wasn't here. "Where's my husband?" she asked, suddenly seeing something in the surgeon's eyes, something held back, that raised her anxiety level even more.

"He collapsed," the surgeon said, easing her down onto the bench. "In the waiting room. While we were working on your son. It looks like a dissected aorta. He's in the OR now. We've got our top cardiac team working on him now. It could have happened anytime . . ." He went through a rough explanation. It was lurking and likely been there for years. Probably congenital. "It just blew."

"*Blew* . . ." Carrie muttered back to him, eyes flooding. *Oh, Rick. Rick. . .*

It just blew.

They let her look in at him. For the next six hours, she had a husband in the OR and her son in the ICU. Both of them fighting for their lives as she raced back and forth, afraid to leave either one for any time. She didn't know who needed her more.

"I love you mountains and oceans," she said to Raef as she sat by his bed, squeezing his small, unresponsive hand. She remembered Rick's vow: *He's going to be all right, Carrie. You know that, don't you?"*

Yes, she had said, *I know that, Rick.* Because you said so.

"You're going to make it, Raef," she whispered in his

136

ear. "You're going to be healthy again, and do all the things young boys do. You know that, right? You know how we love you, don't you?" Her eyes filled with tears. "You know that nothing could happen to you . . ."

She remembered closing her eyes and praying. *"If you save my boy's life . . ."* She was never the religious type, but right now . . . "You can take anything from me. *Anything*. I swear to you . . ."

Not long after that, a nurse touched her shoulder. Carrie turned. "Ms. Holmes, they need you down in the OR . . ."

She looked at the nurse's face for a sign that it was okay.

Rick died on the table. He had a stroke caused by an aortic rupture, and they couldn't stem the flow of blood or get oxygen to the brain. It had probably been there from birth, the doctors said. Through college. Through Iraq. Through law school. Maybe it was the stress of what happened to Raef that caused it to finally rupture, the doctors speculated. Trying to be strong for all of them. The doctors did everything they could.

Now every time she looked in her son's resilient eyes, she saw him.

Rick.

"So what do I always say to you?" Carrie said, pulling Raef close to her. *"C'mere . . ."* The stress of her first day back on the job returned. Losing Martinez. Fielding the call from Steadman. "I need a really big hug."

"I love you mountains and oceans, right, Mommy?" Her arms nestled around him, tears of joy filling her eyes.

"*Right*. Oh, that's *pretty* big!" Carrie said with a halting breath, lifting him off the ground.

And as she held him, the oddest thought wormed into her brain.

What Steadman had said on the phone. As if only to her. "*I swear on my daughter's life, Carrie. You'll know what I mean . . .*"

Yes, I do know what that means, she thought now. She gripped her sweet-smelling boy a little tighter.

"*Whatever it looks like, whatever anyone believes, it wasn't me!*"

That's why the words had hit home the way they did. There was a space in her heart that seemed to open for those very words.

"*I swear!*" Those words meant everything to her.

Yes, she said to herself, hugging Raef. *I know exactly what that means.*

CHAPTER TWENTY

I spent that first night in the Lexus in the empty lot of a large office park.

I also did what that bastard told me to do. I stopped in an Office Max and picked up a couple of disposable phones. I texted the number to Hallie's phone.

Then I waited. I waited until I couldn't hold my eyes open anymore.

No reply.

Earlier, I'd found a tool set in the car's emergency kit and drove around a movie complex until I came across a Honda with Tennessee plates and switched the front plate onto mine. With luck, the owners might not even know it was missing for a while, and even if they did, a stolen, out-of-state plate wasn't exactly the biggest story of the day with everything else going

139

on. And Lexus SUVs were a dime a dozen on the roads.

I hoped this would buy me some time.

I had my first meal of the day from a Wendy's take-out window, chomping down the double burger in maybe three large bites along with a box of chicken tenders and a Coke. I normally watched what I ate and would rather die than stuff down a meal like that, but the day's events had left me empty and ravenous, and, showing up at Ruth's Chris going, *"Table for one, please!"* wasn't exactly an option tonight.

The only plan I had was to assert my innocence and focus on that blue car.

My thoughts drifted back to Hallie and Mike. I tried to think of every possible way he and Martinez might somehow have been connected. Mike was a prominent real estate attorney in town. He would have known police. Then there was the gamecock thing. South Carolina.

But the only real connection between them was *me*.

I turned on the news, basically just to keep me company, until my eyes finally got heavy and I started drifting off to sleep.

What I heard almost sent my heart through my chest.

"The Jacksonville Murder Spree suspect," the commentator said. *"This is not the first time. He's done it before."*

CHAPTER TWENTY-ONE

The news report said that a television station in New England was claiming that as a student at Amherst, I'd been involved in a fraternity hazing accident in which someone had mysteriously drowned.

"*No*," I shot up in the car and shouted. "*No, no, no, no. . . .*"

I pulled out my iPad and clicked on Google news until I found the link. It was from the website of a WNME in Portland, Maine.

How did *they* know what had happened back then?

The article read, *The Palm Beach surgeon wanted in connection with the murders today of a Jacksonville Florida policeman and a successful businessman has apparently done it before.*

My eyes almost bugged out of my head.

A college classmate of Dr. Henry Steadman, a person of interest sought in connection with the cold-blooded killings today, claims that while a student at Amherst College in the 1980s, Steadman and a fraternity brother were involved in the unexplained drowning of a fellow student in a fraternity hazing ritual gone tragically wrong.

Thomas E. Boothby of Bangor, Maine, claims he was a member of a student judiciary board at Amherst called to investigate Steadman's role in the mishap, which occurred at a local swimming hole known as the Quarry.

As Boothby recounted, a freshman pledge at the Chi Psi fraternity, Terrence Gifford, plunged into the lake from a fifty-foot height in the dead of night, struggled in the icy water, with Steadman near him, and drowned. The incident was ultimately deemed to be "accidental," and while Boothby claims, "No one can be sure what actually happened in the waters that night," no charges were ever filed.

"This poor freshman from Minnesota was dragged out at night and ordered to jump into the freezing pond," Boothby, an EPA administrator in Bangor recalled, "which was about fifty feet down. All anyone knew is that three students went up there and only two came back. While there was never any firm evidence to warrant an arrest or expulsion, there was significant drinking going on; other people nearby

142

heard arguing and thrashing in the water." He recalled that although Steadman was ultimately dismissed from the fraternity, he was not asked to leave school.

I felt the blood rush in anger into my face. Who the hell was this guy? *Boothby*. I'd never even heard of him. Whoever he was, he'd twisted the entire thing around. The article also provided details about the events in Jacksonville today and how *the suspect's successful and likable veneer* and *his stature in the medical community* seemed at odds with the heinous nature of the crimes.

"I know everyone feels that way," Boothby went on to say, "but when I heard who it was, it immediately took me back. All I can say is, I always felt something suspicious took place up on those rocks, a lot more than ever came out. So this doesn't surprise me."

School officials have not yet commented on the twenty-two-year-old incident.

"Screw you!" I shouted in the darkened SUV, my blood hitting a boil. A cold sweat sprang up all over my back.

The story wasn't completely made up, at least not technically, but everything else was twisted. Nothing happened up there. Only a tragic accident. The kid fell. He didn't want to go through with it and he panicked up on the ledge. *I* was actually the one who told him

143

he didn't have to go through with it. And "the argument" this asshole was referring to was actually between me and another Chi Psi dude named Luke Chappelle, who kept insisting that if Giffie didn't jump, he could kiss Chi Psi good-bye. The kid tried to break away from Chappelle and head back down when he tripped and tumbled over the edge. I'm the one who jumped in after him and tried like hell to bring him back up. The incident killed me for a while. I almost left school. But it wasn't because I was guilty. We never pushed him. This Boothby jerk had it all wrong. It was a frat ritual. We'd all made the jump multiple times.

I knew this was bad. It was only going to throw more hot coals onto the fire of my alleged guilt. Worse, anyone who happened to believe me would now have doubts.

And it would make it even harder for anyone to believe me about the blue car.

I'd never told anyone about it before. Well, maybe I told Liz once, years before. I mean, it all happened twenty-two years ago. It didn't have any bearing on who I was. And while the event was tragic, I hadn't done anything wrong.

I lay back and closed my eyes, and I realized how trapped I was. How the person who was doing this to me must be cackling with enjoyment.

I was even burying myself now!

CHAPTER TWENTY-TWO

Cars were already streaming into the office lot the next morning as I woke up in the backseat.

I remembered finally falling asleep, still fuming over that Google post, praying I'd wake up in my own bed and that everything in the past twenty-four hours would have been nothing more than a horrifying dream.

No such luck.

I wiped my eyes, reality colliding into me again. Realizing that I was on the run. That my college buddy Mike was dead. That my daughter had been abducted. Kidnapped by a killer who had turned my life into living hell.

I looked up at the car owner's evergreen air freshener hanging from the dash. Other than that, everything was just peachy!

Then it hit me. With the sudden clarity that only comes when your mind is completely at rest.

I went over the sequence of events for maybe the hundredth time: how Martinez was writing me out a summons from his car; the blue car pulling up beside him; how I was thinking how the whole barrage of questions had just been some kind of made-up cover; out of nowhere, the two, crisp pops. The blue car lurching away.

But this time I saw it! Coming into focus as if I was once again looking through my side mirror:

ADJ-4.

That was it! The license plate from South Carolina. There were more numbers, of course, but I was sure it began with those. Not ADF or A4N, or whatever I'd come up with the day before.

ADJ-4 . . .

In the panic of all that happened yesterday, I hadn't been able to fully bring it to mind.

For the first time, I had something to act on. If I could somehow get access to motor-vehicle-department records in South Carolina. I didn't know who to call. An attorney might be able to get it done. The police, of course. *Fat chance of that!* I could call Liz, but I wanted to keep her out of this as much as I could.

Then I suddenly thought of Marv, my business partner in the walk-in clinics. Marv was the ex–VP of Operations in the Lauderdale Hospital system. He knew the world.

Police. Government officials. Movers and shakers. When it came to public records on anything, Marv could get it done.

He'd already sent me e-mails, conveying his shock and disbelief at the news reports and begging me to call him.

I picked up one of the disposables and punched in Marv's number; it rang three times before he picked up.

"Marv Weiss . . ." It sounded like he was on a speakerphone.

"Marv, it's me!" I said, in a hushed voice. "Are you able to talk?"

"Henry. . . . ! Wait just a minute . . ." I heard him get up, probably to shut the office door. Then I heard the tone come off the speakerphone. "Yes, I can talk. Henry, what the hell's going on? This is all so crazy! I know you. These charges can't be true."

"Of course they're not true, Marv! And I know it's all crazy—and I wish I could go into it all right now. But listen; if you want to help me, I need something from you."

"Of course I want to help. *What . . . ?"*

"Marv, first, I want to give you my word—we've known each other a long time—that I didn't do one thing they're accusing me of. *Not one thing.* I swear!"

"You don't have to explain that to me. I know you didn't do it, Henry."

147

"Including that last bit of nonsense from college that came out last night. It's all a crock of shit. But what I have to do is prove it right now, and for that, I need some help."

"I understand. I just can't believe you're in this mess. What line are you calling me on? I didn't recognize the phone. You have to be careful . . ."

"Don't even ask, Marv. I'm learning on the run. I think we're safe. For now . . ."

"I know. I know. I can only imagine . . ." He tried to laugh. "Listen, the local police called here yesterday. They wanted to know if you'd been in touch."

I hesitated a second. "So what's the story on that? What are you going to tell them?" After Jennifer, I guess I was running scared of everyone right now. And I also didn't want to drag Marv into trouble.

He didn't hesitate. "Like you said, Henry, we've known each other a long time. What is it you need?"

Those words were like rain to me in a long drought. The drought of people's trust in me. "That means the world to me, Marv. You've no idea. I've got to locate a car. I saw who did this to that cop. Or at least, I saw his car. I just don't know where to turn."

"You saw it happen?"

"I was looking through my side mirror. The officer had pulled me over for kind of a bogus traffic violation. It was a dark blue sedan. I couldn't tell the make, but I did catch part of the plates. They're from South

Carolina. I couldn't make them out completely, but I'm positive on the first four characters. *ADJ-4* . . . You've gotta find that plate for me, Marv. It's my only way out of this. I know you'll know someone who can get it done."

"*A-D-J* dash four . . . ?" he said, writing it down.

"Yes. I mean, how many plates can possibly begin like that? And registered for a blue sedan?"

"Don't get your hopes up totally. The car could have been stolen."

"I know. I know. Believe me . . ." I'd taken two cars myself in the past day. "But it's a start. It's all I have as a start, Marv. It has to lead somewhere . . ."

"I'll try, Henry, I'll try . . . Listen . . ." He lowered his voice. "I'm sure I'm not the first one to say this to you, but maybe the best course of action is simply to turn yourself in. Let the police pursue this. We're living in America, Henry, not Syria. If you didn't do this, the truth will come out."

"The police up here seem to be shooting first and asking questions later. You ever been shot at, Marv?"

"No," he said. "I can't say that I have. Then how about making your way down here. We'll find you the best representation. Then we can look for your car—"

"Listen, Marv . . ." Hard as it was, I couldn't find a way to tell him about Hallie; about what had happened to her. "I'm sure if the tables were turned, I'd probably

149

be telling you the very same thing. But I can't. Something's happened and I can't. And I can't even share it with you. I know that sounds crazy. You just have to trust me. Not to mention that even if I could— two murders, one of them of a cop, with my means and ability to flee, I wouldn't be getting bail anytime soon. Half the Jacksonville police force saw me in cuffs in the backseat of Martinez's car. They don't have any doubts it's me."

"Cuffs . . . ?"

"There's no way to explain it." And I couldn't now. No time. I just went through it fast as I could. Just enough so Marv could feel the nightmare I'd been through. "Which brings me back to that car . . ."

"Okay. Let me go. So how do I get in touch with you?"

"I'm going to give you a safe number. Or text me. On my cell. I'll call you back."

"All right, all right. I'll get on it right now. But, Henry, you have to promise me you'll stay out of sight until I can get back to you. Then we'll figure out a way."

"I'm not exactly a pro at this, but I'm learning fast. You have no idea what this means to me. I knew I could count on you, Marv. And hey, at least there's one good thing I can think of that's come out of this mess."

"What's that?" Marv replied dubiously.

"You remember a couple of years ago when we

were going back and forth about what to name the clinics?"

"Yeah, I remember . . ."

"Now aren't you glad I convinced you *not* to put my name over the front door?"

CHAPTER TWENTY-THREE

I wasn't sure what to do while I waited, other than stay out of sight. I snuck into the men's room at a Wendy's and washed up. I was gritted out and had no idea how long it would take for Marv to get back to me. Or what the result would be when he did.

Or even what I would do once he found something.

Every time a police car passed by, if they did an electrocardiogram on me my heart rate would be off the paper!

Around 10 a.m., going out of my mind, I finally decided, *The hell with it!* I did have one other option.

I called the Jacksonville Sheriff's Office and said to the operator, "Carrie Holmes, please."

Yesterday, I detected the slightest wavering in her voice, and right now my book was pretty empty on whom I could trust. I wasn't sure what I would say if a secretary answered or if her voice mail came on, but to my relief, Carrie picked up.

"Community Outreach. Carrie Holmes . . ."

"Guess the glory days are over," I said. "Back to the same ol' grind . . ." Then I immediately felt foolish for being so glib.

I was met by a lengthy silence on the line. *"Who is this?"*

"Carrie, please, don't hang up! Or alert anyone," I said. "I just need to tell you something, without worrying if you're tracing this and that I have to hang up. Can we do that, for just a second?"

She still didn't say anything; just let the call go on in silence. I figured I'd misjudged her.

"Carrie, please, I know what you're about to do, but I found something that can help prove my innocence. I know you'd be taking a risk, but just hear me out. Just for a second. I don't have anywhere else to turn . . ."

Still more silence.

Then she said, "Yeah, back to the same ol' grind . . . Dr. Steadman, you should not be calling me," which felt like kind of a miracle, momentarily putting my worries at ease.

"Just give me a second!" I said. "So did you do what I asked? Did you try to find that car? The blue sedan I told you about yesterday. With South Carolina plates . . . ?"

"Dr. Steadman, I told you yesterday, I think you have

153

to turn yourself in," she replied in a lowered, but firm voice. "If you don't, things are going to go very badly for you. I think you've seen that already. And I honestly *can't* be talking to you, other than to say—"

"You didn't, did you?" I interrupted her. "You didn't look for it?"

She didn't answer right away. I heard her release a breath. "No."

I let out one myself. "So are you tracing this?" I suddenly didn't know why I had thought to put myself in her hands and realized I should end the call immediately. But I didn't. "Just tell me. If you are. I don't know why, but I have this sense you're the only one there I can trust."

"You've got no cause to trust me. I work for the sheriff's office, Dr. Steadman. I'm not on your private security team . . . And I'm not your confidante."

"So are you tracing me?" I asked her again. Then I waited. I felt something strangely empathetic in her tone. "Look, I'm gonna put myself in your hands, Carrie. Right or wrong. Maybe I'm stupid. I'm gonna tell you something that can help clear my name. Just please tell me, are you tracing this call?"

She didn't answer.

But I knew what the answer was. She had to trace it. It was her responsibility. And as I checked the time I figured that gave me maybe about another minute and a half before I had to cut it short and move on.

"So how long do I have," I asked, "a couple of minutes
. . . ? Then just hear me out. Why the hell would I kill
those people, Carrie? Why would I kill my own friend?
We were going to play golf, for Christ's sake. I'd known
him since college. He was a lawyer! The only reason I
even went to his house was to get his help in turning
me in. *Check*—I made two calls to him from my cell
phone immediately after Martinez was killed. But he
was dead by the time I got there. I realize I took his
phone and his car—and how that makes me look. But
I needed to get out of there and there was no other
way. And my phone was compromised. And who the
hell was going to believe me anyway after what
happened to Martinez?"

She didn't reply. The clock was ticking.

"And I told you, yesterday, that I was back in my car
when Martinez was shot. He was letting me go; just
writing me up a warning . . . You can check that too.
What possible reason would I have for shooting someone
if they were about to let me go? Not to mention, with
what gun? Last I checked, they didn't let you keep one
on you when you traveled by plane. Has anyone given
three seconds thought to *that*?"

"You could have ditched the gun when you say you
took off after the car," Carrie said.

"But I didn't. And how would I get one? Did I know
in advance that Martinez was going to pull me over?"

"So then turn yourself in, Dr. Steadman. To *me*, since

you seem to trust me. I'll make sure you're treated fairly. You've done wonderful things. In Nicaragua. You built a school there. I saw your daughter's photos—" She suddenly stopped herself, as if she'd revealed too much.

To me, it was the smallest crack in her armor. "You were on my website, weren't you?"

"No," she answered, stammering, as if she'd been caught red-handed. "Okay. Yes. I was."

"Then I'm not wrong, am I? You do have doubts. Carrie, I need you to take this down. *Please.* I recalled the plate number from yesterday. From that car I mentioned. Not the whole thing, but part of it. It began with the letters *A-D-J* dash four . . . There were three additional numbers, but I'm sure that's how it began. There have to be security cameras around. On the lights, or near one of the scenes. The guy headed down Lakeview after he shot Martinez and went onto I-10, heading west. There are *always* cameras! Please, Carrie, I need you to do this for me. That car is the only chance I have!"

I didn't know if I had reached her or not, but I knew my time was rapidly coming to an end and that I'd better get on the move. I put the phone on speaker and the car in gear and headed onto the road. I knew that my partner Marv was a long shot, *if* he even could come up with something. But there was something made me feel that Carrie Holmes was someone I could trust.

She asked, softer, "What did you mean yesterday when you said you couldn't turn yourself in? You mean because you were afraid?"

"Yes, I was afraid, at first. But no, it was something else. I just can't tell you."

"I'm not sure I see how you're in a position to be keeping secrets, Dr. Steadman . . ."

"I can't." Part of me wanted to; I'd sensed that something I'd said yesterday had hit home. But I couldn't. I couldn't take the chance. The stakes were too great if it got out. "All I can say is that it's bigger than whatever happens to me. It's bigger than Martinez. Or even Mike. I wish I could tell you, Carrie, I just can't."

I heard a commotion. Voices in the background. They were probably coming up with my number at that very moment. Just a matter of seconds, then, to hit on my location. Or maybe they already had it! I was playing with fire.

"Did you do this, Dr. Steadman?" she asked me directly. "I knew Bob Martinez. He had a wife and three kids. I want to hear you say it. Did you kill those people?"

"No. I wish I was in front of you so you could see my eyes. I swear, Carrie. I swear on anything. I swear on what I said to you yesterday . . . My own daughter." It hurt to even say it. *"No."*

"And all that stuff that came out about you at college . . . ?"

"All totally twisted," I shot back. "Yes, it happened. That fellow drowned. I was there. But it was an accident. He panicked on the rocks, that's all. I never *killed* anyone. I wasn't even suspended from school. Talk to the people at Amherst. It was an accident. They didn't find a thing. I was even the one who was arguing on the kid's behalf." I turned on the main street, leaving the McDonald's way behind.

"Then what the hell do you think is going on, Dr. Steadman?" I heard exasperation in her voice. "If it's not *you* doing this—who is?"

The words had the feel of an accusation more than a question. And God knows, over the last twenty-four hours I'd asked it myself a hundred times. "I wish I knew, Carrie. But please, just look for that car. That's all I'm asking. There have to be cameras. I guarantee you'll spot it at, or near, both crime scenes. Please . . . *ADJ-4*. Did you at least write it down?"

She didn't reply. I didn't know if she believed me or not. Or if she had been tracing the call all along, and cops were on their way to pick me up right now.

"Did you write it down, Carrie?" was all I could ask.

Suddenly two police cars raced past me the other way, lights flashing, sending shock waves through my heart. Now the answer to whether she'd traced my call was clear. *"Thanks . . ."* I said, and cut off the connection, my disappointment morphing into outright panic. There were sirens echoing all around. I fully expected the cars to do a U-ey, realizing they'd just gone past me, and surround me on the street. Cops jumping out of their cars with weapons drawn.

But they just kept going. Maybe to that McDonald's. Maybe to some other fixed point they had triangulated.

I was still free.

I melded into traffic, getting away from there as fast as I could.

My only hope now was to wait for Marv.

"Great job," Bill Akers said, ducking his head back in. "We missed him. The initial fix was on a fast-food place out on Cassat. We almost had him."

"Too bad," Carrie said. "Bill, you think we ought to check out his story? About that car?"

Akers chuckled, indicating that he didn't give it much credence. "Just let me know if he calls in again. There'll be other chances. He won't get far." He gave her a thumbs-up sign.

She'd done the right thing. *Right?* Carrie wondered after he left. She'd put out the trace. She'd gotten the proper people involved.

Still, she felt an anxiousness come over her.

She looked down at the sheet of paper on her desk. At the partial plate number staring up at her.

Yes, there probably were cameras around somewhere. And yes, it all did seem just a bit improbable. Why Steadman would kill Martinez? Over a traffic violation, no less. While he was letting him go. Not to mention killing his friend?

And with what gun?

Her heart beat nervously. She'd be a fool. A fool to get involved. What with Raef. And she wasn't even a detective.

But, *yes . . .* She slid the number under her desk mat, answering him. *I wrote it down.*

CHAPTER TWENTY-FOUR

Carrie drove, later that afternoon, out to Lakeview, pretending to be on department business, just to see for herself where Martinez had been killed. Her eyes darted back and forth across the steadily trafficked street as it led toward I-10.

She wasn't sure why she was doing this, other than because somewhere deep in her gut, a part of what Steadman had said must have made sense to her. Was it the fact that he'd had no reason to kill Martinez, who *was* in the process of letting him go? She'd checked on that. Or, like he'd said, where would he have gotten a weapon? And why? Or that it made perfect sense for him to go to his friend's house, the only person he knew in town who could help him turn himself in. And no sense at all to kill him. Or was it the good things he had done, which she had read about on his website? Or was it his kind face, which didn't look like a killer's face, and the way he defended himself. Or, lastly, was it what he had said about his daughter? As if he'd known exactly what she had once said about her own son. *Then you'll understand* . . .

Maybe it was that that had hit home the most.

Or maybe it was simply because nothing in Steadman's story fit the profile of a killer. And everything he had said rang true. He was in town to deliver a speech at a Doctors Without Borders conference. Martinez would have been no more than a random interaction. Not to mention this car, this "blue sedan" he pressed so hard on. What would he possibly have to gain if they couldn't find such a car? If it didn't exist. *There have to be cameras*.

But he was right on one thing—Steadman. That there was no one in the department—not a detective or a patrolman or anyone in the brass; not even the guy who mopped the floors at night—who didn't want to see him thrown into a cell for Martinez's murder.

Or who was focused on any other suspect.

No one other than Carrie herself. *Carolyn Rose Holmes*—she smirked to herself as she slowly drove her way up Lakeview—*when did you become the patron saint of lost causes?*

Her heart picking up, she passed the turnoff where Martinez had been shot—Westvale, it was called—and

162

stopped for a second to look. It was still cordoned off with police barriers.

To her knowledge, there weren't cameras on any traffic lights on Lakeview. Which made her task all the more difficult. She'd have to go from business to business and ask around. Kind of like a detective. And do it without drawing attention to herself. At five feet four inches, with shoulder-length strawberry-blond hair, light blue eyes, and a scattering of orange freckles on her cheeks, she didn't much look like a detective.

And she liked that.

Noting the time, she continued west from the murder site toward the highway. The direction Steadman claimed the blue car with South Carolina plates he so desperately wanted her to find was traveling.

She had taken a glance through the witnesses' statements. None of the people who saw Steadman exiting Martinez's car had mentioned the vehicle. Of course the killer would have waited for a gap in traffic before he pounced, and Steadman, rushing back to Martinez to check him out, might have been over him, what, twenty, thirty seconds?

Why do you believe him? Carrie asked herself. *Are you in such a state now that you're a sucker for anyone with a smooth voice who throws on a little charm?*

ADJ-4, right . . . ?

She passed a bank, Gold Coast Savings. They must have security cameras. At least, Carrie figured, ones

163

facing in. But obtaining them might be problematic—given that while she had a perfectly valid sheriff's office ID, it wasn't exactly a detective's shield.

Continuing, she passed a row of fast-food outlets and larger malls, all possibilities. But the big stores were all set back well off the street behind large parking lots.

I-10 was just a quarter mile ahead.

Then she saw a gas station. A tall Exxon sign that suggested that the place might have a fairly sweeping view of Lakeshore Drive.

She decided to turn in.

She parked near the office and asked herself one more time just why she was doing this. Then she opened her door.

She went into the service station's office and asked the guy behind the counter for the manager. He got on the intercom, called out a name, and an affable-looking Indian with a name tag that read *Pat* stuck his head in from inside the garage. "Can I help you?"

"I'm with the sheriff's office," Carrie said. She flashed him her photo ID. Then she pointed toward the road signs. "You know there was a serious incident down the street involving a policeman yesterday?'

"Of course." The manager nodded. "Traffic along here was backed up all day."

Carrie asked him, "Any chance you have security cameras that have a view of the street?"

CHAPTER TWENTY-FIVE

Business was booming for Dexter Ray Vaughn these days.

Booming enough for him to buy, in cash, the run-down row house in Cobb County outside Atlanta that he'd been renting—and fill it with a boss Bose sound system and a sixty-inch Samsung, which, other than a mattress in the bedroom, was pretty much his only furniture. Good enough to buy the tricked-out Ford 450 pickup he was driving lately.

Only problem was, he thought as he glanced around in his T-shirt and undershorts, his wife, Vicki, was always so stoned she couldn't keep the house in any form other than "Early Shithole." And the fridge never had anything in it but vodka and stale pizza. But considering the kinds of customers and business associates he had floating through here on a daily basis, was, like, *Who the fuck really cared?*

The meth lab in his basement was turning out a hundred grams a day, when he got the urge to work. He had a distro network, both in town and even out in the boonies—if you called his half-witted cousin Del, who sometimes ran for him there, a distributor. More like a sloth who sat in the trees farting and scratching himself.

Not to mention the neat, little side business he had going for himself in pharmaceuticals. *Diversified*—just like Warren E. Buffett—he had once seen the word in a magazine at his doctor's office. Local gangs moved some of it locally and provided protection, so Dexter didn't even have to lose sleep at night worrying about the cops.

Shit, some of the cops were his best customers.

Life Was Fucking-A Good, just like the words on the T-shirt he was wearing and had apparently passed out in last night. He'd been partying most of the night and woken up at two in the afternoon on the couch, with a world-class hard-on. Vicki was nowhere around, probably blowing some Mexican up the street for weed. Dex didn't really care. Shit, he could call up a half-dozen meth skanks who'd be over in thirty seconds and go down on him for what he'd left out on the table.

But, he got up and sighed, commerce called. His amigos were expecting more inventory mañana. He had to get to the lab. Dex stretched, still a little wobbly, and took the last chug from a can of warm beer he'd left on the rug.

Man, this steady nine-to-five crap was killing him.

The doorbell rang.

Fuck. Who the hell was there? He groaned. Winston, the Jamaican, was supposed to come by, but that wasn't until around six. Dexter shuffled over to the window, scratching his crotch. He parted the curtain, but was unable to see who was there. He pushed the hair out of his face and reknotted his ponytail, all-presentable like. *"Who is it, man?"* he called, squinting through the peephole. "Speak and be recognized."

"Del sends his regards," the person said.

Fuckin', Del . . . The guy looked like a rube from Okefenokee. *Didn't that pimply bladderhead know better than to send his hicks around . . . ?*

"Del oughta know better," Dexter said, turning the knob and pushing open the bolt. "He—"

And then the door pretty much exploded in his face.

Before he even knew what was happening, this old dude had forced his way in. Heavyset. Arms like fucking ham hocks. Bald on top. Dexter's hand shot to his mouth and there was blood on it. "The fuck you doin', man . . ."

Then his eyes grew wide when he saw a shotgun in the guy's hands.

"Dude, you outta your fuckin' mind?" Dexter blurted

167

at him, thinking he knew about ten people right off the top of his head he could get to blow a hole through this guy as wide as a highway. Stupid fool clearly had no idea where he was.

But then the guy's elbow jerked and the butt of the shotgun caught Dex hard in the mouth. He felt his lip burst open, and when he looked down, he saw three of his own teeth staring up at him from the floor.

"On the couch," Vance demanded, motioning to the dilapidated tweed thing that sat in front of the wide-screen TV.

"Listen, old man, you must be touched!" Dexter said, spitting blood onto his hand. "You don't have any idea what the fuck you're doing here. You think you can just—"

"Sit. On. The. Couch," Vance said again, this time emphasizing each word with the muzzle of the shotgun.

"All right, all right . . ." Dexter said, lifting his palms. "I'm going. I'm going . . . Just keep it cool, old man." He shuffled to the couch and sank down. He wiped blood off his mouth. "Look what you done, dude? What the hell is it you want? You need a boost? *Weed?* X? A little meth maybe? I can get it all. You surely look like you can use some X, there, dude, if you don't mind me saying so. Got no cash—no worries, we can work something out."

"I look like I came here for drugs?" Vance demanded, staring down at him. He grabbed the cane chair that was in the middle of the room and plunked himself down on it, facing Dexter Vaughn, the shotgun dangling loosely from his side. The blinds were already down. "You sold some Oxy to someone named Wayne Deloach, back in Acropolis. Through some poor fool named Del."

"Roxies . . . ? Acropolis . . . ? Nah, never heard of Acropolis," Dexter said, wiping the blood out of his mouth, surely wondering what was going on.

"You heard of *him*, though," Vance replied.

"You some kind of cop?"

Vance shook his head. "Not anymore."

"Then I'm sorry to tell you, I don't the fuck know any Wayne Deloach. Though you're surely right on one thing . . . My cousin Del damn well is a poor fool."

"A dead one too," Vance said, looking at him.

The ponytailed dealer swallowed. Vance could tell from the sheen of sweat that had popped up on his brow that he had gotten the guy's full attention now.

"You said Wayne, right?"

Vance nodded, shifting the gun across from the guy's knee.

"Still, don't know him. In fact—"

Vance squeezed the trigger, sending a casing of Remington 341 buckshot into Dexter's kneecap, causing him to jump up and howl clutching his knee, which, through his jeans, was mostly blood and exposed bone now.

"Look at that! Look what you fucking done, man!"

169

"I'm gonna give you one more chance to rethink your answer about whether you knew this Wayne or not—before you become a dead fool too."

"You fucking busted my knee, you sonovabitch!" Dexter rolled back onto the couch, writhing on the cushions, inspecting the hole in his jeans, blood all over them. "You must be fucking crazy, man. *Ow . . .*"

"That knee'll soon end up the healthiest part of you"— Vance cocked the other barrel—"unless you tell me where your Oxy comes from. I know it was you and I don't give a shit about whatever else is going on. All I want is a name. Whoever it is who supplies you, son. So unless you want to start losing more body parts by the minute and end up on the floor slithering around like a fish in a catch bucket, you better start thinking of some names."

He lifted the barrel again so it pointed level at Dexter's midsection. "I got a big fat target, son. The Oxy, boy. I want a name."

"He's no one! *No one . . . !*" Dexter cried out, putting his palms up for protection. "He's just some jerk-off mule who earns a few bucks bringing them up to me once a month. Hell, it's all small potatoes anyway. What's the big fucking deal?"

Vance squeezed the trigger again and the Remington blasted a hole in Dexter's other knee, taking away much of his shinbone as well.

"*Aaargh,*" Dex screamed, crying now, falling onto the

170

floor and rolling from side to side in pain. His arms wrapped around both his shredded legs.

"The *big deal*"—Vance stood up and bent over him—"is that there are people who are dead, son. People who had a lot more worth in life than you, you miserable mess, because of what you do. And others, who won't get a chance to live their lives out 'cause they were stupid and weak and easily preyed on by the likes of you."

Dexter rolled around on his back, sobbing.

"Now, I can just leave you as you are, son, and you can get those legs mended—maybe—and you may well even walk one day and prey on some other fool's daughter. You'd like that around now, wouldn't you, son, if it turned out like that?"

"Yes," Dexter said, moaning. *"Please . . ."*

"Or we can try another part. Say, right here . . ." Vance held the gun over Dexter's groin. "Shit, probably gonna be useless to you anyway after today . . ."

"No, no, no, no, no . . . !" Dexter covered his crotch, his eyes stretched with panic.

"Then you give me the name, son. Who supplies you. Where'd that Oxy come from . . . You can spare yourself a lot of pain, not to mention eventually getting your head blown off."

"All right, all right . . ." Dexter moaned, sobbing, his face a mishmash of blood and tears. "No more . . . Please, no more. He's no one. Just some mule who

brings it up. Pays for his own use. He's just a mule. That's all."

Dexter gave him the name and told Vance where he could find him.

"Now you gotta get outta here. *Please* . . . I gave you what you wanted." Tears ran down Dexter's face. "Now just leave me. *Please* . . ."

Vance shouldered the gun, and for a moment he almost did leave Dexter be. After all, the guy would likely never walk in a straight line again anyway.

But then Vance stood there thinking for a minute or so, remembering all that had happened and why he was here. And what his vow was. His gaze bored deeply into Dexter's helpless, pleading eyes.

"Can't, son," he admitted sadly.

He drew the gun over the dealer's chest, who put up his hands and started muttering, *"Please, no, don't, don't . . ."* and turned his face away.

Vance said, "Sorry, just not the way it works here."

He squeezed and the recoil lifted his arm all the way up to his shoulders. Dexter's body jumped off the floor, his "Life Is Fucking-A Good" T-shirt with the winking smiley face on it pooling up quickly with blood.

"Someone's gotta pay."

CHAPTER TWENTY-SIX

Carrie left the Exxon station with an envelope full of security tapes from the morning Martinez was killed. A camera had been focused onto Lakeshore, but the angle was wide enough to catch a view of vehicles driving toward the highway.

She drove back to headquarters by way of Avondale, where Mike Dinofrio lived. Whoever killed him had likely driven via I-95 and gotten off at the Riverside Boulevard exit. From there, it was another six or seven minutes to Avondale. Martinez and Dinofrio had been murdered within about thirty minutes of each other, and Carrie calculated it would have taken approximately fifteen minutes or so to get to Dinofrio's given traffic and the time of day. Whoever had done it—either the person in the blue car or Steadman via taxi—would have needed to get there fast.

She exited at Riverside and scanned both sides of the street as she drove past familiar office buildings—the *Florida Times-Union*, Haskell, Fidelity—until the structures along the road grew residential. Under a canopy of old oak trees, she passed the stately, historic homes that lined both sides, looking for cameras.

Nothing.

Eventually she hit Riverside Park, the neighborhood growing progressively more upscale, but still she saw no obvious cameras.

Until she happened on something that gave her hope.

A speed warning. you are going 35 mph, the digital sign read. speed patrolled by automatic camera.

Her heart rose with excitement. It would have definitely caught whoever had passed by two days before.

A couple of hours later, Carrie was back at the office, in the fourth-floor video station, reviewing the tapes. She'd gotten the speed-warning video from a friend who worked at the Transportation Authority. She began, frame by frame, with the tape from the Exxon station near where Martinez was killed.

The camera was focused on the comings and goings at the station, but it also took in the first two lanes of Lakeshore Drive heading west.

This was the best she had.

Carrie fast-forwarded to 10:06 a.m., the approximate time of the Martinez shooting. She sighed that it would have made this process a whole lot easier if Martinez had just had an in-dash camera in his car like a lot of the patrol cars now had.

She rolled the film forward, estimating that it was approximately two miles to the highway from the crime scene, and taking into account the traffic flow, which was steady, the blue car would have had to have passed by the station sometime between 10:09 and 10:11.

If it hadn't turned off sooner.

And if Steadman wasn't lying.

She watched the footage closely. It was going to be difficult to read the full license plate, especially on a car driving in the outer two lanes, because the camera angle wasn't exactly positioned to capture that view. Steadman had said the car was a domestic make. A dark blue. Which wouldn't exactly be helpful since the film was black-and-white.

10:07 . . . Just a steady stream of traffic passing by. Nothing yet.

Carrie advanced the frames. 10:08 . . . At the slower film speed, she studied every car she could. In real time, they had driven by in a flash, the camera picking them up for only a split second.

It was impossible to make out the car color, so she focused on the plates. South Carolina. ADJ-4 . . .

10:09:23 . . . Still nada. She was thinking a car might

175

have already passed by this time. This was starting to feel like a giant waste of—

Something flashed by her on the screen.

A midshade sedan switching lanes. The camera picked it up for only a second. Carrie stopped the tape, rolled back, was able to zoom in. It was a Mazda. Not what Steadman had said, but he'd also said he wasn't sure.

At the higher magnification the resolution grew even grainier. But she was able to make out numbers—at least some of them, though only on the right-hand side of the license plate: 392. The left side was completely obscured.

On the bottom of the plate she could make out a word that made her heart sputter:

Carolina.

Not South or North. The left side wasn't clear.

Just *Carolina.*

It wouldn't be hard to figure out which Carolina; however she didn't know state license-plate colors by heart.

And the plate also wasn't ADJ-4, like Steadman insisted. Nor was it a Ford or a Mercury, whatever he thought it was. The only thing that stood out was the state.

10:09:46. Driving by at a high rate of speed. She wondered if that could be it. She made a note of the time and license numbers and continued forwarding the frames, just in case.

A minute later, another car passed by. This one she

recognized immediately. It was Steadman's white Cadillac STS. Carrie even verified the plate numbers.

He was clearly in pursuit, like he said, chasing the car that had gone before him.

She reversed the tape and replayed the first car over again. There was nothing, *nothing* even remotely suspicious about it. The plate didn't match up, though she couldn't make it out completely. The make was different. If she brought this information to Akers, or one of the detectives, as if it proved something, they'd look at her like she was crazy.

Shit, if she brought it to Raef, even *he'd* probably look at her like she was crazy.

Carrie sighed, filled with frustration. *What the hell are you doing?* she asked herself. This proved zero. She took the Exxon tape out of the player, marking down the one car that had caught her attention.

Then she put in the tape from the speed warning on Riverside Avenue.

Dinofrio had been alive at 10:15, when his wife left to go to her Pilates class. His killing had to have occurred before Steadman arrived, which, according to the cabbie was, 11:02. Accounting for the time it took for him to drive back to the scene, escape the police, ditch the car, walk to the Clarion Inn, find the cab, and drive there.

Calculating the probable time it would take someone to get to Dinofrio's house on Turnberry Terrace, she started with 10:30 a.m.

Carrie started advancing the tape. This one was a whole lot easier. While it was also black-and-white, the camera focused directly on an oncoming car's front grille and license plate.

It *was* a speed trap.

But the work was still slow. There was no exact way to know precisely what time anyone would have passed there. Or, it occurred to Carrie, if they had even come by this route. Who could be sure?

Dozens and dozens of vehicles went by. With no matches.10:35. Carrie started to grow disheartened. *Give it up,* said a voice inside her. *Sometimes people who do bad things don't fit the part. Look at Ted Bundy. He didn't look the part. He could charm the pants off a—*

10:40. Twenty minutes or so until Steadman would have passed by in the cab.

Still nothing.

Then suddenly it came into view. Her heart lurched to a stop.

Oh my God.

10:41:06. There it was. The very same Mazda. 392. This time with South Carolina plates. Perfectly clear.

And this time, Carrie saw *all* the numbers.

Her eyes doubled in size.

ADJ-4, the license plate read. Followed by what she had seen before. On Lakeview.

392.

178

CHAPTER TWENTY-SEVEN

It took to the end of the day, but I did get a text message back from Marv. "Do you have a laptop handy?"

"Yes," I wrote back from a Home Depot parking lot, trying to stay out of sight. "My iPad."

"Check your e-mail."

I found a document there, from the South Carolina Department of Motor Vehicles. I opened the attachment and ran my eyes over it like a starving man looking at a steak. There were names, addresses. All with plates beginning with ADJ-4.

Twelve of them.

Many were from towns I'd never heard of. Edgefield. Moncks Corner. I'd been in South Carolina only twice in my life. Once to Charleston, one of my favorite places, and once to Kiawah Island to play some golf with a bunch of doctor buddies.

Twelve . . . I eagerly scanned the list of names because possibly one of them was the killer I was looking for.

"How did you get these?" I called Marv back.

"Does it matter? I know someone. There's a hundred ways to obtain things like this today. How much do you think a state employee actually makes for a living? But I'm hoping you're simply planning on handing these over to the police after you turn yourself in. I want to repeat, Henry, what you're doing is crazy. I know it seems like you're alone. I know you think this is your only option. But it's not. I did what I said I'd do; now it's up to you. All you're going to do is get yourself killed."

I thought for a second about walking into a police station with my hands in the air and handing them this list. My gut reaction was that the cops would never even stoop to pick it up off the floor.

"I want to thank you for all this, Marv. I mean it. I'll be back with you when I know something."

"My little speech didn't exactly move the needle, did it?"

"I wish I could tell you why I can't, Marv. But the needle's already moved. It's way too late to dial it back."

We hung up and I opened the document again, running my eyes down the columns. Names from all over the state. Four of them were women. Grace Kittridge, in Manning. Sally Ann Jennings in Edgarfield.

A Betty Smith. Moncks Corner. Just to narrow it, I chose to cross them off for the moment.

Two of the plates on the list had expired. One in the past year and the other in '06. Maybe they were just never turned in. Which didn't really matter. They could have been stolen. Just like mine. Hell, for all I knew, the blue car I was searching might be stolen too.

Still, the remote chance that one of these names led to that car was the best chance I had.

I went into the Home Depot and bought a few things with cash. The first two were more throwaway cell phones and the other was scissors.

I went into the men's room toilet stall and started chopping my hair. Each lock of my long brown hair falling into the toilet was like a part of my life that might never come back. I had something I needed to do right now. I had someone who needed me more than I needed my old life. I was no longer someone who had been falsely accused of two murders. I was a dad, a dad who was trying to save the person he loved most in the world. I took one more glance at my old life floating there in the basin— and then I flushed.

I found a cash machine in the store and punched in my account number and password. I requested three hundred dollars. I knew it would likely trigger a response, probably just as it was happening.

Hell, there might even be a police team scrambling as I stood here now.

181

I didn't care.

I wouldn't be around long . . . and where I was heading, it wouldn't matter.

I left, found another ATM at a bank nearby, and took out another three hundred. I stuffed the cash in my pocket, pulled down my cap, and jumped back into the car.

I-95 was only a short drive away. I turned on Sirius radio and found the Bridge. A bunch of oldies I knew.

I called Liz from one of the phones I had bought. I didn't care about the risk. "I want you to know, I have a list. Of twelve cars, whose license plates begin with the number I saw. One of them has our daughter."

"How, Henry?" she asked, surprised, but uplifted.

"Doesn't matter."

The next stop was getting my daughter back. *You just hang on, Hallie. I'm coming.*

Next stop, South Carolina.

PART THREE

PART THREE

CHAPTER TWENTY-EIGHT

The next morning Carrie knocked on Bill Akers's door.

"Carrie, come on in," her boss said, moving some papers around: "There's been some news."

"I've got something as well," she said, pushing back the flutter in her stomach and taking a seat across from him. She placed the folder, which contained photos she had put together of the blue Mazda at both crime scenes, on her lap.

Akers's walls were lined with framed criminology degrees, citations for merit, as well as photos of himself with prominent officials, including the mayor, and a former head of Homeland Security. Which only made what Carrie was about to share with him even harder to do.

She knew she had no greater supporter in the

department than Bill. Truth was the community outreach effort had been one of his own personal initiatives. She also knew she'd need every bit of that support when it came to the budgetary cutbacks she'd heard were coming. She'd worn her most flattering suit, black pants and jacket, and a light blue tee. She wanted to look as proper and businesslike as she could for when the shit would hit the fan later.

"How about I go first?" Carrie said. She took in a breath. "I have an admission to make, Bill. I want to show you something . . ." She put the folder on his desk.

She had struggled all night over showing this to him. She knew what she had done would get her into a lot of hot water: withholding key evidence from the investigation, a murder investigation; and going around on her own obtaining confidential security tapes using a JSO ID.

Not to mention, how she was probably the only person here who harbored any doubts about Steadman's guilt, which she knew, politically, wasn't exactly a home run. She'd pretty much tossed and turned the whole night.

But in the morning, she'd awoken, sure in her heart that she was doing the right thing.

Carrie swallowed. "Look, *Bill* . . ." she began, trying to ignore the photo of Akers with the new Chief Hall, directly in her line of sight, "I've had some thoughts

. . . about what Steadman was saying the other day . . . How certain things just weren't adding up. Like why would he have shot Martinez in the first place? I know the others said he was being belligerent and argumentative, but by the time they all left, things had calmed down considerably, and Martinez was only writing up a warning and about to let him go . . ."

Akers nodded obligingly. Carrie judged his gaze as, disappointed.

"Not to mention where any possible weapon would have come from. I mean, he'd just come off a plane, right? And how there's nothing in the guy's past to suggest he had these kinds of tendencies . . ."

Akers took off his reading glasses. "Carrie . . ."

A look of skepticism came over her boss's face, and she found herself suddenly rushing things, not giving him the chance to interrupt. "Then it kind of seemed crazy Steadman would kill his own friend? Who he knew from college. More likely he was going there because he had nowhere else to go—he told us he only ran from the scene in the first place because the police fired on him. I mean, he did place a call to 911 . . . So I asked around . . . He'd also placed two calls to Dinofrio, minutes after he ran from the crime scene, so it seems possible, doesn't it, Bill, that he only headed there because Dinofrio was the only person he knew in town, not to mention an attorney, which kind of backs up his assertion that he only went there in the first place to turn himself in. And the second murder scene showed no sign of any struggle or altercation—"

"I didn't realize he *had* said he was only going there to turn himself in." Akers looked at her inquisitively. "You certainly sound like you've been following this case closely, Carrie."

"I'm only pointing out that there are inconsistencies, Bill. You know how Steadman kept going on and on the other day about us looking for that blue car? With South Carolina plates?" She opened up the file. "I started thinking—"

"Look, Carrie." Akers pushed himself back in his chair. "I appreciate all your thought on this, but have you given any thought to the possibility that maybe Steadman intended all along to kill his friend?"

"What? Why in the world would he want to do *that*?"

"I don't know. Maybe there was some history between them that will come out. And given what *has* come out, the other night, about his time in college, you may well be wrong about any predating 'violent tendencies.' And it's entirely possible he could have planted the gun somewhere. Off the airport grounds. Maybe on a previous visit."

"A previous visit?"

"Why not? That would give him a perfect alibi, right? To come up here to play golf with him . . . Then he stashed the gun somewhere when he ran from the scene. Or left it near Dinofrio's house. People are searching the areas now. And what if Martinez somehow found something? What if Steadman somehow felt Martinez was interfering with his plan?"

"He was up here to give a speech at a doctors' conference, Bill! Look, there's something you need to see." Carrie blew out a breath, knowing there was no holding back now, and took out the first photo, the one of the blue Mazda racing from Martinez's murder scene. *Here goes the career*, she thought.

Akers put up his hand. "No, Carrie, I think you're the one who needs to see something . . ." He reached to the side of his desk and pushed a piece of paper across to her. "This came in just an hour ago."

Carrie picked it up. It was an invoice of some kind. From something called Bud's Guns in Mount Holly, North Carolina.

An invoice for a Heckler & Koch 9mm handgun.

She saw whom the bill was made out to, and her stomach fell like a ten-ton weight hurled off a cliff.

> Henry Steadman
> 3110 Palmetto Way
> Palm Beach, Florida

Steadman's address.

An H&K 9mm, the same kind of gun that had killed both Dinofrio and Martinez. It was bought at a gun show, in Tracy, which made it perfectly legal to avoid providing certain IDs and background checks.

The invoice was dated March 2. *Just three weeks ago!*

Steadman had lied. He said he'd never even owned a gun. Her breath felt cut in half. Carrie was afraid to lift her eyes.

"So what exactly do you have in there that's so important for me to see?" Akers asked her with a sharpness in his voice. Acting more like a superior officer than a colleague.

"Nothing . . ." Carrie swallowed, her mouth completely dry. She closed the file. "This makes it all pretty clear."

CHAPTER TWENTY-NINE

I had just about made it through Georgia when I heard the news.

I'd spent the night in Hinesville, a few miles south of Savannah. I pulled off the highway in need of a night's sleep and, even more, a shower, and drove until I found a motel that looked even sleepier than me. The woman who checked me in seemed as anxious to get back to the tea she was brewing as I was to avoid her direct sight. Ten minutes later I was bathed and gone to the world, a *King of Queens* rerun on the TV. Glad to just be in a bed after two nights. When I woke up, the housekeeper was knocking on the door. It was close to ten. The news was on, *Libyan Rebels Advancing on the Capital of Tripoli*. I closed my eyes again, wondering if I'd hear an update about me.

What came on almost sent me into cardiac arrest.

"Florida double homicide suspect purchased a nine-millimeter murder handgun at North Carolina gun show."

I shot up in bed, as a pretty, down-home anchorwoman told the world how on March 2, only three weeks ago, I had bought a Heckler & Koch 9mm handgun, apparently the same gun that killed both Martinez and Mike, from a local dealer at a gun show in North Carolina.

I leaped out of the bed and put my face close to the screen.

What I saw was a supposed bill of sale from an outfit called Bud's Guns, in Mount Holly. The report claimed that the weapon had been paid for in cash at the Mid-Carolina Gun Fair almost three weeks earlier, which, it explained, avoided the requirement for a more detailed background check and ID.

My heart almost came up my throat. I'd never been to a gun show in my life! And I'd only been to North Carolina once in the past several years, to Duke University, for a conference on rebuilding facial bone structure.

But there it was. My name on the invoice. My address in Palm Beach. Having paid cash, as if I was trying to avoid detection. Three weeks ago. Before the murders. For the entire world to see!

If there was even a sliver of hope that someone might believe that I wasn't guilty, that was now dashed. My mind flashed to Carrie Holmes. It had taken everything just to convince her that the Amherst incident had been twisted maliciously.

What would she be thinking now?

I reached over to the night table and found one of my disposable phones.

This was part of the setup! It had to be. How could someone have my name and address on a bill of sale, buying the identical gun used in the killings, three weeks before the crime? How would anyone have known I'd be in Jacksonville? How would anyone have planted me there?

Suddenly the truth settled into me and my eyes went wide.

The sonovabitch who had been orchestrating this whole thing, who had Hallie . . . he'd been planning it for weeks.

How? . . . Why?

I turned off the TV and sat back in a daze, mentally rewinding through everything that had happened since the moment I'd arrived in Jacksonville two days before.

Martinez pulling me over; ordering me out of my car; telling me I was going to jail. All those questions, as if I'd committed some serious crime. As if they were hunting someone.

And Mike. How would anyone have known about him? Or put us together? That *that* was where I'd head in a panic? My head was throbbing. *Who? Why?* Were

Martinez and Mike killed merely to make it appear that I was a murderer?

But then I suddenly realized, the bastard had gone one step too far.

I took the phone and punched in the number for the sheriff's office. Carrie had told me not to call her. But I had to. By now, I was damn sure she thought I was guiltier than ever. Everyone would. My heart began to race as I waited for the call to go through. Finally, a receptionist answered.

"Carrie Holmes . . ." I said.

A fear kicked up that she was probably waiting for me. They probably had a trace set up as soon as they heard my call. It might even be a trap. A plant. Knowing I'd call in. I couldn't blame her now.

And I didn't care. I didn't care if the cops barged in here right now and took me away. I just wanted one fucking person in this world to believe me. As long as I had one person to help me clear my name . . .

"Community Outreach. Carrie Hol—"

"I didn't do it, Carrie!" I didn't give her a second to interrupt. "I don't care what it looks like. I don't care how it makes me seem. I didn't buy that gun. I've never been to a gun show. Someone is setting me up, Carrie. That's what I couldn't tell you the other day. Why I couldn't turn myself in.

"But this time I'm pretty sure I can prove it!"

CHAPTER THIRTY

Raef had been put to bed a half hour ago, and Carrie sat with her father over a beer on the screened-in sunporch.

She thought of her dad as a canny old codger. Actually, not old at all. At seventy-two, Nate still maintained a fit and trim physique—an ex–navy fighter pilot and a small-town police chief in New Hampshire for twenty-two years. And out of everyone else she knew, he was usually the wisest, and the one whose perspective always mattered the most. In her gym shorts and flip-flops, Carrie curled a leg up on the wicker rocking chair and faced him, gently shifting the subject from his dim view of Florida's football chances this year. The June bugs were buzzing all around the modest, three-bedroom ranch that looked out over an islet, a couple of blocks off the beach.

"Dad, there's something I have to go over with you . . . Don't answer till I finish. Okay? Then say what you want."

He put down his beer and nodded, knowing this was her way of broaching a serious subject. "Okay . . ."

She told him everything. Her doubts about Henry Steadman's guilt from the start. How nothing quite added up. No motive. No weapon. How he had called 911. That she knew there was some crucial piece of information that he was withholding. The way he begged her to help him. Only her.

She waited to gauge his reaction.

"Finished?"

She shook her head. "No."

"Didn't think so."

She told him how Steadman had called her a second time yesterday. How she'd had some misgivings, and then doubts about her misgivings, which made her father, the ex-police chief, wince, and his eyes registered the seriousness of her involvement.

Then she let out a deep breath herself and admitted how she had tracked down the suspicious blue car Steadman was so obsessed with. The one she could now prove was at both crime scenes.

That was when her dad's nonjudging eyes widened.

Then she told him about the gun receipt in North Carolina, and that it didn't sway her either.

"He claims he wasn't anywhere near North Carolina

that day. And that he can prove it. Look, Dad, I know how this all sounds. I know I've broken a few rules. But someone's setting him up. Someone's gone to an awful lot of trouble to pin these crimes on him, and put him in the middle of something. Nobody wants to hear it, and I'm not sure what to do. Everyone's already got him convicted, and the news about the gun purchase only solidified their view."

Nate nodded, leaning forward, forearms on his thighs. "Is there more? Can I take a sip of beer now?"

"Yeah, take a sip of beer." Carrie sighed. "There is more, but I don't want to completely ruin my case right from the start."

Nate curled a smile, but only slightly. "So what is it you want to know? What I would do if I found out someone on my staff who wasn't even part of my investigative team was having discussions on her own with the suspect and withholding evidence on the case?"

Carrie's stomach shifted. *Probably fire her,* she figured he would say.

He continued to look at her. "Or what I think of your assessment of Steadman's case?"

"I think the first part doesn't need to be gone into too much." Carrie shrugged with a contrite smile.

"Or maybe why you'd be putting your job at risk, what with Raef in there in need of care?"

"Just for the record, I could be out of a job next month because of a budget cutback. Even next week,"

Carrie said. She sat back and pressed the cold beer bottle against her cheeks.

"Look, I can see you believe him, PK . . ." "PK" had been his nickname for her ever since she ski-raced as a kid back in New Hampshire, a twisting of the name of her idol Picabo Street. "But the way you went about it . . ."

"I know." She averted her eyes. Then she raised them back to him. "But the truth has to count for something, doesn't it, Dad?"

"It does . . . The truth does account for something, honey. It's just that—"

"Look"—she swung around and leaned close to him—"everything that happened from the time this guy set foot in town seems meant to pin Steadman for those murders. Why would he beg me to look for those plates? What possible gain would there be for him in that? And then the plates checked out. Why would he risk calling me, believing we'd have a trace on him? He doesn't know me from Adam, Dad . . ."

"*Eve,*" her father said, smiling. "He wouldn't know you from Eve . . ."

Carrie let out a breath, which relaxed her. "Okay, Eve . . ."

"You run this by anyone at the office?"

"I tried to." Carrie sighed. "Akers. I tried to show him what I had, but the mood's pretty tense there, politically, and everyone's worked up over Martinez, and it was all falling on deaf ears. It's pretty clear they don't want to deal with any possibility except Steadman. Especially now that this thing about the gun show has come up. It's damning. So what do I do? Drop my file off on Akers's desk as I'm signing my own termination papers and go, 'Oh, by the way, Steadman isn't your man . . . ?'"

"Or . . ." Nate asked, looking at her judiciously.

"Or . . . I don't know . . ." Carrie said. "Prove it."

Her dad cradled his beer again, rotating the bottle. "You know you've been through a lot, Carrie. You've had things taken from you that none of us should never have to deal with. You've always been a tough little gal, and we've all been proud of you . . . Whatever you've done. But are you sure you're not finding some way to feel"—he hesitated a second as he chose the word—"*important* again in some way. Not important . . ." He frowned at himself. "Maybe that wasn't it. Maybe I mean attached to something. Or simply alive."

"I feel plenty alive, Dad," Carrie said. She looked toward Raef's bedroom. "I feel about as alive as I need to feel right now."

"Then you're boxing yourself into a dangerous place, honey . . . Between what your conscience says, and what the rest of us would say."

There was a long-drawn-out silence. He was saying what Carrie pretty much expected him to say. What anyone rational would say. Of course, "rational" wasn't

199

exactly the operative word in her life lately. And maybe her dad was right—maybe there was just a little need to feel vital again after what had happened to her, and it was this that had opened her a little to Steadman's pleas.

Then you'll understand what I'm saying, Carrie. I swear, on my daughter . . .

But that didn't change what she now was certain had to be the truth.

"So you're sure?" Nate brought her back, looking her in the eyes. "You're one hundred percent sure, Carrie, it was the same car at both scenes?"

"You want to see the photos?" Carrie looked back at him just as firmly.

"No," he answered, leaning back. "I don't need to see the photos. Not if you say so, girl. It's just that . . . this isn't gonna go so well for you, as you say, politically, no matter which way it works out."

"Which way . . ." Carrie cocked her head quizzically.

"Whether you drop it off on Akers's desk. Or whether you do what you have to do. To find the truth."

She stared at him.

Her father winked. "Never let it be said Nate Walsh stood in the way of the truth. Or of his little girl, when she's got a mind to do something. You've got the plate number . . ." He shrugged. "I don't think it would be too hard to find a name behind it. I think we both know a federal agent in Atlanta who just might get you an ID on it pretty quick."

Carrie looked at her father and smiled at him gratefully, the blood rushing back into her face.

"And you damn well better hope they're not stolen . . ." He rolled his eyes. "Which they probably are. 'Cause where the hell would that set your case?"

"I know." Carrie grinned and nodded. "I know."

"So come on . . ." He stood up. He reached a hand for her. "Let's go help your mom clean up . . ."

She took his hand, and when she got to her feet, she looked into her father's eyes, his deep, gray, smouldering eyes, and he put his arms around her and she put her head against his chest.

"Thank you, Daddy," she whispered. "Thank you for believing in me."

"As long as you know the real reason you're taking this on, PK? Why you're putting everything at risk, everything that only a few months back seemed like the world to you. Your position. Your reputation. It's one thing to keep a secret from the job, something else to keep it from yourself."

"Because it wasn't everything, Daddy." She lifted her head off his chest and looked him in the eyes. She knew exactly why she would do it, though the answer had never come so clearly, nor quite this way. "Rick was! And he would do it. He wouldn't just let it go. He'd dig for the truth, right? Wouldn't he, Dad? And right now . . ." Her eyes glazed up a bit and a tear rolled down her cheek and landed on his golf shirt. "Right now what

201

I want more than anything in the world is to make him proud."

"He would be proud, honey," her father said, squeezing her. "He'd have to stand in line to say it, but I promise you, he would be proud."

CHAPTER THIRTY-ONE

"Maryanne . . . ?"

I knew I was taking a chance. I could feel my assistant trying to decide whether to answer. And with all that had come out, I couldn't blame her if she didn't.

Finally, she said hesitantly, *"Dr. Steadman . . . ?"*

"Yeah, Maryanne, it's me. But please—before you say a word, I don't want anyone else to know I'm calling. Is that all right?"

"Yes, of course. Doctor . . ." She lowered her voice. "We're just all so confused about what's going on. But I want you to know, no one here believes a word of it. We all know you couldn't have done those things. We just want to help you prove yourself . . ."

It was like a warm breeze hearing her say that. To know that the people who actually knew me, who worked with me, didn't blindly believe what was being said. Maryanne Kunin had been my assistant for fifteen years. I'd been there for her when her husband lost his contracting company and then a condo they owned in Destin went down below their mortgage.

Now she would be there for me.

"Maryanne, listen, I need something from you. It's important! It's just that no one else can know. That's vital. But there's nothing anyone can do for me right now that can help me more. Can I count on you?"

"Of course, Doctor," she replied almost as quickly as I had asked her.

"Thank you." I felt a lump catch in my throat. My voice cracked a little with emotion. "You just have to know, Maryanne, I didn't do those things they said. Any of them. I—"

"You don't have to say that to me, Dr. Steadman. Just tell me what you need."

CHAPTER THIRTY-TWO

"Federal Bureau of Investigation," the operator answered. "Atlanta Office."

"Jack Walsh, please . . ."

Carrie took in a breath. She had to admit that she felt some doubts about calling her brother. One side of her hoped he would be out in the field and unable to take her call. Another side told her she was doing the right thing. There had been a Steadman sighting the night before at a motel somewhere in northern Georgia. The night clerk had realized that he'd been there only when she saw the morning news after he had gone. Now the woman was all over the news. Carrie was pretty sure she herself knew where he was heading.

Anyway, she decided, the damage was done already.

The real damage was done the moment she withheld that call.

"Special Agent Walsh." Her brother picked up the phone.

"Jack . . ." Carrie said. "Here's one for you: the CIA, FBI, and LAPD are all trying to prove they're the best at apprehending dangerous criminals. President Obama devises a test. He releases a rabbit into a forest and tells each of them to catch it."

She and her brother always started things off with a joke. He said, "Okay . . ."

"So the CIA goes in, and they embed animal informants throughout the forest. They question all plant and animal witnesses. After three months of extensive investigations, they conclude that rabbits do not exist."

Jack chuckled.

"The FBI goes in next. After two weeks with no leads, they burn the forest down, killing everything in it, including the rabbit. And they make no apologies. They say the rabbit had it coming!"

He chuckled again.

"Finally, it's the LAPD's turn. They come out two hours later with a badly beaten bear. The bear is yelling crazily: 'Okay, okay . . . *I'm a rabbit! I'm a rabbit!*"

This time her brother laughed.

"It's making the rounds here," Carrie said. "Thought you'd get a laugh."

"Hey, Car, I was just thinking of you."

She and her brother didn't talk as much as they used to. Mostly they just traded e-mails a couple of times a week on family matters. Jack was two years older; he and his wife, Polly, had two young kids of their own, and half the time he was off on assignment somewhere. So they took a minute now to catch up, about how she was feeling back on the job. And about Raef.

"Pop says he's about ready to get back to school again?"

"Definitely after the summer. He's really doing great, Jack. Listen . . ." She switched from the small talk. "There's a reason why I called . . ."

"I knew that," her brother said. "The joke wasn't *that* good!"

"I need a favor, Jack." She took a deep breath. "I don't want you to ask me about it. About why I need it. I just need you to do it for me. I need you to track down a license-plate number for me."

"Plate number? You guys don't have people down there who do that kind of thing?" His tone was both jocular and a bit suspicious.

"What can I say, dude, budget cutbacks." Carrie sighed, playing along. They always had the kind of relationship where they shared everything with each other. Though Jack was always the great pontificator. Captain of the wrestling team in high school. Debate team. Villanova Law. But this time she wasn't volunteering anything

207

more. But Jack was no dummy. He knew they could get that kind of information in thirty seconds down in Jacksonville. Why would she be asking him to trace the plates other than some reason to keep it out of the office? No doubt his next call would probably be to their father.

"I have confidence you wouldn't be getting the FBI into something they ought not to be in, right, little sister?" Maybe he'd *already* spoken with Nate, she suddenly found herself thinking. "We're all sorry to hear about what's happened there, that officer of yours? The town must be turned on its heels . . ."

"Yeah," she answered, "it definitely is."

"Crazy about this guy . . . Steadman? That his name? He must've just flipped . . ."

She didn't answer directly. Not this time. Instead, after a pause, she just said, "I'm simply asking my big brother for a favor, that's all. If you worked at GE, I might be calling for a toaster."

"*Carrie* . . ." She was sure he was about to say something big brotherly (and probably smart), like, *Just be careful what you're getting into, sis*. Or, *You can't use the FBI for your own private purposes, however justified they may seem to you*.

Instead, he just drew in a wistful breath. "Budget cuts, huh?" He chuckled dubiously. "We're all deep in 'em. All right, give me the plate number. I'll see what I can do. *And, Carrie* . . ."

Here it comes, she thought, readying herself.

"Thanks for the joke."

The fax came in a couple of hours later. With a note attached:

"Here's your favor, sis. How about we say 48 hours—and then I might be asking if I should look into this myself."

The name behind the plate she was looking for. From the South Carolina Department of Motor Vehicles.

ADJ-4392.

She stared at it awhile, glancing at the photos of Rick and Raef on her desk, until a drumming started up in her heart and in her blood, and she knew she was doing the right thing.

Her next stop was Akers's office.

"Bill, I need a little more time," she said, catching him as he had his jacket in hand and was about to leave. "Raef needs some more tests. I know this is all bad timing. It's just that maybe I wasn't quite as ready as I thought . . ."

"How much time are we talking about?" her boss asked, surprised.

"Three or four days." She shrugged. "Maybe a week."

She could see he was disappointed; maybe even annoyed. It had been that way since she went in to talk about her doubts about Steadman the other day. But he put his sport coat on and nodded. "I'll work it out with personnel. But, *Carrie . . .*" He sat back on his desk. "Get done what you need to get done. Then come back for good. We've held your job open a long time. I can't promise I can give you any more sway."

She grabbed a few files she could work on and was almost on her way out the door when she heard the sound of an e-mail coming in.

It was from an address she didn't recognize. Mpkunin119@hotmail.com.

The subject line read, "March 2."

Carrie clicked on it and there was no message, only a document attached. It looked like a page out of an appointment calendar that someone had scanned in.

Suddenly she realized it was Henry Steadman's calendar.

There were a bunch of handwritten notations. "Discuss with Mark!" "Heat tickets 4/10 for JP."

The rest was just his schedule for that day:

> 7:30–10:00 a.m.: OR—Lynda Fields
> 12:30: lunch, Paul Dipalo, U of M board
> 2:30: Patient consult: Andrea Wasserman
> 4:00–5:00: Conf call, Diamond-Murdoch

A routine day, Carrie thought, quizzically, *why would he—*

But then she realized just what the date was and

what it meant—and a warm surge of triumph and vindication ran through her. And she found herself totally unable to hold back her smile.

March 2.

That was what Steadman was trying to tell her the other day, about proving his innocence.

March 2 was the day he was supposedly in North Carolina buying the 9mm gun.

CHAPTER THIRTY-THREE

Vance found John Schmeltzer at a bar in Dania, Florida, just north of Hollywood. It was a dark, sleazy, sixties-style place, set between a Jiffy Lube and a debt company, with a heavily tattooed Hispanic behind the bar. Dog races were on the TV.

Vance wasn't sure he'd ever seen a more depressing place as he stepped in, in his sweaty shirt and rumpled pants, removing his hat.

Schmeltzer was at table drinking a beer in a wifebeater T-shirt and pink shorts. He was thin, with coarse, curly hair, bald on top, and sideburns clear down to his chin. Maybe forty. He was with a couple of other lowlifes who, Vance thought, might have recently crawled their way out of the Everglades, and didn't look a whole lot higher up the food chain than Schmeltzer himself.

Vance walked up to his table. "Dexter Vaughn said I could find you here. He said you could help me with my back. Hurts like the devil. Show me how it works down here."

"Dexter, huh?" Schmeltzer looked at him a bit skeptically, squinting over his shades. "He said that. Not that it really matters . . ." The guy grinned, clearly not sizing Vance up as much of a threat. "That's the beauty of it down here. I know what you've come for and welcome to the Promised Land."

He proceeded to try to raise Dexter by phone, just to be sure, but failing to for obvious reasons, Vance knew—Schmeltzer just said, "Ah, hell with it," and offered to take Vance around. They climbed into a silver Mercedes convertible, Schmeltzer saying how he had to do a little business anyhow, so why not climb on in. "So *how* you know Dex?" he asked casually.

Vance pressed his fingers against the fancy leather console. He felt the gun in his belt dig into his back as he pressed against the seat. "Through his cousin. Del. From South Carolina."

"That's where you're from?"

Vance shrugged. Didn't really matter much if he told him the truth. So he simply nodded.

"*Del?* Not sure I know any Del," Schmeltzer said, squinting over his shades.

"No matter." Vance shrugged, looking ahead. "You probably never will."

"So what's your story?" Schmeltzer asked. "Work accident? Chronic? Got any disability papers? X-rays, you can show? A scrip?"

"Uh-uh." Vance shook his head.

"Man, they really sent you down here cold, didn't they?" Schmeltzer squinted. "Tell me, partner, no secrets here, you even *got* a bad back?"

Vance looked at him and smiled thinly. "Nope."

"Ha! No worries, bro. Your secret's safe with me. You *will* need some kind of story, though. We can do migraines. You're under a doctor's treatment up where you live, right? But you're visiting. I know exactly where to take you. You may have to just spiff the doc a fifty or something. Okay by you?"

"Sure, whatever," Vance said. He sat back. He felt the gun. He felt he was close.

"So relax! Won't be but a while, and that back of yours will be floating in the clouds. Welcome to paradise, dude. Take off that jacket . . . Enjoy the ride."

Vance pushed back deeper into the seat. John got off the highway at Oakland Park Road. In Ft. Lauderdale. The street was busy and commercial. Gas stations. Car dealerships. Fast-food outlets on both sides. Lots of long lights and traffic.

There was something else Vance soon noticed. Pain clinics. Lots of fucking pain clinics. One after another.

"Welcome to Broward County," Schmeltzer proclaimed, noticing Vance crane his neck. "Pharmaland,

USA. More fucking pain clinics on the streets than there are McDonald's. And that's a fact!"

"This is where you get them?" Vance had thought Schmeltzer was going to take him to his source, maybe a doctor who wrote bogus scrips. But this . . . "A pain clinic." He widened his eyes in surprise. This was starting to make him mad. "All legal?"

"Clinic?" Schmeltzer's grin was wide. "Dude, I'm on the VIP list of half the pill mills from here to Palm Beach. For an extra five bills they sell you a gold card. No wait. Back-to-back prescriptions. Everything you need filled directly on-site. Oxy. Vicodin. Muscle relaxers . . . Whatever floats your boat! All you need to be a dealer here is a license to be an MD! These guys are raking it in."

Vance felt his fists clench.

"Some of these places, you can just walk right in and rub your back like you're in pain and they'll lay it all out like a Chinese take-out menu. *Won from Corumn A* . . . Just a drug dispenser. But you gotta know the ropes. And you gotta choose your sources carefully. *Comprende, partner . . . ?* Which is what I do. I used to drive around in some Korean piece of shit. Now look at what we're riding in . . ."

Vance looked around. There were more of these clinics than there were barbecue stops back where he was from. *All you need is an MD? This was how the sonovabitches poisoned his Amanda.* "I'm especially interested in the

215

ones where you got what you gave Dexter," he said.

"*Dexter?*" Schmeltzer grinned, kind of deferentially. "You are? No worries, I'm gonna take good care of you. *And* your back!"

Getting closer to the beach, they passed a more upscale section of office buildings—brick and glass. Vance was feeling himself growing angrier by the minute.

Schmeltzer slowed. "See that one over there?"

Across the street. On the ground floor of a red-brick office building. A fancy glass front.

The Harvard Pain Remediation Centers.

"I see it," Vance said, feeling his pulse start to pound.

"There's the one. You said Dexter, right? Top-of-the-line. There's a real MD on the premises, not some Pakistani just out of med school looking to rake in a few bucks. You need a real prescription. No scrip, they turn you away. But no worries . . ." Schmeltzer patted his pocket. "I know someone there. I got us covered . . ."

"This is where the pills you sold to Dexter came from?" Vance's mood picked up. The Harvard Pain Remediation Center. He felt he was at the end of a long journey. He felt his fingers itch. *You're sure about that?*"

"Dexter. Frank. Hector . . . Got all the bases covered, dude." Schmeltzer pulled into the turn lane and shot Vance a quick glance. "You're not a cop, are you?"

A cop? Vance looked back at him. "No."

"Good. 'Cause you're starting to sound to me like

216

you wouldn't know an Oxy from an Advil . . . And I gotta be sure."

"My daughter . . ." Vance started to say.

"Your *daughter* . . . ?" He cut in at a break in the traffic and pulled into the driveway of the clinic, going behind the store and into a spot with pain clinic written on the concrete barrier.

No one was around.

Schmeltzer shook his head. "Just be glad your daughter's not from down here. More shit in the schools down here than in the damn hospitals. 'Course, I probably don't help those numbers, if I say so myself . . . No age discrimination when it comes to business. That's the Fourth Amendment, right? Everyone gets to pay."

He put the car in park and cut the motor. "Anyway, you were saying . . . ?"

He turned back to Vance and his eyes almost popped out of his head when he saw the gun.

"My daughter ran over a woman and her baby," Vance said, hardening his gaze on John's startled eyes. "Jumped the road while she was high—on OxyContin. Ran 'em over right on their own front lawn. The woman's husband was in Afghanistan. Never even saw his own kid. Not once."

Schmeltzer swallowed. "I'm sorry, mister."

"Her boyfriend gave it to her. Who got it from some leech named Del. Dexter's aforementioned cousin . . ."

A bead of sweat wound its way down Schmeltzer's

temple. "Where you going with all this, friend? You said that Dex—"

"Dexter's *dead*," Vance said. "They're all dead. Del. Wayne. All of them except my little girl, Amanda, who might as well be. She's serving twenty years. And where I'm going with it, friend . . ." Vance said, "is that I traced back the Oxy that twisted my little girl's brain that day, that done ruined her very existence, to you."

Schmeltzer stared back at him, the grimness and resignation on his face suggesting that he realized he only had a few more seconds to live. "This ain't gonna solve anything, you know. They're just gonna get it from somewhere. Fuck, man, they can find it in their parents' medicine chests if they—"

Vance shoved the gun into Schmeltzer's chest and pulled the trigger, twice, the sound muffled, Schmeltzer's torso flung back against the side window with a lung-emptying groan, his eyes glazed, staring at his hands smeared with blood.

"Solves it for me. Anyway, you were right on one thing, though . . ." Vance leaned over and jammed the gun into Schmeltzer's mouth, the dealer's eyes about three times their normal size and stunned, and drew back the action. "Nice car."

CHAPTER THIRTY-FOUR

Vance left Schmeltzer's crumpled body on the floor of his car. He checked himself just to make sure he didn't have blood all over him.

He had found what he was looking for and his search had pretty much come to an end.

Then he left the car and went to the door of the clinic.

He felt a stirring in his chest and his blood was all alive and buzzing, a voice deep inside him telling him that this was it. The end of the line. He had set out to prove that causes had effects and that you couldn't escape the consequences of what you'd done. The sin from the sinner, the Bible said. The wheat from the chaff.

The Harvard Pain Remediation Centers.

This was where his little girl's life got all caught up in the tide that ruined it.

Time to end it now.

Vance stepped inside and looked around. Blond paneling on the walls and a classy, almost Asian feel. All beige and white. In the waiting area, a heavyset black woman was in a chair with a metal walker in front of her. A video was running on a screen. Another woman was seated behind the counter. Pretty. In a blue nurse's uniform. Her blond hair in a ponytail.

"Can I help you?"

The woman behind the counter was looking at him. Vance felt the emotions in his chest start to build. *Can you help me? Can you make right everything that's gone wrong in my life? Can you bring back my wife? My home? My job? Can you bring back my job on the force, which was the last time I felt like a man.*

You can only take so much. Vance looked at this woman, his hand reaching into his pocket, wrapping around the gun handle.

"Just gimme a minute," was all he could grunt.

The woman smiled at him. "First time here? I know it can be a bit unsettling. Here's a brochure that describes the procedures we do here. They're all doctor performed. Dr. Silva on staff is one of the foremost pain specialists in the area. But take your time."

Vance nodded and took the brochure. His blood throbbed. The sweats had come over him. He could do

220

it now. *Do it!* This was the source of it all. A sense of absolute certainty rushed through him.

"Or feel free to check out the video over there." She pointed toward the overhead monitor in the waiting area. "It's only three minutes, and it explains most of the procedures."

"Thank you," Vance said, taking his hand off the gun handle.

He went over to the screen, his heart drumming like a bass drum, *boom, boom*, and tried to listen, as best as he could, to a description of a bunch of procedures he didn't give a damn about. Or could even pronounce.

Epidural steroid injection. Nerve root block. Pulsed radio frequency neurotomy. Stellate ganglion block.

Electromyogram.

His head spun. The only thing you needed to become a drug dealer down here was to have an MD license . . . They were as bad as the ones who pushed the pills. Bloodsuckers. *They were the ones who profited the most!*

He gazed at the doctor who was narrating the video. He sounded smart, almost caring. Probably just some actor. *All a sham!* He looked at the woman behind the counter and wrapped his hand around his gun.

End it.

Vance's chest felt like a furnace. *Now.*

The video came to an end. "Let us know how we can help you . . ." the doctor said, staring at Vance with those earnest eyes.

221

Help me?

He was about to turn back to the counter with the gun in his hand when he noticed the doctor's name.

He wasn't an actor at all. In fact, Vance now realized, he was the one person who should rightfully pay. Not these people here. They were just pegs, like him.

The one who had profited most from Amanda's suffering.

Suddenly Vance felt uplifted, stronger, infused with purpose. He eased the gun back into his pants.

He stared at the earnest, smiling face, sure now where his rage should truly be directed.

The Harvard Pain Remediation Centers of South Florida.

Henry Steadman. M.D. *CEO*.

PART FOUR

CHAPTER THIRTY-FIVE

The first place I went to in South Carolina was a town called Summerville, north of Charlestown.

It was actually a pretty place, nestled among woods of tall pines and, I guess, well named, as the road map said it had been a kind of summer refuge in the 1800s from the stifling humidity and heat of Charlestown.

The name I had was a Donald Barrow. 297 Richardson Avenue. The map said it was just outside of town. The plate number ADJ-496. According to the information I had, it was registered to a 2004 Buick Marquis.

I ordered a sandwich in a local stop on Main Street, which was ringed with budding azaleas, then took it back to my car and drove to the address—an old white clapboard house on a street shaded by tall pines, and ate it, looking over the house, in my car.

I really didn't know what to do. How to handle this.
I wasn't exactly a pro at this. What if it was the right
place? What if the Buick was blue, and I went up to
that door and the face came back to me and I stared
directly into the eyes of the person who had done these
horrible things? Realizing my daughter was there!

And he recognized me! He had to know my face.
What then?

I'd been running that scenario over in my mind since
I'd left Florida.

I wrapped up my sandwich and placed it on the seat
next to me. I tucked in my shirt and took a breath. *You
have to do this, Henry, Never any time like the present, right?*

I left the car and walked up the short walkway leading
to the house and onto the porch, trying to calm my
heart, which was beating fast.

Anxiously I rang the bell.

I heard footsteps inside, and a middle-aged woman
with flecks of gray in her short, curly hair came to the
door.

"Hello," she said, and when she didn't recognize me,
she asked in a pleasant drawl, "Can I help you?"

"Hi." I stepped forward. "Is Mr. Barrow at home?'

"Mr. Barrow . . . ?" The woman hesitated with a
slight look of surprise. "May I ask why?"

I stepped forward. "I was sent by his insurance
company. To take a look at his car."

"His car . . . ?"

"A 2004 Buick Marquis? Plate number ADJ-496 . . . It was in an accident, I was told."

The woman looked at me curiously and shook her head. "There must be some mistake. There hasn't been any accident . . ."

"You're sure?" I asked her again. "Maybe if Mr. Barrow is at home . . . ?" Here in the Deep South people were generally polite and unsuspicious. If I were in South Florida, she'd already be asking to see my ID.

"I'm afraid my father isn't here. He's . . . He's been ill. He's been living in a nursing home in Ladson for the past six months."

"Oh." I stared back, suddenly feeling foolish and intrusive. "I'm very sorry. *Is it here?* Mr. Barrow's car. Any chance I could just take a look at it? I don't understand the confusion. Just to be sure . . ."

The plates could always have been stolen.

She thought about it for only a second, then stepped out and led me around the side of the porch. "It's in the garage. But I assure you, it hasn't been in any accident." She went down another set of steps that led to the garage, pushed a button, and the garage door started to go up.

There was a white Buick in one of the two bays. With a South Carolina plate. ADJ-4967.

"You're right. Clearly, it hasn't been in any accident," I said, shrugging.

"I can assure you, it hasn't been out of the garage in

227

the past six months," the woman said. "Since my father left. For the life of me, I can't see how anyone could have thought . . ."

"No, probably our error," I said. This clearly wasn't the car I was looking for. "I'm sorry to bother you. I hope your father gets well."

"Well, thank you," she said, "but I don't know. He's eighty-six. You know how it is."

"Yes, I know," I said.

I went straight back to my car, before it occurred to her to ask for some ID or for the name of the insurance company I represented. There was also the fear that she might call the police, especially after I noticed her looking at my car.

I drove away, out of town the way I had come, and when I thought I was safe, I pulled into a gas station, my heart still pounding.

You're no Harrison Ford, Henry . . .

One down.

ADJ-4653. That was next. A town named Martinsville.

CHAPTER THIRTY-SIX

"Daddy? *Daddy?*"

I'd heard the ring and grabbed one of the phones from the passenger seat, and saw the call was from Hallie!

I didn't know if I was alerting half the police in Florida, and *I didn't care*! Over the past twenty-four hours I must've tried her cell a dozen times.

I pulled to the side of the road. "*Hallie?* Hi, baby, how are you doing?" My heart beat joyously. "I'm so glad to hear your voice! I'm—"

"Daddy, he just said I could tell you that I was all right, that's all. And I am. But he said he has something to say to you. And whatever it is, Daddy, please do it. He's—"

"Hallie, just hang in there!" Tears sprang up in my

229

eyes and I cradled the phone in both hands. "Your mother and I both love you very much, you know that, honey, and we're going to get you out of there. I promise, honey, you just be brave—"

"Aw, that's sweet, Doc, really it is," a man's voice replied. Everything in my body turned to ice. "I did plan on filling you in on things just a tad more, but truth is, I'm really kind of enjoying thinking of how it is for you out there. Can't go back, can't go forward. How does that feel? You have to admit, that gun show thing was a pretty good piece of work, huh? So tell me, how's it been for you these past few days?"

The ice now turned to fire. *"What is it you want?* Just tell me." I felt myself gripping the phone like it was a weapon. "I'll give it you. Please . . . Just let my daughter go. She's got nothing to do with anything."

"Oh, that's where you're wrong, Doc," the man replied calmly. "She's got everything to do with everything. She's part of you! But don't you be too worried about her. It's you *I'd* be focused on. Hopefully the police aren't checking out where you are right now."

"I told you before, you harm one hair on her head, you sonovabitch, and I'll—"

"So how's it feel, Doc?" He cut me right off. "How's it feel to have your life taken from you. How's it feel to lose everything you hold dear?"

My chest tightened. I couldn't believe the hatred this animal seemed to hold for me. The blame. I was about

230

to say, *Why? What have I done to you? Why are you doing this?*

But before I could get the words out, I heard him say, "More to come. More to come for sure, Doc."

Another click and he was gone.

"Hallie!" I shouted, knowing I was talking only to a machine. *"Hallie . . ."*

I started to cry.

That old bromide came to mind: what doesn't kill you makes you stronger. And what was stronger than a father's will to save his child? Nothing. It coursed through me like a river overflowing its banks, stronger than the urge to have my life back or the will to clear my name. It was everything.

But now I didn't know how I felt. Closer to her or farther away? I didn't know where she was. All I had was this stupid list of cars, and I didn't even know if they would lead me to her. Or to nowhere. The clock was ticking.

And I couldn't even let the people who might find her help me.

I called Liz. She answered on the third ring, expectantly. "Yes . . ."

All I could say was, "I spoke with her, Liz." I felt so alone and helpless. I didn't even tell her I had spoken with him. "She's okay. For now."

CHAPTER THIRTY-SEVEN

"'Manda . . . ?"

It took a moment for her to reply. And when she did it was clearly with hesitation. She didn't seem so happy to hear from him. "Hello, Daddy . . ."

It felt good to Vance to hear her voice. Like he was back home, and on a Sunday, and she came out to ask what he was working on, in the wood closet, and things hadn't happened as they did. "How they treatin' you there, honey?"

"Okay. I guess. I'm learning. My cell mate scares me, though. She's in here for hitting her husband with a pipe and cracking open his head. She makes me nervous, the way she stares at me. I don't belong here, Daddy. You know, I don't—"

"I'm sorry to hear all that, 'Manda." He was sitting

at the desk in his shabby hotel room, looking out at cars shooting by on the highway.

"I just don't. But I've been reading. They got a lot of books here. I'm reading this one about a handsome lawyer from a small town in Alabama named Atticus, who's defending this black man, who the whole town thinks is guilty of rape, but he's not. It's written from the point of view of his little daughter, named Scout. I know he's going to get him off. It makes me feel good."

Vance thought the man in the book sounded like a lot better father than he had been; that Amanda kind of wished he was her dad. It made him feel diminished, jealous of a character in a book he didn't even know. "That's good to hear, honey. I'm glad."

"And I wrote this letter . . . To the husband of the woman I killed. He's in Afghanistan. I told him I don't know why things happen, but that they do, and I wasn't old enough at first to understand my blame in all this, but now I do and how sorry I was. That if I could make it up to him, I would . . . How I would gladly change places with his wife if I could. That it was clear she deserved to live and have a family more than I did. And her baby . . ." Amanda began to sob.

"You don't have to do that, 'Manda. There are others guilty as you. That's why I'm calling . . ."

"Yes, I have to do it, Daddy! I do. It made me feel good. To see myself for what I am. I know he won't ever answer, and it don't matter, but the counselor here says I have to face up to it. To what I did. To make amends—"

"I understand the concept of amends, honey. That's why I'm calling you. I've—"

"So where you been anyway? I spoke to Aunt Linda and she said you haven't been around here at all."

"I've been working on your situation, 'Manda. How to make it right."

"And ol' Wayne; now there's a fellow for ya. He's suddenly not around here either. Just up and split. No one can find a trace of his ass." She laughed bitterly. "I'm sure *you* don't mind that none."

"Wayne's where he deserves to be, Amanda. For what he did."

"Huh, Daddy . . . ?" Her voice focused in more. "What d'you mean?"

"Nothing, honey. I don't mean anything by it. 'Cept he deserves to be gone for what he did to you."

"It wasn't Wayne, Daddy. I understand that now. It was *me*!"

Vance didn't answer her. She just didn't see things clearly, didn't understand about matters of personal responsibility and right and wrong. She still had the point of view of a child, he thought, and it was probably for the best.

All he wanted to tell her anyway was that he loved her.

"You know, I know I wasn't always the best dad, Amanda . . . Like that person in the book."

"You were all right, Daddy. You did what you could."

"I remember I once went to visit you at school. On one of those father-daughter class days. You were maybe eight or nine . . ."

"Funny, I don't remember ever seeing you at school, Daddy. Even once."

"It was back in Florida. I was late. I couldn't get off shift. But I went this one time. I got there, but everyone had left. Someone already drove you home. But this teacher let me go in. To your classroom. All by myself. And I saw this drawing you made. They had it on the wall. I think it was of me. It was a man in a uniform . . . with a blue cap. And he was chasing someone. With a gun. The teacher said it was part of some exercise your class were doing. How you were supposed to draw the person you admired most."

"I remember that, Daddy. It *was* you. *Before* . . . Anyway, I don't recall you ever telling me about it. You probably went straight to the bar afterward and got yourself drunk. You probably told them all about it."

"I probably did." That sounded about right, as Vance recalled. "But it made me realize, thinking about it, that there was a time where you did think of me in that way. As someone you admired some. Who stood up for the right things. Like that character in your book, Atticus . . ."

It took her a while to answer. "I suppose."

"And I was hoping you might think of me like that again. Because that's what I'm doing, Amanda. I'm making it all right again. For you. As much as I can."

Vance had this thought that probably there was a time in all of our lives when we are all of us innocent. When we love our fathers and mothers. Because, what else did we know? When we all want to stand out and be someone good. And do good things. Before the world sets us on our paths and we become who we were.

Even his 'Manda had that inside.

John Schmeltzer too, no doubt.

"So, Amanda . . ." Vance cleared his throat. "I may not be seeing you for a while . . ."

She chuckled darkly. "You drunk, Daddy? You sure are sounding it."

He was about to say no, and the silence grew deep before he could answer. And while it lasted, Vance wished he could say a lot of things to her. Like how he did love her. How he just wasn't able to show it for a long time. Like how he was actually taking care of her now, as he knew he should have taken care of her back then. Making things right.

But instead, a smile crossed his lips, in his dingy motel room in South Florida. A drop of liquor hadn't touched his lips in weeks, but all he said was, "Yeah, honey, I'm drunk."

CHAPTER THIRTY-EIGHT

On the morning he was sure his life would come to an end, Vance stepped through the door into the offices of the fancy medical building in near Palm Beach.

A metal plaque on the wall read, *Dr. Henry Steadman. Cosmetic Surgery.*

He looked around and took a calming breath. The place was decorated to the hilt. *Why would that surprise anyone?* He stepped up to the counter. There was an attractive woman there, in regular street clothes. And a bunch of other women behind her, some in green nurses' clothing; others on the phone, or doing paperwork. He felt for the gun under his jacket tucked into the back of his belt.

"Dr. Steadman," he said. "I have an appointment."

"Mr. Hofer, correct?" the woman behind the counter greeted him pleasantly.

Vance nodded. "Yes."

"Good. There's a bunch of forms for you to fill out. You know how it is. " She handed him a clipboard with several papers attached. "Dr. Steadman won't be very long. Just bring these back up when you're ready. And let me know if I can help you with anything."

He tried to smile, and took it all back to a chair. That woman didn't have to die. She hadn't done anything. None of these people had. He was pleased to find no one else in the waiting room.

No, only Steadman had to die.

He filled out the forms as best he could, and went over what he would say when he saw the doctor. In truth, he hadn't practiced anything. Other than, *You are the man responsible for my little Amanda's ruination. Do you understand that? Do you understand your responsibility?* He'd written it all down, why he was doing this, tried to make his thoughts clear. He had this note on him. He'd hoped people might look on him as a kind of a hero— how he'd stood up. For his daughter. Found the source. And rubbed it out.

If not as a hero, at least as someone with the will to separate right from wrong.

Yes, that was enough, he decided.

He filled out the forms, writing down his real address for once, back in Acropolis, and gave them back to the pleasant gal at the desk.

"Great," she said. "Why don't you come through the

238

door, and we'll bring you into another room and the doctor will see you soon."

His heartbeat picked up. "Okay."

The woman led him down a hall through a maze of medical workstations and examining rooms, into a smaller waiting area where he was told to take a seat. There were magazines and newspapers spread on the table. Vance picked up a "USA Today. Egyptian Unrest Continues for Second Week. Mubarek Refuses to Go."

He wondered for a moment how God would look at him. Whether there was a heaven or hell. He hoped there was. He thought he deserved heaven somehow. Maybe he had caused pain in his life, but life was a balance, right? A balance of good deeds and bad. And he hoped that God would find that he'd done good too. Just like that wave over there in Japan. Or this guy in Egypt. God does bad things too. And—

"Mr. Hofer, my name is Maryanne," another woman said, interrupting his thoughts. Vance looked up. "I'm Dr. Steadman's assistant. He can see you now."

CHAPTER THIRTY-NINE

The doctor's assistant led him down the hall, gesturing him into a corner office.

"Mr. Hofer . . ." The man from the TV, about six feet, longish brown hair, a friendly smile, got up from behind his desk. "Come sit over here. I hope you didn't have to wait too long. What can we do for you today?"

The office was modern and bright, with picture windows that looked out over the Intercoastal. It had a large, built-in bookshelf against one wall, a polished conference table with six chairs, bronze sculptures, what looked, to Vance, like African masks, and a handful of framed diplomas and awards on the walls. One of them was a magazine cover. Everything about the place was expensive, dizzying. *Why not? It was paid for with people's blood, right?*

"Get you anything?" Steadman asked. "Coffee? A Coke? Water?"

"I'm fine." Vance shook his head.

"Okay, then." The doctor glanced at his assistant. "Thanks, Maryanne. We're good. So please, sit down."

There was a credenza behind him with a bunch of photographs and awards on top. Vance tried not to be taken in by the size and the fancy setting. His eye caught a framed magazine cover—"South Florida's Best Doctors . . ."—on the wall. Steadman's picture on it.

"You advertise enough, no telling what they'll give you," Steadman said with a grin, noticing Vance fix on it.

Vance saw why people might be drawn to him.

"So I have your paperwork here," Steadman said. "I see you live up in Georgia." He crossed his legs, palms pressed together. "So what brings you here, Mr. Hofer?"

Maybe this was the time, Vance thought, staring back at him. Why dance around with a bunch of meaningless questions and answers? *Just tell him. Tell him why you're here! Does he know what he has caused? Is he prepared to assume responsibility?* Vance felt the gun digging into his back. Inside, his blood was racing.

Just do it now.

Instead he said, "I've got this thing." He touched his collar. "On my neck. These wrinkles here . . . It's always bothered me."

It was true. His neck had always been prematurely

241

wrinkled. He'd always tried to hide it, always wore shirts with high collars to cover it up. Whenever his photo was taken, he felt ashamed.

Steadman stood up and came around. "Do you mind if I take a look . . . ?" He stepped next to Vance and gently pulled his shirt collar open. "Yeah, I see . . ." He touched his neck. Vance felt a shiver run down his spine and his heartbeat picked up. Maybe he ought to simply pull out his gun and shoot the man dead right now. Why drag this out? He'd waited for this moment so long . . . He wanted to see Steadman's shock and watch him beg when he told him just why he was here.

"Yes, I see . . ." Steadman said. He ran his fingers against Vance's bunched skin. "Okay . . ." He went back around his desk and began to type into his computer. "We can perform what they call a rhytidectomy . . . It's basically a tuck. Just like a face-lift. Same principle. I can pull it up on the screen."

Vance put his fingers against his neck and smoothed out his skin.

Steadman went on: "It's not a spot I generally work on. But I can see how it might bother you. What kind of work are you engaged in, Mr. Hofer . . . ?"

"I used to work for the state police," Vance said.

"A cop?" the doctor asked him, scrolling.

Vance nodded. "Fifteen years. Before I had to move. Since then I ran a lathe machine in a die factory."

"I see . . . And what brings you all the way down here?'

"Your reputation," was all Vance said, picturing how Steadman would be with the barrel of a gun shoved into his mouth.

Like them all.

"Well, thanks; always nice to hear. Ah, here we go . . ." Steadman spun the screen around. There were two photos side by side on it. "My guess is that your skin texture seems fully pliant enough for surgery. If you're interested, I'd like to take a shot of you, do some tests . . ."

A fury began to build in Vance's chest. Steadman seemed like a nice guy, but he was the same as those others who had profited from his daughter's fall. Worse, he hid behind all his big-shot degrees and this fancy office. He would never have to pay. Never. Not unless Vance did what he was here to do.

Now. . .

"I saw you have these clinics . . ." Vance said.

"Ah, pain remediation, yes . . ." Steadman spun the monitor back around.

"I was there . . ."

Steadman's look shifted a little, like he thought Vance was really only here for some kind of pain matter, and not what he'd said at all.

"My daughter . . ." Vance felt behind him for the gun. "Back in Georgia . . . She's—"

243

All of a sudden the intercom came on. "Doctor . . . Sorry to interrupt, but I have someone who says you're expecting his call and that he's traveling—"

"Who is it?" Steadman asked, over the speaker.

"Michael Dinofrio," said his assistant. "He says you know him."

"Yes, tell him to hold on." Steadman turned to Vance. "I'll only be a second," he said apologetically. "I'm heading up to Jacksonville for a medical conference in a couple of weeks and I just need to iron this one thing out . . ."

Vance nodded, his rage starting to recede.

"Thanks! *Mike . . . ?*" Steadman picked up the phone and swiveled his chair around. "How are you, guy? I'm with a patient, so I can only speak for a second. Yes, I'll be up there on the nineteenth as planned. Three weeks from tomorrow. *We're on . . . !* Fantastic! I'll be practicing my putting starting this afternoon! I'm looking forward to it more than I am my own presentation . . ."

While Steadman spoke, Vance noticed the photographs on the credenza behind him. Some of the doc with some celebrities Vance thought he recognized; others . . . One was of a pretty young girl. Looked like a teenager. In a denim jacket with flowery embroideries all over it. Her head was tilted onto Steadman's shoulder. The two of them beaming. Looked just like him. Real nice . . .

And the other—that same girl in a riding outfit and cap, on a horse, captured in midjump. *Beautiful. . .*

244

"Mike, that'll be perfect," Steadman finished up. "You can e-mail me directions to your house in Avondale. I'll be flying up that morning. I'll send you my travel details soon as I know them. Thanks again, buddy. And I can't wait to see you and Gail . . ."

Steadman shifted back around and put down the phone. "Sorry about that. I'm giving a speech up in Jacksonville at a Doctors Without Borders conference in a couple of weeks . . ."

"*Jacksonville . . . ?*" Vance said, blinking.

"Yeah. An old college buddy of mine is a member of this new Jack Nicklaus course . . . Impossible to get onto, know what I mean? So I'll pop up early and we'll get to play a few. You a golfer, Mr. Hofer?"

Vance shook his head. "No."

"Lucky for you!" Steadman leaned back in his chair. "You would think the human race would have evolved enough than to whack a little white ball as far as you can, and chase after it, and call it fun! Dogs maybe."

Vance pretended to laugh, his mind off on a new path now, at its own fork in the road— something new formulating inside him. Even more satisfying.

"Your daughter . . . ?" he asked the doctor, pointing toward the credenza.

Steadman looked behind him and nodded proudly. "My little girl . . . Not so little anymore; that was taken a while back, she's actually nineteen. Just started college last fall. You say you have a daughter yourself . . . ?"

"Yes. 'Manda," Vance replied.

"Then you know what it's like, right?" Steadman shrugged wistfully. "Always our little girls . . ."

"Yes. I guess you'd do just about anything," Vance said, nodding, "to keep 'em from harm." His blood began to throb again, but this time with a rush of delight at the plan he was forming. Far better than this.

Jacksonville.

That was near Yulee, where Vance used to live when he was on the force.

And he knew someone there. Someone who owed him a favor.

A real big favor, Vance recalled.

Three weeks. That would give him time. Things began to take shape in his mind. *I mean, the object is to make Steadman suffer, right?* Just like Vance had suffered. Just like the ball of misery and ill-fatedness that had come to Amanda's door. He could make this greedy doctor see, Vance suddenly realized, just what a chain of woes he had set in motion. To end it here, he now realized, would be far too easy.

"I think I'm gonna have to think about all this," Vance said, rubbing his neck. "Maybe I will take a name from up there. How about I let you know?"

"Of course," Steadman answered, easing back upright. "You know how to reach us. Maryanne will be happy to answer any further questions you may have. As well as the costs."

"Perfect." Vance nodded, looking at him.

Steadman came around the desk. "We'll be happy to print off any information about the procedure to help you in your decision." He walked him toward the door. "In the meantime, it's been a pleasure . . . Very nice to meet you, Mr. Hofer . . ." He extended his hand.

Vance took it, and looked back into Steadman's unsuspecting eyes. "Pleasure's all mine."

CHAPTER FORTY

It all began to take shape for Vance, on his way back to Acropolis, and he felt a renewed sense of purpose and life.

What he had to do to make Steadman properly pay.

Jacksonville. He had three weeks to make it happen.

It was all starting to come alive!

He spent close to a day driving around in his blue Mazda, hashing out the details. Simply killing Steadman now would be far too easy. He had to make him feel pain. The same pain Vance had felt. How it felt to have everything taken away. Everything he had built up in his life. Everything he loved. Cherished. Taken away.

He had to rob the man of everything he once held dear.

Because ultimately, Vance realized, Steadman was no

better than any of the others, no better than Wayne, Dexter, or Schmeltzer. All those fancy degrees and accomplishments . . . put a gun to his mouth and he would shit in his pants like all the rest. Beg. Offer up everything he had.

How else could you make a man like him ever feel remorse? How else could you make him be accountable for his actions?

Vance knew that someone like Steadman felt that the way he was perceived by the world was just as vital as whatever he'd accomplished in his life.

His reputation. His prestige. Take all that away, and he was no better than a shit pile in a dust storm. You had to cut out his heart to make him bleed.

And that's what Vance would do: cut out his heart.

Like Amanda's had been cut out.

And he knew exactly how to do it.

Near Atlanta, he stopped and found one of those Internet cafés. Vance didn't know a whole lot about computers, but the waitress helped him. He looked up Doctors Without Borders and located the meeting in Jacksonville that Steadman had spoken of to his friend. At the Marriott Sun Coast there. On March 19.

And he saw Steadman's name on the list of speakers.

Everything knitted together. There was only one piece he had to add, and he thought he knew just how to do that. He needed some help to fully carry it out. And he knew where to find that help.

He'd waited years to use it.

Near his home, Vance stopped at a diner and found a phone. He dialed 411 and asked for a name. A name from deep in his past.

In Jacksonville.

Once, their lives had come together in a moment that could never be undone. It was more than a bond; it was a debt. A debt that had never been called or forgiven. Or even asked to be repaid.

Until now.

The line rang, and to his delight, a man picked up, kids shouting in the background. "Hello."

Vance said the name that would unleash it all. "Robert Martinez, please."

The Jacksonville cop hesitated. *"Who's this?"*

Vance felt himself hurtled back in time. For a moment all the quiet mediocrity and held-in futility of his life fell away.

"It's Vance. So what do you know, old friend . . . ?"

Silence.

Vance leaned his elbow against the wall. "Been a long time, huh?"

CHAPTER FORTY-ONE

Herbert Sykes.

Vance brought the image of the black man's face back into his mind as clearly as if he were standing in front of him now.

Slim and wiry. Around forty, Vance had guessed. Reminded him of that comedian, Jimmy Walker, who was popular back then. Skin like blacktop, and those big, wide eyes. Slippery like an eel, Vance remembered thinking when he first came upon him. A water moccasin, slithering through the mud, looking for prey.

Except this time the snake bit him.

It was ten years ago.

Vance had just gotten off his four-to-midnight shift, and was finishing off a steak at a diner off the highway, about to head home, when the call came in.

"All available units, ten–twenty-four." A home break-in. In Deerwood. Dispatch said the husband and wife were locked in a closet while the intruder ran through their house. Their young daughter was severely beaten. Possible sexual assault.

The suspect was spotted heading west on Southside in a black SUV. *Suspect could be armed and dangerous.*

Vance could have ignored it; he always knew this. He was done for the night, and on his way home to Yulee. But it was just that the part about the little girl that got him going.

Until that moment, Vance's life had been going in a steady, if undistinguished way. And that was fine with him. He had joined the local force straight out of the reserves. Never more than a high school degree, but he knew how to do what he was told and he didn't back down from trouble when it faced him.

Amanda was nine, and Joyce was working at the county clerk's office. They had a two-bedroom home. Paid things off. Maybe he drank a stage. Maybe he used the back of his hand when his frustrations built up. He was never very good at controlling them.

But they had a life, a good life, simple as it was. They even went away on trips together back then. Myrtle Beach once, and another time to Elvis's home in Memphis.

Vance threw on the lights and siren, tracking the chase on the radio. On a side street, he came upon them, second on the scene.

Martinez was on him first, and already had the guy spread up against his car. A black Land Cruiser.

"Sonovabitch claims he was nowhere near Deerwood," Martinez said, recognizing Vance, a state trooper, but whose beat was local. "But lookie here what the boy had on him."

Martinez held up a black handgun, his thumb and index finger around the trigger guard.

"Sumbitch is a goddamned liar," Vance said, coming around the car with his nightstick. He could smell a piece of shit from a mile away, and this one, with those scared, buggin' eyes and multipocketed North Face jacket, driving a car Vance couldn't afford in ten years, had the smell all over him.

"You like to rob houses?" Martinez asked the guy, shoving him in the back with the stick. "You like to beat up on little girls . . . ?" he pressed. He let the stick slide down to the guy's ass. "Maybe do other things. Put your hands where they don't belong?"

"I didn't do shit to anyone," the guy turned and said. Scared, but still indignant. "I was at my cousin's. I—"

Martinez kicked out the suspect's feet and made him fall to the ground. "Don't you be talking back to me," he told him. Laughing. "I simply asked you a question, boy. So that's how you get your rocks off, playing with twelve-year-olds, you piece of gutter shit."

He kicked him. Hard. In the stomach.

The dude curled up with a loud *ooof*. Then Martinez

253

went after the legs and near his groin. Over and over. The suspect attempting to cover himself up and curling into a ball.

"I didn't do shit!" he yelled out. "I want my lawyer."

"'Course you didn't do shit." Martinez kicked him again. He pointed to the guy's gun. "This is all just fun and games! Right? You lying bastard . . ." He kicked him yet again. "Don't you worry, you don't need no lawyer, rat filth. You ain't ever gonna make it that far, boy, understand?" Martinez kicked him again, and the guy moaned. "So what'd you take from there? C'mon, we know where you were. We know what you were up to."

This time he lifted his boot and stomped on the guy's head.

"Oowww!"

Vance felt his temperature start to rise and his hands squeeze around the club. He leaned over and peeked through the SUV's windows. "I don't see anything in the car."

"Don't you worry about the car," Martinez said to him. He put his boot on the black dude's skull, pressing it against the pavement. "So that's what you like to do . . . Put them slimy, little fingers up a twelve-year-old girl's nightgown?"

"I don't know what you're talking about," the guy moaned, scared shitless, eyes wide. "I wuz at my cousin's. In Westside. Call there! *Ask!*"

254

"He didn't do it." Martinez turned to Vance. "What do you think about that? Says he didn't do it. You didn't do it, huh?" He stomped on the guy's head again, the guy rolling over in pain. *"Fucking piece of shit!"*

That was when another car came up. Lights flashing, radio crackling. Martinez went around to meet it, leaving Vance alone, his blood pressure rising, alone with the pathetic, cowering animal who'd just put his soiled hands all over a twelve-year-old kid.

Slimy, black eel, he remembered saying.

He could smell it. What the guy had done. It was all over him. He could just smell the sick filth all over that eely skin.

"Lemme see those hands?" Vance told him, his fingers wrapping around the stick. At the station, the guy would probably lawyer up. Plead it down to nothing. That's the way it all worked today. Justice, whatever there was of it, had to be administered out here . . . *Here,* you still had to pay up for what you'd done.

"I said show me those hands!"

The guy curled up, not quite understanding. "Look, man, I—"

"I told you to show me those hands! And don't be looking around. No one's gonna help you out here." Vance bent over and whacked him across the back with the stick. Just to let him know he was there.

The slithering eel let a loud grunt, air rushing out of him. Ribs cracked.

255

Vance hit him again. This time up on the neck, his head up against the pavement. "I said, show me those hands!" He reared back and hit him again. Vance wasn't sure what had made him so damn angry. He arrested people all the time. People who'd done far worse. Martinez just seemed to open something in him. Things he'd kept inside for a long time. This sonovabitch eel just seemed to bring it all out.

"You don't seem to hear me, son . . ."

The guy was bloodied. Not answering back now. But Vance stepped on his right shoulder, pinning the guy's arm, and brought the club down on his extended hand, hard as he could, bone and knuckle cracking.

The eel yelped and started to whimper.

"This'll teach you where to put those hands, son . . ." Vance did it again. With the other hand. The water eel howling like a baby now.

Two uniforms ran around to see. "Jesus, Trooper," one of them said, "what the hell you done?"

"Motherfucker reached for something," Vance said, staring into the guy's eyes. "You did reach for something, didn't you, boy? So I boxed his hands."

Didn't matter what he said—in Jacksonville back then, no one was going to buy the story of a black man who was carrying a gun over a state trooper's.

Of course, Vance didn't plan on the whole thing being caught on camera either, some kids who, hearing the commotion, had come to the window of a nearby apartment house, their camcorders catching every second of what went on.

Every second except the part when Martinez took the guy down and kicked the fucking daylights out of him, insisting he was the one.

And how after it was all over, there turned out to be nothing in the car. No loot at all. And it being a Land Cruiser and all, and the car they were after turning out to be a Jeep. And how the sonovabitch *had* been at a cousin's birthday party, not a half hour before, just like he said.

The real suspect was apprehended after a shoot-out around the same time, three miles away.

"He'd done something," Vance said at the inquiry. "I could tell."

But Vance never said a word about what Martinez had done. Throughout the inquiry that followed, when all that footage was shown, including the testimonies of the officers who'd arrived on the scene. Vance just sat there, taking the rap. Immediate dismissal from the force. Loss of benefits.

He just figured, why bring down someone else's life needlessly?

But over the years . . . at his lathe at the plant or lying awake in bed . . . or watching his wife withering away to nothing . . . or hearing Amanda and that pond scum Wayne laughing and giggling and then not saying much of anything down the hall . . . he often wondered:

Why he'd done it?

Then. At that moment. To that man. *Sykes*.

Brought down his own life too.

He never quite came up with the answer.

But whenever he recalled the moment when his life spun away from him, Officer Robert Martinez was always there.

CHAPTER FORTY-TWO

Vance said, "I need a favor from you, Bobby."

"A favor? What are you crazy, Hofer? Calling me up like this? After all these years. If my wife picked up . . ."

"But she didn't pick up. You did, Bobby. And I need something from you. It ain't much. I figured I'm owed that from you. Don't you think so, Bobby-boy?"

"I'm not 'Bobby' to you, Hofer. I'm not anything to you. I've got a family now. I know what you did for me back then. And Lord knows, I guess I am in your debt some. But that was years back. We've all moved on. I can't even talk to you now. I'm hanging up now—"

"No, Bobby, you're not hanging up. Not if you know what's good for you. Not until you hear what I have to say. I ain't looking for much, all things considered. Not so much at all, to make things square."

Vance knew if Martinez was still listening, there was hell in his eyes.

"What is it you want, Vance?"

"How's life been for you, Bobby? Good, I suspect. I hear kids in the background. I think you're still on the job. I figure probably a sergeant by now. Pension. What did you say, we've all moved on . . . ?"

"Not sergeant," Martinez said begrudgingly. "Patrolman, first class."

"Well, ain't that grand. *Me*, Bobby, shall we say I haven't been as kissed by fate. Having fully moved on . . . My wife died. Lung cancer. My kid's a fucking drug addict who's now in . . ." He stopped, deciding not to say where Amanda was. "Been operating a lathe press these last ten years. But got laid off. Guess my temper's always been a thing to deal with, but you know that. Even lost my home . . ."

"I'm sorry, Vance," Martinez said. "I am."

"Yeah, *sorry* . . ." Vance said. "I bet you are. It's just that 'sorry' is a big ol' luxury to me now. Know what I mean. 'Sorry' is like having a bagful of cash. But cash you can't spend. You just look at it. And watch it. And it looks back at you with scorn. Kind of laughing at you . . ."

Martinez didn't say anything.

"So I'm giving you a chance. A chance to square

an old debt. And a damn easy one at that. 'Cause, make no mistake, Bobby, it was *me* who gave you that happy life you're living now. Who gave you those kids I hear. That rank. That pension you'll be spending one day . . . I don't have to explain it all out. *I* gave 'em to you. You understand that, don't you, Bobby-boy . . . ?"

Vance could all but feel Martinez seething on the other end. And weighing his reply. Finally, he came back: "What is it you want from me, Vance?"

"Good." *He had him!* Vance told the cop about this person he owed a comeuppance to. "This doctor. From down south. He got my 'Manda all strung out on these pills. She's done a bunch of bad things. I just want him razzed, Bobby. That's all. You know what I mean. He's coming up your way. In a couple of weeks . . ."

"Razzed?"

"You know the routine. Just take him out of his car. Scare the shit out of him a bit. I've seen you work. I just want him to know he's not so high-and-mighty. He deserves that. Got my little girl all messed up. You have a little girl, don't you, Bob?"

"I do. Becky. She's ten."

"So it should be easy for you. You just think of her. You'll know what to do. I just want you to scare the daylights out of him. You can even bring some pals in on it if you like. Just make the guy feel like his fucking world's falling apart . . ."

261

"And I'm gonna find this guy, *how* . . . ?" Martinez asked. "You said he's not from around here?"

"No. South. Palm Beach. But I'll take care of all that, don't you worry. You just handle your end. You just make him shit those pants, and you'll never hear from me again. We're clean. So what do you say? Easy, huh?"

"When?" Martinez asked, after a bit of time, thinking it over.

"March nineteenth. He'll be flying into the airport. I'll pick him up there, and let you know what he's driving and where he's heading . . . But I think it's near the Marriott Sun Coast Resort. You know that place?"

Martinez said he did.

"Just scare the daylights out of him. That's all I ask. I told you, it's not much. You can even tell him it was from me if you like when it's all over. Yeah, I'd like that. Say hello to him. From Vance. Okay . . . ?"

"And if I do this right for you . . . ?"

"Then we're done. For good. Won't even light a candle at your funeral. 'Course, much more likely, you'll be lighting one for me first."

Martinez didn't laugh. "March nineteenth?"

"March nineteenth it is, buddy. You free? I catch you on a good day, Bobby-boy?"

If Martinez had agreed with a bit more generosity of spirit, or at least a bit quicker, acknowledging his debt, Vance might have regretted how this "favor" would ultimately end for him.

262

But since he didn't, Vance decided not to waste a whole lot of pity on him. A debt was a debt, and Martinez was no angel. No angel at all.

"Just make him soil those fancy pants of his, Bobby-boy."

CHAPTER FORTY-THREE

The last part came to him while he was working with his saw in the toolshed in back of his house.

The Mid-Carolina Gun Show was at the town armory in Tracy that weekend.

Vance drove up. He'd been firing a gun since he was five. Knew how to handle a Winchester 70 hunting rifle, and an M24 bolt-action sniper's rifle too. Sometimes, around his house, he would shoot off rounds at squirrels or possum, just to keep his eye sharp.

But this time he wasn't here just to mill around.

There was a specific dealer Vance had come to see. One, he'd been told, he could deal with. The hall was ringed with long aisles of display booths. Gun dealers, small and large, their wares displayed on backlit walls. Lots of people with their kids milling around.

He found the booth he was looking for along the back row.

Bud's Guns. Mount Holly, NC.

The owner was a ruddy-faced guy in a golf shirt with a thick red mustache. As Vance came up to him, he was occupied with a customer. Vance looked on the pegboard wall among the inventory, for something that might catch his eye.

He stopped at a Heckler & Koch USP 9mm.

Vance took it off the wall; it was attached to a metal wire that ran through the trigger guard. He put his hand around the handle. *Nice.* He checked the magazine and pulled back the slide, feeling the action. Light and smooth. He thumbed the slide release and gently squeezed the trigger. *Click.*

This would do the trick.

Bud freed up and came over with a salesman's grin. "Looking for something compact and reliable, that's a nice piece of equipment there."

"Yeah, I am."

"Accurate too. Less than one and a half pounds. H and K's are used on several police forces around the country. Don't hardly even need to *sell* 'em—they kinda sell themselves, if you know what I mean. I'm pretty sure I could work you up a dandy price."

"It is a beaut." Vance nodded.

"Shoots regular nine-millimeter ammo, or I got these custom, hollow-point, Hydra-Shok babies if you want to blow the door off the barn. I can do seven-forty, if you get me now. Show discount. I'll even throw in a shoulder holster. You won't find a better one here . . ."

"It's nice . . ." Vance pursed his lips, thinking. "But I got this problem." He set the gun down on the counter and looked the dealer in the eye. "Joe Tucker down in Waynesboro said you might be able to handle it for me. Lost my driver's license, if you know what I mean. I was hoping to, I think you know . . . find my way around some regulations. That's why I thought this show might be the right way to go."

The dealer gave Vance a tight smile from underneath his mustache. "I know Joe." He turned his back to the aisle. "I assume we're talking cash?"

Vance shrugged. "If that can get it done."

Bud scratched his walrus-like jaw and nodded. "How 'bout we say, eight seventy-five, and you can take it with you just as is. No questions asked."

Vance picked up the gun and squeezed the trigger one more time. *Do the trick just fine.* "Lemme see that holster."

Bud grinned. "You'll have to fill out an invoice, though. That much there's no getting around." The dealer bent under the cabinet and came back out with a form.

"Got no problem with that," Vance said.

"Here . . ." Bud handed him a pen. "Have a start at the paperwork while I box it up. Mister . . . ?"

266

"Steadman," Vance said to him. "Henry Steadman."

"Pleased to meet you, sir."

Vance began writing Henry Steadman's name under "Buyer" and his address in Palm Beach. Palmetto Way.

"And while you're at it," Vance said, reaching into his pocket and bringing out a wad of bills, "throw in a box of those hollow-points as well."

CHAPTER FORTY-FOUR

From Summerville, I went north on Route 26 toward Columbia, the state capital. Two people on the list of license plates lived up there and another was on the way.

About an hour in I came into the town of Orangeburg. A James A. Fellows lived about twenty miles away in Blackville on Tobin Ridge Road. But I wasn't exactly optimistic, as his plates expired two years ago.

I took the turn onto 301 West to Blackville.

The road wound through a bunch of backwater, roadside towns, basically shacks on the road with a church and a barbecue stand. A boarded-up market with an old sign for something called Knee High Cola actually made me smile. But not as much as the billboard I passed for the New Word Baptist Church, with the pastor pointing at you as you drove by, with the dire warning, referring to the brutal Carolina summer: *"If you think it's hot here . . . !"*

That might've been the first time I truly let out a laugh in days.

I saw the sign for Blackville, and then for Blanton Road, which I knew from MapQuest fed into Tobin Ridge Road.

Truth was, Fellows didn't hold a lot of promise for me, since the plates had expired in August, two years back. As I drove out on the rutted, sun-cracked pavement, I couldn't imagine anyone with any connection to me living all the way out here.

About a mile off the main road, the blacktop ended. There were houses—run-down farmhouses with low fields of lettuce and okra. A couple had above-ground swimming pools. Dog cages in the yards. The occasional Confederate flag.

I passed number 442. Fellows was 669, still a long way down. There was a bend in the road. A dog jumped out of nowhere, running out at me, barking wildly. As I passed, he dropped back and looked after my car like I was driving into hell. A mile farther along, I passed 557. Mostly woods and fields now.

I felt myself starting to grow nervous. Let's say Fellows was the guy. How would I know? What would I even do? Take a picture of the famous blue car? I didn't have a weapon, but it was likely he did! It dawned on me, a guy could get killed out here and no one would even know he'd disappeared.

Finally I saw a red house ahead on the right. On the mailbox was a hand-scratched number, 669. I blew out my cheeks. This was it! There was a beat-up, black pickup in the driveway. More like a rutted clearing in front of the house. There was a two-car garage, open, with tools everywhere, and another vehicle in it up on blocks.

I pulled in. Dogs started barking, and I saw three Dobermans jumping against the wire in a dog cage. Something told me, *Henry get out of here* . . . A huge elm shaded the front of the house. Laundry strung on an outside line.

I heard hammering.

A guy who was working on the front porch stood up when he noticed me approaching. He didn't come toward me; he didn't avoid me either. What he did do was give me a look like he wasn't into visitors.

"Help you?" he said, putting down his hammer.

"Mr. Fellows?" I asked, opening the car door and walking toward the porch.

He nodded. Barely. He had on denim overalls, a sweaty white T-shirt, and a blue cap. He had a gaunt, angular face, a scrabbly-looking, gray growth of whiskers, sharp, distrusting eyes, and as I got closer, a gap in his teeth.

He could have been anywhere from forty-five to sixty.

"My name's Dawson, Mr. Fellows. I'm tracking down a license plate for an insurance company. It appears it was part of an accident." Nervously, I checked my sheet. "South Carolina ADJ-dash-four-three-nine-two. It's registered here to you at this address."

"Accident, you say?"

I felt my heart start to gallop. Fellows surely didn't look like the guy I'd seen through my mirror. And I didn't see any blue car around the house. No surprise there. But what if it *was* him. If he had killed Mike, he would surely recognize me.

And here I was.

"In Georgia," I said, though if he was connected he surely knew this was a lie.

"Georgia?" he said, as if surprised. He spit a wad of tobacco into a paper cup. "You say this plate belonged to me?"

"According to the South Carolina Department of Motor Vehicles," I replied. "But they've expired."

It crossed my mind that the guy could just take out a shotgun and shoot me right here. Instead, he scratched his beard, nodding. "C'mon with me." He took me into the garage. More like an open shed, a car on blocks with the hood open. Tools, cans of oil, tires, hubcaps everywhere. "Sounds familiar. You say expired?"

"August. 2010. You a Gamecocks fan, Mr. Fellows?"

"Gamecocks? Sure." He looked back with a gap-toothed smile. "They're my team. Why . . . ?"

I felt a surge of optimism mixed with fear. He led me around the raised-up car to the back of the garage, where, against the wall, I saw a cardboard box. He kicked it.

Maybe a dozen license plates clattered inside.

"I know maybe I should turn 'em in," he said. "Some do go back a ways. But the DMV's all the way up in Chambersburg. And now and then my wife sells 'em at tag sales and such. Every penny helps these days . . ."

I bent down and leafed through the box. He read the disappointment all over my face. ADJ-4392 wasn't among them.

Fellows shrugged. "I could check inside, but I'm pretty sure you're right about the plate number. Could be anywhere by now . . ." He grinned again. "You're welcome to any of the others if you like."

"No." I forced myself to make a thin smile. "Won't be necessary."

"So this was an accident, you say?" Fellows asked again, walking me back outside.

I nodded in frustration.

"In Georgia, huh?" Fellows asked, his eyes suddenly turning dubious. "So you mind if I ask you . . . you a cop as well?"

"*As well?*"

" 'Cause if you are, that's exactly what I told the one who came by a while back. That someone must've took 'em. Could be anywhere."

272

I looked at him. "A cop came by here earlier. *About this?*" I wasn't sure whether to be excited or alarmed.

Fellows nodded. "Hour, hour and a half ago . . . Looking for that same plate. 'Course, she said it was Florida, not Georgia, and that it was a criminal thing." His gaze seemed almost amused. "Whichever—sure seems a popular one for one day . . ."

"You said *she* . . . ? It was a woman?"

"Pretty little thing . . . *Here*, even left me this card . . ." Fellows dug into his overalls. "Said if I recalled anything, I should . . ."

He brought it out, handed it to me.

It was excitement. A tsunami of excitement. And no matter how I tried to stop myself, I broke into a wide-eyed smile.

The card read, *Jacksonville Sheriff's Office. Director, Community Outreach.*

Carolyn Rose Holmes.

CHAPTER FORTY-FIVE

I stepped into the Azalea Diner, a roadside truck stop next to the Motel 6 a mile or so out of Orangeburg.

There were a couple of locals around the counter; a young family at one of the tables; a large trucker type in a booth draining a cup of coffee.

Then—

I saw her! Or I was sure it *had* to be her. Strawberry-blond hair. *Pretty little thing*, Fellows had said. And that she was staying the night in case anything else came up. The kid at the front desk of the Motel 6 where Fellows said he had sent her confirmed that she was there, and that she'd gone out around half an hour ago to get something to eat. And where else was there to go? I didn't know what I should do. Go right up to her? *Fancy running into you here . . .* The last thing I wanted was to alarm her. Or draw unwanted attention to myself. She had no idea I was anywhere nearby.

But as I stared at her, in the end booth by the window, alone, a cute button nose, freckles maybe, in jeans and a hooded gray sweatshirt that I thought read, *U.S. Marines,* texting on her phone, two things became clear.

One was that Carrie Holmes believed me. *Why else would she be here?*

And *two*—which lifted me even higher—she had the plate numbers! And if she was *here*, they must have belonged to Fellows.

And I had found him too!

Looking at her, I realized that I had never felt as much gratitude toward another person as I was feeling toward her. I realized just how much she had to be risking just to be here. Who, back home, would have even believed her? And then there was the kind of courage it took for her to follow through.

I almost felt the tears sting in my eyes. It was as if I was connected to her in a way I couldn't describe.

I took a table at the other end of the restaurant. I grabbed a menu from the holder and held it in front of my face.

I was petrified that if I just walked right up to her, she might scream—I was still a wanted murder suspect. So I took out the cell number she had written down for Fellows and dialed it.

My heart jumped with excitement. I saw her look at her phone and, curious at the number—it probably read, *Unknown Caller*—answer in a halting tone.

"This is Carrie."

"What's old, rusted, and jangles around a lot in a box?" I asked.

She hesitated, checking the number again, confused. *"What?"*

"ADJ-4392. Or I sure wish it did!"

I watched as Carrie Holmes's eyes went wide.

"How's the food here? I hear it's the best north of Blackville!"

This time her eyes jumped up and darted around the restaurant, finally settling on me, my menu lowering, the cell phone at my car.

I took off my glasses. Peered at her through the four-day-old growth and the golf cap.

Her jaw dropped. *"What the hell are you doing here?"* she blurted.

It sounded a lot more like a demand than a question.

"The same thing you're doing here. I just saw Fellows. He told me you were here. I didn't realize I had the right plate number until now!"

The color began to rush from her face, giving way to a look of distrust or bewilderment. Or maybe even concern.

"I didn't mean to alarm you," I said. "Please, please, don't be afraid. I want to come over and talk. You don't have to worry about me in any way. You know that! Can I do that? Can I come over, Carrie? I—"

"No!" she barked. "Stay where you are!" Then, grasping how ridiculous this all was and that she had nothing to fear, she kind of took a step back and said nervously, "Okay. Okay. But look, I—"

Neither of us seemed to be finishing sentences very well.

She was flustered. A bit unnerved. The same way I was flustered. I pushed out of my seat and headed toward her down the aisle. My legs, a little rubbery. I could see she wasn't sure whether to yell out or jump up and arrest me. And I didn't know whether to hug her in gratitude or make a run for it.

I sat down in the seat across from her.

I couldn't help but grin. "I was right, wasn't I? You found the blue car. You traced the plates. To Fellows. That's why you're here. Which basically means the car *was* at both crime scenes. Just like I said."

She nodded tentatively.

"Which then means you know I'm completely innocent, don't you? You know I'm being set up."

Suddenly I couldn't control my grin.

"Look, all I know is—" She barely got the words out of her mouth when the waitress came up. A little chunky, her hair up in a bun, the name Nanci embroidered on her blouse. She plopped a menu in front of me.

"Well, you two seem to have hit it off . . . Specials are on the board. Chili's Southern style, which means no beans. It's always good. Chicken and biscuits seem to be crowd-pleasers too."

"Just gimme a second," I said to her, maybe slightly abrupt. Then, softening my tone: "How about I take whatever she's having . . ."—pointing to a bowl of soup in front of Carrie.

"Turkey okra," Nanci said. "Crackers . . . ?"

"Yes, crackers! Thanks . . ." She continued to stand around as she wrote my order on her pad.

My eyes went back to Carrie. Both of us seemed to smile.

"You know I wasn't in North Carolina the day that gun was bought," I finished my thought. "The same blue car was at both crime scenes! What was it, a Mercury or a Ford?"

"Mazda," she said, chuckling. "Look, I don't know anything for sure. It's possible you could have sent someone else to get that gun. Gun shows are notorious for being loose with records . . ."

"Carrie . . ."

"And that car at both crime scenes doesn't actually prove anything. It surely doesn't prove you didn't do it, only that there could be some other possible expla-nation. Or that you had an accessory . . ."

"*Carrie,*" I said again.

"What I do know is I work for the Jacksonville

278

Sheriff's Office. And you shouldn't be here, Dr. Steadman. I shouldn't be sitting—"

"Carrie!" I said one more time, raising my voice. "You don't have to be afraid. I know you believe me. *You're here.*"

Her eyes slowly relaxed and she curled her hair around her ear as she blew out her cheeks and leaned back against the padded booth.

And nodded.

I said, "It's okay."

Nanci came back with my crackers and soup. "Bowl's hot," she said, setting it down.

"Thanks."

"And free refills, just so you know."

"Good." I shot her an exasperated glance. "Thanks."

She went away, and Carrie looked at me. She took off her glasses. "What did Fellows tell you?"

"I figure the same thing he told you. That he has no idea where the plates might be. He showed you the box?" I took a sip of the soup. *"Jeez."* It scalded my tongue. "This *is* hot!"

Carrie nodded, holding back a thin smile. "Guess we both got the same spiel."

"So it *was* Fellows?" I said, taking another sip of soup, and I had to admit, after living out of fast-food drive-through windows for the past four days, it tasted good. "Where those plates came from."

She nodded again. "How did you get here?"

279

"Had someone I know spiff a DMV worker in South Carolina. I had them pull everything that began with ADJ-4 . . . Then I worked my way down the list."

"Not bad." Carrie smiled. "Do you believe he doesn't know where the plates went? That he has nothing to do with it?"

"I don't know . . . *You're* the detective . . . But it does mean something though . . . It means whoever *is* involved is from around here. They'd had to have had some contact with Fellows."

"You know anyone from this area?" she asked.

"No." The South Carolina connection stumped me. "I don't."

"So why would someone be doing this to you?" Carrie fixed on me. "If they wanted to kill you, they could have done it at any time. Instead, they went after Martinez and your friend. *Why?*" Her gaze stayed tight on me.

"I don't know. I've gone over this a hundred times. And I still have no idea."

"But the person who did it . . . he not only had to be connected to Fellows, in some way he also had to know about you. When you'd be in Jacksonville. What you were doing there. Where you were headed. He knew about your friend Dinofrio . . ."

I hadn't thought about Mike for a day now and it hurt to bring him to mind all over again. That he had died while trying to help me hurt even more. I nodded emptily and closed my eyes.

I wanted to tell her about the calls. About my daughter. Keeping it from her was killing me inside. She had already put so much of herself on the line for me.

"I'm starting to think, if this whole thing is simply to entrap me, for what I don't know, Martinez had to have been in on it too. I mean, killing him was either a spur-of-the-moment thing, or . . . Or it was planned. That could be why he stopped me and pulled me out of the car in the first place, for basically nothing . . . But how could anyone have known where I'd be? At that exact time? And what I'd be driving?"

"You were followed," Carrie said, her blue eyes fixed on me. "Probably right from the airport."

"*From the airport . . . ?* This is all insane!" I said, cradling my head in my hands. It was wearing on me, but the more I thought about it—the rented Caddie, my destination, Mike—someone must have known. I thought back to Martinez. His insistence about the insurance thing and how I was driving down a one-way street . . . Had that all been meant as a kind of provocation? To anger me? To make me react? *Sir, if I have to tell you to shut your mouth again, it will not go well for you. . .*

Had Martinez been a part of it too, and . . . ? As I racked my brain searching for answers, I suddenly heard those two loud pops all over again and saw him slumped over the wheel.

Had this whole thing been set up to have him stop

me and then kill him—and then have his murder pinned on me?

Light-headed, I pushed myself back against the banquette. "Who could hate me so much to want to cause me this kind of pain? You're right, he could have killed me. He could have done it a dozen times. But he's not trying to kill me. He's—" *He's trying to torture me*, I wanted to say. *He's stolen my daughter!* "*How does it feel to have everything you value taken from you? Everything you hold dear. . . .*" "He's trying to pay me back. For something I did to him. It's like he's got me trapped and he's just toying with me before he comes in for the kill. And it's incredible how my life has somehow managed to fit into their plan . . ."

"Toying with you . . . ?"

I looked at her and drew in a breath, and sat back. I realized how crazy it all sounded and started to make a joke out of it. "Sorry. It's a hell of a lot to go through if someone simply didn't like how their boobs came out."

Carrie's eyes twinkled with an awkward smile.

"I'd have gladly redone them—gratis . . ." I shook my head and smiled. "Anyway, I just want to say, you're very brave. Hell, I know how *I* felt just driving out to that godforsaken place . . . They obviously breed those community outreach gals pretty tough."

She put her glasses back on and smiled at me. "You're proving to be pretty self-reliant yourself. Given your occupation."

282

Nanci came up again. "Everyone doin' okay? Seems you're liking . . ." We both nodded. She asked if we needed anything else, and we shook our heads no. "Then I'll be right back."

I looked at Carrie and something came to mind. From the first time I called her. "So what was it?" I asked. "The first time I spoke with you, you said you were just coming back . . . ?"

"Sorry?"

"The first time we spoke. You said it was your first day back. From being out for a while . . ." I noticed a wedding ring. "Honeymoon? Maternity leave . . . ?"

"No . . ." She tilted her head and shrugged, her expression shifting, lips pressing together in a tight smile. "It was nothing."

"Nothing . . . ?" It occurred to me that maybe she'd been sick, and I shouldn't have pried. "Sorry, I didn't mean to get personal."

"Dr. Steadman, we really have to figure out what the next step is here." Her gaze returned to business now. "You just can't keep on running."

She was right, of course. But she didn't know the truth. All my hopes had been based on tracking the killer through the license plates, and now we had found the source, and that hope was gone. Now there was no next place left for me to go, except to keep running.

I tried to convey with my eyes that there was more

going on than I could possibly explain. "I have no choice, Carrie."

"There is a choice. Look, I know I haven't slept in a night and my thinking might well be off, but we *have* things now . . . We have the video of that car at both crime scenes. We have you in your office, operating, the day that gun was bought. That's all something. We have Fellows—somewhere, somehow he connects to whoever's doing this. This isn't like before. They'll have to check these things out."

"No, you just don't understand . . ."

"You have *me*." Her gaze was powerful and resolute, but then she allowed a self-deprecating smile. "I know that's not exactly like having the attorney general on your side . . . But I can guarantee that these things will get looked into. *And* your safety. You can even do it from up here, if you like. There won't be any guns blazing."

"You're suggesting I turn myself in?"

"What other way is there? We've both done what we can. Let's let the professionals put it together now. Look . . ." she said. "I think you deserve a real detective working for you, don't you agree . . . ?"

"I think you've done just fine," I said. "But I just can't . . . There's stuff I can't tell you."

"You have to, Dr. Steadman. We're done. I don't see any other way."

If I told her the whole story, that the person who

was trying to destroy my life also had my daughter, and it got back to the police, and they looked into locating Hallie . . . I couldn't take the risk.

"I wish I could," I said, and looked at her. "Turn myself in. But that's not an option anymore."

I shook my head, tears of frustration burning in my eyes. Frustration that I couldn't tell her what I knew.

"Then don't you see—then I can't help you anymore, Dr. Steadman. I'm totally in over my head as it is. I can't go on with you." She shook her head. "I shouldn't even be here with you now . . . What I should do is . . ."

"What? Arrest me? You're not even a cop, Carrie. You're in community outreach!"

"What if I screamed, then? I could yell out who you are. I doubt you'd even make it out of this diner. You definitely wouldn't make it to the next town."

I looked behind us, and saw there was a group of good ol' boys standing around near the entrance who, I could imagine, would just love to raise a beer one day about how they had tackled the Jacksonville killer.

"Then scream . . . Go ahead. I'm in your hands. There's your posse over there. I can see them all on the *Today* show tomorrow . . ."

Carrie gave me a pleading, no-nonsense smile. "What? What is it you can't tell me? Look at what I put on the line for you."

"I have to think it over. In the morning. Just put in a little more—"

"So if it's a yes, you'll be at breakfast. And if it's no—you'll be outta here."

I shook my head. "I won't be 'outta here' . . . You put a lot of faith in me to do what you did. I'll do the same for you. I promise." I put up two fingers. "You have my word. I just need to run it all through one more time. Scout's honor . . ."

"Right, like you were ever a scout." She rolled her eyes.

"Accused murderer pack. Tiny chapter." I smiled. "Never meet in this same place . . ."

She looked at me, as if she was trying to read something on my face. How much she could trust me, how much faith to put in me.

"What was it that made you believe me?" I asked her. I moved my hands close to hers. "You had no reason to look for that car. I'm damn sure no one else there would have. What was it?"

"Something you said." She cleared her throat. "Seems kind of stupid now. In light of everything."

"Try me."

She shook her head. "I'll tell you," she said, the twinkling disappearing in her eye, "after we turn you in and they dismiss your case. *Deal?*"

"I guess trust is a two-way street. Takes more than a single bowl of turkey okra, huh?"

"Guess so."

I stood up and left some bills. I smiled and put up

286

the same two fingers. "See you in the morning. Either way."

"Are you in the motel?" she asked me.

I shook my head. "No. Lexus."

CHAPTER FORTY-SIX

James Fellows sat in his padded chair, smoking, long after his wife, Ida, had gone up to bed. And long after he normally would have gone up as well.

He was thinking about the two visits he'd gotten today. One, from that pretty gal who worked for the Jacksonville police. The other . . . he didn't know who the other one really was. Just that he wasn't no claims adjuster. Of that much, he was sure.

Both of them looking into the same set of plates.

Truth was, he didn't have a clue where they'd ended up. (Though now, after he had seen the picture the woman had brought, maybe he had some idea.)

He surely didn't want to find himself drawn into some kind of investigation. Hell, these days, he didn't much like even showing his face in town if it wasn't totally necessary.

Any more than he liked covering up for someone else's trouble.

But he was also the kind of man who stood by his friends. He didn't know just what had been done, but it must be of some matter, he reckoned, if people had come here all the way from out of state.

And he always knew, if there was a fellow who was capable of something, well, the man who drove a car like that, or at least, his daughter's car, he was it. He'd always been kind of a lit fuse. Not one to hold his liquor well. And now, with what had gone on with Amanda, who could even blame him.

Still, it was one thing when they worked together, something else, given what happened, now . . .

Fellows picked up his phone and called. The man's cell phone, the only number Fellows now had. Anyway, this hour, he'd no doubt be asleep himself.

He answered on the third ring, not sounding sleepy at all.

"It's Buck," James Fellows said. "Hope I'm not disturbing you none. Just giving you a friendly heads-up. You been driving your daughter's car around? Down in Florida maybe?"

Vance remained silent for a while before he answered. "Why you asking?"

"These people were up here looking for a license

plate. *My* license plate, in fact. And they seemed to have seen your car. Or *hers* . . ." Fellows laughed darkly. "Seems you got yourself in a lick of trouble, huh, partner?"

CHAPTER FORTY-SEVEN

It was hard to sleep that night. Carrie was kind enough to get me a room so I didn't have to sleep in the car, or show my face again at the front desk, and I lay awake in the spartan motel room, long after *Letterman* and *Craig Ferguson* had ended, hating how I'd had to hold back what was really going on from the one person I actually trusted, and slowly coming to the conclusion that there was no other choice now, at least no better one, than to put myself in her hands and turn myself in.

I was scared to death of what this might mean for Hallie.

But with Fellows's license plate no longer a lead to follow, maybe there was no other way.

And Liz wasn't going to go on blindly trusting me forever.

Tomorrow I could be in the hands of the police. How could I ever trust that they would act with in Hallie's best interests after how they'd already acted to me?

I tossed and turned, feeling like I was hanging my own daughter over a cliff. I had found the source of the license plates and it led nowhere. I had nowhere left to go.

I sat up against the pillow and racked my brain for maybe the thousandth time trying to figure out who had a reason to do this to me.

Certainly Marv didn't. My shares in the clinics didn't even revert to him if anything happened to me. Anyway, he was like an uncle to Hallie. And as Carrie noted, it wasn't like someone was trying to kill me anyway.

In fact, I seemed to be the only one this bastard seemed intent on *not* killing!

I knew I wasn't perfect. I'd played around a bit and screwed up my marriage. Maybe I'd gone for the bucks a bit in my practice instead of devoting myself to saving lives. But I had tried to do good for people. I gave my time and energy and built up a pretty good life. And I was a good dad. *Who could want to cause me such suffering?*

Who could take innocent lives and end them so coldly, just to hurt me?

I was scared. Scared of the decision I had to make. Scared of what might happen. If I told her . . . if I let Carrie know about the abduction . . .

292

Maybe I should just go. In the morning. Not put this one on her. But where . . . ?

Teeming with frustration, I took out my iPad, logged onto MapQuest, and called up the town of Blackville, South Carolina, where we currently were.

The only thing that *did* make sense to me was that whoever was doing this at some point had to have had some contact with James Fellows.

I looked at all the surrounding towns around Blackville. Bamberg. Denmark. Williston. Places I'd never heard of. Perry. Barnwell.

Of course, this person didn't have to have been anyone I might have met. He could be a hired hand. An accomplice. He could live anywhere. I enlarged the map to a wider radius.

Suddenly my eyes focused on something.

Not exactly a "eureka!" moment at first. More like a faint throbbing deep in my memory. I had to clear my head just to narrow in on it. The town.

Acropolis.

It wasn't actually in South Carolina, but in Georgia. Just over the state line.

But I'd seen it before, that name. I just couldn't recall where.

I checked the scale: Blackville and Acropolis were maybe thirty miles apart.

You've seen this name before, Henry. You have. Where do you know it from . . . ?

Then suddenly it hit me.

I'd seen a patient from Acropolis. In Georgia. A few weeks back. I tried to bring the guy to mind.

He was heavy. Bald on top, orange hair around the sides. Ruddy. He had come about something on his neck. Those heavy wrinkles. I pictured it. He had fallen into the memory bin of patients I'd only seen once and never saw again. He had seemed a little odd. As I recalled, I told him I could recommend something up his way, *then*. . .

All of a sudden it was like a jackhammer was drilling me in the chest.

That's when Mike had called that time!

It suddenly was a "eureka!" moment. *Yes, when that guy was in the office, Mike called.* To set up our golf date at Atlantic Pines. I tried to bring it all back. Adrenaline surged through every part of me. I had told Mike I was heading up to Jacksonville to give a speech. *Did I mention a date?*

I couldn't recall. But then I realized it didn't matter. I'd mentioned the Doctors Without Borders conference I was speaking at.

That was enough. Anyone could put it together. And I'd mentioned Mike. I remembered now:

"You can email me directions to your house in Avondale. . . ."

My eyes shot back to the MapQuest map again. I couldn't recall the guy's name, but I did remember his face, and a certain oddness about him. And I damn well recalled where he was from . . .

Acropolis. Georgia.

I didn't know if I was just imagining something. Or if I was fabricating it, out of sheer desperation. I didn't know this person from Adam. I'd never seen him before in my life. It made no sense.

What could he possibly hold against me?

But as I fixed on the map, clouds of doubt and uncertainty opening up in front of me, light shining through the night, I fixed on that town:

Acropolis, Georgia.

Could it be?

CHAPTER FORTY-EIGHT

I did my best to hold off until morning. I barely slept a wink.

At five-thirty I called Maryanne, my assistant.

"Maryanne—it's Henry!" I said. "I realize I'm waking you up, but this is important!"

"Dr. Steadman?" she muttered groggily. I could hear her husband, Frank, stirring next to her, wanting to know what the hell was going on.

"Maryanne, I'm sorry to disturb you so early—but I need something from you. It's important—or I wouldn't be calling you like this . . ."

She cleared her throat and gradually gathered her wits. "What is it you need?"

Frank was probably calling the police on the other line, but I didn't care.

"You remember that guy who came in about a month ago—heavyset, bald, fuzzy reddish hair around the sides. From out of state. I can't think of his name, but he came in about his neck. Wrinkles . . ."

"Yes. I think so," she answered. "Hofer . . ."

"I need his records, Maryanne. As soon as you can get them to me. I need his name and address, whatever he left, as well as his Social. And a photo. I'm pretty sure I took one while he was there. It has to be in the system. I need you to get that for me . . ."

"Sure. Of course . . ." Maryanne stammered. "I'll go right now."

I could hear her already out of bed and in motion. The gears must have been turning in her mind as she mobilized herself because she suddenly asked: "You think he's involved . . . ?"

"Fast as you can, Maryanne! That's all I can say. You have no idea how much is depending on this."

CHAPTER FORTY-NINE

I couldn't wait for breakfast to show Carrie what I'd found. I was far too wound up.

By 6:15, Maryanne had e-mailed me what I'd asked for. The patient's name was Vance Hofer. The address he'd left was 2919 Bain Road. In Acropolis. He'd left a Social Security number as well.

And a photo. I always took one as a "before" shot to scan into my patients' files.

And there he was! My eyes swarmed over the round, pink-complexioned face. The dull gray eyes that seemed to stare off past me with the slightest hint of a smile in them. I'd never seen him before he walked into my office that day. *Was he the one? The one doing this to me? What possible motive could he have to want to harm me?*

Excited, I knocked on Carrie's door with the iPad at a quarter of seven. She opened it just a crack, a towel wrapped around her. "Okay, you're still here," she said. "I can see that. Can you give me a couple of minutes, though? I'm dressing . . ."

"Carrie," I said excitedly, "I think I know who it is!"

The door edged open wider. Her hair was still wet from the shower.

"Something hit me during the night. I just received a file back from my office. A patient's file. I need to show it to you."

"I shouldn't be more than a minute or two, okay . . . ?"

Seconds later Carrie opened her door.

She was in a baby-blue Gator basketball warm-up T-shirt over jeans, her hair combed out a little. A bunch of clothes was strewn all over the second bed. No makeup. If I had been there for any purpose other than to save my daughter's life, I might have thought she looked totally adorable.

"What are you talking about, Dr. Steadman?"

I told her how it came to me during the night, this town where a patient of mine had come from: Acropolis, Georgia. Not a patient actually, a prospective one, and how I'd just bumped into the name kind of randomly as I searched through MapQuest. How he'd been in my office a couple of weeks back at the same time as Mike happened to call about my trip.

I opened the iPad, and showed her what Maryanne had sent me.

"Vance Hofer . . ." Carrie muttered to herself. "Acropolis. I don't understand, what's his connection to you?"

"There is no connection!" I sank onto the bed across from her. "At least none I can identify. Only that you asked last night if I knew anyone from around here and then I saw this town on the map where he said he was from, and it's only about thirty miles from here. And then it hit me that he happened to be in my office the day Mike called in. I took the call while he was sitting right there in front of me. And I'm certain I mentioned the conference I was going to and about playing golf; I'm not sure, but I may even have mentioned Atlantic Pines . . . And I even think I told Mike to e-mail me his address in Avondale . . . I'm sorry"—I could barely hold myself together—"but I'm not really into coincidences right about now . . ."

More seemed to fit together the more I recalled.

"Go on," Carrie urged.

"I remember him being kind of odd . . . I don't know . . ." I got up, my blood racing, like I was on speed. "I can't exactly put my finger on it. Just not my usual kind of patient. He came in about some rhytid tissue on his neck. Heavy wrinkling. I told him what I could do. I even told him I could recommend someone closer to his home if he wanted. That's why I recall where he

300

was from." I stopped pacing. "I never heard back from him.

"But it all kind of fits. It's the *only* thing that has fit! I don't know what his connection to me is, or any motive, only that he was there! He heard all those things on the phone. And he's from fucking *here* . . ."

Carrie nodded, slowly at first. I wasn't sure she was totally buying it.

I told her, "I'm thinking we can take this back to Fellows and see if he knows him . . . ?"

Then she looked up at me, blue eyes beaming, resolute. "I'm thinking I can do you one a whole lot better than that."

She grabbed her cell and found a number on her speed dial, and I sat on the bed, waiting expectantly for the call to go through. The person picked up.

"Jack—I need you to look someone up for me," Carrie said, cutting right to the chase, "and I don't want to have to tell you why, or how come the JSO isn't able to do it for me. I just need you to do this for me—no questions asked. Okay? If it's what I think. . . ."

She stopped herself, and looked at me, one knee curled to the side, like a yoga position. "If it's what I think it is, I may have a headline here for you."

She waited, seeming to gird herself for the barrage she was anticipating.

"I know. I know. *I know all that, Jack* . . ." The last one she exhaled with exasperation. "I can't tell you

that, Jack. And I can't tell you where I am either. Only
. . . Just write this down, okay?" She spelled out Hofer's
name. And his address. And she gave him his SSN. I
heard a trace of excitement in her voice. I knew she
was putting herself out on a line. This wasn't exactly
part of the Community Outreach routine.

My blood throbbed with the certainty that we were
finally getting close to the truth.

"Just e-mail what you have back to me as soon as
you have it. Whatever you can find on him. With a
special emphasis on anything that might have caused
him to become violent, okay? That's not important,"
she said. Then, in answer to another question: "That's
not important either. You just have to trust me on this.
Like ol' times . . . And, Jack . . ." She waited. "This is
important. This has to stay one hundred percent between
us, okay. I need your promise on that." She nodded.
"Thank you, Jack. And I will be careful. I promise . . ."

Carrie hung up and looked over to me, a crooked,
little girl's smile conveying, *I hope that was smart.* That
this was terrain she had never been down before.

Neither had I, for that matter.

"Someone you work with?" I asked curiously. "At
the sheriff's office."

"Brother." She shook her head. "At the FBI."

CHAPTER FIFTY

There wasn't much Carrie and I could do until we got more information on Vance Hofer, and that could take hours.

So we agreed that the best thing to do was to drive back out to the Fellows property and talk with him again.

This time I stayed in the car and let Carrie do the talking. What could I have offered, anyway, that was any more persuasive than a Jacksonville police ID?

Fellows was outside watering plants when we arrived. He didn't seem exactly eager to see who it was who had come back a second time.

The conversation was brief. He was even more guarded and distracted than he'd been the day before, trying to ignore us. But Carrie showed him the photo of Hofer that Maryanne had sent me, which made him brusquely turn away, his glare pretty much saying, *I think it's time for you two to get the hell out of here now. . .*

Then Carrie came back to the car with a look of frustration and disappointment on her face, but also a gleam of something promising too.

"Well . . . ?" I asked her.

"He said he never heard of him. At first." Carrie backed out of Fellows's drive and continued about a hundred yards or so before stopping and turning to me. "But then he basically admitted he was lying."

"How? What did he say?" *This could save me!*

"He asked to see my ID again. Then he told me, 'Next time, come back here with a real cop, and I'll tell you.'"

Carrie's brother reached us back at the motel.

She put her hand on mine, motioning for me to stay silent, and put the call on speakerphone.

"Are you with someone, Carrie . . . ?" I heard her brother ask. My heart was beating so loudly I was worried he could hear me through the phone.

"Don't worry about that, Jack. Tell me what you found?"

"You wanted to know if anything could have possibly made this guy resort to violence?"

"Yeah . . ."

"Well, find your ticket, sis. I think you hit the lottery."

Carrie and I locked on each other's eyes.

"I'm looking through it now. The guy lost his home, a year and a half ago. His wife died, which pretty much broke him. He's been living in a trailer since. Not to mention his job . . . The past ten years he worked as a lathe operator in some metalworks plant in South Carolina which went under . . ."

"Do you happen to have the name of the place, Jack?" Carrie's eyes lit up with anticipation.

I heard the sound of a page being turned. "Lemme see. Here it is. Liberty Machine Works. Bamberg, South Carolina. Mean anything?"

Carrie stared at me hard, her eyes expansive. "Yeah, Jack. It does mean something. That's where Fellows worked as well."

"Who?" her brother said through the phone.

"Never mind, Jack. Sorry." But her look to me was lit with elation. And vindication. Fellows *had* been lying. He and Vance had worked together! That was how they knew each other.

That was how Hofer would have come upon the plates.

"That enough, or you need any more?" her brother asked, as if he were daring her to say yes.

"Keep it coming, Jack. You're on a roll."

"Seems your guy is an ex-cop as well. He was with the Florida State Police for almost fifteen years. Accent on *ex*, though—he was dismissed in an IA investigation back in 1999. He seems to have taken the fall for his

305

role in an excessive-force incident." I heard a whistle. "*I'd say . . . !* It says here he held down a burglary suspect and busted both his hands with a nightstick. All caught on film. It all happened back in Jacksonville. Right in your own backyard."

"*Jacksonville?*" Carrie turned and fixed on me.

"That's right. It was a joint investigation with your very own sheriff's office there. Very public back then. There were other officers involved, but they were all cleared."

Carrie's gaze grew serious, and though she only shot me the briefest of looks, I knew what was in her mind. Because it was in my mind too.

"Jack, is there any mention there of just who those other officers were?"

I heard him leaf through his report. "A couple of reprimands maybe. Hofer seems to be the only one who was directly implicated. Dismissal. Loss of all benefits."

I could read Carrie's mind: If we looked it up, would Robert Martinez's name be there?

That had to be how he and Hofer knew each other. From back on the force in Jacksonville. *Did Martinez somehow owe him? For Hofer taking the fall?*

Everything was beginning to fit together. It was kind of like peeling back a dark curtain and finding a secret, parallel part of your life you never knew existed, but one that was going on all the time, and eventually collided with yours.

Head-on.

It had to be Hofer. Everything fit! He knew where I was going and when. He'd taken the plates from Fellows's garage and gotten in touch with Martinez, his old cohort from Jacksonville, who owed Hofer a favor, so Hofer got him to agree to pull me over. Scare the shit out of me!

And then he'd killed him! Killed his own friend. And then he went out and killed Mike. With a gun he'd probably purchased using my name.

All to make it look like it was me!

But why? Our paths had never crossed until he came in my office. I was a blank trying to put anything together from that time. He had looked at my photos on the credenza. Asked about my daughter . . .

"So, you got enough?" Carrie's brother asked. "You find what you were looking for?'

"Yeah, Jack." Carrie nodded somberly.

"In that case, I guess you don't need to hear the kicker," her brother said, with a slight note of teasing in his voice.

"The kicker?" Carrie said. "C'mon, Jack, no holding back now."

"The guy's daughter was just convicted on a vehicular homicide charge. Two months ago she ran over a mother and her newborn son. She pleaded guilty. Sentenced to twenty years . . ."

It suddenly hit me: Hofer had mentioned something

307

about his daughter in my office. He was looking over the photos on the credenza. He'd noticed Hallie. He asked me—

"Apparently she was whacked out on OxyContin at the time of the accident," Carrie's brother said.

"Oh my God!" I suddenly understood why Hofer had asked me about my clinics. The pain centers . . . *His daughter had been high on OxyContin at the time of her accident.* Somehow he blamed me for what had happened to her. OxyContin had taken a piece of her life. Now he was taking mine.

"I know!" I turned to Carrie. "I know why he's doing this to me."

"Who's there with you?" her brother asked. He sounded alarmed. "Look, I know from Pop what you're doing up there. You're in totally over your head. Do you understand what you're getting yourself into . . . ?"

"I have to go, Jack. But it's okay. I'm not—"

"Carrie, listen to me. I'm starting to get concerned that all this has gotten to you. After what happened to Rick and Raef . . . If you've got something to share, it's time to turn it over. To me, or to the JSO. But you can't be putting your neck out, least of all with someone like this."

"Steadman didn't do it, Jack." Again, her gaze locked onto mine. "This other guy did. Hofer. I'm positive."

I grabbed her phone and put my hand over the speaker. "I have these pain centers. Hofer asked about them. We prescribe Oxy, but only with a doctor's scrip. But a lot of the others are merely shills, storefronts . . ." The color drained out of my face. "Somehow he's blaming me for what's happened to his daughter!"

"I'm sorry, Jack, but I gotta go," Carrie said, taking back the phone. "Don't do anything. I'll call you later, and when I do, I'm gonna be able to prove it. I give you my word."

"Carrie, listen to me, please. This guy—"

She disconnected the line, her face clouded with both resolve and worry.

"You have proof?" I asked.

She nodded, though a little tentatively. "I can get it."

"Where?"

"A couple of hours from here." She started up the car again. "We're going to see a guy about a gun."

"Wait." I put my hand on her arm and stopped her. "Carrie, before you do, there's something you have to know. This guy, Hofer . . ." I took a breath and felt all the anxiety of the last few days finally come to the surface, my whole body going weak and numb. "He has my daughter!"

CHAPTER FIFTY-ONE

Carrie's face went pale. She looked at me, her blue eyes wide, starting to put it all together.

"That's what I wasn't able to tell you," I said. "Why I can't turn myself in. He told me if I did, or if I happened to get caught, or if the news somehow got out about Hallie being kidnapped—he'd kill her! Just like he killed Mike and Martinez. He called me on Hallie's phone—she was away at school—and he put her on. She's terrified, Carrie! You can imagine! She's sure he'll do what he says."

"*Oh God . . .*" I saw her look change from resolve to sympathy and she put her hand over mine.

"That's what I tried to say when I first called you. When I asked about your son. And why I couldn't just give myself in. Any more than I can now. No matter how much evidence we have."

"Why do you think he's so determined to ruin your life?"

"I don't know why! Maybe his daughter came to one of my clinics. You need to have a scrip for Oxy, or be evaluated with a set of X-rays by a doctor, but I don't know, I can't completely control where these things might end up. You know what's going on out there."

"We have to tell Jack," Carrie said firmly. "You can't keep this to yourself any longer."

"No, no!" My heart almost jumped out of my chest in alarm. *"You can't!* You can't!"

"We have to. This is what they do. They're professionals at this. We're just . . . You can't get her back by yourself."

"Can you promise me that word won't get out the minute the JSO finds out I've turned myself in? My name is already on every newscast across the country! You're saying they won't go public when I land in the hands of the FBI? They still think I've killed one of their own! They'll think I just made this whole story up, to shift the blame. I can't live with what might happen!"

"I'm sure I can get Jack to keep it under wraps. These people aren't savages. They'll know what to do. What other possibility is there?"

"I know who it is now. He'll contact me. It's me he wants! Me he's put in this rat's trap. Not Hallie. He's just using her to lure me."

"He'll kill her too," Carrie said, steadfast. "You know he will. You're playing with fire."

I brought my hands up to my forehead. I didn't know what was right. Or maybe I knew what was right, I just didn't want to lose control. Now that I was finally so close.

"Once he tells me where he is, then I can call in help."

"And what if he never calls. What if that phone never rings again. And that's his revenge. How will you live with *that*?"

I didn't answer.

"We need to get the proof," Carrie said, letting her words sink into me. "Once we can prove it's Hofer who's behind it, then you have to let me bring in Jack. Or whoever his team is. I won't walk away from you." She clasped her hand over mine. "I promise. I won't! But this is the only way I can go on with you. This is a murder investigation. I can't withhold evidence. Not if I know—

"You've done everything you possibly can. You found out who it was! But you can't get her back . . ." She shook her head. "Not by yourself. You trusted me enough to tell me this, now you have to trust that we can work out the rest of it. It's the only way."

I think the only thing that scared me more than the unknown surrounding Hallie was the thought of what I would do to get her back once I knew. I also knew it wasn't all my call. Liz had a say as well, and I knew exactly what she'd say. She'd agree with Carrie in a heartbeat.

I nodded, about as halfheartedly as I ever had in my life.

Carrie blew out a breath and nodded too. "We get the proof it's Hofer, and then I call Jack. He'll get her back for you. Are we all right?"

I slowly nodded again, and Carrie squeezed my hand one last time. And I squeezed hers back.

She smiled. "Now let's go see a man about a gun."

CHAPTER FIFTY-TWO

We doubled back to Orangeburg and picked up Interstate 77, which headed north. It was only a couple of hours straight up to Charlotte.

To Bud's Guns. In Mount Holly, North Carolina.

I leaned back and shut my eyes for a while. For the first time in ages I actually didn't feel freaked out. No one would be looking for us in Carrie's Prius. No one had any idea where we were headed.

In a matter of hours, we'd have the proof that Hofer was setting me up.

Carrie turned on the news, and a troubling report came on: I'd been spotted in Orangeburg at the diner. Apparently the waitress, Nanci, had recognized me, after seeing a newscast that evening, and once word got out, the night clerk at the motel did too, and they had found the Lexus I'd stolen.

The report also said that I'd been spotted with a woman. And might be heading north.

Carrie's name would eventually come out.

"Congratulations." I turned to her. "You've graduated from Community Outreach. You're now an accomplice."

"Hopefully not for very long." She smiled at me through her sunglasses. "I intend to set the record straight on that in a matter of hours."

"I'm sorry to have gotten you into this," I said.

"You didn't get me into it. I got me into it. And you know what?"

"What?" I shrugged.

"Whether it's crazy or not, I'm glad I'm here."

"I'm glad you're here too," I said. "Your brother, Jack, however, may not be equally ecstatic when he hears the news."

"I can handle Jack," Carrie said, pressing her lips together. "I always have. Now my dad, the ex-police chief, he's a completely different story . . ."

I dozed for a bit, and when I came to we were on the highway, doing seventy.

"You were out for a while." Carrie smiled, glanced over.

"Guess something's been keeping me from getting my usual eight hours lately," I said back. "Can't imagine what that is . . ."

I looked at Carrie, her pretty blue eyes firm with both determination and resolve, and I suddenly felt something else there, how much courage there was in this tough little package, how much she had risked for me.

"Can I ask you something?" I said.

She shrugged. "Sure."

"I was wondering, what did your brother mean when he said he was worried how everything might have gotten to you. He mentioned Rick. And Raef . . . It made me think, when I spoke to you that first time, you said it was your first day back at the job . . ."

Carrie glanced away, checking her mirror, and changed lanes.

"I know you said you'd tell me, later on, when I turned myself in. But it's not like we don't have a couple of hours here to ourselves . . . *Your husband*?"

"Uh-huh." Carrie finally nodded, letting out a breath. "And my son."

She drove on a ways, still seeing I was waiting for an answer if she felt like giving me one. "Last September, my son, Raef . . ." She drew in a breath. "He was eight. He went into a seizure on the soccer field at school. He lost consciousness. Rick got the call and I was about two hours away . . ."

I nodded.

"I rushed to the ER, but Raef was already in the ICU. A ruptured AVM. You know it?"

I nodded again.

"The doctor said it would be touch and go for the next forty-eight hours. He'd lost a lot of blood flow to the brain. He said Raef was putting up a good fight, but that something else had happened. He sat me down . . ."

She blinked and again pressed her lips tightly together. "Rick was in the OR, undergoing emergency surgery. He had what's called a dissected aorta. You probably know what that is too . . .

"They said he probably had it from birth. Apparently he'd sat down in a chair in the waiting room and all of a sudden he just felt woozy. It had to be dealt with immediately. The procedure took four hours." Carrie forced a smile, different from any I had seen from her thus far. "I had a kid in the ICU clinging onto his life and a husband in the OR who could go either way . . . I kept running back and forth, checking on Raef, holding his hand, telling him to hang on, then I'd would go back up and watch Rick . . ."

I frowned and swallowed. "How did he do?"

"He didn't make it," Carrie said, with the slightest shake of her head. "He stroked out on the table. Like a ticking bomb, they told me. I suppose it could've gone off anywhere. It just happened there. You would have thought . . ." She glanced in the mirror again and shifted lanes.

"Would have thought *what*?" I asked her, noticing the tears shining in her eyes.

317

She shrugged. "Rick did two tours in Iraq. Before law school. He lost a lot of friends there. You would have thought if it was simply a matter of stress, it might've happened over there . . ."

"What do *you* think it was?"

She blinked almost distractedly and shook her head. "I don't know . . ."

She held the wheel with one hand, and I reached out and put my hand on her arm and squeezed. "I'm sorry."

"Thanks. I don't really talk about it much. I suppose it's all still pretty new. Raw . . ."

"I didn't mean to make you go through that."

"Here . . ." She reached behind the seat, pulled out her purse, and opened her wallet. There was a picture of a nice-looking guy with short, light-colored hair, wire-rim glasses, and bright, intelligent eyes. "He was a lawyer," Carrie said proudly. "Damned good one. He handled military cases. Rape. Sexual assault by superiors. Even Don't Ask, Don't Tell defendants . . . He pushed to have them adjudicated in civilian courts. Rick was a stand-up, guy . . . About the most stand-up guy I ever knew."

"I think you do him proud," I said, "when it comes to that measure."

Our eyes met, and we didn't say anything for a few seconds. I saw a Florida driver's license next to Rick's photo. "You mind?"

She shook her head.

I pulled it out. With my new cropped hair and glasses, I kind of resembled him.

"I should probably take that out now," Carrie said. "I guess it still makes me feel like he's still here. There are times I just want to feel close."

"I think you should keep it there as long as you like," I said. Our eyes met. "I think you'll know the right time." I was about to put the photos back in her wallet. "So how's your boy doing?"

"He's doing great," Carrie answered with a resurgent smile. "He's back at home now—at my parents' actually. He suffered some cognitive loss that they've been working on at the hospital, as well as some motor paralysis on his left side. But he'll be back to school in the fall. Little guy's the love of my life. But you must understand that, Dr. Stead—"

She caught herself, in an awkward pause. "Sorry."

I looked at her. "You think it's time you start calling me Henry? Nothing special, it's just that I kind of let everyone who saves my life call me by my first name. It's a rule with me . . ."

Carrie smiled, brightness coming back into her face. "I don't know. Maybe we should keep it like it is for now . . ."

"You're right. Anyway, *Doctor* Steadman will probably get us a better table at the Denny's in Mount Holly if we have lunch there . . ."

319

Suddenly I realized what the answer to my question about Carrie was.

It had to do with what I had said to her that first time I called in that somehow made her trust in me and look for that car. When everyone else had me tried and convicted as a ruthless killer and just wanted to bring me in.

I had asked if she had kids . . . And now I remembered, after a long pause she had answered yes, she did, a son. Her first day back, from such an abominable tragedy . . .

And then I had said: *"Well, then you'll know exactly what I mean . . ."*

Then I swore, on Hallie—the love of *my* life—that I was completely innocent of all the things they were saying.

And somehow that had cut through all the convincing evidence and the rush to judgment. And it had made her believe me. In spite of everything to the contrary. All the evidence, all the crimes Hofer had managed to pin on me—

"What?" Carrie glanced at me staring at her, and it suddenly was like she was reading my mind as she smiled, a bit fuzzily. "So you want me to tell you what it was? That made me believe you that day. Seems a little stupid now, in light of everything, but—"

"No." I shook my head at her, smiling. "I think you just did."

CHAPTER FIFTY-THREE

Mount Holly was a sleepy North Carolina town, like so many I'd been through lately. We made it there by 2:30 that afternoon.

Around Charlotte, the traffic narrowed to a single lane, a bunch of police lights flashing. Carrie pushed Rick's license back to me, saying, "You may want to hold on to this. And while we're at it, maybe this too." Underneath it was Rick's business card.

Worriedly, I started thinking maybe those sightings of me were more dangerous than I'd thought.

But it was just an accident. We passed right on through the line of police cars. The road was clear the rest of the way.

Bud's Guns was located in a small strip mall on the

outskirts of town, in between a wheelchair outlet and a Dairy Queen.

"Ready?" Carrie asked, parking the car and reaching around to the back for her file of photos and my iPad. She took in a breath.

"Totally ready," I replied.

Carrie went into the store, the iPad armed with two bookmarked photos: one, from the *Jacksonville News*, of me, which must have been found on my website. Clean-shaven, smiling, confident, the way I looked just days ago.

And the other of Vance Hofer, which I had taken in my office three weeks before.

I followed her in, but stayed back in the aisle.

A barrel-chested, wide-shouldered guy with curly reddish hair and a thick mustache was behind the counter, just hanging up the phone. Carrie went up to him, resting my iPad on the counter.

"Help you, ma'am?" the amiable gun dealer asked with a wide grin. "Hope I'm not saying something wrong, but you look like just the kind of gal who'd line up pretty nicely with an extended-mag TEC-9."

"Already got one." Carrie smiled, as if he had compli-mented her hair. "You the owner?"

"That be me." He nodded. "Bud Poole. And you . . . ?"

"My name's Carrie Holmes." She pushed her sunglasses up on her head, all business. "I'm with the Jacksonville Sheriff's Office." She flashed her JSO ID.

"Jacksonville, you say . . . ? Been getting a bunch of you folk up here these past few days, you must know what I mean . . ."

"I do . . . Hope you don't mind if I ask you some questions . . . You were at the Mid-Carolina Gun show a few weeks back?"

"I was." Bud nodded again. "Make it every year . . . Some of my steadiest customers are up there . . . But somehow I thought this business was all wrapped up . . ." He shifted a little uncomfortably.

"Just a question or two. Kind of a follow-up. You were the dealer who sold the gun to Henry Steadman?" Carrie opened her file. "An H and K nine-millimeter . . . I can show you a copy of the invoice here . . ."

"Save the effort," Bud said obligingly. "Everyone in the damn country has seen that invoice by now. That was me." He shrugged, his ruddy face sagging a little like an old orange. "Look, I told all this to the people who were up here before. I always do things by the book. Anyone got a problem with it, write your congressman and change the law . . ."

"I assure you I'm not up here to hassle you about sidestepping some red tape, Mr. Poole . . . I just want to show you a couple of photos, and ask if you'd be kind enough to let me know if you recognized the person you sold the weapon to."

"Hard *not* to recognize him," the dealer grunted. "His face's been on the evening news as much as that guy

323

Gadhafi. But like I've been saying to anyone who'll listen, I was busy; it was crowded that day. You make a lot of quick sales at these shows. Everyone has a way of melding together . . ." Bud glanced up and saw me in the aisle. "Feel free to look around. Be with you in just a moment . . ."

"I'm sure they do." Carrie nodded. She placed the iPad on the counter and brought up the photo of me. *"Is that him?"*

Bud stared, fingers rubbing his chin. "I keep saying, could've been in a cap or a beard or something. Or sunglasses. My reputation is my Bible, I always say. But yeah, looks like the guy."

"You're pointing to a picture of Dr. Henry Steadman," Carrie confirmed, "of Palm Beach, Florida, who's been accused of committing those killings down in Jacksonville."

Bud shrugged again. "I can't exactly vouch for what people chose to do with 'em once they pay me the cash."

"Or I'm wondering, is it possible it could have been *this* man that you saw?" Carrie said, switching to the second image on the iPad. "I just want you to look again and think back carefully. I understand that you were very busy . . ."

This time she showed him the photo of Vance Hofer.

Bud didn't have to say a word. His eyes pretty much told it all, fastening on the new face, flickering in surprise and then thought, nodding.

"Just take a close look. I know it's hard to admit you might have been wrong . . ." She switched back to the photo of me. "But what if I told you that *this* person, Dr. Henry Steadman, was actually in South Florida on the day of that sale, operating on a patient in the morning and in meetings for much of the rest of it?"

Bud bunched his lips.

"But that *this* man . . ." She switched again to Hofer. "*Vance Hofer.* Is there any chance, Mr. Poole, that it might have been *this* man who bought that gun from you that day?"

He drew in a deep breath, his ruddy complexion replaced now by a dim pallor, staring and seemingly reevaluating. He tapped his index finger on the counter.

"No one's trying to get you into any trouble, Mr. Poole. Like you said, you did exactly what was required. But I'm sure there are security cameras somewhere that might show Mr. Hofer coming into the hall that day. And not Dr. Steadman. So which person was it," Carrie asked again, "this man or *this* one?"—flashing once more between the two. "Truth is, we're going to have to clear it up at some point, whether here or in front of a jury, where you'd be under oath."

My blood began to race in anticipation, vindication only seconds away, as I watched the wall of Bud's conviction begin to crack, and he cleared his throat, the lump in it almost visible.

"Guess it coulda been *that* guy . . ." he said, flicking

his index finger toward Hofer's photo. "Like I said, it was crowded, and it's always a good show for me."

A sense of elation surged through me.

"Sorry"—Bud scratched behind his ear—"if I gave anyone the wrong impression."

"No worries." Carrie turned and shot a happy glance my way. "I have the feeling you've made at least one person very happy today."

CHAPTER FIFTY-FOUR

For Vance Hofer, there was only one place to go. One place where he felt at home and knew that no one would find him.

He had driven for hours, with Steadman's daughter asleep in the backseat, her wrist bound to the door in his old cuffs from his days on the force, her ankles tied.

When he finally turned on the old familiar road, pulled up to the remote, ramshackle house, the last place he had been before it all fell apart, everything suddenly felt right to him.

It looked a little the worse for wear, the grass over-grown, the porch sagging and stripped of paint, no one doing the chores for a couple of years.

But he'd been happy here.

"Wake up now, darlin'," he said to the girl in back.

327

Vance was proud of how he'd set everything up. Lifting him, he felt, from the speck-like unimportance of his life's past mediocrity.

He was proud, after his visit to Steadman, about the way he had found her up at college as she was coming from the stables, about how he had posed as an admiring spectator who was watching her ride. A picture of perfection if he'd ever seen one. Unlike his own daughter, who's only after-school activities, he suspected, had taken place in the boys' bathroom of the local high school.

And he was proud about how he'd followed Steadman as he got off his plane that day, giving Martinez the heads-up about what he was driving—that fancy white Caddie—and when Martinez might expect him by. How he'd stayed a short distance behind all the way from the airport until he saw the flashing lights and sirens.

Watching it all beautifully unfold.

Surely there were bad things that were a part of it too. Martinez. Vance thought of the cop's look of befuddlement when he turned and saw Vance pull up beside him.

The gun in his face. No clue in the world what was happening. *And then pow. . .*

And Steadman's friend. In that fancy house. How Vance had found him at his desk, the garage door left open, after polishing up his clubs . . .

They would require some lengthy conversations with the Man Upstairs.

But Vance felt he'd done his share of good as well,

bringing ol' Wayne and Dexter to mind, plus that Schmeltzer maggot. Ridding the world of vermin like that surely cleaned it up a lick, and might earn him, he hoped, upon his ultimate judgment, the smallest measure of thanks for making the world a better place.

But he always knew . . . Always knew sooner or later that they'd come for him. Fellows's call showed him that.

Yes, he'd done it well. Still, that didn't quite make them even.

Not quite yet.

He opened the door to the back and uncuffed the girl's wrist. "*What?* Where are we?" the frightened girl called out, pulling back from him. "What are we doing here? Get your hands off me!"

He didn't care—she could kick and scream all she wanted. She could scream until she was blue in the face; there was no one around to hear. He cuffed both her wrists, then picked her up and carried her into the woods, kicking overgrown branches and brush out of his way, a place he hadn't been to in a couple of years but that used to be home to him. He found the shed. There was a lock on the door. His own lock. He set her down and opened it.

"No, no," the girl said. "I don't want to go in there. I don't—"

"Better get used to it," Vance said to her. "It all gets interesting from here."

He picked her up again and kicked the door open, flicking on the one light. Many of his old tools were still on the walls. It was dark and damp, with cobwebs all over.

He opened the storage hut.

"No, no, please," she begged, shaking her head. "What are you doing? Don't. Not in there . . ."

"What'd you think, you were here on vacation?" Vance grabbed her wrists and undid the cuffs.

Pretty as a picture, he recalled. The horse and rider coming around. The beating of its hooves. The rider leaning. Toward the jump. The graceful bunching of the muscles in the animal's hind legs, then leaping, clearing, horse and rider frozen momentarily in midair. Then the landing on its forelegs, without missing a stride.

"What are you doing? What are you staring at?" she asked, trembling.

Pretty as a picture, right?

Vance was all set to throw her into the dark compartment, when that gave him an idea.

CHAPTER FIFTY-FIVE

Carrie and I drove from the gun shop into the center of town, where we got a coffee and sat in the small green off the main street, under a stone pillar commemorating the town's World War II dead. It was a warm afternoon. A couple of kids were riding their bikes, BMX-style, up and down the stone steps. A woman on a nearby bench was feeding a few birds. All around the square and main street was the languorous still-life of the South.

The sudden proof Carrie had just gotten made me both elated and a little scared. Now I *had* to turn myself in. That was our agreement. I had to hand myself over to the very people who'd been trying to kill me just the other day. Back in handcuffs probably and in a jail cell. Interrogated in a room, hoping I could convince them, probably the FBI, that they had to hide that I was innocent. Fending off all the media frenzy I knew would follow.

Not even the Jacksonville police could doubt it now.

"So what do you say," Carrie asked, holding her phone. "You ready to do this now?"

"Yes." I nodded, tossing her a halfhearted smile. Then: "*No*. Listen, Carrie, I don't know how I'm ever going to thank you enough for what you've done. Without you, I would have driven away from Fellows's house, not even knowing it was where the plate was from. And I wouldn't have known a thing about Hofer. I'd still be driving around, confused and panic-stricken."

"You found Fellows yourself. And you would have found Hofer. Let's just say it was a team effort." But I could see the sense of satisfaction on her face too. "So I'm going to call Jack. We're going to explain it to him. From the start. I'm going to ask him to send a team, maybe out of the Charlotte office. We can arrange to meet somewhere neutral. Maybe in the lobby of that motel over there . . ." She pointed toward a Comfort Inn. "Or maybe outside of town, so it doesn't create a stir."

"We can't create a stir, Carrie."

"Or get the local police all involved. That's just what we need, right?"

"Then you can go back to your life . . ." I said. "Community outreach."

She looked at me. "I made a decision. I think I'm

gonna put in for something else. Maybe a detective's shield. It's what I wanted to do all along, I just put it aside while Rick finished up school and then got called up in the reserves . . . What do you think? You think I've got the goods?"

"I think you've got *all* the goods," I said, unable to stop myself from smiling.

"If the JSO doesn't toss me in jail, just on principle . . . *You* might well get out first."

"Look, when this is over . . ." I didn't know quite how to say it. "I'd like it very much if . . . if we could . . ."

"Still pushing for a client?" Carrie's blue eyes twinkled playfully.

"No, that's not what I meant. I . . ."

She stopped me. I saw my own feeling reflected in her expression. "I know what you meant, Doctor . . ."

"*Henry*."

"Henry." She shrugged and smiled, this time, from the heart, and I felt my whole being—the one that had been alone and in the dark, separated from any connection for the longest time—light up like a warm lamp had just gone on. She said, "I hope you get your daughter back, Henry. I'd like to meet her when you do."

"I'd like that too."

"I'm going to call now . . ."

"Okay . . ." I exhaled a breath and nodded.

Carrie shrugged. "This is either going to be one of

333

the most fulfilling things I've ever done—or one of the dumbest. Here goes."

She smiled, punching in her brother's number. We both waited with a bit of anxiousness for him to answer. I know *I* surely did. Carrie looked at me, this time not turning away.

Then I heard someone pick up and Carrie went, "Jack."

She cleared her throat. "Jack, I have something to tell you . . . Yes, I'm okay. I'm in Mount Holly, North Carolina—it's about twenty miles out of Charlotte. And I have Dr. Henry Steadman with me. I want you to know—he didn't have anything to do with the crimes he's been accused of and we now have the evidence to prove it. He's ready to turn himself in. But before you do anything, you have to listen . . ."

I drew an anxious breath and looked past her, toward the main street of the small town where we had left Carrie's Prius, as I went over in my mind what I was going to say.

My thoughts suddenly took the oddest turn, and I found myself recalling images from my marriage with Liz. How I had failed to keep it together. Regardless of whose fault it was. How I had just drifted ever since. Never quite put to the test. But now . . . I looked at Carrie. She curled her hair around her ear as she went on with her brother. Now I was somehow being given a second chance. How life does that. How it provides many chances. Chances to redeem oneself. How—

Suddenly a phone rang in my pocket. Not my cell. One of my prepaids!

Hofer!

I pulled it out while Carrie was on the line with her brother. I saw Hallie's number.

"Hallie?" I gasped.

"Hey, Doc," I heard Hofer reply.

My blood instantly heated, just hearing his voice. "Where's my daughter?" I barked at him—though in some deep place in my heart, I already knew.

"Oh, sorry, Doc," Hofer said, sighing, "she's no longer here."

335

CHAPTER FIFTY-SIX

Bud Poole got on the phone after the woman from Jacksonville left.

He just wasn't sure if he should call his lawyer first—or the police!

He chose the police.

It had been a strange conversation right from the start. Showing him those photos— Steadman and that other guy. Hofer. And how she wasn't even a detective, just some employee at the sheriff's office down there. No badge, only an employee ID.

Even if he had gotten a little carried away with all the attention about Henry Steadman . . . he knew it had shaken him up, thrown him off his game.

And then that other guy, the one who was milling around the aisles. He and the woman had come in together. He remembered how their eyes clearly ran to each other's after he looked at that photo. There was something between them. He saw it. And then the guy looked up and Bud got a good look at his face.

Henry Steadman.

When they left, Bud went to the door and watched them climb into the same car . . . A white Prius.

This was the biggest news Mount Holly had seen since snow.

The lawyer, he could come later.

He punched in the number, and when the duty officer answered, "Mount Holly Police," Bud asked for Lieutenant Pete Toms. Shit, he could've asked for practically anyone there—he'd sold them all a weapon or two over the years.

"This is Lieutenant Toms."

"Pete . . ." Bud said. "Bud Poole. Over at Gun World . . . You're not going to believe who I just saw! That guy from Jacksonville. Steadman. Who's wanted on those murders?"

"Bud, you seem to be seeing him everywhere," Pete replied with some levity.

"I know. I know. But this is different! He just drove away in a white Prius. With Florida plates. He's with a woman. This is for real, Pete," he said, almost huffing on the words. "They just left my store!"

337

CHAPTER FIFTY-SEVEN

I froze, as if a syringe of ice had been injected directly into my veins. "What do you mean she's no longer here?" I shouted into the phone in alarm.

"What'd you think this was—some kind of game?" Hofer said. "I told you, didn't I? You go to the police, you knew what was going to happen. Still have your old cell phone? Take a look. Picture coming through now . . ."

No. No . . . I almost retched right there. How could he have known? Was it Fellows? But he could have only told him Carrie and I were up there at two different times. I grabbed my cell from my pocket. "I didn't go to the police. I swear! What did you do to her, goddammit? What did you do?"

My phone vibrated in my hand. I saw the message come through from Hallie. Tears of helplessness started to burn in my eyes—and of fear. Fear at what I was about to see.

My own daughter. . .

I pressed the open option. The photo flickered for a moment, uploading; then it came in.

It was Hallie. *Oh God. . .*

But to my joy her eyes were open and she didn't appear to be harmed.

Her mouth was taped and her eyes were focused in anger and humiliation, and there was a sign hung around her neck. In her handwriting.

Just kidding, Dad.

My pulse started to calm, like a tide receding, but then the relief turned immediately into rage. "You sonovabitch, Hofer."

Another pause. This time I realized I'd made a mistake. Saying his name. Telling him that I knew. But I didn't care.

"Oh, relax. I was just trying to get a rise out of you, Doc. You can be sure, the call will be for real soon enough. Maybe even tomorrow. So you know who I am, huh? Well, all congratulations to you."

I turned back toward Carrie and she noticed the pallor on my face. I mouthed a single word to her. *"Hofer!"*

Her eyes went wide. I heard her tell her brother she needed a minute, that she'd call him right back.

"Yeah, I know who you are, Hofer. And what you've done. I know it was you who killed Martinez. And Mike

Dinofrio. I know you bought that gun pretending to be me. That's where I am now. Up in Mount Holly. I also know you knew Martinez from back when you were on the force, and that you knew Fellows from work—and that you got the license plate from him. I even know why you did it—your daughter. Because you somehow blame me for what happened to her. And I hope it was worth it, Hofer, because however long it takes, I'm gonna find you myself and wring the life out of you!"

He snickered. "You've been a busy little bee, haven't you, Doc. A busy, busy little bee. But hell, there's only one thing missing. You're up in North Carolina, and all the fun's going on down here. And you don't know where we are."

"What do you want from me, Hofer? Give me my daughter back. Please . . . What do you want me to do?"

"I want you to know what a man is truly capable of, when you take everything he has away from him. What it used to mean to be human."

"I didn't do any of that to you, Hofer."

"Oh, yes you did. Yes, you did do it to me, Doc. You may not fully know it, but you damn well did it and profited from it, probably laughed about it at parties or bought some fancy car from it, it's all the same to me. The man who looks away bears all the guilt of the man who sins. Just like all the rest, Doc, you are accountable . . ."

"The rest . . . ?" He was rambling. What did he mean by "all the rest"? Who had to be made accountable?

"In fact, you are the very source of it, Doc. The heart of the beast. Whether you knew or not, that's no matter. It came from you."

"What are you talking about? What came from me?"

Suddenly I realized what he meant. The OxyContin that his daughter must have been on. At the time of the accident. Had it come from me? Had he traced it?

I felt sickened.

"I'm sorry, I'm sorry about what happened to your daughter. I'm sorry if I played a role in it. But let it be over now, Hofer, please. You want me. I'll go wherever you want. Just tell me where to find you. I give you my word. But Hallie's innocent. Just let her go."

"I'm not getting through to you, Doc. A little baby was killed. Along with her mother. *They* were innocent. Not your little Hallie. They were the ones you made bleed."

"No. It wasn't me. Your daughter did that, Hofer. And surely not Hallie. Please, I'll come to you. I'll do what you want. Just let her go."

For a moment I thought I might have him convinced. In the background I heard my daughter whimpering. He may be crazy, twisted with blame and guilt. But there might still be some speck of human feeling left in him.

"Don't worry, Doc. I've got something nice cooked

up for her. And soon. But for now . . . remember, our arrangement's still on. You remember that, don't you, Henry . . . ?"

"I remember," I said, squeezing my fists, feeling the blood come to a stop in my veins.

"I don't have to remind you, do I? How I'm gonna start with her feet, Doc, by skinning them, and then I'm gonna skin my way all the way along her back up to that pretty, little neck of hers . . ."

I clenched my teeth. "Oh God, you sonovabitch, please . . ."

"And I'll be thinking of you, Doc, thinking of how you poisoned my daughter, every inch of the way. Thinking of how you caused those deaths, and knowing I'm doing good, every second I watch her die. You hearing me right . . . ?"

"Yes, Hofer, I hear you. Just don't touch her. I'm begging you."

"But don't worry. Show won't start until you're here to see it. I promise you. I'll call you again, and we'll figure how we can pick up on that discussion. About the role you might have played in my daughter's life. About accountability. Your daughter and mine . . ."

"Let me talk to her again," I said. "I've done everything you asked. Let me talk to Hallie again. Please . . ."

"Nah, you just get a move on, Doc. Worry about keeping yourself alive. 'Cause you just told me where you are. Bud's Guns, right? And as soon as I get off this phone, I just might dial up the police up there and tell them who I think might be in their town . . . Just for the sport of it. And that would mess up all our plans. Wouldn't it, Doc? Mr. World-Famous Surgeon."

I didn't answer.

"*Wouldn't it?* Mess up all our plans. Must be a bad connection. I didn't hear you."

"*Yes,*" I said, looking at Carrie, seething, "it would."

"Now shoo away. She'll be all right. Least for a spell. I'll take care of her, like she was my own. So best get yourself along . . . Before you don't have any choice. Ta-ta, there, Doc . . ."

I heard one more chuckle and then the line went dead.

CHAPTER FIFTY-EIGHT

"What did he say?" Carrie asked.

"He played a sick joke on me. He told me she was dead. He's going to do it, Carrie, if we don't find him soon."

"I'll call Jack back."

"No." I put my hand on hers, stopping her in mid-dial. "Not yet. He warned me not to do it. There were others, Carrie," I told her. "Martinez and Mike were shot. But he said he'd skin her like the others . . ."

"*Others?*" Carrie's eyes grew frightened. "Oh my God! He's going to kill you, Henry," she said, looking at me. "You know that, don't you? And then he's going to kill her."

"He's got my daughter, Carrie!"

She took my hand and made me sit down. My legs

felt rubbery. Just feeling her steady grip, her smooth fingers massaging and warm . . . it made me feel stronger, like there was some way out of this. "We're going to find a way to get her, Henry. We've got to let him think he's got his way with you. And *you* have to keep demanding proof that she's okay. We're going to get her back. Soon as you give me the go-ahead to bring in people who can handle this kind of thing."

"I don't know," I said, thinking of Hofer's promise. "What if they bungle it? Or if word gets out of what they're planning? Then Hallie would be dead. I couldn't live with that. Think about Raef, your son. What would *you* do?"

I saw by the silent breath she drew that she knew exactly what she'd do.

I had to stay out.

I also knew there was no way we could remain here in Mount Holly. Carrie had already told her brother where we were. If she didn't get back to him, he'd surely get the local police involved. And I didn't know if Hofer had been for real when he said he would alert the local police. It sounded just like him! Then I realized, Carrie had given her brother Hofer's name.

They knew about him! They could easily go to his home. I suddenly realized I might not be able to control the FBI.

I was about to tell her this, that she had to doubly

warn them—not to do anything—when I looked past her, to where we had left the car on Main Street.

My stomach fell off a cliff.

Two local cop cars had stopped next to Carrie's Prius, and a couple of officers were inspecting the car. The plates.

They were on their radios.

"Oh, shit!" My eyes stretched wide.

"What?" Carrie muttered, turning around and saw for herself. "Oh, Jesus, no!"

I think it dawned on both of us at the same time that everything was about to change. That she couldn't cover for me anymore and I couldn't remain here. Not for a second longer. No matter what we had proven. I had to run, and Carrie . . . *couldn't*. I didn't know if it was her brother who had called it in, or Bud. Or Hofer . . . It must have been Bud, I realized, if they knew which car to look for.

But it didn't matter. All I knew was that if they caught me, Hallie would be lost!

I got off the bench, my heart in a frenzy, and started to back away, my eyes fixed on the two cops, their patrol car lights flashing. A small crowd had gathered around. Flashing lights clearly weren't routine here. It would only take a minute for them to scan the area and spot us here.

"I've got to get out of here, Carrie."

She nodded, not trying to stop me. *"Go.* I'll do my

346

best to cover for you, Henry. I'll have to say something . . . I'll explain it the best I can to Jack. About Hofer and Fellows and Martinez. I'll say we split up when I told you that you had to turn yourself in . . ." She had a look of helplessness on her face. But behind it, I saw something deeper. She was scared. *For me.*

"Don't try and call me," she said. "I have your number. The one you called me on at the diner. *Henry . . .*" Tears welled up in her eyes. She was as terrified as I was, and I could see that a part of her wanted to take off with me. My heart was going *ka-bang, ka-bang* against my ribs. If we had seconds more, I would have gone up and hugged her right there. Carrie glanced around at the cops. "You better go . . ."

Suddenly one of them looked our way. He saw us! He put his hand over his eyes to shield the sun. I saw him motion to one of his partners.

"Henry, just go!"

CHAPTER FIFTY-NINE

I ran.

Actually, I started to back away at first, across the green, hoping not to draw any attention. I kept one eye on the policeman who was staring at me suspiciously, no doubt starting to realize that Carrie and I fit the description he'd been given. My other eye was on Carrie, with a sinking feeling in my stomach that I had to run away. I'd only known her, really, for a day, but having to take off, so suddenly, after everything she'd done for me, was tearing at my heart.

Then suddenly the cop called to his partner and took a couple of steps in our direction, and I bolted across the green. Behind me I heard one of them shout: *"Hold it there!"*

The street was heading toward the main road out of

the town, mostly fenced-in yards and old Southern homes, and I didn't see any cover, other than weaving in and out of people's yards, hiding, until I was ultimately caught. I ran onto a small bridge that crossed a river leading into town and peered over the edge, hearing shouts behind me, The small, narrow river ran parallel to Main Street.

I took a quick glance back at the officers, who had now set off after me, Carrie going up to them, and leaped over the stone ledge onto the embankment, slipping on the dry, loose dirt and sliding down the edge, about twenty feet down. I landed on the rocks of the riverbed there, which was more like a narrow stream.

This was insane! I was running from the police all over again. They didn't know anything about Vance Hofer or Bud's Guns. All they knew was that they had a wanted murder suspect here. In their little town.

They could very well start shooting at me!

I looked back up to the bridge and didn't see anyone, but I knew that was only a matter of seconds. The word had probably already gone out to every cop within two townships! I didn't have a clue where to run or how to get out of here. Not just out of this riverbed, but out of town. *Out of the area!* All I could think of was that if I got caught, in this Podunk place—the famous plastic-surgeon murderer!—there would be no containing it. They'd be crowing to every news station in the

349

country! And even worse, Hallie would be at the mercy of that monster.

I couldn't even let my brain wander there!

The river cut behind the main street and I knew, if I kept along the rocks, I'd be in full view and they'd track me down in minutes. It must've been a dry spring here because the river seemed more of a stream and offered no protection either.

I saw a giant, iron spill pipe along the bank, maybe six feet tall and rusted—it seemed to open directly under the bridge. I wasn't sure where it led—only *away,* and that was okay with me. In about ten seconds cops were going to be all over me. I pawed my way down to it, scrabbled over the rocks, and made it to the opening in the pipe under the cover of the bridge, and ducked. The opening was large, about two inches shorter than I was, at six-two height, and I quickly found myself in the cool, dark, iron-smelling cavern just as the two cops who were pursuing me must've gotten to the bridge and peered over.

I heard shouting above me.

It was dark, clammy, and creepily cool in here. I had no idea how far it led or where to. There must be a bend somewhere. I couldn't see an opening at the other end. It was at least a quarter mile. There was a layer of filmy water on the bottom; my moccasins were soaked, not exactly cut out for this kind of thing. I went along in a crouch, a hand on each side of the pipe, knowing that in a couple of minutes the cops would make their way behind me, and praying, my heart ricocheting against my ribs, that there wouldn't be a party to meet me at the other end, complete with dogs and brandishing rifles.

I tried not to imagine the kinds of creepy things that called this place home: spiders, leeches, even rats . . . "Oh God, Henry, how have you found yourself in this fucking mess?" I said, my words echoing against the sides, which were rusted and slick with moss and metallic smelling.

I was about a hundred yards in when I spotted the light of an opening at the other end. I didn't know if I felt lifted or afraid. I just knew I had to make it there before the cops crawled in after me or radioed in re-inforcements.

Okay . . . As the light grew larger I racked my brain for what to do. The thought flashed through me that I could climb out of this tunnel and duck into the woods for a while. Maybe I could call Carrie and she'd be able to find me . . . Then I thought, *Henry, who are you kidding? They'll be all over here, and you're not exactly an outdoorsman.* Liz always joked how I'd be voted off *Survivor* before the first commercial . . .

And there was still Hallie. If I was apprehended, it would be a death warrant for her.

The sad truth began to sink in that, sooner rather than later, I'd be caught. I'd be kept in jail in this stupid town until I could be handed over to the Jacksonville police. No one was going to listen to me; they would only believe I'd concocted this story to save my own skin. By the time they found out that I was telling the truth, Hallie would be dead.

Hofer was going to win.

No, no . . . *You're not going to let him win, Henry . . . You're going to find a way out of this and get to Hallie . . . Do you fucking hear?*

A voice echoed behind me and I spun. The bright circle at the entrance had disappeared and someone was screaming, "*Police! Steadman!* Whoever you are, get down on the ground! There's no way out!"

His words reverberated against the walls.

In front of me the opening looked about fifty yards ahead.

I didn't know if they would shoot. They still weren't a hundred percent sure who I even was. But these small-town cops might well be itching to pull a trigger. I crouched lower and picked up the pace, the opening in front of me growing larger. And then I could see rocks straight ahead, where the pipe met the river, and my heart picked up and I even heard the sound of rushing water.

I heard someone yell, "*Shit,*" maybe a hundred yards behind me. It might have been the heavy one, taking a tumble in the murky water. Meanwhile my feet were cold and soaked, and the opening was in front of me. I had finally made it to the end.

Cautiously, I stuck my head out, and to my joy, I heard nothing—no shouts to get down on the ground! No dogs barking. *No sign of police.* The river wound its way behind the main street, and I could see the backs of shops up on the hill above me. I heard the sound of water picking up speed. I climbed out of the pipe and onto the slick rocks and looked down.

I was on a kind of elevated levee, a makeshift dam with a fifteen- to twenty-foot drop-off to the level below. The town was directly above me, an easy climb back up the rocks. But there were cops up there to contend with. I scurried along the shore, slipping on the slick, wet rocks, until I got close to the edge. I straddled the dam along the embankment, spray rushing up at me, hitting me in the face. I noticed two anglers a couple of hundred yards down the stream, their lines in the water.

I couldn't get across here.

I could jump. I looked over the edge. The rocks were larger and jagged below. But I could do it! I could let the river take me. *But where?* I thought of the movie *The Fugitive.* Harrison Ford had jumped. From a much higher and more dangerous height than this. Into the swirling spray. And the river had taken him. But that was Hollywood. These fishermen would only point out my escape. Assuming the police didn't witness it themselves. They were only a short way behind.

No, I had to make my way back up into town.

I looked up and saw the back deck of the motel Carrie and I had passed while driving through town. I balanced along the edge, took off my jacket, and hurled it as far as I could into the river. It landed in an eddy and managed to catch on a rock. I hoped it might distract them for a while. Make them believe I had jumped, and spend some seconds looking for me.

Then I started to paw my way up the sharp embankment, groping at rocks, weeds, anything that might hold me.

If they came out now, I'd be a sitting duck. I made it to the top and hurled myself over a small retaining wall onto a gravel patch underneath the motel's concrete foundation.

My breaths jabbed like needles in my lungs.

I looked below and saw the two cops who had been chasing me finally emerge from the pipe, shielding their eyes and looking up the embankment, gingerly making their way along the rocks over the dam, scanning downriver.

Then they spotted my jacket. The two of them inched closer to the river's edge and got on their radios, calling it in.

I could see the two anglers downstream, waving at them. Their words were unintelligible, but I knew exactly what they were trying to tell them, pointing up the hill at me.

Finally grasping it, the two cops looked up the hill,

and I ducked behind some brush and rolled away from the bank.

Someone shouted my name!

I spun, and was face-to-face with another policeman, this one young, crew-cut light hair and sunglasses. Maybe forty feet away. He leaned out over the edge above the embankment, his gun drawn. Shouting down to the other two. *"Up here! Up here!"* He was about two storefronts away, his weapon trained on me.

"Henry Steadman, get down on your knees! *Stop!*"

I stood, completely frozen, realizing that he was at an awkward angle leaning over the edge, still maybe forty feet from me.

And more alarming, every cop in two townships was going to be here in about twenty seconds!

I took off, throwing myself out of his line of sight as the young cop squeezed the trigger, a shot ricocheting behind me off one of the posts supporting the motel.

God, Henry, are you insane? He's shooting!

My heart was in a sprint, my thoughts jumbled and unclear. All I could think of was Hallie, and how I had to get out of here . . . And if I couldn't . . .

Well, then it didn't matter what happened to me!

I ran around the side of the motel and hoisted myself over a redwood fence and onto a balcony—the restaurant. I hurried through an open sliding-glass door to the main room, hurrying past a young kid, probably an

off-duty waiter or kitchen help, who smiled accommo-
datingly. "Anything we can do, sir?"

"*No,*" I said, hurrying past him. "No. Thanks."

"Kitchen opens at five o'clock," he called after me.

I rushed out through the dining room, knowing that
the cop who had shot at me was probably only a minute
away, probably followed by several others. Surely the
two who had been in the spill pipe behind me had to
be up here by now as well.

I figured my one reasonable chance was to somehow
get out of town, then call Carrie and hope she could
pick me up somewhere. Or, at this point, hand myself
over to her brother, which all of sudden seemed like a
far better option than ending up in a local jail.

But even that seemed a million-to-one now.

I ran into the main lobby and looked out the sliding
front doors, and saw the cop who had shot at me running
up the driveway, his gun drawn.

Oh no, no. . .

I looked down the hallway and heard the two cops
who'd been behind me in the drain coming up the
outside stairs.

It's over, Henry.

I was cornered. I thought about putting my hands in
the air and ending it all right here. I was so damn beat
from all this running . . . I felt like a prisoner who'd
been forced to hold his arms up, over his head, for
hours, and if he let them drop he'd be killed, and all

356

he wanted to do was let them down, just for a second, to feel what life was like, regardless of the cost or the outcome, whatever fate was in store.

I looked at the guy behind the desk, tears welling in my eyes, and was about to simply say, *It's me! It's me they're here for!* And raise my arms.

Then I realized that I couldn't do that. No matter how much my arms hurt. No matter how long this had to go on.

Because the outcome wasn't about me, but about Hallie.

The cost of dropping them was my daughter's life.

I turned to the guy behind the counter. I said, "Something's going on! There are police all over here. I heard shots. I think the guy they're after is that doctor from Jacksonville. I think I just saw him run upstairs."

The guy looked alarmed and then craned his head to look out the front door, at the policeman coming up the driveway. I went over to the staircase, pretending to head after the culprit, and while the desk clerk's attention was focused on the cop, I ducked down a hallway around the back and found a door marked employees only. Which, thankfully, was open! I slipped through it and found myself in a janitorial staging area, with buckets and mops, shelves stocked with cleaners, and another door that seemed to lead outside to a delivery staging area.

A driverless white van marked CAROLINA PIE COMPANY

was pulled up there, clearly delivering that night's desserts. As I passed by I looked in for the keys.

And then I saw it.

A black delivery guy in a gray work uniform was saying to a hotel employee in the delivery bay, "So this is all, then? Guess I'll see you Monday, sugar." He had a large laundry bin with him, stuffed to the brim with white sheets and linens.

And just outside there was a delivery truck, R&K INDUSTRIAL LAUNDRY, Charlotte, with its cargo door open and a metal ramp leading into the bay. While the driver had the female hotel staffer signing for his pickup, I slipped outside and looked into the truck, its cargo bay filled with identical large laundry bins.

Jesus, Henry, you've got to do this now.

I heard a commotion back inside the hotel—people shouting—and I realized that any second the town's entire police force was going to converge right where I was standing.

I hoisted myself up, crept to the back of the truck, pulled up some dirty sheets from one of the bins, and jumped in, covering myself up.

Now, if the driver could just get on with it and get the hell out of here!

It took a few agonizing seconds, seconds that seemed to stretch into minutes as I lay curled up in the bin, until I heard the grating metal sound of the loading ramp being yanked up and the heavy cargo door slamming shut.

The bay went dark and silent, and all I could do was pray for the driver to get moving!

It seemed like an eternity, and then I finally heard the cab door close and the truck's engine start up. *Yes!* The cargo bin rattled.

Let's go! Get the hell out of here, I begged from inside the bin.

Then the truck lurched forward.

I was sure that at any second I would hear someone order him to stop and the truck brake to a halt.

But I didn't. We just went on. The truck stopped for a second at what I took to be the main street and slowly made a left turn.

My God, Henry, you're going to get away!

I allowed myself a yelp of joy inside the bin as it chugged into third gear and steadily picked up speed, my mind flying back to the motel, which must now be flooded with cops, closing it off from all directions, the three who were first on the scene calling to their partners from the second floor. *"Up here! Up here!"*

I'd made it!

CHAPTER SIXTY

I bounced along for what seemed like an eternity, alternately exhilarated at my escape and petrified that at any second I'd be surrounded by police cars with blaring sirens and the truck would come to a stop.

Joyfully, after about twenty minutes of advancing along slowly and around turns, we went into fourth gear and it felt as if we had now gotten onto a highway.

Probably I-77. Heading back to Charlotte.

I did my best to come up with some plan for what to do. First, I had to get out of the area; then I had to wait for Hofer to get in touch with me. This meant getting myself on a bus headed south, or if I was lucky, doing what I'd done before—finding a car.

Or getting back in touch with Carrie. She would

surely bring the evidence we'd uncovered to the FBI and the police.

But first, I had to call Liz. She was Hallie's mother. She had to know what was going on.

I took my own cell phone—I needed to make sure she would take the call. I was pretty sure the driver wouldn't hear me over the engine noise. It rang a couple of times. It was 4 p.m. and I never knew Liz to leave the office much before six. I knew she'd recognize the number.

Hopefully, it wasn't being monitored by the police!

At last she picked up. "Henry . . . ?"

"Yeah, it's me. Liz, listen, I know who's got her!"

I told her what I'd discovered. About Hofer. And why he was doing these things to me.

His daughter.

The Oxy.

"I spoke with her, Liz. Or at least I saw her." I didn't tell her about the details of the photo. About the ticking clock that was over her head. "She's alive. Probably scared out of her mind, of course. But she's alive."

There was an immediate lift in Liz's voice. "Now we can go to the police!"

"No. We can't. Everything's still the same. I had another run-in with the police. In North Carolina. I was on the line with him and then the cops showed up. It was a million-to-one shot that I got away. You're probably going to hear about it on the news . . ."

"What's that rumble I hear? It sounds like you're in a train station."

"No, I'm not on a train. I'm . . ." I decided not to explain that either. "We still don't know where he is, but I do know he's going to find a way to bring me to him. If we get the police involved now, even in the strictest of confidence, because of how crazy everything is with me, it might blow everything. They may release his name . . . They may still even use it as a wedge to get to me. Anyway, listen, we've already made contact with the FBI—"

"*We*. Who's *we*, Henry?"

"This woman from the Jacksonville Sheriff's Office. Who's looked into my case."

"*A detective?*"

"No. Not exactly a detective, Liz . . ." How could I tell her? That Carrie was from the Community Outreach department. It would make me look like a fool! "Liz, you have to trust me. We're getting close. I don't want to blow everything now. I just don't know how much time we have . . ."

"Henry, I've done nothing for three days! I'm going out of my mind! Now you know who it is. How much longer can you expect me to sit back . . . ?"

"Liz, I'm dying too. I could clear my name in an hour now if I could turn myself in. But I can't . . . I know you have no reason to trust me right now, or to believe me, other than you know that I want Hallie back as

362

much as you. Maybe more! This all happened because of me, Liz. We have to find out where he's got her. Give me one more day."

"Oh God, Henry, you can't be serious, to keep doing nothing. It's our daughter . . ."

"I *am* serious. I'm deadly serious. But until I know where Hofer wants me to go, where he's taken her, we have to keep doing this."

She didn't say anything. I just heard her weeping. My tough-as-nails wife, whom I never saw as much as shed a tear.

"Just bear with me another day, Liz. A day to figure out where he is and what he wants from me. Can you do that, baby? I know what I'm asking you. Is that okay?"

Just then the truck veered to the right and slowed its speed. We were exiting the highway. We were probably nearing its base. In Charlotte.

"Liz, I have to go now. I don't know when I'll be able to call you. But I will. As soon as I can. Soon as I know something."

"Henry, you can't just run out on me like this—"

"Liz, I have to go . . ." We came to a stop. The truck made a right. And then proceeded, as if along an access road. I knew I didn't have much time. And now the driver might easily hear me. I lowered my voice. "Liz, I'm sorry, but I have to run. I'm gonna find her, Liz. I give you my word. Can you trust me on this?"

She sniffled and drew in a breath. The truck went down a short straightaway, never getting out of second gear. I knew we were close. It might be reaching its destination at any second.

Liz said, "Yes. Yes, Henry I trust you. I don't know how much longer I can go on like this, but . . . Get her back for me, Henry. You get this bastard!"

"I will, Liz. I will. You take care."

I pressed off the line. I felt the truck slow and make another right turn. The driver bounced over a speed bump and seemed to pull into a driveway.

Then the truck came to a stop.

My heart was beating with dread. I knew I was in Charlotte.

And there were two possibilities:

Either I'd have to find a way to get back south, where I assumed my daughter was being held captive . . .

Or ten cops would be waiting for me with guns drawn as the cargo bay opened.

CHAPTER SIXTY-ONE

The truck's door rattled open. I peeked out from under the sheet in the back of the cargo bay. Bright light flashed into my eyes.

All I heard was the grating sound of the loading ramp being pulled down to the ground. And the driver calling out to someone, obviously a ways away, "Hey, John. Givens still around? Dude owes me thirty bucks . . ."

"Yeah, man, he's still here. In the spin room. You need help unloading?"

"Thanks. Give me a minute. Need to take a leak."

My blood sped into overdrive. I had to get off the truck before the driver came back. I had no idea where I was.

I climbed out of the bin and crawled up to the front of the cargo bay and looked around. I didn't see anyone.

I steadied a hand on the ramp and jumped down. There were a bunch of similar trucks in the lot and an open slot to a loading bay. I headed off at a steady pace toward the open gate and didn't look back. I didn't hear anyone call. I just walked right through. Like a man leaving prison behind. All the while my heart was thumping.

I took a look around. I was in an industrial neighborhood. Warehouses and light manufacturing businesses. Queen City Restaurant Supplies. J. Crawford and Sons Glass. One thing I did know. We weren't more than a half mile from the highway.

I picked up my pace, hoping no one called me from behind. *Hey, you! You there. What are you doing?*

I let out a loud sigh of relief when I was sure I was free.

I had about sixty bucks left. And no jacket. I had flung that into the river. It was March, and it still got chilly at night. And no more iPad. That was back in Carrie's car. No good to me now.

I could make my way to a bus station and try to hop a bus. But the police might be watching and that would mean putting myself on the street for a while.

I spotted an Exxon station a couple of blocks away. And a sign for I-77, heading south. I saw an overpass and figured that was the highway straight ahead.

I hurried over to the station, figuring I'd use the restroom and find something to eat. That maybe I'd just put my thumb out on the entrance ramp and try my luck.

When I got to the gas station, three cars were filling up. I went into the men's room and splashed cold water over my face, still reeling from the harrowing escape I'd made, and still surprised to see my newly cropped hair and glasses.

In the mart, I grabbed a hot dog and a coffee. I got on the cashier's line.

There were two TV screens above the counter. One was a black-and-white security camera that showed who was coming in and out. I turned my face away. The other had on one of those courtroom reality shows. Judge Roy Brown. As I got to the front and dug in my pocket to pay, a breaking news flash interrupted the programming. A local announcer came on: "This just in . . . Dr. Henry Steadman, wanted in the shooting deaths of a Jacksonville Florida police officer and a local lawyer, was said to be spotted today right here in North Carolina, in the tiny town of Mount Holly, thirty miles east of Charlotte. News Four has received word that a chase *did* ensue with the police, and that shots were fired. There is no word of whether Steadman is in police custody. And there is said to be a female accomplice apprehended there as well. That's all we have for you right now. More on this as it comes in . . ."

I saw my picture flash on the screen. The way I looked a week ago—longish hair, dark glasses, a broad smile. *Carrie, apprehended?* My heart sank. Though I knew they would only want her as a way to get to me.

I threw out a couple of bills for my food and nodded agreeably when the heavyset guy behind the counter shook his head. "Unbelievable, huh?" he said.

"Yeah."

"Better hope he doesn't come in here, if he knows what's good for him . . ."

I had to get out of there now. Not just out of the city, out of the state. It was only a matter of time before the police put everything together. How I'd gotten away. For all I knew, they were searching the whole area already.

I headed back outside and ate my frank around the pumps, watching the cars pull in and sipping my coffee.

Of course, standard procedure on 99 percent of people pulling into a filling station was to take their car keys if they left the car to go inside. But now and then someone left them in the ignition. I'd surely done this from time to time myself.

And that's what I looked for. I mean, I was smack in the heart of the Deep South, right? Everyone was trusting here . . .

The next two or three drivers just filled up their tanks and didn't stray far from their vehicles. A middle-aged woman in a Honda drove in, parked, and went inside the mart, but took her keys with her.

This could be futile.

But then a heavyset black guy in long denim shorts and an oversize Hornets jersey drove up in a gray Buick.

I watched him start to fill up his tank, the keys still in the ignition, then, almost as if it was an afterthought, take a run into the station. Maybe to pay. Maybe to buy a Ring Ding or something. Or use the john.

I tossed my coffee in the garbage and meandered over to his car. I saw the keys still in the ignition. I felt like a creep, loitering around, but I had no choice. Hallie's fate necessitated it. I glanced inside but couldn't see the guy. Maybe he'd gone to the john.

I didn't care.

I disconnected the pump and hopped inside his car. No one seemed to notice.

Heart racing, I hit the ignition and pulled out of the station. If anyone had seen me, no one ran after me. No one shouted.

I hit the light as it was just turning yellow and made a sharp right, following the sign to I-77.

I shot on the ramp for the highway, heading south, whooping with relief and exultation.

In twenty minutes I'd be in South Carolina.

CHAPTER SIXTY-TWO

Carrie was held in the chief's office at the local police station in Mount Holly, looking at pictures of Chief McDaniels fishing and with his grandkids, until they squared her story with the Jacksonville police.

Hours.

Around six, she heard some discussion going on outside. The door opened, and her brother, Jack, stepped in.

He was the last person she wanted to see. "Before you even go there, Jack . . ." Carrie stood up.

He had one of those reproving-older-brother looks on him, like when she'd drunk a few too many beers back in high school (he was always the straight one) or when she left their bathroom looking like a shit storm had passed through it. Except this time it had kind of melded with one of those serious, more official looks Jack had learned at the FBI.

He sank into the chair across from her. "What the hell were you doing, Carrie?"

"He didn't do it, Jack. No one back in Jacksonville wanted to hear me. You can check with this guy Bud at the gun store in town; where Steadman supposedly bought that gun. He never did. Vance Hofer bought it. *Here . . .*" She handed him a piece of paper she'd taken from her bag, Henry's daily schedule for March 2, which he had e-mailed her. "If anyone had done their homework, they'd have known that Steadman was in Jacksonville operating that day . . ."

Jack looked it over, scratching his bushy hair and squinting his intelligent brown eyes.

"It's all pretty clear, Jack. In fact, Hofer just called him earlier today. I have photos of his car in the vicinity of both murder sites. We traced the plate on the car to one of his work buddies. He knew Martinez from that incident you described, and he also knew when Steadman would be in town, and had Martinez stop Steadman and come up with this song and dance about talking back, maybe just to razz him at first, and then he killed him. He also killed Steadman's friend. He admitted as much to Steadman. And apparently there are others as well . . ."

"*Others?*" Jack put the schedule back on the table.

Carrie nodded. "You already know about his daughter.

371

He claims he traced the OxyContin back to a clinic owned by Steadman, so no doubt there are a few gaping holes in the chain of supply that may turn up somewhere. And there's motive. His life was in shambles. The last straw was his daughter. He twisted the blame to Henry—"

"Henry?" Her brother raised an eyebrow.

"Gimme a break, Jack. If anyone back in Jacksonville was doing their police work, they could have found the car at both scenes. They could have checked that Steadman was at his office the day the gun was supposedly bought. They could have asked where he would possibly have gotten a gun, just getting off a plane. Instead of running around pulling triggers . . . Check with this gun-store guy Bud in town. He'll tell you—"

"I've already spoken with Bud," her brother said. He let out a breath and loosened his tie. "Chief McDaniels said he was the one who alerted him, so I stopped on the way in. I also traced that plate back to a guy from that metalworks factory, where Hofer worked—"

"So then you know! You know Steadman didn't do it. So stop making it out like I'm protecting some kind of insane double murderer. I was only doing what the guys with the gold shields back home should have been doing. It was all a setup, Jack. He could be dead . . . *Henry . . ."* She swallowed grudgingly, correcting herself. "I mean Steadman."

"Attaway." He winked at her and smiled.

"But it's gotten deeper, Jack. A lot deeper . . . No one will tell me anything. What's happened? I need to speak with him."

"*Don't.* I've spoken with the JSO. In light of all this, they've agreed to rescind the arrest warrant against Steadman. I mean, *Henry*"—he smiled—"to merely a person of interest and hear out his side. Which should clear him, Carrie. We'll put out a joint APB on this Hofer and—"

"*No, Jack, you can't!*" Carrie's blood rose with a jolt of panic. "You can't release Hofer's name! Like I said, everything's changed. That's why Henry had to run. He got this call—from Hofer. The first one was before I even spoke with him. Back in Jacksonville. Then another this afternoon. Just as I was talking to you about bringing him in."

"What call, Carrie?"

She hesitated, not knowing what was right, pushing the hair out of her eyes. "I don't know, Jack, I can't—"

"*What* call?" Jack shifted closer, his eyes growing more serious. "Sis, I've gone to bat in some pretty serious ways to get you off the hook on this and not any face local, not to mention federal charges for, say, harboring a fugitive, or transporting one across state lines. Abetting a fugitive in the commission of a crime is a—"

"*Jack!*" Tears rose up in Carrie's eyes, tears of confusion and frustration. "You don't understand . . ." She drew in a steadying breath, unsure of what to do.

373

She'd given her word to Henry. But she didn't even know where he was; if he'd been caught or not. Or hurt. No one was giving her any information. Ultimately she had to trust Jack. That he would do the right thing. Henry's daughter's life depended on it. She was almost shaking. "Jack, I have to have your trust on what I'm going to tell you. You need to give me your word."

"*Sis* . . ." Her brother leaned forward and took her hands, which were now trembling ever so slightly, and he squeezed them in his own. "I know you're involved, but if you can't trust me on this, who the hell are you going to trust?"

Carrie closed her eyes and let out that breath she'd been holding in for hours Then she nodded. There was nothing else she could do.

She told him. About Hofer's call when Henry had fled to his friend Mike's house, moments after finding his body. *"How you enjoying this so far?"* And then today. About him having taken Henry's daughter, and what he had threatened to do if word got out. What he had done to others . . .

"He's crazy, Jack. He'll do everything he says. Whatever you do, you can't let his name get out, or else . . . He'll kill her, Jack. *He will!*"

"I understand . . ." Jack nodded, his brow furrowed in thought. His look seemed to say, *No good choices here.* "I'll talk to the sheriff's office. Let me see what I can

374

do about keeping this all under wraps. We still have to find this guy, though . . ."

"Jack, once it leaks out to the press that Henry's no longer a suspect, you know there'll be no stopping them. *Hofer will know!*"

Jack nodded, tight-lipped. "You may have to spend the night here. The JSO is on the way and I'm thinking they may want a word or two with you. Sorry to make you stay here and check out Chief McDaniels' two-foot bass a little bit longer . . ."

Carrie forced a tight smile, not feeling much like laughing. "Thank you, Jack, but the JSO—"

"I've already spoken with them. I think I can assure there won't be any charges, if it all checks out."

"All right, but . . ."

" 'Course, I can't say how they plan on handling the matter internally. Still"—he stood up—"unless they're as dumb as bean curds, I can't imagine that they want their investigative teams totally looking like a bunch of asses on this . . . Who knows, you may even end up with a promotion." He grinned and headed to the door. Then he winked with approval. "I know what you need, Carrie. And good work on this. Whatever it was, you did good."

She swallowed appreciatively.

" 'Course, I can't make any promises about Pop's reaction. I'll leave you to square that one with him yourself . . ."

"*Jack . . .*"

IIcr brother turned.

"Where is he? Steadman. No one's told me a thing. He's okay, right?" She looked unsure. "I'd like to see him if I can."

"Is he okay?" Her brother chuckled. "Your guess is as good as mine, Sis. Right now we don't have any idea where he is. He just disappeared."

"Disappeared . . ." Carrie's eyes grew wide, and she was unable to hold back her smile. "You mean he got away?"

Jack laughed. "Canny little bastard, huh? We're thinking in a laundry truck. We're checking now. But I damn well know where *I'd* be headed if it was Cara who'd been taken and I'd gotten that call."

CHAPTER SIXTY-THREE

I pulled off the highway near Columbia and spent the night in the parking lot of a Fairfield Inn, a couple of miles from the University of South Carolina.

I was glued to the car's radio, and caught several updates on the incident in Mount Holly, but nothing about a car being heisted at a gas station in Charlotte, so hopefully no one had put that together. I desperately wanted to call Carrie, to let her know how I'd gotten away and find out what she'd told the police, but I didn't know if she even had her phone and I didn't want to put her, or myself, at further risk. I didn't know if the police were still chasing me or still believed I was guilty. I only knew I had to find Hofer—*and Hallie*—before the police found me. Before Hofer followed through on his threat!

And as I sat there, huddled in a car in South Carolina, not knowing what my next move would be, not knowing if every cop in the state was looking for my car, I did think of someone who might know where Hofer was.

His daughter. Amanda.

I did the old McDonald's drive-through thing again for breakfast burrito and located the nearest library, and I was at the small stone building when it opened at 10 A.M.

The woman at the information desk pointed me to two computers in a kind of reading room, a bunch of magazines and newspapers arranged neatly on a round table. The old, large-monitor Dell warmed up creakily, taking me to the state library homepage. I clicked over to Google and typed in "Amanda Hofer."

Dozens of items came up. The first, from the *Lancaster County Crier*, which I assumed was the hometown paper.

"LOCAL TEEN, 19, KILLS MOTHER AND BABY"

Then below it: "Said to be on Painkiller at Time of Accident. OxyContin and Xanax Linked to Auto Double Homicide."

Farther down, "Local D.A. Seeks Murder Conviction in Tragic Double Homicide."

I scanned the details, about how elevated traces of OxyContin and Xanax had been found in Amanda's blood as she drove to her cosmetology class that morning. How she had been seen driving erratically through traffic. How she had driven right off the road and onto the victim's lawn, bouncing off a tree and right up to the house, where she mowed down Deborah Jean Jenkins and her two-month-old son, Brett. How the child's father was in the army serving in Afghanistan and had never even seen his newborn son in person.

As I read the actual details, my heart filled with compassion for this man, and for a moment I had to stop and take a couple of breaths, my thoughts finding their way to Hallie, who was around the same age as Amanda Hofer.

Then I scrolled farther down and found what I was looking for in the *Atlanta Constitution:*

"TEEN AUTO KILLER PLEADS TO TWO COUNTS OF AGGRAVATED VEHICULAR HOMICIDE. RECEIVES 20 YEARS"

It showed Amanda, drawn and pale-looking, as she was led from the courthouse.

To begin her sentence at the medium security Pulaski Women's Prison in Hawkinsville, Georgia.

That was exactly what I wanted!

I switched to the website for the Georgia State Prison System, clicked on "Women's Institutions," and immediately found Pulaski. It wasn't far from I-75. A two- or three-hour drive from where I was.

Visiting hours were from 11 A.M. to 4 P.M. All visitors had to present a valid photo ID.

I reached into my pocket and pulled out Carrie's husband's license that I had taken.

And his business card. *Attorney-at-Law.*

I knew it was a long shot, but that's all I had right now.

I looked again at Rick's face. Okay, hardly a perfect match—I had blue eyes; his were green. His hair a bit lighter.

Still, it could work. I mean, we weren't exactly talking the supermax at Florence, Colorado, here . . . This was a medium-security women's prison in backwoods Georgia. Probably a work-farm facility.

And it had to be the last place on earth anyone would be looking for me.

CHAPTER SIXTY-FOUR

Vance Hofer stood above the circular saw in the remote woodshed. He eased a two-by-four along the line, splitting it seamlessly down the grain line. He liked how it felt, like he was back at the mill before everything fell apart. He used to come out here back then, and his wife, Joyce, would make something cool to drink and Amanda would bring it out, asking, "What are you making out here, Daddy?" and he would just go, "Nothing. Just thinking." The bright sparks and whine of the serrated blade were like a hymn in church to him, making his thoughts clear.

He raised his goggles and wiped a thick mixture of sweat and sawdust off the back of his neck.

Vance accepted that his time had come, but he had one final act to see through. *They may build but I will tear asunder*, the Good Book read. *They may repent, but all judgment is still mine.* He knew he had done things to warrant judgment. Some had seemed to rise up from someplace deep inside him, like steam from somewhere deep in the earth. And some just felt justified. But this last thing . . .

He had decided that Henry Steadman was the root of all that had gone bad in his ruined life. The man had no true sense of what he had done, no deep contrition. Only selfish regret at having lost his easy life. And so he had to pay, like the rest had paid. And Vance had devised something good, something that would make him beg and cry before he died. That was a vow, Vance reflected as he eased another plank through the blade. One he'd take to the grave.

He gathered the remnants into a pile, the smell of raw, split pine like incense to him. He brought them over to the chipper. Not a big, fine machine, like what they had had at the plant, which could reduce a full-grown tree to pulp as fast as you could feed it. But it would do what he asked of it. Vance felt there was a beautiful magic to the job it did—the way it transformed something palpable and real one minute into the smallest of inalterable parts the next. It hummed as it chewed up the disparate pieces, raising a foul-smelling dust like vapor.

Purification in its truest, most elemental form.

A shout came from the locker in the back room. He

almost didn't hear it over the chipper's noise. *"Please . . . Please . . ."* the girl called out. "Let me talk to my father!"

"Keep quiet, child, if you know what's good for you," he called back, feeding the split pieces of wood into the chipper's mouth. "You hear I'm busy."

His own daughter was no better than a whore and deserved all that fate had levied on her. Still, life didn't degrade its victims in a vacuum, Vance thought. Evil had to be drawn out of you, by an agent, a snake. And then let loose in the world. And then the only way to remedy it was for it to be purified. As well as all who had touched it. That was the only way to make it go away . . .

He fed the split wood into the machine, rendering it into its natural, purified state.

Pulp.

He had never fully appreciated the wonderful magic of it until now.

From the shed, the girl cried out again, only a muffled noise above the chipper's grating whir. Truth was, he could hear it all night and it wouldn't sway him now.

"Let me out. I'm begging you. Please. Let me call my father. He'll give you whatever you want. Can't you hear me in here? *Please!*"

Go at it all you want, Vance said to himself. *That's about all you have left in this world. And don't worry, you'll see him soon enough. That I promise.*

383

She yelled and yelled again as he continued feeding the wood, returning it to its natural state. Eventually her voice became like daggers in his ears. Reminding him of things he didn't want to hear. Things he had put away forever.

He paused the chipper with the foot pedal, got up, and went over to the locked shed door, and slammed on it with all his might.

"Shut the hell on up, Amanda!" he yelled.

CHAPTER SIXTY-FIVE

Pulaski was a three-hour drive.

I'd called and left my name with the visitors' center, identifying myself as Rick Holmes, an attorney from Jacksonville, and saying that I wanted to meet with Amanda Hofer. I stopped at a men's haberdashery store and picked out a sport jacket straight off the rack along with a white dress shirt. I wore them out of the shop.

The prison came up out of nowhere, about twenty minutes south of Macon, a town I recalled from my Allman Brothers stage, and was ringed by a barbed-wire fence and a handful of guard towers. The only times I'd ever even been inside one was during med school, at Vandy, where I did some procedures on inmates, but not like this.

Of course, this wasn't exactly San Quentin and we

were in the middle of nowhere, and Amanda Hofer wasn't exactly the Unabomber—not to mention that I was relying on the fact that no one ever assumes someone is trying to break into prison.

At just before 1 p.m. I left the car and headed toward the main entrance. Inside, on the left, was a sign marked VISITORS. My heart started to pound. At the counter, I waited behind an African-American family; the mother, in jeans and a tight halter top, seemed to know her way around, and her two talkative boys in NFL jerseys. I told myself to calm down. When they were done, I stepped up to the heavyset woman in a khaki guard's uniform behind the counter.

"Richard Holmes. I'm here to see Amanda Hofer."

The guard checked over the log. "Are you carrying any firearms or any other weapons? If so, you'll have to check them here."

I shook my head. "No."

"Any food, paraphernalia, or materials you're planning to leave with the inmate?"

Again, I shook my head. "No. None."

She began to fill out a visitor's form. "May I see your ID?"

I pulled Carrie's husband's license from my wallet and passed it across the counter, along with his card, identifying me as an attorney, and waited, sure that the guard was able to hear the bass drum that was booming in my chest. If there'd been some kind of meter measuring heart rate or agitation aimed at me, the needle would be off the chart!

Instead, she just looked them over, glancing at me once, and slid them back. No request to see anything else. No alarms sounding—or guards rushing out with their guns drawn.

Just: "Up from Florida, huh? Warm down there as it is up here?"

"You got off easy," I said with a grin, sure it was a trick question, and realizing I hadn't checked the weather back there in days.

The guard laughed. "Wait till July and you won't be sayin' that . . ." Then she got on a mike. "Can you bring up 334596 to Booth Three?" she asked, then pushed across an admittance form for me to sign.

I was in!

"Go through the door on the right and down to Booth Three," she instructed. "Remove anything metal from your pockets inside. Enjoy your visit." She looked beyond me. "Next in line . . ."

I went through the door and then through a security station, with a metal detector and a long metal table, like I'd seen in courthouses. I emptied my pockets: just my three cell phones and my wallet. Another guard checked my paperwork and then pointed me through. "Down the hall. Booth Three is on the left."

I took my things and proceeded down the hallway. I came upon a row of ten or twelve visiting booths—four-foot-wide compartments with microphones and a Plexiglas wall separating the inmate from the visitor.

I went over for about the tenth time how I was going to play it, hoping it would work. I had absolutely no idea how Amanda would react. But I was here. I'd gotten this far. And Hallie's life depended on it.

A door on the back wall opened and a pale-looking girl in a purple jumpsuit stepped in. She looked across the glass and clearly didn't know who I was or why I was here. For a split second I thought she might turn around.

But she didn't. Two khaki-clad guards stood against the wall. Amanda Hofer shuffled over and sat across from me. She wasn't bound, and her face was kind of gaunt and pale. Her light brown hair was straggly and held in place by a band. Her eyes were kind of dull gray and like a deer's, fearful and mistrusting. She didn't look a day older than Hallie and my first thought was that I couldn't help but look at her as any father might, thinking, *Jesus, twenty years. . .*

"I know you?" she asked blankly.

"No." I passed her Rick's business card. *Come on, Henry, pull this off!* "I'm a lawyer. From down in Jacksonville." She looked it over, more like an uncomprehending kid than a drug-hardened felon.

"I never been to Jacksonville." She shrugged, looking back at me, and said in a deep drawl, "So why you here?"

I had practiced over and over on the long drive down how I would handle this, even though I knew from the outset that it had a slim chance of success.

"I'm a claims attorney," I explained. "There's been a settlement in a court case from years back. Involving your father." I knew about the situation down there with the police. "Vance Hofer, correct?"

"That's him," Amanda said, kind of indifferently. "What he do, win the lottery or something . . . ?" She curled an amused smile.

"No, nothing fancy like that. But there might be some kind of restitution for him pending. I just need a sign-off on some paperwork. Problem is, we've been trying to locate him, with no success. Three ninety-four Partridge Row? In Acropolis?'

"That's where we live. Where we used to live anyway," Amanda corrected herself. "Just a trailer. We lost our home a few years back. After my mom died."

"Sorry." I tried to find a way to win her over. "I was hoping you might help me out. We've called; sent a registered letter. He hasn't responded. It's pretty important actually. We've been down every other path."

"Truth is, I don't have a clue in hell where my father is, Mr. . . . Holmes. Nor would I give a damn even if I did. I'm afraid you've wasted your time coming all the way up here."

I frowned. At least one thing was clear—she surely

wasn't covering for him. "Do you mind if I ask when the last time you saw your father was, Ms. Hofer?"

"*Saw* him . . . ?" She bunched up her lips. "Months. Not since my trial. Bastard hasn't shown up here once. S*poke* to him . . . ?" She shrugged. "Maybe a month or so ago. He called. He sounded pretty strange. Like he had made up his mind on something. Haven't heard from him since. The sonovabitch could be dead for all I know or care. Sorry—but we're not exactly a Disney World commercial, he and I . . . You know what I'm sayin'? Hope you got a million bucks lined up for him, Mr. Holmes. Would serve him right if you did and he was dead. And me . . . Well I sure as hell won't be spending any of it anytime soon. Sorry . . ."

She put her hands on the counter, about to get up.

"You must have some idea. Did he say where he might go? Or do you know where he could have headed? This is a matter that has to be taken care of now."

She shook her head. "I wish I could help you, Mr. Holmes, but—"

"*Please. . . .*" Our eyes met and I knew she heard the desperation in my tone. "Please, just sit down . . ."

Haltingly, Amanda let herself back down in the chair, looking at me even more curiously. "You're not exactly sounding very legal-like there, Mr. Holmes, if you know what I mean . . ."

"No." I nodded, swallowing. "Truth is, I'm not." I

took a breath. "And my name's not Holmes. I only used his card and ID as a way to get in here. I needed to talk with you, Ms. Hofer . . . *Amanda*, if that's okay . . . Because someone's life depends on it. Someone very close to me. Just hear me out. Then you can go. *Please . . ."*

She didn't respond one way or the other, but she continued to sit there, curling her hair with a finger, her dull, dishwater-colored eyes growing slightly more alive and interested. "All right."

I lowered my voice. "Whatever you may think, please don't react or get up. Just let me tell you why I came. My name is Steadman, Amanda. *Doctor* Henry Steadman. Does that name mean anything to you?"

Her eyebrows lifted in surprise, and she looked at me closely, offering me a thin, dubious smile. "This is a joke, right?"

"No. It's no joke, Amanda. I wish to hell it was." I kept my eyes on her. "So you know what I'm accused of."

"I watch the news."

"Then you know that the police are looking for me. And then you know I'm putting everything I have on the line to sneak my way in here and talk with you . . .'Cause right now all I have is my freedom. You can turn me in anytime you like. You'll probably get a reward or something. But someone's life is on the line. My daughter's life, Amanda. She's just a year younger than you. Her name is Hallie. Will you hear me out?'

391

She pushed back a strand of hair, shaking her head. "Mr. Holmes or Steadman, or whatever your name is, you must be totally crazy . . ." But she nodded.

"Thank you." I pressed my lips into a tight smile. "I don't know exactly where to begin, and I don't have a lot of time. Amanda, I'm going to tell you some things you may not want to hear. But they're the truth. The gospel truth, so help me God. And the first thing is: I didn't do any of the things I've been accused of."

She curled a grin. "I heard that before. Everybody says that in here . . ."

"I know." I smiled again. "I figured. But I swear it's the truth. And I don't mean to shock you by what I'm about to say next, but it's your father who's done them, Amanda. Not me. Your father had a policeman drag me out of my car in Jacksonville and then he killed him. He also killed a friend of mine in town. To make it look like it was me. He even bought a gun, in North Carolina, at a gun show, and used my name and address . . ."

She drew her eyes wide. *"Why?"*

"I know how this must sound. And I wish I could explain it all to you right now . . . But let it be enough to say that I spoke with him just yesterday, and he's admitted it all—every last detail—at least to me. Somehow he blames me for what happened to you. Because I own a series of pain clinics down in South Florida and he's become convinced that the pills you were on at the time of your accident, the Oxy, came from me. My clinic . . ."

By that point I expected Amanda to shout out for a guard. But instead, her eyes grew wide and a little angry. Not in denial, or at least that wasn't what I was detecting. But in agreement. Corroboration. She shook her head. "That time I spoke with him, he said some things that didn't make sense to me. About how people had to be made accountable. For all they'd done. I said, 'What kinds of things, Daddy? What're you talking about?' He sounded like he was drunk. But he said he wasn't. He just said he was going to be taking care of some things . . . Almost like he was sayin' good-bye."

"Amanda"—I leaned closer—"I know how this sounds, and how hard it must be to hear . . ."

"How it sounds?" She grunted a laugh. "How it sounds is like you're talking about my ol' man. That's all it sounds. I asked about Wayne, my old boyfriend, and he said, 'Don't you worry about him none . . .' He went on about it being him feeding me all those pills. And it wasn't. It kind of scared me. And what's really scared me is I haven't heard a word from Wayne since . . . Not here or even written—"

"Amanda, your father told me that there were others who he did things to. Who he said he made pay. He described what he was going to do to my daughter . . ."

She sniffed and shook her head. "That crazy-ass son-ovabitch . . . He's got a host of hate in him."

"Amanda, that's not all." I hushed my voice and leaned in closer. "I can already prove everything I just told you. And I wouldn't even *be* here if it wasn't that . . ." I drew in a breath. "That it's not just about me. When he called the other day . . . it wasn't just to gloat or ask how it feels that he's ruined my life. He has my daughter, Amanda! He put her on the phone. He has her captive. I don't know where. He wouldn't say. He said he'd let me know when the time was right. But she must be terrified. You can imagine. And he said if I got caught, or if I gave up his name in any way—that he'd kill her. Just like he's killed the others, Amanda. That cop. My friend Mike. Probably Wayne as well . . ."

She sat there staring blankly.

"Amanda, I need to know where he might have her. That's why I'm here. I'm sorry I lied, but I had to get to see you somehow. And I didn't know if you would hear me out or trust me. So you see I'm desperate, Amanda. I'm dying. You must have some idea where he would be. *Look . . .*"

I reached for my wallet and took out a photo. Of Hallie. In a UVA T-shirt, with her favorite jumper, Sadie. Her pretty face all lit up. I think it was the week she got accepted. Every time I looked at it, I could still see all the hope and excitement in her eyes . . .

"She rides. She's expert at it. They want her to compete in college."

Amanda stared at it. Something pleasing and pure in the way she looked at Hallie, almost as if Hallie were some idealized version of who she might've become. If things had been different.

Then she pushed it back under the glass. "He'll do it," she said. "He's just crazy enough to do what he says. I could hear it when he called. It was like he was tellin' me good-bye . . ."

"If he has Hallie, it has to be somewhere remote," I said. "He has to be able to keep her concealed and make sure no one is around to hear—'cause I know my little girl would fight. To the bone. It has to be someplace he'd be familiar with and feel secure. He only saw a photo of her in my office a few weeks back, so I don't think he's planned it out for months. So it has to be somewhere he would know. Can you think of any place? You're my only hope."

Amanda's eyes remained steady, and when she blinked, there was some certainty in her gaze. "He has this place. It's kind of a toolshed, where he would work. For hours sometimes. Back at our old home. In Acropolis." She shook her head. "He was always keen on that place. It all kind of fell apart for my father when we lost it. It was his pride and joy. Bank owns it now; it's at the end of a long road and no one ever bought it, as far as I know. There's nothing around it but wetlands and woods, so there's no one—I don't think anyone even knows it's there. And there's this locked closet, attached, where he would keep supplies . . ."

My heart thumping, I pushed Rick's card back through the glass along with a pen from the counter. "Can you write down the address?"

Amanda shrugged. She started to write—a slow, block cursive, almost like someone who hadn't gone past the sixth grade.

3936 Cayne Road
Acropolis

When she was done, she looked back up at me, her eyes shining now, with what looked like innocence. "His heart is in that place. I can't think of nowhere else he would go."

"Thank you," I said. My chest was expansive. I remained there a moment just staring at her, as she pushed a wisp of hair out of her eyes and gave me a hopeful smile.

And with it, I knew we were both thinking the same thought. *What if it had all been different?* What if she had grown up with someone else, someone like me? And with a sister like Hallie. Would anything have changed?

"I like horses," Amanda said. "There was a time he used to say to me, 'You scamper just like a racehorse, Peachy.' *Peachy,* that was his name for me. 'Cause of my light hair."

Then the pallor of disappointment crawled back into her eyes. "I hope you get him, Dr. Steadman. And when you do, you make sure you do what it is you have to do to get your girl free. You don't hold back for me. That man . . . He wants to hold those to task who are accountable. You make sure you start with him. You make *him* accountable. You do that to him . . . for me!"

I nodded. Then I stood up. "I'm gonna come back and see you again, Amanda. Maybe if this all works out, we'll both come. Hallie and me."

"Maybe," she said, shrugging, and she got up. "*Guard!* In the meantime, you just go do what you have to do to get her back."

CHAPTER SIXTY-SIX

I basically ran out of the prison, my body alive with the possibility that I knew where Hofer was.

I knew I should alert the police. Not the local police, in Acropolis. Not with my name out there as a fugitive and my daughter's life on the line. But maybe Carrie's brother. The FBI. Of course, there was always the chance Hofer wasn't actually in Acropolis at all, and then I'd have nothing. And everything would be blown.

The bastard had made it clear with that photo of Hallie. Whatever he had planned for her was happening very soon. I realized then that there was no doubt in me—none at all—that I was going to go get her myself.

I turned on the car and plugged "Acropolis, Georgia" into the Buick's GPS. I knew it was north and east from the prison, near the South Carolina border. The route came up. It read, two and a half hours. I could drive there first and figure out my options once I arrived. I already felt close to her. *Hallie, I'm coming! You just hang on, baby.*

I felt a power I had never felt in my life take hold of me and it wouldn't let me go.

I got ready to go, but first I found my cell phone and made two calls. The police could come and get me now for all I cared. They could track me down, follow me—I would lead them right to my daughter.

The first call was to Liz. She picked up on the second ring. "Henry . . ."

"Liz, I said that I'd get back to you, and I just want you to know, I'm going to get our daughter."

The second was to Carrie.

My blood was pumping as I punched in her cell number. I didn't care who was monitoring. I didn't care if the fucking FBI was sitting at the table playing mah-jongg with her.

"My God, Henry!" Carrie answered, clearly elated to hear my voice. "I was so worried. I didn't know if you had—"

I cut her off. *"Carrie!"* I knew what she was feeling as she realized that I was alive, because reconnecting with her, I was feeling the same way. "Where are you?"

"Driving back home. The chief wants a meeting with me. I'm halfway through Georgia."

"Turn around."

"Turn around?" She hesitated. "Why?"

"Because I think I found him, Carrie! I know where Hofer is!"

CHAPTER SIXTY-SEVEN

Two detectives from the Jacksonville Sheriff's Office had driven up earlier that morning, and Carrie had pretty much laid it all out for them: Hofer; the bogus gun purchase; his daughter's accident; his relationship with Martinez from years before: and the tapes she had of his Mazda at each of the two crime scenes. As well as his call to Henry yesterday. How could she not tell them, whatever promise she had made to Henry?

And she also told them about Hallie.

Dubious as they were, they listened intently, writing it all down. Every piece of it pretty much exonerated Henry.

And she got their promise not to release anything until Hallie was found.

Now she was making her way back down I-95, back

home, to a meeting with Bill Akers and the chief, where they might well take her report, commend her for finding the truth, then tell her on the spot that she could pack her things and leave . . .

When Henry's call came in. *"I know where Hofer is!"*

"How?" she asked, slowing, shifting to the right lane.

"I went to see his daughter. In prison. It's a long story, Carrie, and you actually helped make it happen. I'll tell you about it when I can. But she told me Hofer has this shed behind his old house in Acropolis. The one he lost after his wife died. Now the bank owns it. No one's living there. She says the place is kind of a sanctuary to him. It's deep in the woods, and has some kind of locked storage compartment attached. That has to be where he is. And where he's got Hallie. I'm heading there now!"

"Wait!" Carrie tried to think it through. If Henry went there alone, he'd likely get them all killed. He was the one Hofer wanted. And calling the local cops to get there ahead, who knew what they would believe or how they would handle it? They might well bungle it. They didn't know the truth yet. This was Jack's terrain. There was also the possibility that Hofer wasn't even there. Then they'd be alerting the police; everything would be out in the open. "Henry, listen, you can't go there on your own. You can't."

"I *am* going, Carrie. Just like you'd be going. If it was Raef."

402

A tremor of apprehension and dread started to quiver inside Carrie.

She had been expressly ordered to stay out of this now. The JSO had a lot of damage control to do. Chief Hall was expecting her in his office. Her cell phone was probably being monitored as well, so in minutes they might know Henry had called. *This is crazy!* She'd be putting everything on the line. Her reputation. Her career . . . the thimbleful that was left of it.

She saw a sign for an exit coming up in a mile. *Hell, she was probably going to get fired anyway. . .*

"Where is it?" Carrie asked, pulling into the right lane. "If you're going there, I'm coming too."

Henry hesitated at first. And she knew exactly why. It was because he knew she would come! It was because he was feeling how she'd put herself on the line for him. And it was because he wanted her there with him.

Why else would he have called?

"You have a GPS," he said. "Head back up toward Augusta and take State Road 24 to Acropolis." He gave her the exact address: 3936 Cayne Road. "I'm about two hours away."

"You're probably an hour ahead of me," she said, looking at the navigation map.

Then she said: "I had to tell them, Henry. All of it. Even about Hofer's call. I'm sorry, but there was no way around it. Now they just need you to come in so they can hear your side. They promised it would all stay inside until I meet with the chief. So you can't do anything till I get there. Promise me that. You'll get yourself killed, and likely Hallie as well. So you just wait for me, and don't do anything crazy. Then we'll figure out what to do, okay?"

"I'm sorry, but I think it's too late for that. I think this already qualifies as crazy . . ."

"Then *crazier*," Carrie insisted. "You hear me, don't you, Henry? I need you to tell me okay."

"Okay," he agreed. But there was something more than acquiescence in his voice. She couldn't put her finger on it, but it was deeper. She felt it. She saw the exit, and readied herself to turn around under the underpass and head back the other way.

"You wait for me, goddammit!"—stopping at the light and plugging the address into the GPS.

CHAPTER SIXTY-EIGHT

The tiny backwoods towns all melded into one. Jessup. Statesboro. Waynesboro. Places I'd never heard of and might never again.

I drove in a daze, fueled by my dread over Hallie and the anticipation of finding her and what I would do when I got there. Once I knew for sure that that's where Hofer actually was, we could turn it over to the police or the FBI. They were the best chances of getting Hallie out of this.

I knew Hofer didn't *really* want Hallie—he was using her to lure me there!

Around 4 p.m., Carrie called again and I seemed to have about a forty-minute lead on her. I tried not to go too far above the speed limits. All I needed was to get pulled over in some local speed trap. And in a stolen car, no less!

Finally, I began seeing signs for Acropolis.

That's when my blood really started to race and I realized I had no idea what I'd be finding there or even what I was getting myself into. I just prayed I'd find my daughter alive.

The GPS told me to turn off onto Seaver Lake Road before I reached the actual town. Part of me expected to run right into a gathering of cop cars and flashing lights, from Carrie's call. But there was nothing out here but open fields, and animal pens and barns. Barely even a road sign.

My nerves began to fray. Hofer had said he would call. So far he hadn't. Did that mean that something bad had happened? What if I was too late? What if Amanda was wrong, and he wasn't even here?

Seaver Lake Road was bumpy and rutted, with weather-beaten trailers intermittently dotting the sides. Flatbed trucks and old-clunker vans pulled up in front of them. Dogs ran out to the road, barking after me. A couple of people who were around stared after the car as I drove by.

At the lake, about a mile and a half down, I ran into Cayne Road.

I was here. I'd never exactly played the hero in life. I played baseball in college, but never got the game-winning hit. I worked on boobs and eyes, never saved a life on the table, never had to risk my own life.

Until now. I was about to face off against someone who had killed, someone who was driven by hate and revenge. I began to think about how terrified and panicked Hallie must be feeling, held captive by someone who was surely crazy. And that fueled my resolve. I still didn't see any sign that anyone had arrived at the scene ahead of me. I thought maybe I should call Carrie and let her know I was here, but I decided just to go on. Hofer had no idea I'd be coming. I figured that was the one thing I actually had going for me. Surprise. I decided I would just get there and make certain they were actually here. Then I'd wait for Carrie.

Hang together, Hallie, I said to myself, seeing a weathered ranch-style house at the end of the long, rutted drive and a mailbox with 3936 written on it.

It won't be long now.

CHAPTER SIXTY-NINE

It might once have been nice; it might have been the home of an actual family. But scrub and tall weeds now covered the yellowed lawn, which clearly hadn't been cut in years. A wire fence bordered the property, sagging at spots where the wind had knocked it down, a wooden gate hanging from its post. It bordered a dried-up field of what might have been hay, and the back was ringed with dense woods.

Amanda said the bank owned it now, but if they did, this was one property they had written off their ledger long ago.

Farther on, on the shoulder of the road, I saw a blue Mazda, the same Mazda I had seen pulling away from Martinez's police car. The same one, I was sure, that Carrie had found on the tapes of both murder scenes.

Hofer was here.

Which meant Hallie was around here too.

I left the Buick on the edge of the road, out of sight from the house. I had no idea if Hofer was inside, or if he'd seen me drive up. Or if he was deep in the woods in that shed Amanda had described.

This is it, Henry. . .

I thought about calling Carrie, but she would only tell me to wait, and my blood was pumping. So I went around the side, hugging the thick brush to stay out of sight. I got about fifty feet from the house, and didn't see any lights. What I did see was a hefty Realtor lock on the front door, making me doubt that Hofer was inside.

I continued around to the back, searching for a clearing in the woods.

I saw a path leading straight from the weed-filled backyard, but I worried I might be spotted if I took it. There was a rotted-out jungle gym in back, and an aboveground pool, filled with crushed pinecones and weeds.

I crept around the side. Twigs crackled under my shoes as I made my own path through the woods, ripping branches out of my way. I didn't know what I would do if I found this shed—only that my daughter was likely to be in it, as was the sonovabitch who had taken her.

You just go do what you have to do to get her back, Amanda

409

had told me. The dead spark in her eyes was unmistakable. *He's got a host of hate inside him.*

I pushed through the brush until I didn't see any sign of the house behind me. My shirt, the one I had worn to the prison only hours earlier, clung to me with sweat.

Then I saw the tiny wooden shed deep in the woods.

No light on inside it.

No sound coming from it.

But I knew they were there. Call it a father's radar.

My heart started to pound. It had a slanted roof and one window and what looked like a storage hut attached to it, as Amanda had described.

The door was slightly ajar, left open maybe in the hope of a breeze to ease the stifling heat. And I knew that's where he was. With my little girl. Only thirty yards away.

I saw a rusted metal pipe on the grass. I picked it up. It was covered with moss and crusted rust.

As I held it, it occurred to me that we all have a certain capacity for violence if you dig down deep enough. If someone threatens what really matters in your life . . . If you went past fear and worry and dread . . .

And Hofer had dug down as deep as was possible in me.

I knew exactly what I would do with that violence if I got the chance.

410

I went back into the woods until I was sure I was out of sight and pulled out my phone.

I relished saying the words I'd wanted to utter since this whole sick and crazy business started:

"I've got him, Carrie."

CHAPTER SEVENTY

Sonovabitch. . .

Vance leaned against the window, smoking, and suddenly caught sight of Henry Steadman, not forty yards away, hiding in the woods.

Well, whaddaya know. . .

Vance was a man who could read you the name off a dog's collar at a hundred yards at night, while Steadman probably wouldn't know what breed it was if it was sitting on his lap. But there he was, nonetheless—Vance was sure of it—peering at him.

How the hell did he find his way here . . . ?

Vance put out the smoke, went over to the storage closet, and unlocked the door. It was dark and damp in the cramped space, and the girl was both surprised and clearly frightened. She came out kicking and scratching at him. *My, my, such a pretty little thing.*

"What's going on? *No,* get off of me!"

"No whimpering now, darlin'," Vance said, pinning her arms. "You're gonna get to see your daddy just like I told you. Only a little sooner than we thought."

"Daddy!"

Her eyes stretched wide in surprise and Vance could see that she was just about to shout his name, so he hit her across the chin and her cute little eyes rolled backward, a stream of blood coming from her lip, and when she sagged in his arms, he picked her up, rolled off a length of heavy tape, and stretched it tightly across her mouth.

"Now scream all you want, angel. But your time's up. This time it's for real!"

He placed her down against a table, and grabbed the length of rope he had especially measured out, and wrapped the girl's wrists, hog-style, so they were bound in front of her, and then sat her up, a leg on each side of the feeder bench of the circular saw, looping the rope through the winch on the blade's axle and then tugging, making sure it was all tight.

He pulled the starter pedal over to where he'd propped her, slumped forward, and gave it a test run with a little pressure.

The jagged blade whirred and came to life.

Perfect.

He went back to the window and peered out again

for Steadman. He didn't see him right then. Which didn't matter. Didn't matter how he got here or who he brought along.

Or how many of them there were.

He was ready for them all.

He had separated all the chaff from however much wheat his poor life was ever going to produce. *This is all for you, honey,* he'd said to Amanda. I did what I said I'd do. I brought them all to their knees. For you. I punished them all who took away what was yours. Your life to live out. Your innocence. I took care of it, darlin', the only way I know how.

I took care of it for you, Amanda.

He heard the girl moan slightly and start to come back to consciousness. Then he picked up his phone and punched in Steadman's number.

You want to play it out, Vance thought with a smile, staring out at the trees, listening to the phone ring. He checked his gun.

All right, then, let's play it out.

CHAPTER SEVENTY-ONE

I tried Carrie twice—but she didn't pick up. Maybe she was going through a stretch with no reception, which was easy out here in the boonies.

But just as I hung up, my own phone rang.

I was about to say, *Carrie, listen . . . !* When I saw the caller ID: *Hallie Steadman*.

It was him.

I let it ring, nervous that control of the moment had been wrenched from me, not certain what I should say.

Then I realized: *He doesn't know I'm here! He's calling to tell me where to go.* I had the advantage after all.

And I was going to hear my daughter's voice again!

I pushed the green button. *"Yes."*

"Hey, Doc, how's the weather where you are?" Hofer

said with a chuckle. "I said I'd be back in touch. So I'm ready for you now. You want your little girl, don't you?"

"Let me talk to her," I said. "You touch a hair on her head, and I'll kill you myself, Hofer. Put her on."

"In a minute. In a minute . . ." he replied. "So where are you now? I think it's time we meet up again."

"Doesn't matter where I am," I said. "Put Hallie on."

"Well, I hope you're not *too* far away," Hofer said with a drawn-out sigh, " 'cause you'll miss all the fun. It's starting *now*, Doc. As we speak. I was sure you'd want to hear . . ."

"What?" I felt my insides gnash together with alarm.

"Yeah, you heard me. Now. *Here*, say something to your daddy, honey. He wants to hear that you're okay . . . If you can even hear her, over this damn saw . . ."

I heard a chilling, whirring roar start up that sounded like nails being ground up and spit out.

"Daddy!" Hallie's voice came on. "He's going to kill me, Daddy! Daddy, you have to help me, *please* . . ."

"Hallie, you just hold on!" I shouted back, my guts wrenching. My fingers wrapped around the metal pipe.

"Hear her, Doc?" Hofer came back on. "She's saying you better get here quick, 'cause all the fun . . ." The saw blade started to whir again, and Hofer elevated his voice above it. *"It's happening now!"*

I almost lost it, hearing Hallie's cries. I couldn't wait for Carrie anymore.

She would be too late.

"Hey," Hofer said, almost cackling, "don't you want me to tell you where we are?"

I didn't need to know.

It was happening now!

I ran. I clicked off the phone and grabbed the pipe, rage and desperation and fear all jumbled up inside me.

I sprinted out of the woods, heading for the shed's door.

I had no idea what I might have to face in there. If Hofer had a gun, he could just blow me away. I figured I had one thing going for me and that was the element of surprise. If I was even figuring . . . I wasn't thinking of anything except saving my daughter.

Then I heard her scream.

I yelled out, *"Hallie! God help you if you've hurt her. . . ."* Tears flashed in my eyes.

I reached the door, my mind and blood a rampage of wanting to kill him. I bolted through, rearing the pipe above my head, ready to swing at anything that moved.

I saw Hallie—fear and anguish and now shock all over her beautiful face—bound to a kind of bench. A trickle of blood ran down her chin, but otherwise she seemed okay. For a split second our eyes met and it was one of the happiest sights of my life. But then it all fell apart as she screamed in terror, *"Daddy, watch out!"*

I spun, wildly swinging the heavy pipe behind me, hoping to connect with Hofer.

Instead all I felt was a bludgeoning blow to the back of my skull, and my knees buckling gave way, blackness filling my head. I found myself on the floor. I fixed on my daughter and a biting fear ran through me that I had let her down.

And then Hofer stepping over me as I blacked out completely.

"Well, now "we're just one big happy family now, aren't we, Doc?"

CHAPTER SEVENTY-TWO

My eyes opened foggily. My head was ringing, the sound alternately loud and pounding and then distant like in an echo chamber. I didn't know how much time had passed. I was propped up against a wall. I blinked, pain throbbing in my head—then it all came back to me.

Hofer.

Hallie.

Why I was here. I raised myself up, jolted by this body-shaking spasm of dread.

Then I heard his voice.

"I wouldn't get any ideas, Doc. Not unless you want to see your little girl here dead."

The first thing I saw was Hallie, which for a moment felt like heaven to me. She still seemed okay. The next thing was Hofer, positioned directly behind her on the bench, which I suddenly realized was the feeder bench for a circular saw, a gun to the back of my baby's head.

She was trembling. A trickle of blood ran down her chin. "Daddy, listen to him. Do what he says. He's crazy . . ."

"She's right. At least, about the 'listen to him' part. *The rest . . .*" He shrugged. "That you'll have to decide yourself."

"Let her go," I said to him, shifting in pain. I wasn't bound. Just leaned beside the wall against the leg of a worktable. My eyes shot around, looking for something I might use if I had to. I saw an ax, hanging on a Peg-Board. A hammer. Both were far out of reach. "It's me you wanted. I'm here. Let her go. She hasn't done anything to you."

"Oh, that's where you're wrong, Doc. In fact, she's done everything to me. So tell me, just how did you manage to find me?"

"I don't know," I said, shrugging. "Blind luck."

"Don't push me, Doc." His face went blank and he dug the gun into the back of Hallie's skull.

She winced, shutting her eyes, tears escaping from them. "Daddy, please . . . Don't let him do it. *Please.*"

"*No,*" I begged. "Hofer, don't . . . In the name of God . . ."

He wagged his gun at me. I assumed it was the gun that killed Martinez and Mike. "You oughta recognize this little baby, Doc. You the one who bought it, right?"

420

He laughed. "Well, I'm not surprised—I figured that would be the first thing that came out. You have to admit, I did have you all going there for a while, huh? All those things fit together just like honey and a bee. That thing about you in college, at that swimming hole . . . Lord in heaven, how could I even make that one up? So how did you find me? And don't bullshit me, now"—he winked—"unless you want to find your girl's brains all over your lap."

I made a sudden move, and Hofer raised an eyebrow warningly, motioning me back against the wall with his chin.

"Your daughter. I went to see her," I said. "In prison. I posed as a lawyer and told her I had something for you. A monetary settlement. I said I couldn't find you, and she told me you might be here."

"*Settlement?*" Hofer grinned, as if amused. "So where is it? Show me the money?"

I just looked at him.

"Shit, there weren't no money . . ." He grunted, curling a sly grin. "Damn, they will shit on you if you give 'em the chance. The women . . . Nothing you can do about it. You sure you don't want me to blow her head off right now and . . ."

He cocked the gun and Hallie shut her eyes and squealed.

"*No.*" I started to lunge toward him. "*No.* No, please . . ." Tears filled my eyes. "I'm begging you . . . I called

421

the police. There's no way out. Let her go. Let her go and take me. They'll be here any second."

"No matter." Hofer shrugged dully, evincing a slight smile. "Let 'em come. It's over for me anyway."

He looked at me, and for the first time I saw with aching clarity just where this was leading. Where it had been leading from the start. What had begun as a twisted but fatherly attempt to right the wrongs he believed had befallen his daughter had now just fallen into a free fall descent into malice and self-destruction.

"So what do we do?" I looked back at him.

"I don't know . . . Sit back. Wait a spell. Trust me, you're in for quite a sight." He pressed the pedal with his foot and the large saw blade spun into motion. Hallie jerked forward, pulled along on the feeder bench. She let out a scream, terror flashing in her eyes, her arms suddenly dragged toward the blade, held back only by Hofer. *"Daddy!"*

"Stop!" I shouted, lurching toward her. I had to get her out, and I had to do it now. Hofer shifted the gun toward me. I bubbled to the surface out of every pore on me, but there was nothing I could do other than have him shoot me down. I felt shame and anger thinking he had outwitted me. *"Please*, don't, no," I begged, hot tears burning my eyes.

Hofer lifted his foot and caught Hallie by the shoulder. He grinned, all pink in the face and seemingly pleased with the entertainment.

I exhaled a breath, grateful for the momentary reprieve.

I looked at Hallie, who was now sobbing, helpless and afraid, trying my best to convey some ray of hope to her. I looked around the shed and focused on that ax. I'd be shot, I knew, but maybe I could somehow get to him first and free Hallie. I wasn't going to let him kill us without a fight.

"I love you, peanut," I said to Hallie.

She forced a terrified smile through her tears. "I love you too, Daddy."

I inhaled a final breath, seeing the gun at my daughter's back, Hofer's foot bobbing on the pedal, his eyes empty of anything but insane gloating and the urge to see me die.

Which made us equal.

This is it, I said to myself. *Go!*

Then I felt my cell phone vibrate.

CHAPTER SEVENTY-THREE

Carrie jumped out of her car, at the end of Cayne Road. The last time she had heard from Henry was more than forty minutes ago; then she'd gone through a dead patch.

She locked on the two cars. Hofer's, the one she had seen in the two videos. And a gray Buick—the car Henry said he was now driving.

They were both here.

She'd tried his cell a dozen times over the last twenty minutes—and now she felt herself getting scared.

She called Jack and told him her location. He told her not to do anything herself—that he would handle things now and she was not, by any means, to venture in there. But Carrie said sorry, she couldn't promise him that right now.

She hung up with him begging her: *"Carrie! Carrie, listen!"*

Then she called 911 and reached the local police. As calmly as she could, she told them where she was and why she was there. The dispatcher on the other end seemed like she'd never handled any emergency of this magnitude before. No way she understood the gravity of what was happening.

Carrie told her, "You send a team out here now!"

Then, checking her gun, she made her way toward the main house. A red, run-down, ranch-style home. She saw the heavy Realtor's lock on the front door. Didn't see any sign of activity or lights inside.

She didn't like what she was feeling.

Cautiously, she inched her way around back, toward the woods. Where Henry said Hofer's shed would be.

It was dark in there and plenty creepy. Carrie went a step at a time through the dense brush and branches, which she had to clear out of the way. Her pulse pounded like a big bass drum inside her. She had never done anything remotely like this in her life.

She begged her hands to stop trembling.

There it was. Hofer's shack. A thin glow of light coming from the window. She looked around. *Henry, where are you?*

"Henry?"

A feeling of dread fell over her as she slowly advanced. The door was ajar. She didn't hear a sound coming from inside, which made her heart beat only faster. She thought about waiting for backup to arrive, then she thought something terrible might have already happened, and she couldn't take it any longer.

She was ten feet from the door. *Henry, you better not have done anything stupid in there. . .*

CHAPTER SEVENTY-FOUR

My phone vibrated three times and then it stopped. I had no idea if Carrie was nearby or out on the road. Or if she had alerted the police, which now I was praying she had.

I glanced at my watch, thinking that if she was forty minutes behind me, she might already be here.

Which meant she'd seen the cars. And when I didn't answer the phone, she would put it together.

This might be my way out!

Hofer sat there with the calm, resigned look of a man who had already made his pact with God. No matter whom Carrie had alerted, I glanced at my daughter and knew that this was going to end badly.

"I'm sorry." I looked at Hofer. "For what I did. To Amanda. I'll do anything I can to make it up to her.

She'll be out— she'll have a life at some point. Let Hallie go. I'll make sure she has whatever she needs . . ."

"You're talking money?" Hofer said.

I nodded. "Money. Education. Whatever she needs."

Hofer scratched at his orange hair, for a moment even seeming to consider it. Then he snickered, kind of fatalistically. "You're a doctor. You're smart. I thought you'd see by now . . ." He looked back, tossing me a wistful smile. "This don't have nothing to do with my daughter anymore. Or yours."

"Then what *does* it have to do with?" I shouted back, looking at my daughter helplessly bound, her body just feet from that blade. "What? *What?*"

"*You, Doc.*" Hofer's pink face grinned. "It's about you. Maybe it started like you said . . . Back at some point, it made sense, how people just dragged my little girl down the wrong road. But then it kind of hit me—in that fancy office of yours that day, where I guess you now know I went to do this then, looking at all those pictures of your beautiful life and all your fancy degrees—how people like you, it all just came so easy, didn't it? Whereas people like *me* . . ." He arched his brow. "Well, let's just say, things went a different way.

"And then I started to realize there, how every step of the road, every time I thought I might just make it, there was always someone like *you* blocking the way. Whether on that police disciplinary board that started it all going; or at the mill when they closed it up; or at

428

the bank or the medical insurance company . . . Someone is always there with a smile and a handshake before they take whatever you have, every last piece of dignity and humanity. See what I mean? And that's what you are, Doc—someone standing in my way. Yes, my Amanda's troubles may have led back to you. But I know if it wasn't you, it would've been someone else. But it's kinda nice, how it all just came together, staring at your little girl here in your office . . ."

"Let her go, Hofer," I begged him. "You started all this saying it was about making the right people pay. Well, make me pay. You wanted me. I'm here. Look at her." Hallie was trembling in his arms. "She's just a kid. Just starting out. You and me, we've seen where life goes. I'm begging you. She didn't do these things to you. There must be some shred of mercy and feeling left inside. Let her go . . ."

"You make a good case . . ." Hofer bunched his lips, as if weighing my plea. "But sorry, ain't gonna happen, Doc. Ain't how it's gonna go."

That's when Hallie started to whimper.

I looked at her. "I'm so sorry, baby . . ." I wanted with everything I had in me to reach out and hold her in my arms. "I'm so sorry I dragged you into this."

"I'm sorry too, Daddy," she said back. Tears were streaming down her cheeks. "I knew you would come for me. I never believed for a second you had done those things . . ."

I smiled. "Of course I would come for you, baby . . ."

Hofer wrapped his meaty forearm around her shoulder. "Well, nothing left but to get on with the festivities, don't you agree . . . ?"

He leaned against the pedal and gave the blade a whir.

I couldn't wait any longer. I couldn't just sit here and let him do something horrible to my daughter. I jumped up, determined to do anything I could to protect her, and made a lunge for the ax on the wall. As my fingers got within a foot of it, I felt a burning blow rip into my side, throwing me back against the wall and onto the floor, my hand at my side.

Blood all over it.

"Daddy! Daddy!" Hallie screamed hysterically.

"There ain't no chance," Hofer said, almost as if he'd been taunting me to go for it. One hand holding Hallie, the other wagging the gun at me. "Only reason you're still breathing is I want you to see what happens next. *Angel* . . ."—he hit the pedal, the blade jumping to life—"say your prayers, if you have any. But it was sure nice watching you ride . . ."

"No!"

He was about to release her, her arms already jerking forward, when the shed door crashed open.

Carrie stood in the doorway, her arms extended, her gun trained directly at Hofer. At his head, as his body was completely blocked by Hallie.

430

"Let her go." Carrie's gaze was like a wall of stone, reflecting some part of her being I hadn't seen before. "You let her go now, Hofer, or so help me God, you'll die here on the spot."

She glanced my way for only a fraction of a second, her eyes widening at the sight of my hand holding back the blood. Then she shifted back to Hofer.

"*Die here* . . . ? Oh, you're just a little late to the party, darlin'. We're *all* gonna die here! Me. The doc." He dug the barrel of his gun into Hallie's skull. "Sorry, you too, angel . . ." Then he shifted his gaze back to Carrie. "And you! The only real question is how that's gonna happen, and where . . ." He stepped on the saw pedal and the jagged blade began to rev and whir like an engine starting up, Hallie lurching forward with a scream. " . . . That's where we still have a few things to discuss."

"There's nothing to discuss," Carrie said, squinting through the sight, taking a breath. *"You let her go."*

Hofer grinned at her. "You better be confident, darling. Right, Doc? That's your little girl's life she's playing around with." He wrapped his arm around Hallie's neck and drew her near. "Even if you happen to hit me, for her sake you better be damn sure I don't fall forward and my foot happens to find that pedal and I let go . . .'Cause if it does . . ." He shook his head grimly. "Well, let's just say you don't want to be responsible for such a sight. Would she now, Doc . . . ?"

Carrie's eyes shifted slightly in my direction, and I had no choice but to nod ever so slightly.

Then she went back to Hofer, pulling back the hammer. "I am confident."

Their gazes met, Hofer snorting and shaking his head. *"Well, then . . ."*

Carrie squeezed, her finger barely moving, the recoil jerking under control.

Hallie screamed, and for a second I was sure she had been hit, and I lunged . . .

Hofer's head barely flinched.

He still had the same, smug expression on his pink face, though his head snapped back ever so slightly, and a dime-size black dot appeared out of nowhere in the center of his forehead, his eyes gently rolling back into his skull.

He seemed to hold there for a moment, his gaze becoming vague and his smile, however sensate, seemed to settle on me, laughing, as if to say: *You still lose!*

Then he pitched forward.

And in the sudden surge of elation I felt as I realized that he was dead, I saw with growing horror that the threat he'd made seconds ago was about to come true.

His weight pushed forward onto the pedal, and Hallie lurched out of his thick arms, the saw blade starting to whir and rotate. Hofer rolled off the bench to the side, his ample girth covering the pedal, and

Hallie was dragged forward by her arms as she started to scream.

"Hallie!" I yelled in horror as I saw what was unfolding.

Carrie got there first, desperately trying to roll Hofer off, but he was way too heavy for her and something, his belt, or his shirt, seemed to be caught on the thing.

Hallie pulled against her binds, arms first, but it was futile. She kept inching forward. Her beautiful face was twisted in horror. *"Daddy, please!"*

I leaped to Carrie's side and frantically tried to help roll Hofer off, but the sonovabitch's deadweight wasn't budging.

Carrie shot me a panicked glance. *"Oh my God, Henry!"*

Not even feeling the fire from the gunshot in my side, I dove over to the tool board, Carrie straining to hold Hallie back, and grabbed the ax.

I'd never swung one in my life, and surely not with my daughter's life on the line, her face contorted in screams, and my adrenaline racing off the charts. I raised it above my head and brought it down with all my might onto the rope near the wheel axle.

Nothing. It clanged off the blade and into the wooden bench.

It didn't sever the rope.

"Daddy!" Hallie was hysterical now, and I was too, Carrie straining with everything she had to hold her back, to gain precious seconds, but we were losing . . .

She continued to be pulled forward, now about two feet away.

I pulled the ax out and swung again.

This time I hit home, twine unraveling.

But it still didn't snap.

Hallie was now barely a foot away from the serrated, whirring blade, her face flushed a deep red and her eyes like round, horrified orbs. *"Daddy, quick! Please!"*

I raised the ax one last time, praying to something I wasn't sure I even believed in, but whom I begged to give me the strength. *This was our only chance.* The saw's chilling whir and my daughter's frantic screams combining in an awful wail.

Please . . . Please, God, I begged, and brought the ax down for a third time.

It snapped.

I felt the twine sever, Carrie yanking Hallie off the table with only inches to spare, both of them falling onto the floor.

For a second everything froze. I didn't hear crying or exulting. I didn't know if everyone was safe. My breath was trapped somewhere in my body. I had zero sensation in my side. I was drenched in sweat, my shirt matted with blood. I was scared to utter Hallie's name. I was scared that Hofer was about to rear up and the whole thing would begin anew.

Then I heard weeping.

Hallie weeping. Not in pain, but joy. Sobbing from

434

shock and happy relief. I ran over and untied her wrists and took her in my arms like she was three years old again. Squeezing her with all my might, both of us smeared with sweat and blood and tears. I began to shout. Exulting now. And laugh. Sobbing and saying at the same time, "Baby, you're okay. You're okay. *It's over. It's over, sweetheart* . . . You're okay."

I was afraid to believe it myself.

Until the pain hit me, and I buckled.

Carrie ran over to me and eased me against the wall, but I was still clutching Hallie.

No way I was going to let her go. Ever.

"Daddy, I love you, I love you . . ." she cried into me.

"I love you too, baby!" I pressed my face against hers.

We slid down to the floor. That's when I first heard the wail of distant sirens. The three of us, we just slid slowly down, holding one another, afraid to let go, my daughter's trembling face buried into my shoulder.

"They're coming!" Carrie said to me, jubilant. "They're coming!"

"Yeah, they're coming!" I nodded, resting my head back against the wall. And I could only smile, grateful tears pooling and shimmering in my eyes. Holding my daughter as tightly as strength would let me. Totally impervious to the pain.

Looking at Carrie.

Those ecstatic blue eyes were about the prettiest thing

I had ever seen, and I let my head drop against her, unable to do anything but smile and laugh with everything I had in me, and wince a little.

And cry.

CHAPTER SEVENTY-FIVE

I won't even pretend that my injuries turned out to be life-threatening.

The bullet went through the oblique muscle of my back, about as favorable an outcome as I could have hoped for. It would keep me off the golf course for a while. And out of the OR.

But I knew I had enough to keep myself occupied for the next couple of weeks.

After the police arrived, Hallie and I were rushed to the Richmond County Medical Center in Augusta, thirty miles away. We both went in the same EMT van, Hallie receiving oxygen and glucose, and Valium intravenously for the shock.

Lying on the adjoining gurney, I held on to her hand the entire trip. Except for the day I first held her in my arms, I don't think I've ever felt a deeper understanding of what it meant to be a father.

We called Liz on the way. Another tearfest. It almost made me feel as if we were a united, happy family again. Past the shoals of jealousy and bitterness that I hoped would never bar our way again.

We told Liz where we were being taken, and Carrie said the FBI would send a plane and fly her up there now, Liz's choked, grateful voice on the other end barely containing the unstoppable flood of joyous tears that lay behind it. *"Thank you, Henry. Thank you . . ."* she kept saying, in a fervent—and reproachless—tone I hadn't heard from her in years.

There was nothing stronger in this world, no greater driving force, than the urge to protect your child.

We got to the hospital—Hallie to the ER to be stabilized. Me, into surgery.

All they really had to do was clean and irrigate the wound. It took just a little more than an hour.

After recovery they let us share a room. Hallie slept off the Valium. I just lay there watching her. Relishing the sight. I knew the next few days would be hectic. I knew I was in for police interviews and camera crews and maybe even the morning news shows.

Henry Steadman, the "boob dude" of Broward County.

I couldn't help but laugh.

Every once in a while my mind flashed back to my

final sight of Hofer back in the shed. Much as I wanted to despise him, I wasn't sure I could. Twisted as he was, he was acting as a father too, a desperate one, at least in the beginning. And I wondered, my mind drifting in and out, if the very things I held dear hadn't been taken from him one by one—his career; his family; his dignity—would he have gone so off-kilter? Would he have just lived out his life? Were there millions of him, teetering on the same isolated precipice where life could go either way, made bitter by life, but trudging on?

There was a knock on our door, and I figured one of the doctors had come to check my wound.

Instead, Carrie came in. Still in the same baby-blue sweatshirt and jeans.

I looked at her and felt a rush of warmth come over me. "Hey."

"Hey." She smiled back at me. "Doing better I see."

"Nothing I can't patch up later when I'm back at the clinic." I grinned.

Carrie smiled too. "How's she doing?" she asked, looking at Hallie.

"She's doing swell. She's been through a lot, but she'll be fine. In the end. You ought to know." I knew she probably couldn't wait to get back to her own son.

She nodded. "Guess I do." She sat down on the edge of my bed. "I've talked to the sheriff's office. They're sending a team up here to chat with you."

"*Chat*, huh?"

"I don't know if I'm exactly the person to speak for them, but I'm pretty sure you're in the clear."

"*Whew*. Just when I was getting used to dodging bullets."

"They're sending Rowley," Carrie said. "Since you guys seemed to get along so well . . ."

She gave me a held-back smile, but there was something beautiful in her teasing blue eyes.

"Everyone's been telling me 'well done,'" I said. "But the truth is, you're the one who deserves all that. Not me . . ."

She pressed her lips together, shrugging it off.

I took her hand. "So thank you. Without *you* . . . there's just simply no way I'd be on *Good Morning America* Tuesday morning . . ." Carrie giggled. I looked over at Hallie. "I look at her and I wish I could think of a way."

"I've, uh, actually been giving some thought to getting my eyes done." She held back a smile again. "Maybe just around the edges. *Here* . . ."

"No." I shook my head. "I don't advise it. I don't want you to change one single thing. Carrie . . ."

"Uh-huh?"

I brushed my hand against her cheek. I don't know what was in my mind, but I stared into her beautiful blue eyes and probably never felt more gratitude or closeness to anyone in my life.

My voice caught with emotion.

"I just wanted to say . . . that I wouldn't be here . . .

Hallie wouldn't be here . . ." I didn't finish the sentence. *"Just thanks."*

"I know," she replied, and put her hand on mine.

We lingered there a moment. Until we both became a little self-conscious.

"I have something for you . . ." I said, and tried to move, but pain lanced through me. "It's over there. In my pocket." I pointed to my pants, folded over a chair.

"I'll get it." She went over and reached inside. *"Forty dollars!"* She widened her eyes in mock appreciation. "You're sweet!"

"Keep digging. I think there's another ten in there."

She laughed, and eventually came out with what I was hoping she would find.

Her husband's driver's license.

"It got me into the prison to see Amanda. So I guess, without it, who knows how this thing might have turned out."

She held it in both hands, nodding a bit wistfully. "I told you he was the most resourceful guy I knew."

"You did. And I think he'd be proud of his wife."

Carrie smiled, a little blush coming into her face, and then she opened her purse. She reached for her wallet to put the license back, back from where she had taken it that first time in the car. But then she seemed to hesitate. Instead, she tucked it into the side pocket of the purse. As if she was putting it safely away for keeps.

Not just away, but behind her.

Then she caught me staring at her and gave me a rosy smile.

"I think I'll keep it where I can never lose it again." She tapped her chest. *"In here."*

"A good spot," I said, and then we didn't say anything for a long time.

Epilogue

Boaco, Nicaragua. Five months later. . .

"Mira!" I said to the beaming thirteen-year-old girl in the hospital bed. Look at you!

Pilar had smiled a lot before the operation, but now, in her hospital gown, her bandages just removed, that smile was a mile wide.

Maybe for the first time in her life.

She had lived her entire life with a grossly distorted mouth and jaw. Now she looked like any happy teenager, or would soon. I had to do one more procedure to smooth out the cleft around her upper lip. One day, it was possible no one would even know.

"Tu es hermosa, Pilar!" I said proudly. You're beautiful! "One day you will be the prettiest girl at the dance."

She blushed shyly as her mother came up to me and

put her arms around my waist and gave me a tearful hug.

"*Gracias, gracias, doctor,*" she said, laying her head against my chest. Then she began to speak rapidly in Spanish, most of which went over my head, other than the words *regalo de dios*, which meant "gift from God" and *angel de cielo*. Angel from heaven.

"It's an honor," I said, my hands to my heart. Then, "*Ella es mi hija,*" pointing to Hallie.

This is my daughter.

Excited, Hallie went up to Pilar. "Look how beautiful you look!" She had been helping the girl learn English for the past weeks.

The young girl beamed with a light in her eyes. "*Gracias.* I mean, thank you . . ."

Hallie pulled out her camera. "Do you mind? *Una fotografía . . . ?*"

"*Sí!* Yes." Pilar nodded brightly. I stepped away so that her mother could come next to her.

"No, Dad," Hallie said, with one of those "duh" kind of smiles, "she wants it with *you!*"

Pilar nodded. The mother nodded as well.

"*Con mucho gusto!*" I said, and sat down next to her. I took her hand and leaned in close.

Hallie pressed the shutter.

She showed the digital shot to Pilar, who grew excited. "I'll send it to you," Hallie said.

"Thank you so much, misses," Pilar said haltingly again.

"Hallie," my daughter insisted. Then, glancing at her watch: "Dad, look at the time!"

"We have to go," I said apologetically to a chorus of even more *graciases*. "Everything *es perfecto*. I'll be back to see you tomorrow!"

We hurried out of the hospital, Hallie strapping her bag around her shoulder, and jumped into the old Land Rover I was driving here, which was on the street in front. I started it up. Out of the central square with its old church and government center. Over cobblestone streets, which quickly turned to gravel as we pulled out of town.

Stone buildings gave way to metal-roofed storefronts and huts. Fruit vendors on the sides of the road hawking their bounties. Kids kicking a soccer ball on bumpy fields. And those beautiful green hills that surrounded the village.

"That smile was worth a million dollars," my daughter said.

"That's the way I kind of feel about yours," I said back.

After it all was over, Hallie took the rest of that semester off from school. She'd go back in the fall, but not to UVA. At least not now. She'd transferred down to Lynn University, which was close to us. I perfectly understood. It had taken a couple of months of coddling and feeling close, a couple of months of not wanting to be alone. Or even ride.

But after the headlines went away and the

investigations were completed, after months of counseling and a lot of time with Liz and me, we saw signs of our old Hallie returning. The one with the quick laugh and easy smile. The one who trusted people. Now she was even starting to ride again. She'd even found a beautiful chestnut Appaloosa here in Nicaragua.

"Oh, don't get all emotional on me again . . ." Hallie smiled with a roll of her eyes.

I was doing that a lot these days, getting emotional. I still hadn't gone back to operating at home. I couldn't. Not yet. Not that kind of work. I knew I would soon. Maybe after the summer. I just didn't care about it right now.

Not with Hallie and what I was doing down here.

"You better move it, Daddy-o, you don't want to be late."

"Late" was a relative term down in Central America, but I agreed. "No. Not today."

I pulled ahead of a cart and oxen that were hogging the road, pushing the Land Rover into fourth gear. We drove another mile or two until there was nothing around us but green mountains.

Until we hit a plain, lettered sign: AEROPUERTO.

Basically just a dirt landing strip. With a hut and a wind sock and fuel pump, which was usually empty. The kind of aircraft that came in here, four-seaters from the capital or forty-year-old cargo planes carrying medicine and food, didn't need much more.

446

We turned in and pulled up right next to the runway. We waved to Manolo, the chubby airport master, whose job it was basically to sit around all day directing traffic that never came and see if anyone needed fuel.

"Ah, Doctor. Henrique," Manolo exclaimed. *"Cómo estás?* Your plane, it will arrive here very soon."

"Buenissimo," I said, scanning the sky.

In a couple of minutes, we heard the drone of an aircraft somewhere high above us and Manolo pointed to a glint in the sky. *"There . . . !"*

It circled around the valley and came in from the west. There wasn't a cloud in the sky. Or a sound.

Other than the sound of my heart. *"Excited?"* Hallie asked.

"Yeah." I looked at her and couldn't pretend otherwise. "I am."

The plane came down, landing along the bumpy strip, and pulled up to a stop directly in front of our car.

Someone opened the door, and the steps were attached to it.

First, a local came out carrying a heavy burlap sack. Probably grain or flour.

Then I saw Carrie.

She was in a white, V-neck tee and khaki shorts, her hair underneath a straw cap, which she had to hold on to in the propeller draft.

And Raef.

The second I saw her I knew my time alone was

447

probably at an end. Though she probably didn't know that yet. Or maybe she did. Our eyes met, lingering a second in anticipation, and it was the second best smile I'd seen that day!

"Welcome to Boaco, señora!" Manolo announced. "Place of the Enchanter."

"He says that to everyone," I said. I went up to her. "Kind of an official duty. But he's right. Amazing things do happen here, *Detective* . . ."

"Not quite yet," Carrie said. "Another six weeks. But close . . ."

"Down here, things happen in their own time. So close works for me!"

I gave her a kiss—which kind of lingered. I couldn't help myself. I knew Hallie and Manolo were probably giggling. I held her close, so she could feel the excitement in my heart, and I felt hers too.

"And, Raef, I'm Henry," I said, kneeling down and putting out my hand. "I know all about you. And we have a bunch of cool things lined up. And this is Hallie. I think you remember my daughter?" I said to Carrie.

Thank-yous had been said a hundred times on news shows and in person, and Hallie went up and hugged her and Carrie smiled. "Yes, I think I do."

Looking at Hallie and Raef, with the suns of their two new lives dawning inside them, I suddenly had a feeling that I might never leave this place. That I had found what mattered.

That it didn't matter if I ever went back or not.

And I found myself squeezing both their hands. And I looked at Carrie and saw what both of us had done to bring our children here.

On my daughter's life, I remembered saying. *I swear . . . You'll know what I mean. . .*

All the rest . . .

"You all right?" My daughter looked at me, a little funny. She turned to Carrie and sighed. "He kinda gets weird like this, lately . . ."

"Yeah, I am," I said, putting my arm around her. Around Carrie too. "I'm perfect."

The rest was all clutter.

Acknowledgments

This all actually happened—being pulled out of my car, cuffed, told I was under arrest and going to jail, and thrown into the back of a police car while other police vehicles arrived on the scene—incredibly, while on book tour in Houston. (Whoever said writing was a noncontact sport!) Even the threatening, 9/11-type questions that were hurled at Henry were directed at me.

Fortunately, my situation had a far more benign ending than the one in this book—both for me *and* for the "arresting" officer, who I think is walking around in good health these days. I am told that the officer was suitably reprimanded for his actions, and for that, my thanks go out to Chief Thomas Lambert of the Houston METRO Police and his investigating team, who, upon receiving my detailed letter describing the event, launched a full investigation, culminating in a formal apology that cited his officers for improper conduct. I applaud him for going way beyond what I would have expected which was to simply back up his officers, and, for it, I am certain incidents like this will be far less frequent in the future.

In addition, I praise the local police forces of Broward and Palm Beach counties in Florida, who in the past year have cracked down on the "pill mill" businesses there, making tragic stories like this one much more difficult to take place.

So in the process of putting poor Henry Steadman through these travails, I am indebted to several people who helped make the outcome far more exciting—and I know, more believable: To friends Liz Berry and Dottie Frank, and Facebook friend Amy Ogden for local color and background around Jacksonville and South Carolina; to Andrew Peterson for gun prep 101, never my strong suit; to Dr. Greg Zorman for his topnotch medical counsel, *par usual*; to pal Roy Grossman and my wife, Lynn, who always reads my stuff before there's even an ending or a pub date; not sure they ever know how the final product turns out!

To my terrific editor, Henry Ferris, and my agent, Simon Lipskar, who together came up with a wonderful save on this! And to the entire team at William Morrow and HarperCollins—always appreciate all of you, however behind the scenes.

And lastly, with deepest gratitude to Drs. Nelson Bonheim, Harvey Seidenstein, and John Setaro for keeping this ol' heart of mine, which has a lot more stories to bring forth, beating and vibrant and well!

THE BLUE ZONE

THERE ARE NO RULES IN THE BLUE ZONE.

They were the perfect family. And he was the perfect family man.
One day changed it all.

Arrested for racketeering, Ben Raab must take his family into
America's Witness Protection Programme. Only his eldest daughter,
Kate, chooses to stay on the outside. But the Programme's perfect
success rate is about to come to a shocking end. A case agent is
tortured to death and Ben vanishes. The one person who
might be able to find him is Kate.

Pursued by killers, forced to question everything she knows about
her life so far, Kate is plunged into a terrifying existence
for which nothing has prepared her.

Most people would call it certain death.

The FBI calls it The Blue Zone.

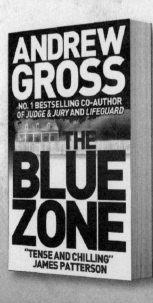

RECKLESS

THE SENSELESS SLAUGHTER OF A FAMILY.
A FINANCIER'S TRAGIC SUICIDE.
A SIMPLE PHONE CALL WITH TERRIBLE CONSEQUENCES.

Three seemingly separate events – that may be linked. From small-town America, through Wall Street to Central Europe and London, the threads of evidence can be followed – if you're good enough. Fortunately, Ty Hauck is. Ty, a former police detective uncomfortable with his new status as a 'security consultant', also has a powerful personal motive: a promise to one of the dead, April Glassman.

Joining forces with Naomi Blum, a beautiful, ambitious US Treasury trouble-shooter, they dig deep into the dark heart of what might be one of the cleverest – and most dangerous – conspiracies the world has ever seen...

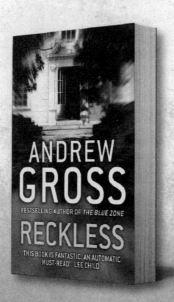

KILLING HOUR

A YOUNG MAN'S SUICIDE.
AN ELDERLY WOMAN'S MURDER.
A CONSPIRACY STRETCHING BACK DECADES.

Dr. Jay Erlich's life is perfect: a wife and children he loves; a successful career. But a call comes that changes everything. His troubled nephew, Evan, has killed himself and Jay's brother is in despair.

Jay flies to California to help out, and is soon convinced Evan's death was no suicide. The police want him to leave the matter alone but he is determined to dig deeper. When his investigation takes him on a journey into his brother's shady past, Jay finds himself caught up in a world of dangerous secrets and ruthless killers…

THE DARK TIDE

GET UP. KISS YOUR FAMILY GOODBYE.
GO TO WORK. DIE…

They say bad luck comes in threes. But for Karen Friedman's family, bad luck is just the beginning.

It starts with her husband Charlie's investments going wrong and the sudden death of a much-loved family pet. Then one morning Charlie takes the train to work – straight into a lethal terrorist blast. For Karen and their children, all that remains of Charlie is a shared past.

Or is it? When the Friedmans begin to receive terrifying threats, Karen turns to Detective Ty Hauck for help. Hauck's family fell apart too, after a tragic accident he still blames himself for. Now he's determined to keep Karen's family safe. But what Hauck doesn't know, is that the people who investigate Charlie have a way of ending up dead…

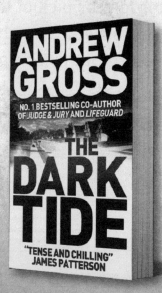

Killer Reads.com

The one-stop shop for the best in crime and thriller fiction

Be the first to get your hands on the **latest releases, exclusive interviews** and **sneak previews** from your favourite authors.

Browse the site and sign up to the newsletter for our pick of the **hottest** articles as well as a chance to **win** our monthly competition!

Writing so good it's criminal